MANY WANT IT . . . ONLY ONE CAN BUY IT.

LIZ LACEY—the famous artist was ready to kiss fame and fortune goodbye, to sell Apartment 3B and follow her heart to Majorca, far from the maddening crowd . . .

HUGH CASSIDY—he thought he could have Liz and his brilliant TV career, thought cash, clout, and love could buy the apartment—and the woman—he couldn't afford to lose . . .

CLAIRE MORAN—she was a dutiful wife to an abusive husband until tragedy drove her to freedom, a successful career, and the dream of Apartment 3B—down payment on destiny . . .

LAINEY CONROY—the glamorous, sophisticated publishing executive was looking for love—at arm's length—only a heartbeat away from another woman's man: in Apartment 3B . . .

CECILY CLARKE-CONROY—it was the perfect perch for the Iron Butterfly, a social *coup*, one-up on the sister-in-law she loathed. She'd sell her soul to outbid—and outclass—Lainey . . .

DOMINIC KENT—until he met Lainey, married life had him disillusioned and restless. Now, with a new lease on life—and love—all he wants is a place for the two of them to call their own.

ALSO BY PATRICIA SCANLAN:

CITY GIRL

# PATRICIA SCANLAN

## APARTMENT 3B

A Dell Book

Published by
Dell Publishing
a division of
Bantam Doubleday Dell Publishing Group, Inc.
1540 Broadway
New York, New York 10036

All characters and incidents in this book are fictitious and any resemblance to real people or to actual events is entirely coincidental.

ISBN: 0-440-21276-6

Reprinted by arrangement with Poolbeg Press Ltd.

Printed in the United States of America

Published simultaneously in Canada

July 1993

10   9   8   7   6   5   4   3   2   1

OPM

This book is dedicated to family and friends, without whom I couldn't have written it.

To my mother, my rock of support.
To my Dad, the best in the world.
To Mary, my sister and best friend.
To my brothers Donald, Hugh, Paul and Dermot and their wives, who are always there for me.
To Yvonne, the best sister-in-law a girl could have.
To Fiona and Caitriona, my beautiful nieces.
To Catherine, sister-in-law to be, who read the manuscript and gave me great encouragement.
To Maureen, my godmother, who spoils me rotten.
To my Aunts, Ita, Lelia, and Flo
who always make a fuss of me.
To Ger, Janet, Ann and Anne the best of friends,
who kept me going and gave me lots of pampering
when the pressure was on.
To Michele, who told me all about Saudi.
To Annette Tallon, of the Dublin Centre for Complementary Medicine, who helped me change my life.
To Alil, a great friend.
To Aidan, for all the legal advice. (Paris, here I come!)
To Albert, who taught me all about PCWs.
To Brian, who is always getting me out of fixes.
To Dr. Frank Fine, who's always there in my hour of need.
To Henry a.k.a. Harry who can live with the slagging!
To Paddy and Derek, my two good buddies.

And finally—
To all my friends in the Library Service, but especially to the staff of Finglas Library: Mrs. Grogan, Alil, Ger, Rose, Bernadette, Martina, Christy and David. Great workmates and great friends.

## Acknowledgments

When I sat at a blank screen I always said a little prayer, "God, please inspire me." He never failed. Thank you, God.

To all in Poolbeg, but especially to Jo, my editor, and to Breda, my sales and marketing manager, who cosseted me through this book.

To Margaret Daly and Kim Murray, who always do a terrific publicity job.

Instead of seeing the rug being pulled from under us
we can learn to dance on a shifting carpet.

*Thomas Crum*

# CONTENTS

## The Nineties

## Tuesday, 23 April, 1991

## The Decision

# TUESDAY, 23 APRIL, 1991

# THE ESTATE AGENTS

"**W**here's the file for Apartment 3B?" Hilary Purcell muttered to herself, knowing that His Nibs, as she disrespectfully referred to her boss, would be requiring it later. Having located it, she placed it on the desk in front of her and returned to her typing. The phone rang.

"O'Malley, Costello and Ryan. Can I help you?" Hilary cursed silently as she made yet another typing error. On the phone an angry tirade assaulted her ears. "Just one moment. I'll put you through to Mr. O'Malley," she said sweetly. She was damned if she was going to deal with the angry client on the other end of the phone. Typical, of course. On their first meeting, John O'Malley had told the client that the firm took 2 percent of the selling price. He omitted to mention that the 2 percent did not include the price of the signs and photograph of the property and the advertising. Not to mention the 21 percent VAT. So the poor unfortunate on the other end of the phone had got a much heftier bill than she had budgeted for.

Hilary had had so many phone calls from shocked and irate sellers that she had decided to let the partners concerned handle them. Why should she have to listen to such abuse on the pittance she was being paid! If only she could win the Lotto! Hilary propped her chin on her hand and a faraway look came into her eyes. She'd pay the mortgage on her parents' house, buy a villa in the South of France for herself, give her brothers a couple of thousand each, and tell John

O'Malley exactly where he could stuff his job. She wouldn't even give him a day's notice. She smiled at the thought. She might even misplace a few files, make a couple of phone calls to her brother in the States, and be positively rude to the clients. Her humour began to improve immensely. Tomorrow she was definitely going to buy a few lottery tickets and if she won she wasn't going to tell a soul except the family. She certainly didn't want to be inundated with begging letters!

"Miss Purcell!" Her boss's suave tones interrupted her reverie. "I want you to ring Mr. White and tell him that we've accepted his offer for the Santry property. Then ring Miss Carey and tell her that someone else has put in a bid of a thousand extra for the house in Donnycarney."

"But I thought we'd sold the Santry house to the Morrisseys," she said, thinking he had made a mistake.

"Contracts weren't signed. We'll return their deposit to their solicitor," he replied briskly, turning to stride back into his office.

Swine! she thought. He'd gone and pulled the rug out from under the Morrisseys by selling to the highest bidder and they'd had their heart and soul set on that house in Santry. And she knew quite well that no one else had put in an offer for the house in Donnycarney; it was just a ploy to make Miss Carey pay an extra thousand. On second thoughts, if she won the Lotto she would buy out O'Malley, Costello and Ryan, through a broker of course, so they wouldn't be aware of her identity. And when the firm was finally hers, she'd call a meeting and personally sack her boss. This exquisite thought got her through the morning until her tea break. Then John O'Malley appeared beside her again.

"Miss Purcell . . ." How she detested that voice! "I want the file on Apartment 3B in Mountain View, if you please. I presume you contacted the interested parties to tell them what time the viewing was arranged for?"

"Yes," she said coldly, handing him the file.

"And you've informed Mrs. Lacey that I'll be there fifteen minutes beforehand?"

"Yes, Mr. O'Malley," Hilary almost hissed. Hadn't she been working with him long enough to know what to do when there was a viewing?

"How many have confirmed?" He perused the file. "Hmm . . . Hugh Cassidy, the TV personality. Mrs. Claire Moran, Mrs. Cecily Clarke-Conroy, Ms. Lainey Conroy. Are they related?"

"I don't know really. A Mr. Dominic Kent made all the arrangements for Ms. Conroy." Hilary managed to refrain from informing her boss that, unlike him, she was not inquisitive enough to go into clients' personal histories on the phone. Honestly, John O'Malley would ask you what you'd had for your breakfast! If Mrs. Clarke-Conroy and Ms. Lainey Conroy were related, so what! Maybe the two of them were having an affair with the man called Dominic Kent. Anything was possible. There were plenty of men buying apartments and town houses for their mistresses. You saw a lot of goings-on in the estate agency business. She wouldn't put it past John O'Malley to indulge in a bit of blackmail. The crook that he was! She knew that he madly fancied Liz Lacey, the famous artist who was selling Apartment 3B. Hilary got the impression that his interest wasn't reciprocated. He thought he was a bit of a ladies' man. But Hilary wouldn't touch him with a ten-foot barge-pole. Just the thought of his marblelike hands with the wet fishy handshake gave her the shudders. And he had a way of looking at you and a way of making remarks that were very close to sexual harassment. If he didn't stop annoying her, she would report him! It would be worth it to knock that smirk off his face.

"Very interesting indeed." Her boss gave a supercilious smile. "I'm off to sell the apartment. I'll be back some time in the afternoon. Take my messages. Good-bye, Miss Purcell. Be good!"

"Good-bye and good riddance!" Hilary spat as she watched her boss get into his BMW. At least she had her office to herself for a while. She hoped that selling Apartment 3B would take up a good chunk of his time as, unfortunately, he had no other appointments that afternoon and would be under her feet for the rest of the day. If Tim Costello was out, she'd nip in next door and have a chat with his secretary.

Who would buy the apartment, she wondered. Hugh Cassidy? He was a bit of all right. Ireland's most eligible bachelor, even more popular than Pat Kenny. Claire Moran from Drumcondra? She'd sounded nice on the phone—a gentle sort. That Clarke-Conroy one had sounded like a right stuck-up bitch with her posh accent. She knew all about the percentages and the VAT and the extra costs. John O'Malley wouldn't mislead *her*. And Dominic Kent! He sounded like a right dish. With that absolutely gorgeous deep voice. Whoever bought 3B, she'd most likely meet him or her as they'd have to sign papers. It would be very interesting indeed to see which of the viewers would become the new owner.

# THE SELLER

*L*iz Lacey's blue eyes snapped open and immediately she was wide awake—that was the kind of person she was. Through her pale lilac drapes, she could see that the sun was shining. Good, she thought with satisfaction. She had read somewhere that sunshine always helped to sell a property and besides, it would show off her balconies to advantage. People were coming to view her apartment today and Liz wanted them to see it at its best. The estate agents had postponed the viewing twice and the strain of keeping the place immaculate was beginning to tell. Liz was not the world's tidiest person. "Out of sight out of mind" was her motto. If anyone looked under her bed they'd be horrified.

To think that she, Liz Lacey, artist extraordinaire, darling of the media and jet set, girlfriend of one of Ireland's most famous and eligible bachelors, never knew what she was going to find under her bed, never mind in the bottom of her mirrored closets. Liz grinned as she remembered the battles she had had with her good-natured mother.

"What's pickling under the bed today?" her mother would inquire each Saturday morning as a cleanup got under way. When Liz bought her luxury apartment, she had resisted strongly the suggestion made by her sister-in-law Eve that she buy a bed with drawers in the base. Under the bed saved her so much hassle. Being without it would be like not having her handbag, which weighed a ton and was almost an extension of her body.

Leaning out of bed to pick up the large bulging Italian leather bag, Liz dipped a hand in, rummaged, skirted a tube of paint and a box of charcoal sticks and found her Filofax. Both bag and Filofax had been a present from her great Spanish friend, Incarna, who tried her best to organise Liz. If she were left to her own devices, she would write down appointments on the back of envelopes. Liz flicked through the address section until she found the estate agent's number. She might as well ring and confirm, in case they had decided to postpone the viewing once again. If they had she would bloody well give them hell. Maybe she would have been better off just selling privately, but it had seemed so easy just putting it in the hands of an estate agent. At the time she didn't realise that there were two people she knew who were interested in buying.

One of them was the mother of Hugh Cassidy, her partner of many years, but by the time that Hugh realised that she was really serious about getting out and changing her life, she had already put Apartment 3B in the hands of the estate agents and signed a sole agency agreement with them. She had also disappointed Dominic Kent, her neighbour from downstairs, who had approached her upon hearing the news that she was selling, to tell her that Lainey Conroy, *his* partner, was anxious to buy a place in Dublin and that Apartment 3B would be perfect. Liz had immediately agreed to let Lainey view the place and Dominic had contacted the estate agents for details and to make an appointment on Lainey's behalf. So she was going to be bidding against Hugh's mother. Well, it couldn't be helped. Hugh should have known she meant what she said about getting out. And she wasn't going to disappoint Lainey now that she had made the arrangement. Liz liked Lainey, one of the most elegant women she had ever seen, very glamorous and sophisticated but with a delicious sense of humour. Apartment 3B would suit the well-travelled woman of the world very well. Lainey was the kind of woman who *should* live in an apartment like 3B.

Fortunately, Hugh was always very fair minded and he

told her to have as many people as possible view the place in order to get the best price she could. Liz didn't know who else was coming. No doubt Mr. Suave would be along in his grey pin-striped suit, showing just the right amount of cuff, his neatly manicured hand holding on to his Gucci briefcase as though the crown jewels reposed there. She just couldn't take to John O'Malley of O'Malley, Costello and Ryan, Estate Agents. He was much too smooth for her taste. Well, let him sell Apartment 3B. He had told her that he had several very interested viewers and he would certainly get the best price for it; all she knew was that she wasn't going to be there. She couldn't bear to be around as people looked at her apartment, so she had made an appointment with Nikki and Susan across the road in Kris Morton's to have her hair done and have a full beauty treatment. It was her little treat to herself. She'd miss her sessions at the elegant pink, grey, and black salon but she'd be back in Ireland regularly, commuting from the little whitewashed villa in Majorca that now awaited her. Now that she had made the most momentous decision of her life, she was anxious to leave the past behind and begin living her dream.

Her eyes took on a faraway look. It wasn't how she had ever thought she would end up. Her finger caressed the smooth wedding band on her left hand. Hugh had never been happy about her continuing to wear her wedding ring. It irked him, this link with her past, but although she loved Hugh in her own way, and he loved her in his, Liz would never love anyone as she had loved Matt, her tall, quiet, good-humoured husband. Sighing, Liz drew aside the duvet, and walked across the thick pink-and-grey carpet to her balcony. How ironic life was, she mused a little sadly. Here she was, owner of a luxurious apartment that she was going to sell for a huge profit, successful beyond her wildest dreams, and she would turn her back on it all to have lived forever in the little flat near Harold's Cross Bridge, whose threshold Matt had carried her across as a deliriously happy new bride. To live with Matt and have his babies was all she had ever wanted but fate had decreed differently.

"Ah, Liz!" she chided herself aloud. It was rare for her to dwell on the past and what might have been. She was much too positive a person for that. Still, so much had happened in the last two months and now, with her life about to change so dramatically, it was inevitable that her thoughts would turn towards the past.

She was doing the right thing. She had thought it through over and over and discussed it with Don and Eve, her brother and sister-in-law, without whom she would never have contemplated making the move. Her face softened into a smile as she thought of Eve, her sister-in-law. How lucky Don had been in his choice of wife. Eve was one of the warmest, most generous, and loving human beings Liz had ever met. From the moment Don had introduced them it was as though they had been friends all their lives. It was Eve who had let her share every moment of her pregnancies and who made her feel very much a part of her family life. Fiona and Caitriona, her two beautiful nieces, were like her own children and they were her greatest joy in life. Now Eve was expecting her third child.

She grinned as she remembered their last outing. She had taken Fiona, aged six, and Caitriona, almost three, into town, brought them into one of the pound shops on Henry Street and told them they could pick five toys each. Fiona loved the pound shops and it had taken her an hour to make up her mind about what she wanted. Each toy was picked up, examined minutely, put down, then picked up again. Caitriona had no such problems. She knew exactly what she wanted: dolls, dolls, and more dolls. Watching the excited happy little faces of the girls holding their bagged purchases gave Liz the warmest glow, and without further ado they trooped across to Marks and Spencers where she proceeded to buy two beautiful dresses for the pair. They then hit McDonald's for the highlight of their special day and they had tucked into burgers, chips, and milkshakes with great gusto.

"I'm weelly alighted," Fiona informed her aunt, wrapping two little arms around Liz's neck and almost choking her with a hug. Liz tried to hide her smile, Fiona couldn't yet pronounce her r's and sometimes got her words a little wrong. How could she not melt when her beloved niece would say things like "Liz, if I wake up in the miggle of the night and I'm stiff scawed can I get into your bed?" This was when she had her two nieces staying on a "holiday" night with her. Caitriona had woken at six-thirty, lifted Liz's eyelid and demanded to know if Liz was awake. When Liz had groggily urged her to go back asleep her niece had informed her matter-of-factly, "But my sleep's all gone!" There was nobody else on the planet who would induce Liz to get up at that unearthly hour, but she was putty in the hands of Fiona and Caitriona.

She'd miss them so much. That was the one big drawback of the step she was taking. But summer holidays were long and Eve and the children were going to stay in the villa, with Don coming out for a shorter period. They would have a marvellous time. All these years of doting over her nieces had kindled in her the desire to have a child of her own. From the time she first felt her niece kicking lustily against her mother's swollen belly and held the hours-old baby gently and gazed in awe at the perfectly formed little face with the rosebud mouth and startlingly blue eyes, Liz had got terribly broody. Now, at thirty-four, this feeling was stronger than ever.

She gazed out at the view from her balcony, smiling to herself. She supposed she would miss the apartment; it had suited her needs so well, this luxurious penthouse with its superb light which fulfilled her requirements as an artist. Still, that was the joy of being an artist. Have brush, will travel. Liz could work at her job anywhere she chose. And for the future she had chosen to work and live in a villa in Majorca.

"You won't be going anywhere if you don't sell this apartment," she told herself briskly. Leaning an elbow on her attractive sand-coloured balcony wall she tried to see what a first-time viewer would see. Because Apartment 3B was perched high on the Washerwoman's Hill in Glasnevin, the view was impressive. Liz could see the clear outline of the Dublin Mountains straight ahead of her. It was one of those gorgeous April days when the sky was a Mediterranean blue and the outline of the mountains was etched so clearly that you almost felt you could reach out and touch them. She could see the distinct shadings of field and bog which never failed to delight her. That was one of the joys of living in Dublin: the countryside was only a bus journey away. The rooftops of the city, dwarfed by the mountains, shimmered in the early morning sun. To the left and a little behind stood the Bon Secours Hospital, its grounds perfectly manicured, sheep grazing contentedly near the wall that divided it from River Gardens, a luxury apartment complex. To her right was the pyramidal grey-blocked building that housed the meteorological service headquarters.

Her eyes wandered back to her own home. Lush landscaped grounds four floors below her were a blaze of cherry blossoms, nodding golden daffodils and tulips, and vivid purple heathers. An ornamental stream flowed rhythmically over decorative boulders giving a soothing ambience. It was a plush, elegant complex of just a score of apartments, in four blocks: in each block a penthouse, two two-bedroomed apartments and two one-bedroomed apartments on the ground floor. The complex boasted an indoor swimming pool, tennis courts, and a pool room. Liz often used the facilities and they were a great selling point. Liz had been lucky with her apartment—of that there was no doubt. She had bought during a bad slump in property and got the place at a bargain. Now prices had risen dramatically and she was in line to make a fairly hefty profit. It was this that had finally decided her to move to Majorca. Property there was very cheap and she was getting a three-bedroomed villa with a small swimming pool for a price that would leave her with a nice tidy amount of savings from the sale of Apartment 3B.

Liz went back in, caught sight of her reflection in a mirror and smiled ruefully, running a hand through the soft raven curls that framed her small heart-shaped face, a face dominated by bright blue eyes which were fringed by long black lashes. Not beautiful in the conventional sense, Liz had an animated face that made men stop and look twice, her eyes mirroring every emotion she was feeling. The faint lines around them etched from her thirty-four years of living added to the character in her face. Small and petite, she aroused men's protective instincts, but Liz had no need of protection. Time and trauma had proved that she was well able to look after herself.

"Get a move on, girl," she ordered, knowing full well she had a colossal amount of work to get through. The previous night she had called a meeting of the other residents in her block to resign formally as secretary of the residents' committee, something she was only too delighted to do. The hassle she had had this past year, chasing up maintenance fees from Al and Detta, listening to Maud and Muriel complain about Derek's parties. Only Dominic had been a model resident. Well, good luck to them in Mountain View; she was leaving them to it. Liz was off to Majorca and a new life despite Hugh's hurt protests. Still, he was getting used to the idea and the bond between them would never be broken, now that they were going to be parents.

Liz squared her shoulders, then made her bed, had a quick shower and ate some yogurt and muesli standing at the kitchen counter. She rang the estate agents to confirm the viewing time and sat down to type out the minutes of the previous night's management committee meeting. In little over a month, with any luck, she'd be toasting herself in the sun.

# THE RESIDENTS

*D*etta and Al Shaw sat at their breakfast counter eating toast and margarine. Both of them drank black tea because it saved on the milk. They were worried. Liz Lacey was selling the penthouse above them and God knows who might buy. Probably some rich old bitch who had loads of money and who wouldn't mind if the maintenance fees went up. Last year had been horrific; the fees had gone up 10 percent. They'd had to get a new Chubb lock on the front door because that silly old bat Muriel on the next landing lost her keys and her name and address were on the key ring. It was only right and proper, as Al told the meeting last night, that if it happened in future, whoever lost the keys would have to pay for the lock. Then Maud, the other old biddy, had decided they needed fire extinguishers and blankets on every landing, not just in the foyer. That had cost an arm and a leg. And now there was talk of getting the outside painted. At least Al had taken over as secretary of the management committee and he might be able to stall things for a while until they got a bit of money together.

"You're mad to be buying an apartment," their parents had told them, but Al and Detta, yuppies to the death, would hear no arguments. Weren't they the envy of their friends and colleagues? Wasn't an apartment in Mountain View better than a semi-detached house out in God knows where! After all, Al held down a prestigious job as information scientist in Hanley and Mason, a huge pharmaceutical company. Detta was a lowly library assistant under his command. And how she loved being commanded by Al. She loved him, loved his power position, and hoped fervently that by marrying him she might advance her own career. To be an information scientist was her dream ever since she had started work in Hanley and Mason. Just think how impressed they'd be up in Kincasslagh, her home town. It would be almost as good as being related to Daniel O'Donnell! It would be a great help with the mortgage too; an increase in salary was badly needed.

A howl from the children's bedroom shook Al and Detta out of their moody introspection.

"Lee, what are you doing to Candine? Leave your sister alone!" snapped Al. He was trying to decide which suit to wear, the light beige, or pale grey. The school of library studies from UCD was coming on a visit and he wanted to make an impact. After all, these were information scientists of the future. Some of them might even end up in Hanley and Mason.

"Ouch, let go of my hair!"

"I'm telling Mammy on you! Maaaamyyy."

"TRALEE!!!" yelled Al. There was silence from the adjoining room. When her father used her full name, Lee knew he meant business.

"We'll just have to give the children more quality time, darling," sighed Detta.

"A clip on the arse would be more like it," muttered her husband.

"Oh, Al," his wife murmured reproachfully as the video intercom tinkled to announce the arrival of Tina, the nanny.

"Come on, that group from UCD are coming today. I want to be there early. Let's get dressed and out of here ASAP."

Detta smiled adoringly. She loved it when her husband ordered her around. They'd manage if the maintenance fees went up, Al would provide. She just hoped that the new owner of Apartment 3B wouldn't want to make huge changes in the place and wouldn't mind children.

On the landing below, Muriel Doyle and Maud O'Connor, her sister, were arguing vigorously about who was to use the bathroom first.

"Muriel, *I* was up first. Therefore *I* get to use the bathroom first. Kindly get out of there immediately," Maud commanded, inwardly raging that Muriel had managed to sneak in in front of her yet again.

Muriel, working on the assumption that possession was nine tenths of the law, refused to be ousted. "*I* put on the immersion," she retorted triumphantly from behind the locked door. That would teach Maud manners, Muriel decided, as she went about her early-morning toilette. She was really annoyed with her sister.

Last night they had attended the meeting in Liz Lacey's penthouse and Maud had got quite tipsy. As they left, that . . . that lothario Derek Sinclair on the next floor had been smirking in a superior manner at them. It was most vexatious to the spirit. And him only a rented. Everybody else at least owned their apartments. God knows what kind of character would buy 3B. Liz might have been an artist, and everybody knows artists are supposed to be a bit wild and eccentric, but they had been pleasantly surprised. Liz Lacey had turned out to be a real lady. If someone like that upstart Sinclair bought the apartment, she and Maud might just as well sell up and go elsewhere.

It had been a mistake, a big mistake, selling her little cottage with its lovely flower-filled garden, to buy this place with Maud. "You'll be great company for each other, Mum. It will be much better than living on your own," her son had enthused. You mean you won't have to worry about me, she thought dryly. It had been the perfect solution for everyone— except her.

Maud was childless. She had lost her husband and couldn't wait to sell their old damp house in Drumcondra.

She wanted to buy an apartment in Mountain View, but couldn't afford it. Nieces and nephews and Jim, Muriel's son, had waged a . . . campaign . . . was the only word to describe it, to get Muriel to sell up and buy with her sister. They had succeeded and Muriel was now more unhappy than she had ever been in all her seventy-three years. Each day was a series of battles. Some she won, some she lost. This morning she had won so far. Now she wanted to make sure that she got the seat by the window. Liz had said that all the potential buyers of Apartment 3B were coming to view today and she wanted to make sure she got a good look at them. Drawing a deep breath, Muriel unlocked the door and marched out of the bathroom. "Age before beauty, dear," she said sweetly to her infuriated sister who stood, arms folded, at the other side of the door.

"The dirt before the brush, dear," hissed Maud as she slammed the door and locked it behind her.

It was going to be one of those days!

A jet of steaming water cascaded down Derek Sinclair's back. He stood in his shower soaping the lovely body entwined with his. Nuzzling the girl's earlobe he smiled. This was absolutely his favourite way to start the day. Pity those two old broads upstairs couldn't see what he was up to; that might stop them complaining about his parties. He grinned. Maybe frustration was their problem. Well just right now, it wasn't his. "Baby, you are beautiful," he murmured in his best Richard Gere imitation as he drew her closer to him and they began to make love for the second time that morning.

Later, when she had gone, having refused breakfast— dieting she said—he sat down and had his own. In the bright light of morning he conceded to himself that she might have been a little overweight, well maybe half a stone! Derek had no such problems and he tucked into a hearty fry. Wait until he told the guys at work about this little cracker. He had really hit the jackpot last night at Adam's party. He nearly hadn't gone, with that blooming meeting that Liz had called.

Pity she was leaving really. He had always fancied her but she treated him like a kid brother. Sometimes he got the impression that she didn't take him seriously at all. And him an ace money broker, a hotshot whiz kid. Maybe she felt twenty-six was a bit young; she was, after all, a bit past thirty. It didn't bother him—he had always liked older, mature women, as long as they were sexy. And Liz Lacey was sexy. So was that Lainey dish old Kent across the hall was snuggling with; she was sexy too, sexy as hell.

You've a good appreciation of women, Derek old son, he told himself as he put his dishes in the dishwasher, ran a comb through his Peter Mark permed hair, and picked up his briefcase. Whistling, he let himself out of the apartment. He checked his mailbox in the foyer: two letters, one a bill, the other from his mother in Swinford. A fleeting hint of guilt assailed him. Mam would really be horrified if she had seen him this morning. She still thought he went to mass, for God's sake!

He shoved the letter into his pocket. He'd read it later. He was a man of the world now, on his way to being the next Donald Trump. He had devoured *The Art of the Deal* from cover to cover. He knew where old Trumpy had gone wrong of course. Overextended himself with the casino in Atlantic City. Derek would never have made the same mistake. It was badly advised. Now if *he* had been advising Donald Trump . . . Whistling to himself, Derek Sinclair began to imagine a scenario where he was adviser to one of the world's best-known business tycoons. He was completely unaware that Maud and Muriel had him under a scrutiny that the KGB would have done well to match.

Michael Smurfit would want to make sure he didn't make the same mistake, Derek decided. Maybe he'd give old Micko a ring. This scenario lasted until he got to his car, when he discovered to his dismay that he had a flat tyre. Using every curse in his repertoire he took off his jacket and rolled up his sleeves. Old Horton would eat the head off him for being late again this week. Blasted car! Pity he couldn't afford a new one. But the rent he was paying for this pad had him almost wiped out. Twenty minutes later, begrimed and oily because he'd had really to struggle with the bolts, the pretender to Donald Trump's throne drove out of Mountain View. As he did so, he noticed the For Sale sign. He wondered who would buy 3B. A thought struck him as he headed towards Phibs-boro. Maybe someone like the doll in the coffee ad might move in. Aha!! The bottleneck at Cross Guns Bridge ceased to worry Derek as he began to imagine the scenario in which he welcomed the beautiful new tenant to Apartment 3B.

# THE VIEWERS

# Hugh

$H$ugh Cassidy snorted in disgust as he read the item in the *Irish Times* about a well-known couple who had been busted for possession of cocaine. He knew them vaguely. If Liz saw it, she'd be saying, "You'll be next." She was always going on at him about his little . . . habit. It was one of the reasons they were splitting up. The other was that he wanted her to come to the States with him, to be with him and share the most important event in his career, an event that was just about to take place. An American TV network was at this moment drawing up a contract for him to sign and Liz was refusing to go Stateside with him. Women! He'd never understand them.

Hundreds of women would give anything to be in her shoes. He had letters and panties and the likes from them to prove it. Only the day before he got the most pornographic letter he had ever read, in which the writer, female, had told him in language that almost brought a blush to his cheeks, what she would like to do with him. She had included a black wisp of satin panty that stank to high heaven of cheap perfume. The letter was postmarked Donegal. Liz had roared laughing. Hugh smiled to himself. Liz was one girl in a million—he'd known that the minute he'd met her.

His celebrity status hadn't fazed her one bit. In fact he'd had to put up quite an argument even to get her to go on a date with him. And eventually he had succeeded. But he'd had to fight hard before they had finally begun a loving and caring relationship. Now, no matter what happened in the future, there would always be a bond between them.

If only he could persuade her to give up this half-baked notion to go painting in Majorca and settle there. He was meeting her later, after he had interviewed a politician accused of taking bribes, and before he presented prizes in a community games event and wrote his column for *Review*, the upmarket arts magazine. He was taking his mother to the viewing of Liz's apartment organised by the estate agent. She had expressed a wish to sell the old family home and move in to something smaller and more compact and when Hugh had established that Liz was deadly serious about selling up and moving on he suggested to his mother that she might consider buying Liz's apartment. She had reacted enthusiastically. Of course it was too late to do a private deal with Liz; the estate agent had been engaged before he'd had his brain wave. But he really didn't mind. Business was better done properly and professionally. It was just a pity that the estate agent would take a good whack out of whatever price the apartment fetched.

Running a hand over his stubbled jaw, Hugh finished his coffee and headed for the bathroom. He had a busy day ahead and dawdling around his Donnybrook Mews wouldn't get anything done. He must call into Quinnsworth in Mount Merrion at some stage. There was nothing in the fridge and his daily was on holidays. Maybe he'd cook Liz dinner for a change. She much preferred dinner *à deux* to going out to any of Dublin's trendy eateries. Of course he loved eating out. Eat and be seen was part and parcel of maintaining a high profile, and Hugh Cassidy's profile was the highest around. He intended it to be even higher.

Twenty minutes later Hugh was shaved, showered, and out the door. Chicken Kiev would do fine for tonight, or maybe moussaka, Liz loved his moussaka. He pointed his Saab in the direction of RTE. It was six-thirty A.M.

# Claire

Claire Moran added her daughter's birthday card to the ones already displayed on the chipped mantelpiece of her Drumcondra bedsit. It was a beautiful card, thoughtfully chosen, and on it her daughter had written simply, "Mum you are the best. Love, Suzy." It was postmarked Singapore.

She was so lucky to have a daughter like Suzy. It was incredible that she, who had suffered such traumas in her young life, had overcome them all, stood on her own two feet, and was now sailing her way around the world, a globe-trotting nineteen-year-old stewardess with Cunard.

When Claire was not much more than Suzy's age, she had been a wife and mother, totally dependent on her husband. Looking back on it now from her eyrie of independence, she wondered how she had stuck it for so long. Of course she had known no better. She hadn't even realised for years of her marriage just how unhappy and unfulfilled she was. Claire shuddered, thinking of her past and the person she had been, so unquestioning and passive. She surely had changed, though. Claire was not the innocent, obedient young wife of nineteen years ago. By God she wasn't!

She might have lived the last ten months alone in her Drumcondra bedsit, a far cry from the large redbrick house in Glasnevin that had been her marital home for so many years, but she was her own woman. At thirty-eight years of age, Claire Moran was a woman of independent means. She smiled ruefully. Well, better late than never. Besides she was certainly only hitting her prime. She had never felt as fit nor looked so well. Thank God she had got over her guilt about spending money at the hairdresser's or in a beauty salon. Up to a few years ago she had always done her own hair. "What would you be wasting money going to a hairdresser's for? Sure isn't that what you were when I married you?" Sean, her husband, had once asked in genuine surprise, when she asked him for the money to go and get her hair done. They had been going to his youngest sister's wedding. She had never made the request again.

Claire should have known better, of course. Sean had no time for female fripperies, as he termed them, assuring her that she looked much more wholesome and natural without that muck that women put on their faces. Her soft chestnut hair, shot through with glints of gold, had been worn in a bob throughout the years of her marriage. Claire ran long fingers through her silky locks, feeling the feathery layers slide through her fingers. Oh, she was a changed woman all right. Physically as well as mentally. Gone was the bob, in its place a sophisticated layered style that framed her oval face. Well-defined arched eyebrows, tinted to match her hair, emphasised wide hazel eyes that were flecked with green. Her skin, creamy and unlined, belied her thirty-eight years, and only the faint lines grooved around her mouth gave a hint to the hardships she had endured.

Sipping her tea, Claire moved over to one of the windows of her high-ceilinged room. It was early yet and the street was still quiet; only a scrawny cat yowling as he slid out of a dustbin broke the silence. A cherry tree, its branches laden with delicate pink blossoms, grew outside her window. For the past few weeks, Claire had spent a few minutes each morning gazing on its beauty. It was only a short time that it was in bloom. She wouldn't be here this time next year. Maybe not even this time next month. She felt a little tingle of excitement. Today was the day, the day she was going to view Apartment 3B. What luck that it had come on the market just when she was in a position to buy it. How many times had she passed the Mountain View complex and wished she could afford to live there.

"Go for it, Mum!" her daughter had urged when Claire had told her of her plans. It would be ideal for both of them, really, if Claire could buy the apartment in Glasnevin. At least Suzy would have a proper bed for the times she came to stay, instead of having to sleep on the sofa bed as she did in the bedsit. Mind, she had done a lot with the room, she thought proudly, casting an eye around. Decorated in lemon and white, it was a far cry from the grim-looking room she had first set foot in ten months before. It had been truly awful. The previous tenant had obviously been colour-blind or in a very depressive state and the olive green and brown colour scheme had been the most unwelcoming sight she had encountered in her quest for a place to live. Weary, heartsore at the shambles that was her life, Claire had taken the room. The rent was not exorbitant, she liked the street, and somehow she had known that her life would change—and for the better.

As her life had changed, so had her bedsit. Out went the olive and brown and in their place, a light lemon and white that made the room seem twice as large and *so* airy and bright. It was incredible, the difference that a coat of paint had made, and psychologically the change had given her a lift, helped her a little to come out of the frightening depression that she had lived with ever since that awful terrifying day. Claire's eyes darkened in pain and sadness. Who could believe what had happened. David, her lovely, quiet son. How could he have done such a thing?

Stop it right now! Claire made the image go away. She must never look back. She and Suzy had made a pact about this the last time her daughter was home and it had helped. Today of all days was not the time for painful memories. Today was a day to be positive. Taking a deep breath Claire walked over to her tiny kitchenette which was hidden behind Japanese screens, and rinsed out her cup in the cracked sink. Briskly slipping out of her nightdress, she pulled on a tracksuit, inserted her aerobics tape into her video and began to do her workout. She knew the routine well and the gentle stretching movements that had made her body limber and supple came easily to her. Doing the exercises always cleared her mind and refreshed her. It was hard to believe that a year ago she had been a physical wreck. She'd even started to believe that she was a hypochondriac.

Thank God for Emma Morris and her acupuncture clinic. She had made such a difference. With her gentle but firm guidance, Claire had taken control of her life in a way that she had never thought possible. Her energy levels were so high now that she was rarely tired, unlike the drained exhausted person she used to be. Sean would never have got used to her. That was twice now that she had thought about her husband, and the surprising thing was that she no longer felt the surging hatred, the bitterness. Claire sighed deeply. It had come as a shock to her to discover how hard and unforgiving a person she could be. She had seen a side to herself that had frightened her. Even her father, who had treated her mother so badly, who had made her own life a misery and whose graveside she had stood at without shedding a single tear of regret at his passing had not ignited such passionate hatred as she had felt towards her husband. It was no wonder she had nearly cracked up, carrying the burden of such violent emotions, repressing them, swallowing them down inside her. She knew what hell was like; she had been there. If Emma Morris had not taught her to release the past and let it go, she wouldn't be here today, eager and excited at the step she was going to take, hoping to buy an apartment for herself and her elderly mother to live in.

Imagine, owning her own home! Decorating it to her taste. Having a double bed all to herself! Claire grinned. She would definitely get a double bed for the apartment if she bought it. She'd had enough of single divans. With a double bed, you could spread yourself out, read the papers in comfort, not having to dive after the supplement that invariably ended up on the floor. And the bathroom! Both bedrooms had their own bathrooms in Apartment 3B. Oh, the joy of not having to share! Not with husbands, children, or tenants. It was a long time since she had lolled in a bath. The bathroom she shared here was hopeless. The immersion was small and so the bathwater barely came over the top of her thighs. You wouldn't stay in it for long even if you were so inclined. When she lived with her husband, his thrift had precluded the taking of luxurious soaks. His Puritan spirit was offended by waste or self-indulgence so she had got into the habit of a quick five-minute wash that was not in the least pleasurable. Oh yes, she had so many things to catch up on, so much to experience and enjoy. Thank God, Suzy and Rosie, her best friend, had made her see sense about taking the money.

"You're entitled to it, Mum!" Suzy had exclaimed over and over again. "It's yours as much as his. You've contributed a lifetime to him and the house. Don't dare feel bad about taking that money!"

It had surprised Claire that her daughter was so vehement. But then Suzy was a different young woman from what she had ever been. So independent of spirit. So eager to experience life. How had she and Sean ever managed to produce a daughter so different from them? Again sadness engulfed her. David, her son, had been like her, even in looks. The big hazel eyes that had the same trusting direct way of looking at you, the same rich chestnut hair . . . "Oh David, David, why did you do it. Didn't you know I loved you?" The cry was torn from her, the tears slid down her cheeks. She didn't try to prevent them. "Cry, cry plenty if you have to, it's much better to let it all go," Emma had told her many times at their sessions and indeed it was a relief to cry, to feel her feelings pouring out of her instead of her repressing them as she had once done.

Claire sat quietly on the tatty carpet of her bedsit, her aerobics forgotten about. It was a while now since she'd had a good old bawl, and that was a good sign. It must be the day that was behind it. When David was small, he always made her some little special thing or drew her a picture, on her birthday. Children could give such joy and such sorrow. Taking a deep breath, Claire wiped her eyes, blew her nose and rewound the video.

She'd want to get a move on, she thought briskly. She

had some clients to visit before she left for her viewing appointment. It was wonderful to be a working woman again. The satisfaction of earning her own salary was indescribable. Sean had been so against her going back to work and, looking back, Claire could see how absolutely threatened he must have felt as he saw his power over her being eroded. Mercifully, she had stuck to her guns. It had been a lifesaver going back to work after so many years. How lucky she was to have a friend like Rosie. Now they were in partnership together and business was booming. Wasn't it strange that such a simple idea could have taken off so quickly? The notion of CALL 'n' CUT had come to her one day when an old-aged pensioner had come into the salon where she worked and confided chattily in her.

"I've got a bird's nest on top of my head, dear. Please do something with it. I couldn't get down the past few weeks because I'd an awful dose of asthma. Mind ye, if I look bad, Betsy next door looks as though she's got a hayrick on hers. She broke her leg, ye know, and can't get out. She's looking for condensation from the Corpo."

Claire hid a smile. Mrs. O'Neill sometimes got her words a little mixed up. It was like the time she had come in to the salon, a little the worse for wear, the sherry fumes unmistakable. Seeing Mrs. Burke, with whom she was engaged in a long-running feud, sitting, hair dripping, just about to have her rollers inserted, she sniffed loudly and said, "I'm particular about who I have me hair cut with. Some people just lower the tone of the place."

"Shut up, you drunken old virago," Mrs. Burke retorted, stung.

"Watch who you're insulting you or I'll sue you for definition of character," Mrs. O'Neill retorted haughtily, staggering ever so slightly as she weaved her way out, leaving Claire, and everyone else in the salon, speechless. Life was never boring with the likes of Mrs. O'Neill and Mrs. Burke. Softhearted, as always, Claire had called into Mrs. O'Neill's neighbour and given her a shampoo and set at home. The elderly lady had insisted upon paying and rather than upset her Claire took the money, understanding the old lady's desire for independence. From then on, she was frequently asked to come and do some of the elderly people's hair at home. It was quite obvious that the need for home hairdressing was there. The sick, elderly, housebound, were all people who called on her for service and it was because of this that CALL 'n' CUT was born.

In casual conversation with Rosie, she had mentioned the need for a mobile hairdressing service and her friend thought it was a brilliant idea. Claire had never thought of it in terms of a business, but Rosie, who was a very successful business-woman, had seen the potential and done her market research. It had paid off. Between them they had bought a small salon, got business cards printed and launched CALL 'n' CUT. Soon they had to employ another hairdresser, so successful was their venture. They were extremely busy but Claire revelled in it, so delighted was she by what they had achieved. It was all her idea, it was working, she was in business and things were really looking up.

A knock at her door startled her out of her reverie. It was Pete, her neighbour from across the hall, bearing a cheerful bunch of daffodils. "Happy Birthday," he grinned, planting a kiss on her cheek. "Rick and me are treating you to dinner tonight so don't go making plans."

"Ah, Pete!" she gasped, overwhelmed.

"Ah Pete nothing! We're only going to Some Like It Hot, but they do a lovely chicken in pitta bread." The young man smiled affectionately. "And anyway we're just keeping in with you because you give us free haircuts."

Claire laughed. "You pair!"

"See you later then?" He raised a questioning eyebrow.

"Sure thing," she agreed, cheerfully waving after him as he walked out the front door on his way to college. A thought struck her and she smiled broadly. You'd never know, she might have good news to tell them tonight if she liked what she saw at the viewing. She was dying to see Apartment 3B.

The last time her mother was up from Knockross, they had walked around the grounds admiring the superb complex, little thinking that they might one day be hoping to buy one of the luxurious apartments. Molly would be thrilled if Claire and she could buy it. Claire had seen a few places already but as far as she was concerned, Apartment 3B would be ideal for them and she had her heart set upon buying it. Humming to herself, she started to get ready for her big day.

# *Lainey*

*L*ainey Conroy fastened her seat belt and sat back in her seat, waiting for the British Airways BAC 1-11 to take off from Rome's Fiumicino Airport. Idly she wondered just how many flights she had been on. It must be well into the thousands by now. Not that long before she had been winging her way around the world as an air hostess with Eastern Gulf Airlines. It had been hard work, that was for sure, but she had seen the world and saved enough money to buy her own apartment. It was thanks to her job with Eastern Gulf that later today she would be going to view Apartment 3B with the intention of buying it. Lainey couldn't wait. She watched the BA hostess explaining where the exits were and demonstrating how to operate the oxygen masks and life jackets. Once when she had been doing the very same thing her life jacket had inflated and she'd had to stand like the Michelin man with her face straight, finishing the demonstration while her colleagues fell about laughing at her dilemma. Lainey smiled at the memory.

People thought it was such a glamorous job, all that travelling and staying in top-class hotels, but they didn't know the half of it. Not, of course, that Lainey was going to let on to the people back home that it had been anything other than a prestigious career. She was looked up to in the village. People pointed her out, impressed by her designer clothes, her sophisticated woman-of-the-world air. She was a long way from the little country hick who had first come to Dublin in search of a job. No! Lainey chided herself, well maybe not a hick, she had never been a hick. She had always been the one people followed, always the class leader.

With a roar, the jet raced down the runway and they were airborne. Not a bad takeoff, she noted absently and smiled, amused at herself. Relaxing in her seat she unclipped her belt and accepted a drink from a smiling steward. She hoped that no one had bought Liz's apartment yet. What a pity she hadn't known that the other woman had intended to sell before she put it in the hands of the auctioneers. They could have come to a private arrangement and done a deal between them. From what Dominic told her the price Liz expected to make was just within her range.

Her eyes softened as she thought of Dominic Kent. They'd been lovers for almost nine years now and the thought of seeing him always gave her a warm glow. She had met many men in her lifetime, dated a few, but there were only two men that she had ever truly loved and one of them it had taken a long time to get over.

Still the little dart to the heart after all these years when she thought of Steve McGrath. His rejection of her still rankled. Every time she saw him with Helena, his wife, she hated him. Many times she had told herself to forget him, forget the past, but she could not. Not even Dominic would ever erase Steve from her heart and mind. It was as though she needed the bitterness to spur her on to succeed. Each promotion, each goal achieved on the ladder of success was to show Steve that she could do it, that she was better off without him. If she had married him she would have ended up still living in Moncas Bay, mistress of Fourwinds, trapped forever in the seaside village. Oh no, she had done much much better for herself. She had travelled the world, attained class and sophistication, far more than Helena McGrath ever had, for all her affluence. Helena would be deeply impressed when she heard that Lainey had bought an apartment. No, a penthouse sounded even better. Lainey was sure she'd be pea green with envy.

She sighed. How could she still be so foolish, at her age? What difference did it make if Helena was consumed with envy or not? Why did she spend half her life hoping to make Steve regret that he hadn't married *her*? Even if he were free, she'd never marry him now. Not after loving Dominic. Dominic had cherished her, Steve had used her. Was it a waste of a life? Should she have married and had children of her own? She was now thirty-five so her biological clock was slowly but surely ticking away. If she were honest, having children didn't appeal to her. She had grown too selfish now, too used to her independence. Lainey didn't feel in the slightest bit upset at the thought of not having any. She wasn't at all maternal and she made no apologies to anyone about it. She was what she was and people could like it or lump it. She would never be happy married now. If Steve had asked her to marry him way back, deep down she knew she would have agreed, but he had married someone else. At least she knew that she would never marry for the sake of getting married as some of her friends had done, terrified when they reached thirty without having a ring on the finger. Better to end up on her luxury shelf than to live with someone who was a last resort.

This was probably the reason her affair with Dominic was so successful. He was married and could never marry her. No doubt that was one of the first subconscious reasons she had been so attracted to him, that and the fact that he had helped her regain her self-esteem, which had been so deeply bruised and battered when Steve ditched her. What a nightmare that period of her life had been. Still she had overcome it. She had prospered and made a good life for herself.

But at what cost? The thought came unbidden to her mind. Lainey picked up the inflight magazine and tried to concentrate on an article about the Seychelles. She did not want to think these thoughts. Facing the truth about her inadequacies was never pleasant and lately she seemed to be doing a lot of it. This restlessness, was it caused by getting older. Was she having a mid-life crisis? Surely thirty-five was too young to start the menopause. God Almighty! what was she thinking? The menopause happened to middle-aged women. Thirty-five was young. She'd better get out of this ridiculous humour before she landed in London.

A smile lifted the corners of her firm, lip-glossed mouth. Maybe she would treat herself to some La Perla lingerie, or maybe a little Janet Reger black number from the duty-free shop before she caught her connecting flight to Dublin. Dominic would love it, and the luxurious feel of satin and silk against her skin always made her feel like a million dollars. It almost costs a million dollars, she reflected, smiling, but to hell with it, she deserved a treat. Steve would have loved it too. Oh, for heaven's sake! she grimaced in exasperation.

Of course it was always the same when she was going home to visit Moncas Bay. It had been a few months since her last visit. She hadn't even made it down for Christmas, she was so busy in her new job as sales and marketing manager of Eagle Publishing. It had been one of the longest periods she had ever spent without returning to the place of her birth. No doubt she would meet Steve and see the desire that was always there when he looked at her. It was there in his eyes. The time he had seen her in that nothing of an emerald bikini, her skin tanned and glowing after a stopover in Santorini, her body far more curvy and sensual than Helena's could ever be, he had wanted her. She saw the hunger of remembrance in his eyes, and was so proud of the way she had walked past him with a casual "Hi Steve" to where Tony Mangan was waiting with a drink for her. Damn him, if she wasn't good enough to marry, that was his loss. He had dropped her for Helena and her money and if he was regretting it, it was too late now. Not that he hadn't done well for himself with the monied Helena.

Steve McGrath had taken over his father's ramshackle hotel, rebuilt it, and by dint of very hard work turned it into a grade-A hotel with one of the poshest eateries on the east coast. Only people with money could afford to stay and eat in Fourwinds. He also owned a large trailer and camping park about a mile away from the hotel and this investment was making him a fortune. Steve McGrath was, by all accounts, a paper millionaire, and she would have been his wife had she had money and come from a family which had so-called "class." Helena was a physican's daughter while Lainey's father had been a postmaster.

Lainey had been so sure that Steve loved her as she had loved him. She had given him everything . . . everything. And he had taken it. No girl had ever loved a man as she had loved Steve, but love wasn't enough. Was it ever? Look at Dominic. His wife was a fool. She had driven him to the arms of another woman through sheer neglect. Dominic would never have had an affair with her if his wife had treated him as a husband and not as a meal ticket. Some women could be so foolish it was no wonder that men looked elsewhere for love and affection. It took so little to make Dominic happy. It hadn't been the sex that kept Lainey and Dominic together although the sex was good. It was the sharing, the need for mutual affection after each of them had suffered rejection by the person they had loved. In each other they had found a measure of contentment that had deepened into a love that had lasted for nine years.

Dominic wanted to pay half the cost of the apartment, but Lainey was adamant. She wanted to buy the place herself, finally to have somewhere that she could call home after years of moving from one place to another.

She had always planned to come back to Ireland. The years spent travelling had cured her of the desire to settle on foreign soil. She had met so many people on her travels who had emigrated, only to find they hated being away from home and longed to return. Many of them had given up good jobs too; it wasn't unemployment that had driven them away. She had met one couple in the States, both of whom had given up permanent well-paid jobs to live in New York. The wife was working as a waitress, making good money, but up at five-thirty each morning to do so. The husband was an elevator attendant. At home he had been an electrician. It was something Lainey came across again and again and it amused her. Neither one of this pair would ever have taken jobs such as these in Dublin.

Well, she had taken the job with Eastern Gulf Airlines to make money. At least she was honest about it, and she had made money, good money, and seen the world too, but her aim had always been to come home and try and get back into publishing despite her dramatic resignation from Verdon Books.

That had been one of the most impulsive decisions of her life, but she couldn't take the bad management and sexism that had ruined all the good work and effort she had put into making that company the success it was when she had been sales and marketing manager. Being unemployed had been a most unsettling experience and she had vowed to make enough money to buy a place of her own and have money at her back. Well, she had more than succeeded and today she was going to view Apartment 3B with the intention of buying as soon as possible.

Lainey smiled to herself as the jet flew across France. Liz's apartment would be perfect. She would be in the same complex as Dominic, yet she'd have her own place where she could close the door and do as she wished. It was a good address, a mile and a half away from the city, and she liked it. It would impress the Moncas Bay set no end and that was always a little added bonus. The postmaster's daughter had done well for herself and Lainey was just the girl to let them know it, to rub their noses in it. God knows they had rubbed her nose in it for long enough, the parochial little snobs. She sighed ruefully. Honestly, at this stage of her life she should no longer feel the need to impress them at home. Being honest with herself she knew it had taken a long time before she got over the sense of inferiority she had grown up with. Now to the outside world she gave the impression of being sophisticated, a glitzy career woman who had it made. A totally together woman, as some would say. And most of the time she was. Only when she knew she was going to visit Moncas Bay did the old emotions surface.

No doubt she'd bump into her brother Simon, who was being extremely cool to her since the row at her other brother's wedding. What a poor joyless man he had turned into since he had married that bloody snob, Cecily Clarke. If there was one person Lainey really detested it was her sister-in-law Cecily. Coming down from Dublin with her airs and graces, acting as though she was Lady Muck and she only a Dubliner from somewhere off the North Circular Road. Oh, she hadn't flown from a very high roost no matter what she let on. An excuse for a lady. Tall, dyed blonde, cold, selfish, and affected, Cecily had come to live in Moncas Bay as Simon's wife, revelling in the keep-up-with-the-Joneses life-style that was enjoyed by the small socially elite set that lorded it over the rest of the Bay's inhabitants. Simon, an utter slave to his wife's whims, had little time now for his family, preferring to forget what he considered his not very well-off past, as he swanned around Fourwinds, smoking cigars and dressing for dinner with his wife, having G&Ts with Steve and Helena and the rest of the "in" set.

Simon and Cecily were so impressed by the pretentious crap that went on with the "in crowd" in Moncas Bay that it was laughable.

Lainey wasn't. She just played them at their own game. She almost laughed as she imagined the expression on Cecily's painted little rabbit face when she heard about the penthouse in Dublin. That would kill her altogether. What she lived in, though you would think it was the Taj Mahal from the way she went on about it, was a *Bungalow Bliss* style bungalow on the wrong side of the railway line. They didn't even have a sea view.

God knows, Lainey had tried at the beginning to be

friendly to Cecily for Simon's sake. And Cecily had certainly used her to worm her way into Fourwinds, but the other girl's immense snobbery and her moody rudeness had been too much to handle. Cecily was wildly jealous of Lainey and every time she heard that she was jetting in from wherever, she would nag Simon into giving her the car to go to Dublin to buy clothes in Brown Thomas. Arklow and Wexford, the nearest towns to Moncas Bay, were far too downmarket for Cecily Clarke-Conroy to shop in. Lainey had been amused at her sister-in-law's immature behaviour at first, but as time went on it got a bit wearing. The thing had come to a head at the wedding of Lainey's brother, Martin. There had been what Saddam Hussein would call the mother of all rows.

Still, seeing Maura and Martin and Joan, her sister, and her parents would be nice. Seeing Steve would be bittersweet as always, but for Cecily, she would wear the cerise and black Yves Saint Laurent suit that she had treated herself to. What Maura knew but Cecily didn't, was that it and many of her other designer label clothes had been bought secondhand in a classy swap shop in London.

As the BAC 1-11 began its descent into Heathrow, Lainey took out her makeup bag and retouched her lipstick. She studied herself in the mirror. Naturally blond hair drawn back in a chic chignon, highlighted green eyes ringed by thick black lashes that stared uncompromisingly back at her. Her lovely pout of a mouth curved in a grin. You're a bitch, you know, she told herself, imagining the desire in Steve's eyes and the envy in Cecily's and Helena's as she strolled into Fourwinds, tanned, slim, and exceedingly glam in her Yves Saint Laurent cerise and black two-piece, the owner of a new apartment if she was lucky. The world was her oyster. She had a challenging job that entailed plenty of travel. Right now she was returning from a trade conference in Rome. She was financially secure, an independent woman. And Dominic would be waiting. Maybe going home wasn't so bad after all!

# Dominic

Dominic Kent sped past the Rock of Cashel at seventy miles an hour, eager to get to Dublin. Lainey was flying in to Dublin later in the morning and he wanted to surprise her at the airport. Usually she left her car in the long-term car-park but she was having it serviced and he had told her he would be there despite the fact that she assured him she'd get a taxi. Today, for some reason, he wanted to be there when she walked through Arrivals. Besides she wouldn't have much time to waste. Today was the date of her appointment to view Liz Lacey's apartment.

He'd been so surprised to hear that Liz was selling up. It was a pity he hadn't known beforehand and he and Lainey could have done a private deal with her. It would be perfect if Lainey bought Apartment 3B. If only she would let him buy it with her! But she was determined to buy it herself. Typical of his independent partner. Trust him to pick a woman who was totally self-sufficient. The most unmistressy mistress, to use that old-fashioned sexist phrase! Other women would be thrilled to have their lovers offer to buy them an apartment. Lainey would have none of it. She would buy her own, thank you very much. Well, independent or not, he was crazy about her and he was dying to see her. Even after all these years of being together it was always special when she returned from abroad or when he came back up to Dublin not having seen her for a few days. He might be fifty-two but Lainey made him feel like twenty-two. Tonight was something he was looking forward to!

Had it ever been like that with Rita, his wife? He couldn't really remember after all these years. It certainly wasn't like it now. She had barely been awake when he slipped out of their bedroom at the crack of dawn that morning. There was a time, many years ago, when she would have made sure that he had a cup of tea at least. Now it wouldn't even cross her mind. He sighed. What a killer apathy was in a marriage. Not that Rita would ever have thought that she was apathetic, or indeed that their marriage had a problem. She was so busy on her committees, so engrossed with her children and grand-children, so consumed with everybody else that she hadn't time to think about their relationship. It had never even crossed her mind that Dominic would be unfaithful, and if she had known that he'd been having an extramarital relation-ship for the past nine years she would have asked in genuine wonder, "But why?"

He frowned. It was not what he had ever thought he would end up doing. It had caused him many sleepless nights but when he met Lainey, somehow it just seemed as though they were fated to love each other and be together. And things had worked out so well for them. His customs and clearance agency demanded that he spend half of every week in Dublin, where he had one office, and the other half in his home city of Cork. When Lainey was home he always arranged to be in Dublin, and Rita had no reason to suspect it was anything other than business that drew him there. She had no idea that he owned an apartment in Glasnevin. She still thought he slept in the bedsit adjoining his office. That *was* where he slept when she made one of her rare visits to the capital or if any of the children were coming for a visit. But damn it, he was fifty-two years old, a successful hardworking business-man and the apartment was his only bit of luxury. Not that their home in Montenotte wasn't luxurious, it was. But the apartment was his haven, his retreat from the world, a testa-ment to his success. Not bad for a fella who had started out with nothing.

He glanced at his watch. Nine-thirty. Damn, he'd meant to get the news at nine. He switched on the car radio. Gerry Ryan was talking about condoms. Typical! Still, it reminded him that he must stock up himself. No, he didn't want to

listen to Gerry Ryan. What was Gaybo on about? He was
trying to talk to Joe Duffy, but the line kept breaking down.
Dominic decided none of them could beat Joe O'Reilly on
Radio South but he had passed its range so he inserted a
cassette into the tape and relaxed to the soothing sounds of
*Madame Butterfly*. Humming to the music he pressed his foot
a little harder on the accelerator, his rugged face creasing into
a smile as he thought of his reunion with Lainey.

# *Cecily*

*C*ecily Clarke-Conroy smiled to herself as she slipped
into her Georges Rech dusky-pink pleated culottes. Culottes
were the "in" wear in the Bay this year and she had got them
on sale in Monica Johns for £100, reduced from £200. A Guy
Laroche navy linen jacket, a pair of navy Bally shoes, her
Italian leather bag and she was right. Today Miss Lainey was
going to get a right smack in the gob and Cecily was going to
enjoy every moment of it. And she was dressed to the nines to
rub salt in the wound. Lainey wasn't the only one who wore
designer clothes!

Cecily smiled at her reflection in the mirror. She'd had
her dyed blond hair cut in a bob. Bobs were the "in" hairdo in
the Bay this season. Helena McGrath had had hers done first
and the rest of the set had followed suit. What one did, they
all did, and Cecily was right there in the middle of them.

If only Simon had built a bigger house. When he became
successful, she had pleaded with him to buy a house on the
Bay Road, the Fifth Avenue of Moncas Bay, so to speak. But he
had stubbornly resisted the suggestion, declaring that he
didn't want to overextend. Of course they should have done it

years ago, but her dental-surgeon husband was always a bit cautious with money. You'd think he was having a tooth extracted whenever she presented her cheque stubs to him after one of her little sprees. Cecily smiled at her little joke. Well if he wouldn't buy a mansion on Bay Road, and wouldn't build a bigger house, he was damn well going to buy that apartment in Dublin.

Actually he had been quite amenable to the idea. It had been a brain wave on her part, really. She would never have thought of it were it not for Mrs. Conroy, her mother-in-law. When they had bumped into each other in the supermarket Mrs. Conroy mentioned casually to her that she'd had a letter from Lainey saying she was going to view an apartment in Dublin with the intention of buying. Cecily had felt a surge of jealousy. An apartment! Her sister-in-law would swan around more than ever, doing the career-girl stuff. It was sickening! *Sickening!* It was bad enough having to look at her in those fantastic clothes with her permanent tan every time she came home. But to have to listen to her going on about her apartment! Life wouldn't be worth living.

And then the brain wave had struck her! Couldn't she and Simon do with a base in Dublin? What with Andrew having started boarding school in the capital a few months previously, it would be perfect for when they wanted to go and visit instead of having to do the round trip in the one day, or stay in her parents' two-up two-down. Cecily didn't like staying at home. She never liked being reminded of her roots. Besides, she informed her husband, her son would need somewhere to stay when he went to university. It would be an investment. It would be ideal for them, and it would be just perfect for when she went up to Dublin for her little shopping trips. Not even the McGraths had an apartment in the city. Cecily and Simon's social standing would rise notches among the set.

Simon had been surprisingly and gratifyingly agreeable. The idea of their being the only couple from the Bay to own a place in Dublin had swung it for her. Simon liked to impress as long as it didn't cost him a fortune. Buying an apartment would be a good investment taxwise and although it might be a bit pricey, it would be worth it, he informed his thrilled wife. Of course he didn't realise that Lainey was interested in buying an apartment, and he certainly didn't realise that his wife had got an exact description of the apartment Lainey was interested in purchasing, through sneaking a look at her sister-in-law's letter. These little snippets of information had been kept very close to Cecily's flat bosom.

It had really been very simple to find out which apartment in Glasnevin Lainey was interested in. Cecily had rung all the big estate agents in Dublin until she found the one selling the apartment fitting Lainey's description. If Lainey was interested in it, then it had to be classy. Although it was hard to swallow, she knew that her sister-in-law had such good taste. Apartment 3B in Mountain View sounded so impressive. Convenient to the city and practically beside the new Dublin City University, it was perfect. Even more perfect was the fact that Simon had a big dental operation to perform and couldn't make the viewing. She was going alone. She wouldn't let Madam Lainey get the upper hand in this battle. Cecily wanted Apartment 3B and she was going to get it!

# THE SIXTIES/SEVENTIES

# *Liz*

*L*iz Clancy sat sprawled in an easy chair in the company of her mother and her sister, Christine, urging Bjorn Borg on to victory against Jimmy Connors in the Wimbledon men's final. Although she was up for Borg, and he was winning quite easily, compared to the previous year's marathon five-set struggle, Liz felt a sneaking admiration for Connors as he grunted his way through his serve. The man never gave up. They had been so disappointed the previous day that Navratilova had beaten Chris Evert in the women's singles.

"He made a bit of a balls of that, if you'll excuse the pun," Christine said with a grin as Connors smashed a serve into the net.

"Christine Clancy!" expostulated her mother, laughing. They cheered as Borg aced a shot right down the line to clinch victory.

"Feel like knocking a few balls around?" Liz asked her sister, as they watched the young blond hero being presented with his prize.

"Sure," Christine agreed, "let's hit Johnstown."

Johnstown Park was just across the road from them and had a dozen tennis courts. The girls played tennis there often. They ran upstairs to the bedroom that they shared and Liz pulled on a pair of green shorts and a T-shirt. Christine, being the better tennis player, slipped into tennis whites. "You just want to show off your tan," Liz accused her.

"If ya got it, flaunt it," the incorrigible Christine said, grinning as she delved into her wardrobe to find her sneakers. Christine's wardrobe was a sight to behold. "Modern art," her sister called it. A mixture of books, clothes, shoes, dolls from her childhood, and God knows what else resided there. It was the bane of her mother's life, but as Christine explained, she knew exactly where everything was, and to prove it, she held aloft her sneakers. "I knew they were in there somewhere," she exclaimed triumphantly as she tried to close the bulging doors.

Liz laughed at her efforts. "Christine, it's time you did a bit of a clean out. It's nearly as bad as when Dr. Devine came for the visit."

"Oh, Lord, don't remind me," groaned her sister, guffawing at the memory.

They had both come down with a terrible stomach bug and their mother had asked the doctor to call on them. Fortunately the bedroom was fairly tidy, and Liz had tidied it even more by shoving her artwork, charcoals, and paints under her bed. They lay, pale and wan, awaiting the doctor. Dr. Devine was shown up to their room by their concerned mother, grinned at the pair of them and called them malingerers. He then informed their mother that he quite understood why she would want to get rid of the pair by poisoning them, but that there were other methods she could use and that he would explain later. In spite of themselves the girls had to laugh. Liz, who had suffered the worst, was given an injection, and as she lay watching the doctor take her sister's temperature, an almost imperceptible movement caught her eye. A gasp of horror was stifled as she saw Christine's wardrobe doors start to bulge. It couldn't happen now! How mortifying! Her mother would have a fit! Liz lay on tenterhooks awaiting the avalanche as Dr. Devine chatted away to Christine. The bulge was starting to get bigger. The doctor stood up and walked over to the window that was at right angles to the wardrobe.

"You've a nice view of the mountains here," he commented. Oh, God, he was going to be buried under a mountain in a minute if he didn't move away. Please, please go, Liz prayed, and almost started to giggle. It had happened to her father once. He had come into their bedroom one night during a storm to close their window, when the doors of Christine's wardrobe had burst open and a stream of articles and clothes and tennis racquets had erupted. "I feared for my life, it was worse than Vesuvius," he later told their long-suffering mother. Now it was going to happen again! Only this time it would be the poor unsuspecting doctor who would get the fright of his life. Liz caught Christine's eye and nodded towards the wardrobe and saw the shock of awareness dawn on her sister's pale face. Her eyes widened, her mouth a horrified oh. Christine slid down farther under the covers and waited. "No gallivanting for a week, girls," the doctor warned as, mercifully, he took his leave of them, considerately closing the door behind him. He was halfway down the stairs and the girls were halfway out of the bed when the wardrobe doors burst open in glorious abandon. "God Almighty, that was close!" gasped Liz weakly. "Quick!" panted Christine, shoving stuff back in, "before Ma arrives up and sees this." It had been a near thing, and there had been a massive clean out the following weekend. Looking at the wardrobe with a practised eye, Liz could see that it was cleanup time again. Next weekend, they decided, as they strolled happily towards the park.

Life was good, thought Liz, as she walked beside her sister, bouncing a ball on her tennis racquet. She was twenty-one, single and free, and just out of art college, with her whole life ahead of her. She was already getting work as a result of the exhibition the college held for graduating students, and her portfolio had been commented upon most favourably. Next week, she was starting a mural for a wealthy family in Howth, and she'd been commissioned to submit the cover design of a book to a big publishing firm. If they liked her work, she'd really be flying high. Some of her friends had gone into advertising, but Liz much preferred the idea of working freelance as she didn't like to be tied down. And she was so lucky to enjoy living at home. She got on well with her parents, unlike so many of her peers who couldn't wait to get flats. And as for Christine, her younger sister by two years, there was nobody who knew her better.

They had to wait for a court so they sat watching the other players. "Would you look at that." Her sister nudged her and she turned to observe two young men in white shorts and T-shirts and tennis sweaters. Confidently they strode on to the court and the younger man bounced the ball on the line and began preparing to serve. Raising an elegant arm, he threw the ball in the air, missed completely and almost knocked himself out. "Eat your heart out, Borg!" murmured Christine as Liz tried hard not to laugh.

"What are you doing tonight?" Christine inquired.

"Ah there's a bit of a party on in Joseph Ryan's house. We're all getting together. Do you and Liam want to come?" Liam was Christine's boyfriend.

"Sure, it might be a bit of fun," agreed Christine as they took a vacated court and began to play tennis.

"Oh, you play tennis do you?" Liz heard a bearded young man, with a gold chain and pale lemon jacket, chat up her sister as Liam went to get them both a drink. "I play in Fitzwilliam myself, it's rather hard to get in there."

"Oh!" said Christine coolly. "I play in Johnstown Park in Ballygall. They're corporation courts and *anybody* can get a game . . . if ever you're stuck."

The bearded one, looking absolutely horrified at the idea of playing on a corporation tennis court, fingered his chain nervously. "Jolly good, that sounds nice," he murmured unenthusiastically as he excused himself to "mingle."

"I love taking the stuffing out of phonies," Christine said unrepentantly, with a laugh.

"Me too," agreed Liz. "And this party's full of them."

"You don't like Picasso!" The man in the purple silk shirt and matching headband almost shrieked in dismay over the din. It was later, and Liz, bored witless, was beginning to have thoughts about going home.

"No!" she retorted. "I think he was one of the biggest con artists going, himself and Salvador Dalí. A three-year-old could do what they did."

"Don't you like modern art? Don't you admire the genius of Rauschenberg, Beuys, Tàpies?" He was thunderstruck at the idea of an *artist* not liking modern art.

"Can't abide it," said Liz cheerfully. "There's too much of the emperor's new clothes syndrome, if you ask me."

"Who do you like, then?" he challenged, shocked by this shameless philistinism. Liz had no problem there, "I like the Impressionists, Manet, Monet, Seurat, Renoir, Degas. I love Gauguin but my favourite of all is Norman Rockwell."

"Norman Rockwell! My Gawd how . . . how middle-class!" the modern art aficionado exclaimed. Liz watched in fascination as his purple headband slid down over one eye. He was fifty if he was a day, but he dressed in the style of the sixties, and she was sure he must have gone to Woodstock. He was an art lecturer in one of the technical colleges. "Share a joint?" he drawled, producing some pot.

"Thanks. I'd prefer a cup of tea. If you don't mind, I think I'll go and make one," Liz said mischievously, hiding a smile as her listener almost got lockjaw.

"Norman Rockwell . . . tea . . . what are young people coming to?" the aging hippy muttered as he took a drag of his joint and went to find another nubile young lady to try and impress.

"I wouldn't mind a cup of tea myself," a deep voice in the region of the crown of her head murmured. Liz turned and looked up into a pair of twinkling blue eyes. *Hmmmmmmmmmm,* she thought to herself, he's gorgeous.

"Would you now?" she said, laughing.

"I sure would, and I can't stand modern art and I love Norman Rockwell . . . whoever the hell he is."

"You mean you were eavesdropping?" she said in mock disgust.

"I certainly was," agreed the young man shamelessly, holding out his hand. "Matt Lacey's the name and I'm gasping for a mug of tea. The kitchen's that way." He pointed help-fully with the other hand.

"I'm Liz Clancy"—she smiled back, glad now that she hadn't gone home—"and I make a mean cup of tea!" They shoved and pushed their way through the throngs. Catching Christine's eye, Liz winked before disappearing into the relative peace of the kitchen. The only occupants were a couple necking behind the door, and a young girl, out for the count under the big pine table. The lovers, seeing that Liz and Matt were not to be intimidated into departing, moved out into the back garden, leaving just the gently snoring young woman.

"Some party!" Matt said with a grin as he filled the kettle.

"You can say that again." Liz laughed as a loud shriek emanated from the bedroom above them. She studied him as he opened cupboard doors looking for mugs. He was tall, lean, with close-cropped tawny hair and blue eyes flecked with gold, and Liz decided he was a guard, a prison officer, or a soldier. The hair was always a dead giveaway. His voice had the lovely soft West of Ireland lilt that you could listen to for hours and, looking at his firm chiselled features, she decided that he would make a great subject for a portrait. Never one to beat about the bush she said directly, "I'd like to do your portrait if you'd let me."

Matt looked at her in surprise. "Would you now!" he teased her. "So you're an artist!"

Liz grinned back at him. "Yes, I am and you're a guard, a prison officer, or a soldier."

"Aha, a bit of a detective as well, I see," he remarked, smiling, as he made the tea. "There, get that inside you and then you can bring me home and show me your etchings." He handed her a mug of steaming hot tea.

Liz took a welcome sip. "Mmm, mother's milk." She sighed in satisfaction. If there was one thing she loved it was a decent cup of tea.

"Do you live in a garret like all the best artists?" he inquired, his blue eyes meeting hers with a smile.

Liz took another sip of tea. "No, I live at home, actually."

"Oh!" He seemed surprised. "And where's home?"

"Is all this going to be taken down and used against me in evidence?" Liz raised a questioning eyebrow.

"If you want me to come and sit for my portrait I'll have to know where you live," he pointed out reasonably.

"I live near Glasnevin. That's on the Northside," she added helpfully. The party was in Terenure and he, being from the country, might not be thoroughly familiar with the capital.

"I just think I might be able to locate it," he teased her. "Working as a policeman means that at least you get to know the city."

"Where are you based?" Liz asked curiously.

"Kevin Street, and I'm from Spiddal," he said, forestalling her next question.

"Ooh, Spiddal!" she said with a sigh. "How on earth can you settle down in Dublin after living in a paradise like that?"

Matt shrugged and drained his mug. "I'm the kind of person who can live anywhere. I'm adaptable. And besides I can always go back for holidays and it makes it all the nicer."

"And what is a nice Connemara guard doing at a wicked party like this? You know that people are taking . . . substances . . . and things?"

He laughed, a good hearty laugh that made her laugh as well. "Joseph is my cousin and he asked me along. And as for the substances . . . well I'm here to rescue nice young girls like yourself from crazy purple-clad art lecturers. Would you like to be rescued?" He raised an inquiring eyebrow.

Liz smiled back at him. There was something about him that she really liked—there was no nonsense nor anything pretentious about him, a thing she found so refreshing. "I'd love to be rescued," she assured him. "Excuse me for a second. I'll just tell Christine my sister that I'm off."

"How will she get home? Has she got a lift?"

"She's with her boyfriend. He's got a car so they'll be fine," she told him, liking him all the more for his concern.

Christine and Liam were chatting with another couple

and when Christine saw Liz she grinned. "Who's the hunk that made off to the kitchen with you? If it wasn't for himself here"—she dug her beloved in the ribs—"I'd have tried to get him for myself."

"That's lovely," Liz said, laughing.

"All's fair in love and war, honey," Christine drawled. "Come on, tell me everything."

"All I know is that he's a guard from Connemara, working in Kevin Street and he's very nice." Christine couldn't keep the smile off her face.

"A guard! Love the uniform! Shame about the hair!" her sister teased her. "Go on with you and don't stay out all night. If I'm awake when you get in, bring me up a cup of coffee!"

"Sure thing," Liz agreed. "See you later!"

She didn't in fact get home until six the following morning. They left the party, and Matt, a gentleman, opened the door of his beat-up Toyota. "This has seen better days, but I'm saving for a new one," he told her, grinning, as he pressed down a spring that had shot up in the driver's seat. Her own seat was fine.

"You'll probably get a Merc or a BMW with all that over-time you're getting."

"Not with the tax I pay. Come on and I'll see if I can afford a fish and chips."

"Yum yum," she enthused. Now that he mentioned food she realised that she was quite hungry.

"Would you like to go to a restaurant?" He glanced at his watch. "It's not too late."

"Oh, that would be lovely," Liz said demurely. "We could try the Mirabeau. The food is fabulous!"

Matt's eyes widened but he said évenly, "Why not?"

Liz tried to keep her face straight but it was impossible, "I'm only joking!"

"You brat!" He grinned back, showing lovely even white teeth.

"Fish and chips will do fine."

"Are you sure now?" he said seriously and she had to

resist the urge to throw her arms around him and plant a big kiss on his mouth. He was an absolutely gorgeous guy—that was for certain.

"Sure I'm sure. Drive on, Macduff, to the nearest chipper," she ordered.

"We're not just going to any old chipper," she was informed smugly. "Have you ever tasted Burdock's cod and chips? They're the best chipper in Dublin . . . in Ireland even, and I should know. I'm a connoisseur."

"Oh, yeah, I've heard of them," Liz replied. "They only open in the evening, isn't that right, and they do their chips in a special oil."

"That's them. They have this traditional recipe that's been passed down from father to son, I think," Matt said, as they drove along the Grand Canal, the yellow melon-slice moon reflected in its gently undulating surface.

Liz sighed, always moved by the beauty of nature. "Isn't that a lovely sight? Look at the light. I wish I could capture that on canvas."

Matt smiled across at her. "I must bring you over to the West with me sometime, that's where you'll get your light and your sunsets and moonrises."

"I spent a couple of weeks in the West, one summer while I was at college. It wasn't half long enough, though."

"Well, play your cards right and we'll see what we can do!" her chauffeur said as they turned off the canal and headed towards Burdock's. There was a queue halfway down the street, but it was worth it for the melt-in-the-mouth cod and chips that she and Matt consumed sitting together on a canalside seat.

"Oh, Matt, that was absolutely scrumptious," Liz said, licking her fingers with pleasure.

"Better than the Mirabeau?" he teased her.

"Oh, much!" she said, pinching one of his chips. They sat contentedly in the warm night breeze talking easily to one another and it seemed to Liz that she had known him all her life.

"Would you like to come for a walk beside the sea," Matt asked her, "or do you have to be in at a certain time?"

Liz smiled. "My parents don't put any restrictions on me. They trust me and I respect them, so I don't have to be in. Besides, you know, I'm a big girl now. I'm twenty-one."

"My God, a geriatric artist!" he said in mock dismay.

"What age are you, smarty?"

"Now she's asking me my age! How unladylike."

"Thirty!" she guessed.

"I am not!" he retorted indignantly, "I'm only twenty-eight just gone."

"Practically middle-aged," she said triumphantly as they walked back to the car and drove out to Dollymount. They walked for miles, hand in hand, inhaling the fresh salt tang of the breeze, laughing and teasing and telling each other about their lives and their families. Matt had a widowed mother and a sister and brother living in Spiddal and another brother in the States. He was close to his family, another plus decided Liz, who was very family oriented herself. She liked men who looked after their mothers. They watched the sun rise over Howth, enjoying the magnificent spectacle as the sky turned pale pink and orange, the reflection dappling the shimmering surface of the sea.

"Will I see you again?" Matt asked a little later as he escorted her up the path to her front door.

"I'd like that very much," Liz answered truthfully. A broad smile creased his face and then he bent his head and very lightly kissed her on the lips.

"See you tomorrow then?"

Liz laughed. "You're a fast mover, Matt Lacey."

"I'd want to be to catch you! I'll collect you at seven."

"I'll be waiting," she assured him. Instinctively, she knew that this man was going to be very important in her life.

"Did you have a good time?" Christine inquired groggily from her bed as Liz removed her clothes and slid gratefully under her welcoming covers.

"I sure did, Christine," she told her sleepy sister. "I think I'm in love!"

"Oh, my sainted aunt, go to sleep and you'll be all right in the morning," Christine said reassuringly, giving an enormous yawn. But Liz was already fast asleep, a smile curving the corners of her lips.

## Monday, May 21, 1979

"Congratulations, Mrs. Lacey," the doctor smiled at her. "You're approximately seven weeks pregnant." Liz sat like an idiot, beaming from ear to ear as the news sank in. She was going to have a baby, she was going to be a mother, and Matt, gorgeous kind sexy Matt, was going to be a daddy. Floating on cloud nine, Liz left the surgery and started to walk home. She couldn't wait to tell her husband. How she would last until he came off shift tonight she did not know. She'd have to tell him first, and then her parents and Christine and Don and Eve. A December baby, due just before Christmas. Matt would have to play Santa Claus!

It was a lovely warm early summer's day and when she reached Harold's Cross Bridge, she decided to sit by the canal for a little while to recover herself. Liz liked living in Harold's Cross. It was a friendly area, not far from the Kevin Street Garda Station where Matt worked, and she loved the canal, the site of their first meal together. Liz grinned as she remembered that first night with Matt, when they ate the fish and chips from Burdock's. They'd had many a single serving from the chipper since. Her thumb caressed the three-banded Russian wedding ring that she wore on her left hand. Imagine she was married for over three months! Where had the time gone?

She'd known practically from the beginning that Matt was the man for her, and he had confessed himself that once he started dating her he was a goner. He had asked her to marry him on Christmas Eve, five months after they had started dating. It had been so romantic. A warm glow spread through her at the memory. They had been standing right beside MacDowell's Jewellers on O'Connell Street, looking at the glittering Christmas trees, and listening to the carol singers who were singing "Adeste Fidelis", and it seemed to Liz that she had never felt so happy in her entire life as she did that Christmas Eve with Matt's arms around her. She just wanted that moment to go on forever.

"I'll be back in a second. I just want to get a paper," Matt murmured. "Just stay there, okay?"

"Okay," agreed Liz, it was no hardship. She loved listening to the carol singers; they really put her in the festive mood. Five minutes later he was back, edging his way through the throngs, a broad grin on his handsome face. Liz grinned back, she just loved this guy so much. "I want you to close your eyes and come with me," he instructed. "I'll lead you!"

"What are you up to now?" she said suspiciously. That Matt, he was always up to something!

"Just trust me, I want to give you a little surprise. Now close your eyes . . . please, Liz!"

"Nut!" she exclaimed, kissing him full on the mouth.

"Mmmm," he murmured, kissing her back. They stood, arms entwined, oblivious of the milling crowds. "Come on before we're had up for indecent behaviour," Matt said huskily, his eyes warm with desire.

"Oh, Matt!" Liz said and sighed, her knees feeling deliciously shaky. Matt was the most fantastic kisser! He never failed to turn her on.

"Close your eyes, you minx," Matt commanded and she obeyed happily. If Matt had told her he was taking her to the moon, she would have gone, she was so crazy about him. She felt him leading her through what seemed like a door, for the noise and singing faded and there was a quietness about the place. "No peeping!" he warned. "Now sit on this chair and keep your eyes closed." He eased her down on to a chair. She was agog with curiosity. Where in the name of God was she? Were people looking at her? She heard a sound, another person whispering to Matt, and then he was telling her to open her eyes, and she gasped at the sight that met her eyes. She sat in a jeweller's surrounded by trays of the most beautiful diamond engagement rings. Her eyes met Matt's.

"Will you marry me, Liz?" he said, and she burst into tears. Through the downpour, she could see the look of consternation on his face and the young assistant's.

"What's wrong?" Matt was mystified.

"I . . . I'm so happy," she blubbered.

Relief suffused her boyfriend's face. "Oh, for heaven's sake! I thought you were going to refuse me. But what are you crying for?"

"I always cry when I'm happy," sobbed Liz, "and I've never been so happy in my life."

The young assistant, beaming again, said delightedly, "Oohh, this is so romantic I could cry myself."

"Please don't," said Matt, laughing.

Managing to compose herself, Liz looked at the sparkling array in front of her. The rings were all so beautiful.

"Pick whichever one you like," Matt urged, putting his arm around her. She tried on this one and that one, and this one again and finally decided on a lovely classical solitaire set in a band of gold. "I'll put it on your finger tonight," he told her as the assistant wrapped up the precious package and handed it to him.

Liz had never been so happy as she was that Christmas. They made love for the first time in his cold, gloomy bedroom, with its lumpy single bed, but Liz hadn't been cold, Matt had kept her warm, covering every inch of her with his strong lean body as they snuggled together under mounds of quilts and blankets. It had been the most exquisite time of giving and taking and sharing pleasure, and Matt, her quiet good-humoured Matt, had surprised her with the depth of his passion for her, making her gasp with pleasure, arousing her to a frenzy with his lovemaking. His hands so gentle and strong traced paths of fire along her body until she had felt as though all her insides were turning to molten liquid. Matt was her first, and when he came inside her, Liz cried aloud with pleasure. Hers had been a wonderful first time. So many of her friends had confided in her that they had been disappointed, but Liz had always known that with Matt it would be perfect.

Sitting on the canal bank, with the sun warming her face, Liz felt ripples of desire running through her as she remembered that wonderful night. There had been many wonderful nights since then. Nearly every night was a wonderful night, and tonight when he got home from work, it was going to be extra wonderful. "Oh, Matt, hurry home," she murmured, getting a strange look from two little boys who were fishing in the canal.

Just under the arch of the bridge she could see one of her neighbours, Will, feeding the stray cats. He waved at her, and she waved back. Will was a pet. He owned a house a few doors down from where they had a ground-floor flat, and he had given Matt a push one day when the car wouldn't start. When it still wouldn't start, he had run Matt up to work, and invited Liz in to taste his homemade avocado-and-tuna dip. It was delicious, and from then on they were firm friends and Liz was provided with a constant supply of his speciality. He was a great handyman, and seeing Liz and Matt up to their eyes in decoration, had arrived one Saturday unannounced, with his own brushes and paint stripper, and had proceeded to organise them in no uncertain terms. He kept them at it until the work was finished and before they knew it, their ground-floor flat had been turned into a light airy home. Wait until Will heard her news, he'd be thrilled for her. Liz really got on well with her neighbours. There was a good community spirit on her street and everybody looked out for everybody else. Even though it would be a while before they were able to afford a mortgage for their own house, she was happy where she was. Happier than she had ever known she could be.

Matt was such a good man. He had spent a fortune on his mother's house, getting a new roof and an indoor toilet and bathroom built for her and he had also helped put his sister through university. That was the reason he was still living in a flat when she met him, and not in his own house. And such a cold and miserable flat. Liz was so glad they had got the place in Harold's Cross where they even had a garden. Don and Eve had bought them a patio set as a wedding present, and Liz was looking forward to eating outside. They'd tried it a few times when the weather was really fine and it had been a joy. There was something about eating outside that really gave you an appetite and just a few days ago they'd entertained Don and Eve, Christine and Liam and Will to a scrumptious chicken supreme, with loads of crispy garlic bread and red wine. Then they'd all played Scrabble with much arguing and teasing and laughing. It had been a lovely evening, one of many such that she'd had since she had got married.

God! It was hard to believe that she'd been married three months. She'd wanted to marry on Valentine's Day and the event had been a happy, homely affair. Liz had been adamant that she didn't want a whole load of fuss and faddle. She and Matt weren't the kind to want to impress neighbours and relations with a big do—they just wanted their loved ones and friends to have a happy day out and not to be worrying about whether they had to wear hats or who they were sitting beside at the meal.

One of Liz's friends, Triona, for whom she'd been brides-maid, had had a fiasco of a wedding a few weeks before Liz. Her mother had insisted on a big affair. "I wouldn't give it to the relations to say we couldn't afford it," she informed her daughter. They had had the whole shebang: red carpet, Rolls-Royce, champagne reception. It had cost a fortune, and it was the most boring wedding Liz had ever been at.

"No way!" said Matt later, as they danced to a deadly dull band that was murdering "Love Me Tender." "There'll be none of this carrying-on at our wedding. Triona's up there almost in tears, the best man is plastered and has insulted her mother and all the aunts are giving out plenty, I'll be lucky if there isn't a fight, and I'll have to do my guardian of the law bit!"

Liz giggled. It was a shame for her friend, but it really was funny that all that money had been spent, and for what? Despite the fact that it was a so-called top-notch hotel, the meal had been a disaster, served over an hour and a half late. Liz had been really shocked to see that they were served packaged soup and that the vegetables were watery and overcooked. The band was a trio of potbellied swingers in their forties who couldn't hold a note, the wedding cake which had cost the earth was as dry as the Sahara, and no one looked as though they were enjoying themselves. Liz had seen people glancing unobtrusively at their watches as if to say, how much longer? Well, Liz was having a quiet wedding with about sixty guests in Clontarf Castle, and if people didn't like it they could lump it!

As she strolled back across the bridge towards home, she smiled to herself. It had been a beautiful wedding, hers and Matt's. She had woken up to find it pouring out of the heavens, despite the statue of the Infant of Prague languishing in the front garden. "Don't worry, it will be fine for the photos. I just know it," Christine said firmly, seeing her sister's crestfallen face. The sisters had a long lazy breakfast before heading off to the hairdresser's to get their hair and faces done. Liz was damned if she was going to get into a fuss. After all this was her last breakfast at home. Through the clouds, Liz could see the sun trying to shine through.

She had promised Matt faithfully that she would not be late, and so at ten minutes to two, she was all ready to step into the Rolls that came as part of the package with the hotel. In a white satin creation made for her by Eve, and which hadn't cost a fortune, Liz looked like a million dollars, beaming from ear to ear as she took her father's arm and walked to the car. She was just so happy she wasn't a bit nervous. They reached the church and Christine, who was waiting at the steps, came over to the car, looking a bit harassed. "The lads haven't arrived yet. Go around the block again," she instructed the occupants of the Rolls.

"Looks like you've been left at the altar," her dad chuckled, as the driver put his foot on the accelerator.

"Dad!" exclaimed Liz, half amused half annoyed.

"I'm only joking! They're probably stuck in traffic somewhere. And of course you had to be on time. Couldn't trust you to be traditional." Her father smiled, giving her hand a squeeze.

"I hope nothing's wrong! It's not like Matt." She worried aloud.

"Nothing's wrong. Now sit back in this dream of a car and make the most of it."

By the time they had gone around the block three times, Liz was getting frantic. What was wrong with Matt? He'd never stand her up. Matt had more integrity than any man she had ever known. He must have been in an accident. His mother must be frantic inside the church. God, please don't let anything have happened to Matt, she prayed silently in the back of the Rolls, her hand clutching her father's. "Don't be getting upset now," her dad said reassuringly, although he was beginning to get worried himself. The driver, used to these situations, drove yet again towards the church at two miles an hour. This time, instead of Christine waving them away to complete another circuit of Ballygall, she beckoned to them with a broad grin. Mightily relieved, Liz whispered a prayer of thanks to the Almighty.

"Puncture," murmured Christine as she arranged Liz's billowing veil. At least it had stopped raining. "Matt's in bits. He's really upset about being late," she told Liz as they prepared to have a photo taken. "And Mick had a big streak of grease down his face. Fortunately I got my hands on him before he went into the church. Poor Mrs. Lacey was in flitters but all's well that ends well, so smile for God's sake!" she instructed crisply.

"I suppose Mrs. Boyce and Mrs. McNulty were having a field day," Liz murmured, as the photographer danced around looking for the best shot.

"Nearly having orgasms!" said the irrepressible Christine. "It would have really made their week if you had been stood up. Imagine the mileage they'd have got out of that!" Mrs.

Boyce and Mrs. McNulty were the two local gossips, and no wedding, funeral, or christening escaped them. They practically lived in the church.

"If bloody Patrick Lichfield doesn't take this photo soon, I'll scream," snapped Liz through clenched teeth.

"That would really thrill Boyce and McNulty. Go on, I dare you!" Christine grinned.

Liz laughed, the photographer clicked, and then she was walking up the aisle on her father's arm as all eyes turned to watch.

Matt stood at the altar, his blue eyes serious as he waited for her to reach him. "Sorry I was late, Liz," he whispered as her father gave him his daughter's hand.

"Were you?" Liz asked, wide-eyed with pretended innocence. A look of relief washed over the face of her husband to be as they turned to face the priest. Mick, the best man, gave Liz a broad wink and she winked back. And then the priest was saying, "Dearly beloved brethren, we are gathered here in the eyes of God to join Liz and Matt in holy matrimony . . ."

All the tension eased from Liz and serenity enveloped her as, watched by their loved ones, she became Matt's wife. Some moments would always remain with Liz: Matt's intent serious face as he tried to get the ring on her finger. "It's all right, Matt, you don't have to break her finger," the priest said soothingly as the congregation laughed. Christine and she catching each other's eyes after the priest had pronounced them man and wife and starting to cry. The hugs from her family and Matt's at the sign of peace. Matt's great bear hug, the best of all.

Letting herself into the flat, Liz felt a lump in her throat at the memory. It had been such a happy day, and as she told Matt when he asked her to marry him, she always cried when she was happy. The reception had been a great success. Clontarf Castle was a lovely venue for a wedding and the meal was superb. That homemade soup . . . she felt a pang of hunger as she remembered. A thought struck her. Maybe she was starting to get cravings. Thrilled with herself, she did a little dance into the sitting room that looked out onto a flower-filled patio. The difference the hanging baskets made. She and Matt had bought a load of them and Will was forever giving them potted plants. A scarlet geranium blazed against a whitewashed wall and Liz, sitting down at her patio table, was reminded of Greece. They had gone to Mykonos for their honeymoon, a fortnight in paradise.

Their rooms had led out onto a flower-filled patio, and at night the scent of jasmine and bougainvillea had been exquisite. From the patio, they stepped on to the beach and they had spent the time bathing and eating and making love. In the evening, they would stroll along the beach to Nikos's Taverna and watching the moon rise over the Aegean, they would eat moussaka and baklava and drink the lovely red house wine, serenaded by the bouzoukis. It had been a perfect holiday and Liz had come home glowing and a half stone heavier. Maybe she'd make a moussaka tonight. Yes! That's what she'd do. She'd have a special dinner, and crack open a bottle of wine, although she would of course abstain. Now that she was pregnant, she must think of the baby.

Liz spent the afternoon working on the plans for a mural she had been commissioned to do by a big insurance company. She had been so lucky to secure the commission. Interested in new talent, the chairman had been to the exhibition of work at the College of Art. She and several others out of her class had been invited to submit designs, and Liz's had been selected. It was a real break. Not that she hadn't been busy, she had. Liz had not stopped working since she graduated, but this was a biggie and was bound to get her noticed. With the fee she was getting, they'd be able to start house hunting.

She worked, engrossed, utterly happy. Once her hand slid down over her tummy and she said, "Hello, baby, your mam's working real hard and when I've done this I'm going to do a mural for your nursery and I can't wait to see you." She had read that you should talk to your baby in the womb and play music to soothe it. Well, that was no hardship, Liz always played instrumental music when she was working. Right now the mellow sounds of Acker Bilk playing "Stranger on the Shore" wafted onto her patio.

Matt rang at six and it took every ounce of self-control she possessed not to blurt out the news of their impending parenthood. "You sound real bubbly. What are you going to spring on me now?"

Liz could tell that her husband was smiling at the other end of the phone. "We got the phone bill," she informed him, rubbing her stomach gently. She wondered if the baby could hear anything or feel anything yet. Really! she was so ignorant about babies and motherhood. She was going to go to the library tomorrow and read up about it all. Oohh, she was so excited!

"The phone bill! What's so exciting about the phone bill?" Matt demanded.

"I love getting letters through the door, even if it is a boring old bill. It's the boring old life I lead. Any bit of excitement makes me bubbly." She grinned.

"I'll make you bubbly when I get home," her husband assured her in that lovely sexy Connemara accent that she could listen to for hours.

"Hurry home, Matt, I miss you," she said huskily, as desire ripped through her.

"I will," he promised.

By ten o'clock she had the moussaka ready, the aroma permeating the kitchen, making her mouth water. At least she wasn't having any awful morning or evening sicknesses. If anything, she was even more healthy than usual. Liz studied her reflection in the bathroom mirror as she towelled herself dry after a quick shower. Her blue eyes were so bright and healthy, her skin glowing, her hair, freshly washed, shining and luxuriant. She knew she had never looked so well in her life—people were always saying it to her. Marriage to Matt had been the greatest thing to happen to her and things could only get better with this beautiful baby inside her. She slid a royal blue silk camisole top on, and stepped into a matching pair of French knickers. Matt loved French knickers: they were a real turn-on for him. Wrapping herself in a matching negligee, she dabbed some White Linen behind her ears, between her breasts, and on her wrists, slipped her feet into mules and sashayed out to the kitchen feeling like a film star. The wine was chilling, the candles were ready to be lit, Matt should be up the road from Kevin Street any minute. She switched on the news and sat down in her comfy cane rocker to wait for her beloved.

There were awful things happening in the world. What would she do if something ever happened to Matt? Don't be daft, she told herself, wishing he was home. He was very late tonight. Maybe there was trouble at the station. It was a tough old life being a guard. People didn't hold them in respect any more. Life on the beat was much more dangerous than when Matt's father was a sergeant in Connemara. Only a month ago, Matt had arrived home with a black eye and a razor cut on his hand—he had been attacked by someone he was trying to arrest. Liz had nearly had a fit but her husband had just shrugged it off. Some little delinquents had thrown rotten tomatoes at him yesterday and ruined his shirt. But he had laughed at her anger and said that if it was the worst that happened to him wouldn't he be all right? He loved his job. His father had been in the gardaí, and his grandfather before him.

Sometimes Liz felt it was worse on the wives and mothers. They were the ones who sat and waited. It was a horrible job in the winter. Many was the morning that Matt had crept in at seven, frozen to the marrow after the night shift on the bike or on the beat, and she would wrap herself around him and thaw the coldness out of him with the warmth of her body. Matt loved that. He said it was worth it to be out in the wind and rain knowing that she was there waiting to warm him up. Liz smiled happily to herself. He wasn't on the beat tonight and it wasn't a night of wind and rain, nevertheless she'd warm him plenty. Tonight was going to be one of the best nights of their lives . . . if he ever got home. The dinner was going to be ruined. Where on earth was he?

That bloody car, the one that had let him down on his wedding day! It would just have to go and that was all there was about it. It really was time to get a new one. Maybe they'd have enough to buy one now that he had finished sending his sister to college. Matt was so good to his mother and family and Liz didn't begrudge the money one little bit. She'd do the same herself if the positions were reversed. Both of them knew the joy of having a close family; it was a bond that brought them even closer. Just wait until her mother and father and Mrs. Lacey heard about the new baby. The first grandchild! The excitement would be mighty.

A ring at the doorbell startled her out of her reverie. Relief flooded through her. He must have forgotten his house keys, the brat. "It's about time!" she said in mock anger, flinging open the door.

But it wasn't Matt.

"Mrs. Lacey," said Sergeant Daly, her husband's superior. "I'm afraid there's been a bit of an accident!"

## Tuesday, December 25, 1979

Liz had been awake all night thinking about Matt and the baby. Remembering how this time last year they had so romantically become engaged. Remembering the plans they had made for what would have been their first Christmas together. Liz's hand slid down over her flat stomach. Who could believe how cruel fate could be? She bit her lip to stop it trembling. But it was no use. "Oh, Matt, Matt, why did you leave me, why did you have to die?" she sobbed aloud. "Why did you do this to me, God? What did I do to deserve this? We were happy, we were going to have a baby. Look at all the horrible vicious drug dealers, murderers, and tyrants in the world, why don't you punish them? Why did you have to take Matt and my baby from me? Matt was a good man. What did he do to deserve to be killed?"

How many times had she asked these questions since that nightmare day in May when the station sergeant had told her there had been an accident. The terror and panic she felt as she hurriedly dressed and sped away to the Meath Hospital in the squad car would never be erased from her mind. A drunken driver, Sergeant Daly had told her, tight-lipped. They had to pass Matt's car on Clanbrassil Street, and when she saw the mangled remains of the Toyota, she turned pale and thought she was going to faint. He'd been so near to home and her loving arms. When she saw him in intensive care, hooked up to monitors and intravenous equipment, all the colour drained from his face, his eyes closed, she thought he was dead, and almost died herself. "Matt, Matt, I'm here. I'm with you. I love you, Matt. Darling, we're going to have a baby," she whispered in desperation over and over, willing him to open his eyes, to give her his lopsided grin. But he just lay so still and silent and unmoving. He had severe head injuries, the stoical doctor told her. He had seen it all before and he cursed the drunken bastard that was going to make this shocked frantic young woman a widow. He'd probably get a suspended jail sentence and lose his driving licence for a year while she would be left to try and repair the ruins of her life.

The nurses had been so kind to Liz. As had Sergeant Daly, who had seen to it that her family and Matt's were notified. Before long her parents and Christine were there to keep vigil with her as she watched the life drain from her husband. Never had she felt so useless, so powerless. "Don't let him die, please God, don't let him die!" she begged over and over as she sat at Matt's bedside, holding his hand. "Don't die, Matt. Wake up please," she pleaded. "I need you. The baby needs you. Oh, Matt, we're going to be so happy, I know we are. Just open your eyes for me, darling. I know you can hear me." A thousand times during that long long night she told him that she loved him and the next morning she refused point-blank to leave his side for rest.

When his mother and sister came, having been collected

off the Galway train by Christine, Liz wept for the first time as she saw the frail old woman lean over and kiss her son and whisper, "It's me, alanna. It's all right. Mam's here!" Hope battled with despair as the hours passed and they did their best to comfort each other. Mrs. Lacey whispered her rosary as she sat beside her son and Liz knew that it gave her mother-in-law comfort. She could not pray. She was too shocked to pray. She felt as though she hated God.

It was Eve who was with her when Matt died, without having regained consciousness, Eve who held her as she cried aloud in anguished terror when her husband gave a shuddering sigh and passed away.

"No! No! No!" Liz screamed as the nurses gently told her that he was dead. "Eve, he can't be dead. It's a mistake. He just can't be. We're going to have a baby, Eve. He's just asleep. Look at him!"

"Oh, Liz!" exclaimed Eve as she held her devastated sister-in-law and tried as best she could to console her. The next few days were a living nightmare for Liz. The funeral had to be arranged, the burial place decided. Liz had never even considered such a possibility in her carefree days, so when Mrs. Lacey, crying softly, said, "I suppose you'll be wanting him buried in Dublin, pet," she could only stare blankly.

"I suppose so," she agreed numbly but when she thought about it, she knew it was wrong. Matt would hate to be buried in the city. Connemara was his home, not this whore city that had taken everything from him and on whose streets he had been killed. Besides, she had only known and loved Matt for a short and precious time, his mother had loved him all his life. Let her have him back where he belonged. Even in her darkest hour, Liz's generous nature, that had made Matt adore her, shone through.

Later, when she tried to remember details of the funeral, she couldn't. It all seemed like a dream. The mass seemed to go on for an eternity and the time afterwards was just a blur. All she could remember was her hand being shaken over and over by people she was too numbed to recognise, then the guard of honour formed by his colleagues as his coffin was placed in the hearse in preparation for the long journey home to Connemara. Only as Matt's coffin was being lowered into the grave did it really sink in that her husband was dead. "Matt! Matt!" she gasped aloud in shock, unable to grasp what was happening. Everything wove away from her, the sky spun dizzily. She saw her mother's concerned face and tried to speak but couldn't, and slumped into Christine's and Eve's arms in a faint. She came to in the car with Eve cradling her head in her lap and Christine trying to get her to sip a glass of water. She felt ghastly.

"We're going back to Mrs. Lacey's now and you're going to bed," Eve said firmly.

"I can't. All the neighbours and relations are coming in," Liz replied, her voice weak.

"They won't mind at all. Now be a good girl and do as you're told," Eve said soothingly.

"Eve's right!" Christine agreed as she held the glass to her sister's lips. "You're exhausted and you've got to think of the baby!"

Tears slid down Liz's face as she rubbed her hand gently over her stomach. "Poor little baby," she whispered. And Eve and Christine, catching each other's eyes, wept with her.

The next day, Liz drove home to Dublin with her parents. She and Mrs. Lacey had talked long into the night, all about Matt, in the way that people do who are bereaved. They parted, clinging to each other for long moments in shared grief, each knowing what the other was going through.

That night in the single bed of her girlhood, with Christine asleep across the room from her, Liz ached for her husband. How cold and lonely her bed was without his strong arms around her. How strange to be at home again as if her marriage had been all a dream. What would she do now that Matt was gone? She knew she could never go back to stay in the flat again. It would be too painful. The memories would be unbearable. Too tired to think straight, Liz fell into an exhausted sleep.

Two days later she had a miscarriage.

It was work that kept her going. Doggedly she worked on the mural that she had been commissioned to do, blotting out every other thought. She gave up the flat and moved in with Don and Eve in the large house they had recently bought near her parents' home. They had an extra suite of rooms and with characteristic kindness they decorated it beautifully and helped her to move all her belongings from the flat in Harold's Cross.

The only thing of Matt's that she kept was his favourite grey-flecked sweater. As the nights got cold and winter crept closer she wore it in bed over her nightdress and derived some comfort from it during the restless dream-filled nights during which she tossed and turned and was eaten by bitterness and despair. She turned in on herself, withdrawing from people, as she sought to come to terms with her grief. Eve's loving patience with her never faltered and often she would come and sit with her in the evening, listening as Liz ranted and raved and railed against her lot.

The people in the insurance company that had commissioned the mural from her were more than kind. The managing director told her to take her time and work at her own pace and not to hesitate to come to him if she had any problems in executing the mural. Finally the day came to actually start painting. Her design had been accepted very enthusiastically and on paper it looked impressive. But would it look as good when it was painted on the wall. She fretted, uncharacteristically lacking in confidence where her work was concerned. She need not have worried. Once she started all her doubts fell away as the mural, covering a selection of some of the most important episodes of Irish history, came to life. As she put the finishing touch to the motif of St. Brendan setting off on his voyage she felt a tingle of satisfaction, the first positive emotion she had felt since her husband died. As the mural took shape and expanded, her old confidence in her work returned and she wielded her paintbrush vigorously. But in the evening when she walked through the revolving door and out into the bustling city, her heart became leaden again and depression dogged her.

She found herself unable to be near a baby. It pained her physically to see a smiling little bundle and she tormented herself with thoughts of what her own child would have been like. Would it have been a boy or a girl? Fair haired like Matt or dark like herself? She would wonder aloud to the long-suffering Eve. When a girl friend gave birth and she went to visit her in hospital, she disgraced herself by running from the ward, sobbing as though her heart would break.

More than anything she dreaded Christmas. As the season drew nearer and the lights went up in town and the shops started selling Christmas cards her depression got worse. Had she still been pregnant it would have been time for the birth and the thought haunted her. If only she hadn't had the miscarriage she would have had a baby, a living breathing part of Matt. All she had ever wanted in life had been Matt and his babies and now she had nothing . . . nothing. Unable to face Christmas at home, and unwilling to spoil it for her family who were desperately concerned about her, she told her mother she was going to spend it in Connemara with Mrs. Lacey.

"Maybe that's a good idea, love," agreed her mother as she hugged her gaunt and traumatised daughter to her. She worried so much over Liz, whose weight had dropped alarmingly and who looked pale and dull eyed and so unhappy.

"Would you like me to come with you?" Christine offered supportively. But Liz refused the offer. Christine had Liam, her boyfriend, to think about and it wouldn't be fair to drag her to the wilds of Connemara for Christmas. And besides, Mrs. Lacey was elderly and catering for another guest wouldn't be fair to her either.

The two women cried when they saw each other again, as Mrs. Lacey drew Liz into the cosy little cottage out of a howling banshee of a wind. They hugged each other tightly and then Matt's sister and brother were kissing her and she was made to sit in front of the fire while the tea was brewed.

Outside the branches of the trees rattled against the windows as the winds whistled and howled along the valley between the mountains. But the house was solidly built and snug and had weathered many a storm and in the soft fire glow, tired after her journey, with a mug of tea in her hand and a plate of buttered homemade fruitcake and scones, Liz sat in Mrs. Lacey's rocking chair and was glad she had come.

Mrs. Lacey and she sat and talked until late, and for the first time since Matt died, Liz slept soundly in the soft comfortable bed with its snowy white sheets and warm feather quilt, in a tiny room under the eaves, snug against the raging storm. The next day, Christmas Eve, she went with her mother-in-law to visit her husband's grave. The sight of the well-kept grave with its wreaths of holly and poinsettia that Mrs. Lacey had made herself made Liz feel utterly alone and unbearably sad. She tried her best not to think of the previous Christmas when she had been so exquisitely happy, tried not to think of Matt and the baby but the memories were stronger than her desire to forget and she wished with all her might that she was dead too. Death had to be better than this torment. That night she did not sleep. She tossed and turned and lay wide-eyed as the moonlight cast its pearly glow along her bed. She could see the stars and tried to lull herself asleep by counting them but the process only gave her a headache. Heavy eyed she watched the dawn light up the eastern sky. Then, in spite of her misery, the artist in her marvelled at the magnificent colours that only a Connemara dawn could produce.

Downstairs she could hear her mother-in-law moving around her kitchen making last-minute preparations for the Christmas dinner. Wrapping herself in a warm quilted dressing gown, she stepped down the wooden stairs to join her. They drank a cup of tea and had some homemade brown bread, sitting companionably together. "We'd best be getting ready for mass," Mrs. Lacey murmured sadly. "Matt loved going to Christmas mass. He loved the carols." Left to herself, Liz wouldn't have set foot in the church. She had not gone to mass since her husband was killed. If God could allow a drunken driver to murder her husband and get away with it and take away the life of her much-wanted unborn child when so many children were being aborted or neglected and abused, well Liz wanted nothing to do with him. In fact she had ceased to believe that God existed. Only that she would not dream of hurting Mrs. Lacey, she would have stayed at home.

As she sat beside the elderly woman in the packed little church listening to the choir singing "tidings of comfort and joy," a huge lump came to her throat and tears slid silently down her face. "Help me, Matt, help me please," she pleaded silently. Beside her, her mother-in-law reached out a comforting hand. She got through the mass somehow and when it was over and they were outside in the fresh blustery wind that reddened the nose and chilled fingers and toes, she turned impulsively to Mrs. Lacey and said, "I think I'll walk over to the grave. I'd like to be with Matt for a while."

"You do that, child. It might help you a little. I'll be waiting for you at home."

Liz smiled at the motherly woman and leaned across and kissed her weather-beaten cheek. "I know where Matt got his lovely nature from." Huddling into her sheepskin coat she turned her face to the wind and walked in the direction of the graveyard. Her hair whipped around her face, and she could feel the tang of salt from the breeze blowing in off the wave-tossed Atlantic. Liz breathed deeply. It was a wild fresh morning and the breeze helped clear her head which was heavy and throbbing after her sleepless night. The rhythmic roar of the sea as it crashed against the rocks near the coast road was somehow soothing and she walked along the road feeling strangely relaxed. Reaching the small graveyard, she paused and looked around. The Atlantic was on one side, the brown peaty mountains on the other and the sky a deep cobalt blue that no artist could ever capture. Liz gave a small smile. She had been right to bury Matt here and the thought gave her comfort. Standing beside her husband's grave, she gently rubbed the marble headstone. "Hi, Matt," she whispered. Was it her imagination or was it the breeze whistling through the trees but she could have sworn she heard him say with a smile in his voice, "Hi yourself."

"Don't be daft," she chided herself aloud but as she stood there she no longer felt alone and a gentle peace seemed to ease the heartache that she had lived with since his death. She stayed for a long time thinking of all their happy times and although her cheeks were wet with tears as she left to walk home, Liz no longer had that awful leaden feeling that had so oppressed her. Somehow it had lifted. The sadness she had been drowning in for so long seemed more bearable somehow. Matt would be glad about that, wherever he was. He would have hated to see the soulless, spiritless person she had become.

That afternoon, after the dinner dishes had been cleared away, Liz sat by the living-room window, her paintbrushes by her side. The sunset was magnificent and she worked furiously, anxious to capture it before night extinguished it. It was the first time she had painted anything spontaneously since Matt had died. When she finished she felt a little of the old exhilaration. "It's beautiful, alanna, really beautiful." Mrs. Lacey smiled as she stood at Liz's shoulder with a mug of steaming tea and a thick chunk of fruity Christmas cake.

"It's yours." Liz smiled back warmly.

That night in her bed under the eaves she lay in that restful state of half sleep. It must be the air, she decided, because she couldn't keep her eyes open, that and her sleepless night last night. How right she had been to come and spend Christmas here where Matt was all around her. She had been so comforted today. At least she had the memories of that wonderful time with Matt. Some women would live a lifetime and never know the happiness that she had known in the short time they had been together. That was something she would always have to sustain her. That and her work. Today she had felt something of the old satisfaction and that was a good sign. Her mural was going to be officially unveiled in the spring. It had already been greatly admired and three people wanted to see her to commission work from her as a result. There was going to be a big reception and the media were to be invited. Careerwise, she supposed, she couldn't start off the eighties any better. It could never compensate for the loss of Matt and the baby but it would channel her energies and keep her sane. Snuggling down into the warm bed she rubbed her cheek against Matt's sweater and fell asleep.

# Hugh

Sunday, March 17, 1974

*H*ugh was in his element. All around him, cheering green-clad crowds watched the New York St. Patrick's Day parade pass along Fifth Avenue, which had a thick green line painted down its centre in honour of the occasion. Hispanics, blacks, East-coast sophisticates, and native New Yorkers were all Irish for this one crazy good-humoured day.

Just a little down from where he was standing, Hugh watched a brawny mounted policeman reach down and pluck a little boy out of the way. "Here, Mama, keep your kid on the sidewalk or he'll get hurt," he said in the broad Kerry brogue that he had never lost.

Perfect! thought Hugh, motioning his cameraman to follow him.

"Sir, I wonder if you would mind doing a brief interview with me? I'm from RTE and I'm doing a programme about St. Patrick's Day in New York."

"RTE!" snapped the policeman. "Never heard of 'em!"

"Irish Television," Hugh explained.

"Ah, why didn't you say so, laddie? What do you want to know then?" The rugged cop smiled. "Sure amn't I Irish myself!" Hugh suppressed a grin as he prepared to interview the man.

He'd been dead lucky to get the assignment. Poor old Bill Deasy had been scheduled to do the item but had dropped dead of a heart attack on his way to Dublin Airport. Hugh happened to be in the programme office when the news came through and had immediately offered to do the programme. "You won't get there in time; the flight's probably left Dublin by now," the editor said glumly.

"Listen!" said Hugh authoritatively, knowing that this was his big opportunity to make it. "Hire a chopper, fly me to Shannon, and I'll catch the flight there. And ring Aer Rianta and tell them to hold that plane until I get there."

The editor stared at him as though he were mad. He thought it over. "Good thinking," he drawled laconically, his fingers busy dialling a number. Five minutes later Hugh was out of the studio like a bullet as he hailed a taxi to get him home. Grabbing his passport, a change of underwear, and a clean shirt, he told the driver to take him back to RTE to rendezvous with the helicopter. Two hours later he was outward bound over the Atlantic Ocean, en route to New York. Hugh couldn't hide his exhilaration. This was his big chance. He was sorry about poor old Bill Deasy. But *c'est la vie* as the French would say.

"Ready to roll," said the cameraman and Hugh began his interview. He spent the whole day and most of the night interviewing anybody of Irish extraction that he thought was interesting and although he hadn't slept in twenty-four hours, he didn't even notice, so intent was he on getting as much material as possible. This was gold dust, he kept telling himself. He had enough material here to make a documentary instead of the ten-minute slot needed by the TV station. If only he could persuade them to make a documentary out of it, what an achievement that would be and what a boost to his developing career! In the meantime he had made some valuable contacts here in New York. This was where it was all happening and this was where Hugh Cassidy intended to make it big, he decided, as he hailed a taxi and returned to his hotel after a night spent touring the pubs in which the Irish congregated.

Hugh rang down to room service, ordered a big juicy steak, French fries, mushrooms, onions, and a bottle of wine. He was ravenous! He hadn't eaten all day. Twenty minutes later his order arrived. Hugh tipped the waiter and tucked in. The steak was half an inch thick and melt-in-the-mouth juicy. New York was amazing! Imagine ringing room service at four in the morning at home. Ha! No, this was where he wanted to be. He'd bide his time at home until the moment was right and then he'd come back here. Contentedly, he finished his meal and sat down to watch TV. He was too wound up to sleep. He'd sleep instead on the flight home tomorrow. The sheer number of TV channels was incredible. Surely out there, somewhere, he could make his mark.

Saturday, November 27, 1976

Fastening his seat belt as the Aer Lingus 737 made its approach to Dublin Airport, Hugh yawned. He was dead tired. He'd been up since five-thirty. He'd caught the first flight to Heathrow and was in London before the shops opened. It had been a hectic day but he'd got the material he needed for his article on the Peace People.

They had held a march through London, ending in a rally at Trafalgar Square. He had managed to arrange interviews with the Archbishop of Canterbury, Cardinal Hume, and the cofounders of the three-month-old Ulster Peace Movement, Mairead Corrigan and Betty Williams. An interview with folk singer Joan Baez was an added bonus. His deadline was six in the evening and he had sat in his hotel room writing like a maniac, before finally telexing the finished item to the Dublin office. A full-page article with his own byline gave him a great sense of satisfaction. Once the plane landed he had to rush over to RTE to record an item about the peace march for a radio programme the next day. Then he was to drive to Bray to present the prizes for a young writers' award at a reception hosted by a local bookshop.

It was all go these days, but things were beginning to happen and he was starting to make a name for himself. He had even become something of a minor celebrity. More and more he was being asked to present prizes and open fêtes and the like. It was handy money, although a bit time-consuming if he had to drive halfway across the country. Bray was just fine. He'd be back in Dublin in no time.

Going through customs he was spotted by an old friend from college. "Hugh! Good to see you! How's it going? Come on, let's go somewhere for a jar."

It was with regret that Hugh said no. Noel Murray was a joker, and many was the drunken night they had spent sowing their wild oats while they were students. Now, dressed in an immaculate business suit with a briefcase at his side, Noel looked the epitome of success. He was working in computers —and cleaning up on it too, Hugh surmised, as Noel strode towards a gleaming new BMW in the twenty-four-hour carpark. As they parted, he said to Hugh, "There are a few friends dropping by tonight. Why don't you join us if you get the chance, Hugh, old boy."

"Sure thing," Hugh agreed. He could do with a little light entertainment. One thing about Noel, he gave great parties.

"See you later then." Noel handed him a card. "Here's the address. I've moved since I saw you last."

"See you later, mate." Very nice, Hugh whistled approvingly. A fancy Ballsbridge apartment, no less.

He made the party by eleven-thirty, and everything was in full swing. He saw beautiful women with come-on looks in their eyes. He'd score tonight no problem! Plenty of booze and lashings of beluga! Noel certainly knew how to throw a bash. It was a pity he was so tired though, these last few days had been really hectic. Hugh stifled a yawn as he liberally smeared caviar on a cracker. "Tired, Hughie boy?" Noel grinned, appearing beside him with a beautiful redhead at his side.

Hugh grinned back. "I'll be fine after a bit of chow. I didn't get much of a chance to eat all day. I think I'll have some of that salmon."

Noel winked. "I've got something that will set you up for the night. Come with me, my weary friend. Excuse us a mo, Donna." Putting an arm around Hugh's shoulders, he led him down a luxuriously carpeted hall and into the master bedroom. "Like my water bed?"

Hugh guffawed. "Christ! who do you think you are—James Bond?"

"Mock not. The birds love it. Believe me it really turns 'em on." Hugh did not doubt it. Noel motioned towards the marble bathroom. Once inside, he shut the door, opened a cabinet and produced a small flat mirror on which lay some white powder in neat white lines. Cocaine, Hugh guessed instantly. Rolling a fifty-quid note the other man expertly snorted a line.

"The best of stuff," he enthused, handing Hugh a note. "You won't need sleep for forty-eight hours. Here, try some."

## Monday, November 12, 1979

Hugh sat at his desk and stared out at the miserable day outside. Torrents of rain poured from the sky, hitting the pavement below with a vengeance. It was not the best day to be having his first book published. He hoped the rain would stop before the launch later that evening. Sighing, Hugh returned to the task in hand. He had been working since six that morning, it was now eight-thirty and, as Winnie the Pooh would say, he was getting "rumbly in his tumbly." He'd just finish this article on emigration and then he'd have breakfast. Head bent, he returned to his typewriter, his fingers flying over the keys. An hour later with a sense of achievement and satisfaction he switched off the typewriter and stretched his cramped muscles. That article would pay next month's mortgage anyway and the other two that he had finished would cover the car insurance and tax. After all the years of scrimp-

ing and scrounging he was finally making a name for himself.
RTE was giving him more and more work, as were the papers.
He now had a regular column in one of the Sunday papers,
and was paid a retainer by it. That retainer was a lifesaver.

As he sat eating muesli and yogurt he wondered if he
should give Karen a ring. Things weren't going too well with
them recently and she had been very cool with him on Sunday, going home to her own place instead of staying over as
she usually did. She said he wasn't giving her enough time,
that the only time she ever saw him was in nightclubs and
restaurants and that they were never alone. Hugh sighed in
irritation. Couldn't Karen understand that this was part and
parcel of his job, that he had to see and be seen. Didn't she
realise that it was a jungle out there, for God's sake, and that
you had to fight for every job that came your way. Nobody
ever made their mark sitting by the fire every night and he
wanted to make his mark. By God he did; he wanted to be
right up there with Gay Byrne and Brian Farrell and the rest of
them. And he didn't want to stop there—he wanted to make
it big in America. America was where the megabucks were
and there was an opening for Hugh Cassidy there—he knew
it. With the trend in emigration steadily rising, there'd be a
hell of a lot of young Irish on the East coast of the States by
the mid-eighties. That's where he'd make his pitch. That's
where he'd get his foothold. Johnny Carson look out! And if
Karen didn't like it, well that was tough!

He shook his head. Women amazed him. Here was
Karen, working as a researcher in RTE, travelling around the
country, meeting loads of interesting people, a bright articulate young woman who considered herself to be liberated. She
was always going to these women's consciousness groups, and
women's lib meetings and yet, behind it all, Hugh knew that
if he asked her to marry him she would say yes, and have no
qualms about giving up her career. Behind it all, she was as
traditional as the rest of them, despite the lip service she paid
to women's liberation.

Picking up the glossy hardback that lay on his coffee

table he flicked through the pages. *Positively Irish* was the title, and he had written about Irish men and women who had made their mark the world over. From St. Brendan to Tony O'Reilly, they were all there, the text accompanied by beautiful illustrations, many of them in colour. It was a quality coffee-table book and the indications were that it was going to sell very well indeed. It was just in time for the Christmas market and the advance orders were rolling in.

Of course he had had to get it published in London. It was such a shame! The major publishing houses he had approached in Ireland had liked the idea but could not afford to spend the money. "Hardback *and* colour! Too expensive, Mr. Cassidy." And as for spending money on advertising! Forget it! Hugh knew that he'd be asked in his interviews why the book wasn't Irish-published and he'd have no apologies to make. Publishing was a cutthroat business and if they weren't prepared to take risks and have some forward vision that was their problem. Hugh had written the book to make money, not for literary acclaim. He wanted it to sell worldwide by the thousands, not the measly five hundred that one of the Irish publishers had offered to publish, with black and white illustrations. His publishers now wanted him to write a series of these books. *Positively Scottish* would be his next commissioned one. Things were looking up all right. There was even talk of a TV series coming out of the book. Just as well he had got himself an agent. Marion Browne was a tough old bird, but one of the best and she'd get things moving. It was worth paying her 10 percent of his earnings.

It was Karen who had advised him to get an agent. If only she would stop pushing him to make a commitment he wasn't yet ready to make. He hadn't led her on; he'd been straight from the beginning. Why did she want to change the rules all of a sudden? He was a good partner: he shared responsibility for contraception, he always went to the women's clinic with her, and since she said she wanted to give up the pill, he had used condoms even though he hated the things. All their bills were shared and he did his own washing. Why did she suddenly want to go all respectable, hinting about getting married? This was the brave new world. She had as much control of her life as he had so why change the status quo?

Hell! He'd better get a move on, he decided, catching sight of the time. His publishers had five interviews lined up for him in the Shelbourne. It would be strange having to answer the questions rather than asking them. He tried Karen's number. It was engaged. He'd try again from the hotel. Hugh wondered if she was going to come to his launch. If she didn't, it would probably be the end for them. Honestly, you'd think she'd be happy for him that he was starting to succeed instead of moaning about never seeing him. It wasn't as if he expected her to stay in by the fire the nights he couldn't meet her. He wouldn't mind if she went out having fun with her friends. He wasn't a dog in the manger. But when he tried to explain this to her, she got mad, really furious and accused him of not caring about her. You just couldn't win with women, that was for sure. Sighing, he left his two-up two-down in Inchicore and headed for the city.

# *Claire*

Sunday, August 13, 1967

Claire Doyle knelt beside her mother at first mass in the small village church of Knockross. Molly, her mother, was deep in prayer, her rosary beads slipping silently through her fingers as she recited a decade during communion. Although it was early yet, only eight o'clock, it was clear that it was going to be a scorcher of a day. Rays of warm sunlight shone through the stained-glass windows of St. Ibar's Church, creating swirling patterns of light on the faces of the congregation as they went to receive.

Claire knelt, observing them. There was Mrs. O'Dea, the biggest hypocrite alive, devouring the statues, doing six rounds of the stations a day, and then reporting poor old Jim Casey to the tax people for doing a bit of painting and decorating on the side, while drawing the dole. What business was it of hers anyway, the nosy old bat! Poor Jim had an ailing wife and a mother who wasn't the full shilling to look after, God help him. No fear of Ma O'Dea being short of a penny, and her husband, the publican, raking it in. Claire hated O'Dea's pub. Her father spent most of his life there and only she and her mother knew what they had to put up with. Her father was the village drunkard, although there were a few more who could claim the title. She turned her head and glanced down at the back of the church.

There he was, Billy Doyle, florid, hung over from last night, and thirsting for his first official drink of the day, although knowing him, he'd already had a nip from one of his numerous small bottles of whiskey. He stood, flat cap in hand, with a crowd of men from the village. When mass was over, they would congregate outside Griffin's shop, gossiping, smoking, commenting on the people going in and out, while they waited for the pub to open. Her father would be the first in. He was an alcoholic, that was for sure, but Claire could not bring herself to feel pity for him. A lifetime of rows and fearsome drunken rages and his abuse of her mother had made her hate and fear her father. She felt her mother's eye upon her and turned again to face the altar. Rosie Lynch, a friend from school, was coming down the aisle, hands joined demurely together, head bowed, looking as though butter wouldn't melt in her mouth. She winked at Claire as she passed and Claire suppressed a grin. It was because of Rosie Lynch that she hadn't ventured to receive holy communion herself. No doubt her mother would have something to say about that when they got home. She sighed deeply. She supposed she'd have to go to confession next Saturday. That meant being in a state of mortal sin for a week. She should have gone last night but she had just lost her nerve.

What would she say? "Bless me, Father, for I have sinned. It's two weeks since my last confession, Father. I back-answered my father, I told lies to the girls at school when they asked me where I got the bruise on my arm. And I . . . I . . . was guilty of oral sex, Father." There! It was said. She could slip it in between the others and maybe he wouldn't even notice. Oh, he would! He would indeed, Father O'Toole was a holy terror. Once she had confessed to impure thoughts, and he had wanted to know if there had been actions with them. She didn't know what he was on about. All she had done was imagine Paul Newman was kissing her and you'd think she'd gone and lost her virginity or something. "How many times?" he had inquired sternly. Plucking a number out of her head, she had stuttered "E . . . eight, Father," and he'd had a sharp intake of breath and told her to say five decades of the rosary! What would he do when he heard about the oral sex? She would possibly be refused communion! Could you imagine the shame of it, going up to the altar rails and being turned away in full view of the villagers. It just didn't bear thinking about.

If only Rosie hadn't smuggled in that book to school. You could have left, she argued silently with herself. But she had been too fascinated, as indeed had the rest of the class, as Rosie sat on the teacher's desk during their lunch hour and read aloud instructions about "how to do it" from a book on the facts of life she had discovered on top of her parents' wardrobe. A pin could be heard drop, as Rosie calmly instructed them on how to use a condom, a diaphragm, and something called KY Jelly. There had been lime jelly for sweet when she went home and she just couldn't face it. Then Rosie had read out something about oral sex. It seemed that the Church did not approve of such practices, although the author felt that if both partners consented, it was all right.

The arrival of Sister Regina had put a sudden stop to Rosie's fascinating and informative lecture. But the damage was done. Claire and the rest of them, by listening to Rosie reading such a book about sex, had gone and indulged in it. It had to be oral sex, Claire had reasoned. Oral was the mouth, and sex was well . . . sex, and they had spent the entire lunch period discussing it, talking about it orally. So there it was. Oral sex. Obviously some people got very excited by talking about sex and that was why the church frowned on it. None of the others seemed too put out about being in a state of sin. A thought struck her. Rosie must have gone to confession and been absolved. *She* hadn't been refused communion, so maybe it wasn't quite as serious as Claire had thought. Giving another sigh, she leaned her head on her hands and waited for the priest to give the final blessing. They'd have to wait for a few minutes while her mother said her last few prayers and then mass was over for another week.

It took her a few minutes to get accustomed to the bright sunlight after the subdued light of the church. Outside, people mingled, greeting each other cheerfully, exchanging little bits of news and gossip. Her mother, drawing off her lace mantilla, handed Claire a pound and told her to go and get the Sunday paper while she had a few words with Mrs. Cassidy.

Claire hated going into Griffin's shop while all the men stood outside it. If only her mother would let her get a bra like the other girls in her class. After all she had turned fourteen and her breasts were unmistakably budding. Old Mickey Hayes was always staring at her with a dirty leer on his face. Once they had been at a school fair in the hall, and there had been a huge crowd around the wheel of fortune trying to get tickets before the next spin. Mickey Hayes had got behind her in the crush and started rubbing himself against her. She had actually felt his thing against her buttocks, the dirty old bastard. Even now she felt sick at the memory, her cheeks hot and flushed as she walked slowly across the churchyard. Why did men do things like that to girls? Why did they think they had a right to touch and feel, even complete strangers. Lena Murphy had been walking down a crowded street in town and a complete stranger had put his hand on her breast as he passed her by. Lena told the girls the next day at school that she had almost puked right there and then on the spot. And she felt so dirty after it. Claire had known exactly how she felt, and she had told the others about Mickey at the wheel of fortune.

And then Anita Morrissey had burst into tears and told them that her father came into her room at night and did dirty things to her. It was terrible. They didn't know what to say and poor Anita had really howled as they tried to comfort her. Rosie, always calm, cool, and collected, had tried to get Anita to tell Sister Anne, who was the kindest nun in the school. But Anita was adamant. Her father would kill her if she told and anyway she was going to run away to Dublin to her sister, who had left home to get away from her father. The only thing was he'd probably start on Sheila, her youngest sister, who was only ten. Maybe she'd try and get Sheila to come to Dublin as well. Anita had tried to tell her mother about what was going on, but her mother had told her not to be telling lies and that she was ashamed of her daughter for talking about such things. Poor Anita was in bits and they all felt so helpless.

A while later, she had run away to Dublin, and there was a rumour going around that she was pregnant. Little Sheila, who had seemed to be a happy enough child, was now pale and anxious looking, so he must have started doing dirty things to her. Rosie was so worried about it she went to Sister Anne and told her what Anita had told them. Father O'Toole went to see Mr. Morrissey, who had chased him off the farm with a pitchfork, yelling blue murder at him. Sheila still seemed white faced and tense and old man Morrissey still had the nerve to go to mass on Sundays.

Claire hunched up her shoulders and folded her arms as she neared the shop. Her heart sank as she saw old Mickey Hayes, standing, pipe in his mouth, hands in his pockets, grinning at her. "Fine girl ye are," he commented. The others, including her father, laughed. Claire ignored them, head down as she shoved her way into the crowded shop. If only she had the nerve to tell him to . . . to fuck off! God, if her mother ever heard her using that swearword she'd be disgusted. Still, she smiled briefly to herself as she took her place in the queue, he hadn't got away scot-free. After Claire told her friends at school about her experience at the wheel of fortune, they decided he had to be punished. A few nights later, half scared, half elated, Claire climbed out of her bedroom window after dark to meet Rosie and a few of the others. Rosie carried a tin of bright red paint, purchased in Waterford that day after school. They had all contributed to the cost and Rosie had managed to sneak a paintbrush out of her father's shed. The villagers of Knockross had woken up the next morning to find the ball court and the gable end of Mickey Hayes's house daubed in bright red paint.

THIS IS A WARNING TO MICKEY HAYES! MICKEY HAYES IS A DISGUSTING OLD PERVERT! HE IS IN DANGER OF CASTRATION IF HE CONTINUES HIS DIRTY DEEDS!

It was signed NEMESIS.

There had been uproar in the village. Griffin's shop had been rife with wild rumours. The parish priest had spoken from the pulpit of wanton vandalism, and Mickey had gone on a binge but no one had ever guessed who the culprits were.

"What can I get you?" Andy Griffin was interrupting her reverie.

"Oh . . . the *Sunday Press* and the *Independent,* please," she responded, handing him the money. On the counter in front of her, a cat walked delicately across the cooked ham, sniffing curiously.

"Get ta hell outta that." Andy swiped at the cat as he handed Claire the papers.

"Are you going to the hop tonight?" Mickey squinted at her as she made her way out of the shop. "Will ya save a dance for me? Yer a fine figure of a girl."

Claire's lips tightened furiously. God! She'd prefer to

walk through a fertilizer pit than to have that guy dancing with her. "Would you ever get lost!" The words were out before she could stop them and it gave her immense satisfaction to see him nearly swallow his pipe. Head held high, she walked across the street to rejoin her mother, amazed at her bravery. It was a pity she hadn't the nerve to add "pervert" to the sentence, but still, "get lost" was better than saying nothing.

"Was there a big crowd in Griffin's?" Her mother was inquiring.

"Just the usual." Claire smiled at her.

"You didn't receive this morning!" Molly's tone held the faintest hint of reproach.

"I . . . I felt a bit faint. I think my period is coming," Claire explained, lying through her teeth.

"Oh! Well, maybe you should lie down," Molly advised sympathetically. She knew her daughter suffered badly with her period.

"Maybe I will." Claire's response was noncommittal.

"Well, come along anyway, I'm starving for my breakfast."

"Mmm, me too," her daughter agreed enthusiastically, forgetting momentarily that she was supposed to be stricken with preperiod pains.

"I thought you weren't feeling well!"

"I'm not," Claire hastily assured her, "but I always feel better after eating something."

"Will you be able for a fry?"

She nodded, wishing she had used some other excuse. If there was one thing she loved, it was Sunday breakfast.

Three quarters of an hour later, Molly and she were ensconced in their small sunny kitchen partaking of rashers, sausages, eggs, and pudding. It was a Sunday tradition, theirs alone, as Billy never came home after mass. Claire looked fondly at her mother, who was reading one of the papers. Grey haired, careworn, Molly Doyle had known precious little happiness in the sixteen years of her marriage. At forty-two, she looked a decade older, thanks to her drunken tyrant of a husband. And yet she would never say a word against him, would never argue with him as he hurled abuse at her. And she would not let Claire criticise him either.

"He's your father, Claire," she would say quietly. "And as such, he's due respect."

*Respect!* She wanted to shout, I've no respect for him, I hate him for what he does to you. But she never said it, because it would upset her mother. So she just buried all her hatred inside and vowed she would never marry a man who drank.

"Isn't it a shame about Vivien Leigh?" Molly was saying. "She died last month. She was a beautiful woman, God rest her."

"Ah, that's a pity!" Claire was sorry to hear of the actress's death. Scarlett O'Hara was one of her greatest heroines, so fiery and tempestuous, unlike her own timid self.

"Do you remember we went into Waterford to see *Gone With the Wind* and we had a meal afterwards?" Her mother smiled.

Claire smiled back. "That was a good day, wasn't it?"

They had had a rare day out. Molly had been putting a little bit aside for ages and fortunately Billy hadn't managed to get his hands on the few pounds. "I enjoyed that day immensely, dear." Her mother's face lit up at the memory and Claire vowed that as soon as she started working, she would bring her mother into Waterford every week to go to the pictures and maybe have tea in a café, if she could afford it. When she was working, her mother would never want for anything again, she'd never have to turn blouses and dresses and coats. She'd had that same old coat for the last ten years, although it was always kept immaculate. A surge of love flooded through her and she leaned over and kissed Molly's faded cheek.

"Oh! . . . Oh . . . what was that for?" her mother said in a fluster, a pleased pink suffusing her cheeks. They were not as a rule a demonstrative family.

"You're a great mother," Claire said shyly.

"And you're a good caring daughter," Molly responded. "Now run out and pull a few carrots out of the garden for me, like a good girl. It's time I got some work done." Claire did as she was bid, unaware that her mother was standing watching her from the kitchen window, great big tears rolling down her cheeks.

Four hours later, the smell of roast beef, Yorkshire pudding, steeped peas, carrots, and roast potatoes, wafted through their small cottage. Claire was setting the dining-room table with her mother's Sunday tablecloth, the lovely hand-embroidered one that she had done several winters ago. The table was set for three but Claire knew it was pointless setting a place for her father. He'd come rolling in around three, after the pub closed. Her mother would have the dinner on the table at a quarter past one on the dot, but would end up tight-lipped and tense, unable to enjoy her own dinner, wondering what kind of humour her husband would arrive home in.

Every Sunday it was the same. Wouldn't her mother ever learn? Claire wouldn't give him a dinner if she were in Molly's shoes.

At a quarter past one on the dot, Claire sat down with her mother to their dinner. Her father's was keeping warm over a saucepan.

They sat in silence, Molly giving an occasional look out of the window to see if there was any sign of her husband. Claire could see her getting more tense by the minute and her own food began to taste like sawdust. Even the delicious apple-crumble that her mother served up for sweet didn't taste any better. Damn him! Damn him! Damn him! she swore silently as she cleared away the dishes. She wanted to go out, to go for a cycle or call down to Rosie but she wouldn't leave her mother alone to face him.

At ten to three, Billy came stumbling through the gate. He was drunk. Claire's heart began to beat a good deal faster and her throat closed up. "Get me me dinner," Billy ordered, falling into an armchair. Silently Molly obeyed. Billy stood up, swaying, and moved over to the table where his place was still set. Greedily he began to shove forkfuls of roast beef into his mouth, the grease dribbling down his chin. He was repulsive looking, and Claire turned away to stare out the window.

"What have you got a puss on ye for?" her father demanded irritably.

"I haven't," she said curtly.

"And that reminds me, miss, I've a few words to say to you."

"Whist now, Billy, and eat your dinner," Molly said tightly.

Her husband's face grew red with fury. "Are ye telling me to whist in me own house?" he roared.

"Billy, Billy, the neighbours will hear you." Molly's face was pinched and white.

"To hell with the bloody neighbours. I don't give a fiddler's fuck for any of them," he shouted. "None of them are good enough to lick my boots. Do you hear me, you stupid bitch?"

"Eat your dinner, Billy," Molly said wearily.

"Eat me dinner! I don't want me fuckin' dinner now! Here's what you can do with this heap of crap!" he cursed, picking up his plate and hurling it at the wall. Claire and Molly stared in horror at the lumps of meat and gravy and veg sliding down the wall over the fireplace to mingle with the shattered pieces of one of Molly's best china plates.

"And you, you little tinker you." He turned and stabbed a finger in Claire's face. "Don't let me ever hear you backcheeking any of my friends again. If Mickey Hayes wants a dance with you, you'll bloody well give him one, or I'll take me belt to you. God damn you with your bloody airs and graces. I've a good mind ta take you out of that convent. All they're doing is fillin' your head with notions. It's out working you should be, and not sponging off me, you lazy little bitch." He gave Claire a shove out of his way, glared at his wife and grunted. "Call me at six, I'm going to bed. And fix me something decent for me tea!" Lurching out of the room, he slammed the door behind him.

Claire met her mother's eyes. "Go out for a while, child," Molly said weakly. "I'll clean up this mess."

"No! I'm not leaving you!" Claire whispered.

"Go on with you now. He'll sleep for the rest of the afternoon," her mother instructed her firmly.

"Will you come for a walk, then?" Claire asked her.

Molly shook her head. "I'm tired, dear, I think I'll have forty winks in my chair, and besides I've a bit of mending to do. Go on with you now, go down to Rosie's!"

Heartsick, Claire let herself out of the cottage. Mounting her bike, she caught Mrs. Daly across the road giving her a sympathetic smile. No doubt she had heard the whole episode. With tears of shock, hate, and fury blurring her eyes, she cycled along the winding country road that led to Rosie's house. So engrossed was she in her misery that she never noticed the enormous pothole ahead of her. Before she knew what was happening she was somersaulting over the handlebars of the bike. She hit the ground with a thump and knew no more.

"Are you all right? Are you hurt? Wake up now!" A man's voice was coming at her from a distance. Groggily, she opened her eyes, and just as quickly closed them again as the sky spun crazily. "Oh, dear," she heard the man mutter. She felt arms around her, and a handkerchief wiping something wet and sticky from her face. "Wake up like a good young woman!" the voice said anxiously. Opening her eyes again, Claire saw the concerned face of Sean Moran, one of the village schoolmasters, peering down at her. Once again, dizziness assailed her, and she passed out.

### Wednesday, December 23, 1970

Claire hummed away to the air of "The Yellow Submarine" as she swept up the mass of black curls at her feet. Boy, was she glad the salon was closed and the last customer finally permed and sent out a new woman. It had been really hectic the last few days but then tomorrow was Christmas Eve and it was only to be expected.

"Turn down that racket, will you!" Mrs. Molloy, her employer, called to her. That racket! Didn't Mrs. Molloy realise that the Beatles were a group the likes of which the world might never see again. Their breakup had been a tragedy. Rosie and the girls in her old class had been devastated. Turning the dial on the radio a little lower, Claire swept on. Rosie and the girls would be on their holidays, of course. Not like her, up to her eyes. They all envied her her job and wages, but if the truth be known she would have preferred to stay at school and gotten her Leaving Certificate. Her mother had pleaded with her father to let her finish school but he was having none of it.

"She can bloody well go out to work. Isn't her Inter enough for her? It's not as if she'll have to work for long. When she finds some fool like me, she can go and get married and raise a family. What the hell will she be needing more schooling for?" Billy Doyle wanted to know.

"But Billy, she could go to university! She's very intelligent. Look how well she did in her exams," Molly protested. Claire had got seven honours in the Inter, all grade As.

"University my hat!" snorted Billy in derision. "Where she'll get more airs and graces and fancy ideas. Anyway men don't like blue-stocking women. Let her get to hell out to work and find a man for herself and stop living out of my pocket."

"But Bil—"

"I don't want to hear another word about it," roared Billy, giving his wife a shove as he headed off to the pub.

"It's all right, Mum! Honestly! Don't be upsetting yourself. Please!" pleaded Claire as she put her arms about her softly crying mother.

"If only I had a bit of money of my own," Molly wept. "I'd send you to school *and* university. I'd make sure you didn't end up like me."

"Ah, Mum!" Claire was crying now. Tears of anger and frustration for her mother whose life was governed by the whims of her drunkard husband. If only she had money she'd take her mother away from Knockross, and away from that bastard who called himself her father.

That had been just over a year ago, and Claire had started the new decade as an apprentice hairdresser with Mrs. Molloy in Waterford. Really a lot had happened to her in the last year. She'd grown up. She had taken her mother to Dublin for the day and they'd had a great time. And she had started dating! Two men had kissed her in 1970!—Jim Reid and Sean Moran, who was taking her to the pictures tonight. A dart of sadness struck her as she thought of Jim.

She had met him at a dance to celebrate the New Year and it was the best evening of her life. At first she thought she wouldn't be able to go. Her father had arrived home polluted and forbidden her to go to the dance. "Stay at home and help your mother!" he ordered before falling in a heap on the kitchen floor. Together, Molly and she had dragged him into the bedroom and managed to get him onto the bed. Molly had taken off his shoes and thrown a quilt over him. The fumes of whiskey were so strong from him that they almost gagged. He had gone on such a bender that Christmas, the worst he had ever been on, and both of them had bruises to prove it.

It had been a nightmare as usual and Claire had been tempted more than once to take a knife and stab the life out of him as he lay in a drunken stupor. She had confessed this temptation in confession once and Father O'Toole had looked at her as if she were insane, and told her that she was in a grave state of mortal sin for harbouring such murderous thoughts. From then on, she kept her murderous thoughts to herself. In fact, if it wasn't for her mother she would only go to confession once a year as was required for her religious duty. Rosie Lynch had given up going because Father O'Toole had told her that she was leading her boyfriend Finbarr into temptation and that she was "an occasion of sin" for Finbarr.

"What about Finbarr leading *me* into temptation?" Rosie exploded indignantly after confession. Rosie and Claire and some of the other girls had gone down the Rock Road for a sneaky fag in the ten-acre field. "That old sourpuss anyway," she referred irreverently to the crotchety parish priest. "If a woman came near him he'd die of fright! Well, I'm not going to confession again to give him his thrills! Anyway, if I told him the whole truth he'd denounce me from the altar!"

The rest of them were agog.

"Did you do *it*?" Mary Morrissey exclaimed.

Rosie nodded proudly. "Last night in the back of his mate's car."

"The whole way?" Sheila Conway stuttered, aghast.

"The whole way!" Rosie assured them.

*"What was it like?"* they all chorused excitedly, marvelling at her fearlessness.

"Oh, it was wonderful!" Rosie couldn't resist boasting. After all, she was the first of the set to become "a woman." "Well, it hurt a bit at first and it was a bit messy, but the second time was better," she amended honestly.

*"The second time!"* the girls shrieked in admiration. "Gosh!" said Claire, a bit taken aback. They had discussed "how far to go" and "going the whole way" but none of them had ever taken the irreversible step. In fact in Sheila's and Claire's case the question was academic as neither of them had a boyfriend.

"Were you protected?" Mary Donnelly, the practical one, enquired.

"Well . . . not really," Rosie admitted. "But I worked it out. I don't think it's my fertile time."

"You're mad!" expostulated Sheila. "What about all those hundreds of thousands of sperm. They swim all over the place and they can live for ages, you know!"

"I know . . . I know . . ." Rosie was a little irritated. "Don't take all the good out of it, Sheila! The next time we're going to use French letters. Finbarr's friend is going to get some for him."

Claire thought Rosie was exceedingly brave. Even with a French letter, she wouldn't go the whole way, if she was ever lucky enough to be in that position. She'd be petrified of all those sperm. Knowing her luck, one of them would be sure to escape. The thought of her mother's reaction would be enough of a deterrent for Claire. The shame of her daughter's unmarried pregnancy would wound Molly, far more than her husband's drunkenness ever could.

"Would you say he still respects you?" Sheila ventured timidly. She had no experience whatsoever of boys.

"Don't be daft, Sheila! This is 1969, not 1769. I'm a swinging sixties girl, heading for the seventies! Women are equal to men. Ask *me* if I respect *him*?"

The girls gazed at her in awe, Rosie was truly superb! A liberated woman. They longed to emulate her.

It was Rosie who had introduced Jim to Claire at the New Year's Dance. Molly had urged her daughter to go. "Don't mind your father. He's asleep for the night and he won't know if you're here or on the moon! Go now and wear that lovely dress you bought in Dublin!"

Claire hadn't been very enthusiastic. Her Da had taken all the good out of it as usual. But as she cycled over to Rosie's with the precious dress in her carrier basket, she began to feel excited. Rosie had invited them all over to her house to get ready and have a cup of tea before they went. Mrs. Lynch opened the door to her knock. She was a warm motherly woman, always laughing, and Claire really liked her. "Come in Claire, pet. We thought you weren't coming!" Martha Lynch exclaimed, drawing her in out of the cold. Rosie's house was decorated with lights and balloons and decorations. There were always people in at Rosie's—her brothers and their friends and the neighbours. It was open house at the Lynch's and Claire envied her friend so badly. She rarely had friends in, afraid her father would arrive in drunk and mortify her and her mother. She wouldn't have a bit of peace with him.

"I was a bit delayed," she explained.

"Well, run upstairs now and change with the rest of them and come down for a bite of supper before you go," Mrs. Lynch instructed her. The sound of girlish giggles greeted her as she sped up to Rosie's room. The scent of perfume, makeup, and cigarette smoke enveloped her as she opened the door.

"Claire! come on, where were you?" exclaimed Rosie, pulling her into the room.

"Delayed a bit." Claire smiled at the sight of Rosie, hair in rollers, white face mask covering her features so that all that could be seen were two gleaming eyes.

"Your Dad again?" she enquired sympathetically. Claire nodded.

"Ah, come on! Forget about him for tonight. We're going to have a ball! Aren't we, girls?"

"Yeah! Yeah! Yeah!" said Mary and Sheila, giggling. "Tonight's the night!"

"Let's see your dress," Rosie urged Claire. "I'd love to be left school and earning my own money. Come on, we're all waiting for you to blow-dry our hair."

Claire laughed as she unwrapped the dress. Since she had started working in the hairdresser's, the girls, even Rosie, really looked up to her, and she was always in demand for blow-drying.

"Oh, Claire! It's fab!" cried Sheila using her favourite expression of the moment.

"Gorgeous!" agreed Mary.

Claire waited expectantly for Rosie's comment.

"Sexy!" her friend said, grinning. Claire grinned back. It was a gorgeous dress, a mini in a lovely shade of blue, with a daring sweetheart neckline. Her mother had been a bit dubious about it when she had bought it in Penney's in Dublin, but seeing that her daughter really liked it, and seeing that it was her own hard-earned money, she hadn't protested too much. It was the most glamorous dress that Claire had ever owned and it made her feel so sophisticated.

The girls dressed and put on their makeup with lots of

giggling and teasing, smoking a shared cigarette and feeling as if they really were sophisticated women of the world. Knockross had never seen anything like them before. At around nine-thirty, they all trooped downstairs to a tasty supper prepared for them by Mrs. Lynch, then they all crowded into Mr. Lynch's car. Rosie, her two brothers, and the girls drove the half mile or so to the hall in the village where the dance was being held. Now that she was wearing the mini Claire was beginning to have doubts. It was so short! She hoped to God that Mickey Hayes would not be there.

But there he was, leaning against the door with his pipe clenched between his teeth, his Wellingtons polished specially for the occasion. His eyes nearly popped out of his head when he saw Claire, but she ignored him, and Rosie, glaring at him, whispered, "Don't worry! If he takes one step in your direction, he'll have me to deal with!"

"What will you do?" Claire whispered back.

"I'll kick him in the goolies!" Rosie growled. Claire soon forgot him as she and her friends, intent on having a good time, stepped out onto the floor and started to dance to the sound of Big Bob and the Bad Boys, the band for the night. All around the walls and the doors, the men watched, lowering the pints, fuelling their courage to ask for a dance. Old Paudi Leary, a crony of Mickey Hayes, came ambling over to Rosie, as the girls watched giggling.

"Would ye care to step out?" The smell of him nearly finished Rosie, who couldn't help wrinkling her nose.

"No, thank you!" she said, cool but polite.

"Huh," muttered the smelly one. "I suppose a ride's out of the question then?"

Astounded, the girls gaped at the drunken old bachelor. Then Rosie said furiously, "The only ride you'll get, Paudi Leary, will be in a hearse from Flanagan's Funeral Parlour if you don't get away from us this minute!" As he shuffled back towards the door, supping his pint, the girls let out a guffaw.

"You won't get a better offer tonight, Rosie!" Sheila spluttered.

"Shut up, you!" Rosie grinned, her good humour reasserting itself. They resumed their dancing and a little later, when the slow sets were on, made their way to the bar to try and get a drink. Rosie, sophisticated to the hilt, ordered a vodka. Sheila, a little less brave, daringly ordered a shandy made with beer while Claire and Mary, both hating alcohol because of alcoholic parents, stuck to lemonade. Rosie's brothers and their friends came to join them and then Rosie was introducing Jim Reid to Claire and she found herself staring into a pair of hazel eyes that were smiling into hers.

"Can I get you a drink?" Jim was asking politely.

Claire, eying her empty glass, supposed he would think her an awful fool if she asked for a lemonade at her age so she said just as politely, "No, thanks, I'm fine."

"Ah, come on, just one. What are you having? What's in your glass?"

"Coke," she answered shyly.

"One Coke coming up," he said cheerfully. Rosie winked at Claire behind his back and Mary and Sheila positively drooled. Claire's hands started to sweat, ruining her carefully cultivated woman-of-the-world image. She was disgusted with herself. He was nice, though. A little bit taller than her, with a head of gorgeous black hair that any girl would envy. He had a nice smiling face and he seemed very polite. It took him a while to get through the crush and by that time both Sheila and Mary were being chatted up and Finbarr, Rosie's boyfriend, had arrived.

"Here you are." Jim handed her the ice-cold Coke and she took a grateful sip.

"Thanks," she murmured, wishing she could say something scintillating and witty.

"Good dance, isn't it?" He smiled.

"Great," she agreed.

"You left school, didn't you?" he enquired and she noticed that he too was drinking Coke. Maybe there was Bacardi or something in it, though.

"Yeah, I did. I just started working as a hairdresser in Waterford a couple of months back."

"Nice!" He smiled at her.

Claire smiled back. "What do you do?"

"I'm an apprentice electrician. So if ever you need a plug changed I'm your man."

"And if ever you need your hair cut I'm your woman." She laughed, feeling more at ease. He really was very easy to talk to and her hands had stopped sweating. The band started to play a slow set and then he was asking her to dance and they were out on the floor and Jim was holding her in his arms. It wasn't the first time that she had danced with a man but Jim was different. He didn't maul her or press her against him really tightly, he just held her gently, chatting away the whole time.

"Don't you drink?" he asked curiously.

"No! My dad's a drinker and it kind of put me off."

"Oh, I see." Jim's expression was kind. "My dad's a drinker too, I don't drink either."

Claire's eyes widened. "Really!" she exclaimed. Wasn't she lucky to have met someone who understood. Jim and she stayed together the rest of the night and she had never felt so happy, or had such an enjoyable evening.

"Have you gone off on a dose?" Rosie whispered when she caught her friend alone—Jim had excused himself and gone to the gents.

"Yes," she whispered back.

"Goody!" smiled her best friend, giving her the thumbs-up as Finbarr whirled her around the floor.

A polite cough caused Claire to look up and she saw with a start that Sean Moran, a teacher from the village, was smiling at her. She smiled back. When she fell off her bike a few years back, it had been Sean who had come to her assistance and brought her to Ardkeen Hospital. He had called once to visit and she had felt so mortified. She didn't know what to talk to him about, so they just talked about school. She had given herself an awful bashing that day—cracked ribs, broken arm, black eyes. Sean had told her that he was sure she was half dead.

"Hello, Claire. How are you?" the teacher inquired.

"Hello Mr. Mor—Sean," she amended. He had told her to call him Sean.

"You're looking very nice tonight. How's the job going?"

"Oh fine, fine," she assured him.

"I was ah . . . wondering perhaps, if you would consider doing your Leaving Certificate on your own?" He stood, arms folded, sandy hair flopping over his pale blue eyes, studying her intently. "You did very well in your Inter Cert, after all."

"I never really thought about it," Claire admitted.

"Well, I think you should give it some thought. I'd be very willing to give you tuition in the evenings."

"Oh . . . oh thanks very much, Mr. Moran!" Claire was quite taken aback by his offer.

"Sean!" he reminded her with a faint smile.

"Oh . . . yes . . . Sean." She felt a bit of a fool calling him by his first name when she was so used to calling him Mr. Moran. He must be at least thirty-five. She didn't know if she wanted to study with him. How much did he intend to charge? She might not be able to afford his fee. Of course her mother would think it was a marvellous idea.

"You'd want to give me your answer soon, you know. You'd want to start as quickly as you can to get the syllabus covered."

"Em . . . er . . . what would your fee be, Sean?" she asked hesitantly.

The teacher looked horrified. "Good heavens, Claire, I wouldn't charge. I just feel you should make the most of your potential. If you like, call around to my lodgings some evening after work and we can discuss it."

"Okay," she agreed, relieved to see that Jim was heading back towards her.

"Good! Good! And ah . . . Happy New Year, Claire."

"And the same to you, Sean. Good night."

"Who's he?" Jim asked.

"One of the teachers from the primary school."

"Was he chatting you up?" he laughed.

"No, he wasn't! He thinks I should do the Leaving on my own. He said he'd help me study."

"Good idea," Jim agreed. "There's no harm having a go. But I think he fancies you. He was looking at you the whole evening."

"Give over!" Claire blushed scarlet at the idea of anyone, let alone Sean Moran, fancying her.

"And why wouldn't he be looking at you? Aren't you the prettiest girl here tonight?" Jim was smiling down at her. "Can I see you home?"

"Yes, please," she murmured, thrilled by his compliment. She wondered if he would kiss her. She really hoped he would. She'd only ever been kissed once, by Tony Carroll, a rushed furtive affair after a school dance and she hadn't really enjoyed it, Tony had nearly choked her by ramming his tongue down her throat, but he seemed to have liked it a lot. Kissing Jim would be different, she was sure of it.

It would be like something out of a Mills & Boon romance, her current favourite reading material. She and the girls devoured them and the most flattering thing they could say about a man was, "he's a real Mills & Booner." There weren't many "Mills & Booners" around Knockross, although they were all agreed that Father Kennedy, the new curate, was an absolute dish. He had been on the missions and had to return because of recurrent malaria. He had been posted to Knockross to help Father O'Toole, who was growing feeble in body if not in mind. With his tan and his hooded blue eyes and his black hair with just the slightest hint of grey at the temples, all were agreed, he was the perfect hero. And completely wasted in the church in their opinion! Practically all the readers of romance fantasised about tempting him with their nubile bodies and his leaving the church to marry them. All the young females of the village, and quite a few of the older ones, abandoned Father O'Toole's ten o'clock mass for

Father Kennedy's later one at eleven, much to the dismay of Mickey Hayes and Paudi Leary who enjoyed standing at the back of the church watching the young ones going up to receive.

Jim was a bit Mills & Boony too, she decided as they walked hand in hand up the road towards home. Claire had said good night to Rosie and told her she'd call over the next day.

"I'll be dying to hear all the news!" Rosie winked.

Claire hoped she'd have some news to tell her. Was Jim just being polite by walking her home or would he want to see her again? Was she actually going to have a boyfriend? She felt like doing a little dance up the road. She was just going to enjoy the walk home, she decided. As her mother was fond of saying *"Que sera, sera."*

It was a real crisp cold winter's night. Their breath was freezing in the air. The stars seemed so near in the black velvet sky that she felt she could reach out a hand and pluck one down. The moon, a silver sliver, hid coyly behind chiffon wisps of cloud and in the ten-acre field, an owl hooted.

"Isn't it a beautiful night?" Claire said happily. "Don't the stars look so near?"

"Look at the plough." Jim pointed. "Imagine you can see that at night in any part of the world. I wonder how many people are looking at it now?" Whoever was looking at it couldn't possibly be as happy as she was, Claire decided. What a wonderful way to start off a new decade. Maybe her whole life was going to change.

A car passed them, slowed down and reversed. Sean Moran opened the driver's window and poked his head out.

"Can I give you a lift anywhere? It's a mighty cold night!" Was it? Claire hadn't noticed.

"We're enjoying the walk, thanks all the same," Jim said politely.

"Well, good night then. And Claire," he gave her a tight little smile. "Don't forget to call next week."

"I won't!" she promised "Good night."

"He fancies you, I'm telling you," teased Jim.

"Ah, stop it!"

Putting his arms around her, Jim laughed. "Mickey Hayes and Paudi Leary nearly got heart attacks when they saw your mini. Sean Moran is trying to muscle in. I've got my hands full, I can see. But you know what?"

"What?" she smiled.

"I'm the one that's walking you home!" Bending his head, his lips met hers in a long, passionate, and very romantic kiss.

An hour later, after a walk that should have taken, at the most, fifteen minutes, a dazed and happy Claire walked with Jim beside her up to her front gate only to stop in horror as she saw Billy Doyle, furious and still drunk, waiting for her.

Oh, God! Why are you always picking on me? she screamed silently as Billy lurched towards them.

"Where the bloody hell were you, and I after telling you not to go out tonight?" he yelled, grabbing her by the arm. "I'll teach you to disobey your father!"

"Now just a minute, Mr. Doyle!" protested Jim heatedly.

Billy tried to focus bleary eyes on the younger man.

"You mind your business, you young whippersnapper. And get out of my garden or you'll feel the toe of my boot!"

"Please, Jim, go now. Please! It'll be okay," Claire whispered, dying with shame that he should be a witness to her drunken father's uncouth behaviour.

"I think I should stay," Jim said firmly.

"Get out!" roared Billy.

"Please, Jim!" She was crying now.

Reluctantly Jim turned away as her father shoved her through the front door.

"You impertinent little bitch, bringing that gobdaw back to my house," he shouted, spittle drooling down the side of his mouth. "*I'll* learn you!" Taking his belt off he lashed out at her, striking her on the face and legs. The stinging lash of the strap was nothing to the pain in her heart. Jim would never want to see her again. Her father had ruined things for her yet again. Hatred that had been repressed for so long finally erupted.

"I hate you. You drunken fucking bully. You're a . . . a bastard . . . a mangy slob of a bastard and I hate you!" she yelled as his fury increased and the lashes got more frantic.

"Don't" . . . lash . . . "you" . . . lash . . . "talk" . . . lash . . . "to me like that!" Billy put all his weight into striking her with his belt as she stood there screaming at him.

"Stop it Billy! Billy, I'll call the guards—I'm telling you!" A white-faced Molly launched herself at her husband, dragging him away from Claire, who had collapsed onto the floor under the violence of his blows.

"That one gets out of my house tomorrow; I've had just about enough of her," Billy said viciously, as he rethreaded his belt through his trousers.

"And I'll be with her," sobbed Molly, wringing her hands.

"Ah, good riddance then!" her husband grunted, staggering into the bedroom.

"Claire! Claire child, are you all right? It was all my fault, I didn't think he'd wake up but he did. Claire, love, are you all right?" Molly was frantic at the sight of her battered daughter at her feet.

"I'm all right, Mum." She tried to whisper, but her mouth felt as though she had lead in it and she could feel the hot wetness of her own blood. Molly tried to lift her up, and eventually Claire managed, with her mother's help, to get to the bathroom.

"I think I'll have to get the doctor for you, Claire," Molly whispered, horrified at the sight of her daughter's wounds.

"No! No Mum, it looks worse than it is," Claire said weakly, catching sight of her black and purple face, swollen to twice its normal size. Between them, they managed to bathe her cuts but the pain was excruciating where Molly touched them gently with disinfectant.

"Get into bed now, Claire. We'll talk in the morning," Molly whispered, tucking the sheets around her daughter.

In the dark, alone, heart pounding, hot tears slid down

her cheeks. What was she going to do? Her father had told her to get out and anyway after tonight she didn't want to stay at home. But where would she go? And what about Jim? Would he ever want to get in touch with her again? Claire cried herself to sleep.

The next morning she awoke in agony. Her body ached all over and she could barely drink the tea that Molly brought her. Of her father there was no sign. Molly said he had left the house after his breakfast. Gone to visit his mother, he told her. He gave no indication of remembering anything about the night before. "Should I call the doctor?" Molly asked worriedly. "You're in an awful state."

"I'll just stay in bed today and I'll be all right. Honest, Mum," Claire assured her. She'd be mortified to have Dr. Nolan find out what had happened to her. She lay cocooned in her comfortable bed. Claire loved her bed and bedroom. It was the place she could escape all her worries. Billy never set foot in it so it was a true haven. Molly had painted it pink, her daughter's favourite colour, and a fluffy white sheepskin rug covered the gleaming polished floorboards beside her bed. A poster of Paul Newman, her absolute favourite star, faced across the room at her, his famous blue eyes twinkling down. Next to the poster a picture of the Virgin Mary and the Infant Jesus. On her old-fashioned dressing table lay Claire's recently purchased lipstick and eyeshadows, her pride and joy. She loved experimenting with makeup but took care not to wear too much in case her father would notice. Outside, the rain lashed against the window panes and a howling gale made keening eerie sounds. Her mother had lit the fire in the bedroom and Claire lay watching the flickering flames casting giant shadows on Paul Newman, wishing she could stay there forever.

Later, coming out of a half sleep, she heard voices at the front door, just down the hall. Molly slipped into the room. "It's Rosie. Will I tell her you're sick? You don't want her to see you in that state, surely?"

Claire shook her head and winced. Every movement

caused her pain but she didn't mind Rosie seeing her. Rosie was her best friend, she shared the good times and the bad. But even Rosie found it hard to contain herself when she saw the way Claire looked.

"Jesus Christ! Claire! Are you all right? Girl, you should be in the hospital!" she exclaimed in concern.

"Shush, Rosie. I don't want Mum getting upset," Claire whispered.

"Oh, the bastard, the dirty bastard." Rosie was nearly crying as she took Claire's hand. "You've got to get out of this house. You can't put up with that just because you go to a dance and bring home a fella! Jim told me about it."

"Jim did!" Claire blushed in shame.

"Yeah, he was really mad. He wanted to come back and see if you were okay but I persuaded him not to. I thought it might make things worse."

"Thanks, Rosie," Claire murmured gratefully.

"He wants to know if he could call and see you at work. He wants to ask you out again but he doesn't want to call to the house in case it causes trouble."

Tears welled up in Claire's eyes.

"Oh! what's wrong? Does it hurt?" her friend asked in concern.

"Oh, no . . . no it's just I'm so glad Jim wants to see me again after . . . after last night. I'm just happy, that's all." Claire gave a little laugh as she wiped away her tears. Jim had seen her humiliated by her father. Seen her at her worst and he still wanted to meet her again. Well to hell with Billy Doyle! She was going to see him and Rosie was right—she couldn't continue to live at home. She'd have to get a flat or lodgings but at least she wouldn't be in fear of her father.

A week later, her body healing, her bruises fading, Claire sat in an attic room in an old house in Waterford, surrounded by all her worldly goods. It was a nice bright little room with a good view of the harbour. Rosie's aunt owned the house and Claire was taking up lodgings with her. The only thing that worried her was leaving her mother alone to put up with Billy.

She had tried to persuade Molly to leave her husband. "Please come with me, Mum. We'd manage—I know we would."

"I couldn't leave him, dear. It's my duty to stay. Father O'Toole told me so in confession. I married him for better or worse. He's my husband and who'd look after him?"

"Let him look after himself!" Claire retorted bitterly.

"Claire, I'll be all right," her mother said cheerfully. "Don't worry about me. I'll have great peace of mind knowing you're in a good warm clean place with Rosie's aunt. Sure I'll be able to come and have tea with you at the weekends. We'll have great times going around the shops." But at night when Claire, tired after a hard day's work, lay in her new divan, she worried about her mother and wondered how she was getting on alone with Billy.

True to his word, Jim had called in to the salon, ignoring Mrs. Molloy's disapproving gaze. "Will you come out with me tonight?" he said softly so that the older woman couldn't hear. "What time will I collect you? You'd better give me the address. Rosie said you'd taken lodgings here in the city."

Claire nodded and gave him the address and directions and then he was gone and she was standing grinning foolishly to herself, until Mrs. Deegan squawked at the sink, and she realised that the lather had gone into her eyes.

The next few months were the happiest of her entire life. The strain caused by living with Billy vanished and her true fun-loving nature started to emerge as her self-confidence increased. Rosie and Finbarr and Jim and she had some of the greatest times, going for drives in Finbarr's old car, going to dances and having fun. Rosie's aunt didn't mind Jim calling to the house and he was a frequent visitor for tea. Each weekend she cycled home to see her mother, who was always delighted to see her. Billy never spoke two words to her.

She got the surprise of her life when Sean Moran walked into the salon one day. He must have heard about why she left home—the whole village knew—because he never passed any remark about the fact that she was now living in Waterford.

"Did you ever give any thought to doing the Leaving Cert?" he asked as they stood outside the door watching the traffic going by. Claire had asked him to come outside. She didn't want Mrs. Molloy knowing her business and it was obvious that she was dying to know who Sean was.

"I thought it might be a bit awkward now that I'm living in Waterford," she murmured.

"I'll tell you what," he said kindly. "I'll drive in to Waterford two evenings a week if you like and we could study in your lodgings." He seemed so eager for her to take the exam that she felt it would be churlish to refuse and so, twice a week from seven until nine, she began to study the Leaving Cert syllabus with Sean Moran. To her surprise she rather enjoyed it.

The bottom fell out of her world when Jim called one night looking grim and upset. His employer had collapsed and died and Jim was out of a job. For weeks he tried to find employment but the one job he did land had terrible conditions and pay much lower than what he had been earning.

One evening they were walking hand in hand along the harbour. Jim said suddenly, "I'm getting out, Claire. I'm going to Australia. I've a brother over there. At least I'll be getting decent money." Claire felt as if her heart had shrivelled up and died. She had fallen in love with Jim, although he did not realise it, and now he was going away from her.

"I'll miss you," she managed to say, afraid she was going to disgrace herself by bawling.

Jim hugged her tight. "I'll miss you too, but we'll write and you can always come out and visit," he promised. She never forgot the day he left for Dublin Airport. The pain in her heart seemed almost physical as she kissed him for the last time. His parents were driving him to the capital and they waited in the car as he bade his farewell to her. "I'll write, Claire, I promise," he told her, hugging her hard. Mrs. Molloy sniffed sceptically. Claire stood waving at the doorway as he drove down the street, knowing she'd never love anyone the way she loved Jim Reid.

That night she disgraced herself in front of Sean Moran. He was explaining the points of geometry to her when to his consternation she burst into tears. Silently handing her a handkerchief, he waited for her to compose herself. "Maybe we won't do any more tonight if you don't feel up to it," he said calmly. "Would you like to come for a drink and tell me what's troubling you?"

They went to Ryan's down the road and she had told him about Jim leaving. "Aah," Sean said knowingly. "I see." Claire stared at the sandy-haired man sitting opposite her. He was a bit dry, to be sure, but he was kind in his own way and lonely. He didn't drink either, she noted, watching as he took a long draught of his 7-Up. At least she'd have her studying to keep her occupied in the long lonely nights ahead.

Jim wrote, as promised, a glowing epic about how much he was enjoying his life in Australia. "I miss you," he wrote. "Hurry up and save enough to come over." She wrote back by the next post, giving him all the news. His reply took a bit longer to come and he had only written a couple of pages but she sent a ten-page missive anyway. Each day from then on she would watch for the postman, heart beating a little faster as he came to their gate, only to feel an intense disappointment as he passed by. At last the awaited reply arrived, a page of rushed writing. Deep down, Claire knew that Jim was making a new life and that the new life didn't contain her. When Sean Moran asked her to go to the pictures with him one evening, she consented. When he kissed her, she kissed him back. She knew what it was to be lonely and so did he. They had that much in common at least. Her life took on a routine: studying with him two nights a week, the pictures every Friday and home to visit her mother on a Sunday. Rosie was always there for her. Rosie didn't care much for Sean but she kept her own counsel. She told herself that Claire had been hurt by Jim and Sean Moran was just a stopgap until she got over him.

That was why Claire was going to the pictures with Sean the day before Christmas Eve. They were going to see the smash hit *Butch Cassidy and the Sundance Kid* and she was looking forward to it. It might take her mind off the thought of spending Christmas at home. It was the last time she'd see Sean over Christmas as he was going home to spend the holiday with his parents in Drogheda. He arrived all of a fluster, realising that he had left his wallet back in Knockross. He wouldn't dream of letting Claire pay and nothing would do him but to drive back to the village for his money. "You can call on your mother while we're here," he told her.

Walking up the pathway with Sean behind her, Claire wondered if Billy were at home. She opened the door with her key and called out a greeting. Molly did not respond. Maybe she was out feeding the dog in the back, Claire thought, walking into the kitchen. She got the fright of her life. Molly lay, head on the kitchen table, not moving.

"God! Mum's sick!" she said frantically.

"She's not sick, Claire!" Sean spoke slowly and bemusedly, seeing the whiskey bottle on the table. "She's drunk!"

## Wednesday, June 30, 1971

The sea breeze whipped Claire's hair around her face as she stood on the deck of *The Lady of Man* passenger ship watching Howth slip by as they headed towards the Dublin docks. It was hard to believe that she was coming home. The week on the Isle of Man had gone by so fast. But she had had a lovely time and Sean had treated her like a queen during their week's honeymoon. She looked down at the gold wedding band and the diamond solitaire on the third finger of her left hand and smiled. So here she was, Mrs. Sean Moran, a married woman, an innocent virgin no longer.

Sean had surprised her with his passion. Usually he was so reserved, so much in control. But on their wedding night, in the small Dublin hotel off the quays where they had stayed before going to the Isle of Man, he had been a different man to her. To be honest she had been a bit anxious about their first night together as man and wife. When they were courting, Sean had always been very circumspect. After all he was one of the schoolmasters and he had to be careful not to give any hint of scandal, so they had never been very intimate. She had felt very shy as they undressed for bed together that first night. It was the first time a man had ever seen her in her nightdress. Rosie had given it to her as a present. It was white satin, with the thinnest little straps, and it was so revealing. But she had promised Rosie she would wear it, and when Sean came out of the bathroom in his maroon pyjamas and saw her, he had given a sort of a gulp and stood as if rooted to the spot. Claire blushed furiously and dived under the covers of the double bed. They stared at each other and she felt that he was as terrified as she was. Finally Sean broke the silence.

"Claire, you look so beautiful. I'm a very lucky man." He eased himself into the bed beside her and they sat smiling shyly at each other. Then he took off his glasses, switched off the bedside lamp and put his arms around her. In the dark, hesitantly and then passionately as desire overcame him, he made love to Claire. He told her over and over that he loved her, that he wanted her, that he had dreamed of her ever since he had first encountered her that day she had been knocked off her bicycle and as his breathing quickened and his endearments became more passionate, Claire had found herself responding to him with a pleasure that amazed her. It was just like Rosie had said she'd feel, all tingly and wet and melty. She was thrilled with herself. She felt so powerful that she could arouse her husband to such heights of passion. As her confidence grew, her inhibitions eased. It was such a pleasure to have a warm male body so close to you, to have arms around you and to be able to put your arms around someone back. It was just a little bit of a pity it was all over so fast and that her body felt somehow unfulfilled. But as she lay in the dark listening to Sean's satisfied snoring she gave a happy little sigh.

That morning she had been Miss Claire Doyle, a girl. Tonight she was Mrs. Sean Moran, a woman. It had been a lovely day and a lovely night, much nicer than she had anticipated. Even her wedding, which she had been dreading because of her father, had turned out well. Of course eleven o'clock was too early to be pissed out of his skull—that was one of the reasons she had decided on a morning wedding rather than an afternoon one. In fact ever since that day Sean and she had discovered her mother drunk, Billy Doyle seemed to have eased off a little on his own drinking.

Even though the night was warm, Claire shivered at the memory of that night. Her mother had passed out at the table with a half bottle of whiskey at her elbow. It was the most horrific shock Claire had ever had. Sean had helped to lift her mother to bed and then she told him to go, in case her father came home drunk.

"I can't leave you here alone with the two of them!" Sean declared.

Claire pleaded with him. "Sean, honestly, it would be better if you go home before he comes in. Please!" It was with great reluctance that he did go and for that, she would always be grateful to him. Her mother lay, mouth agape, breathing harshly, and when her father came home, and saw the state of her, and the half-empty whiskey bottle, the shock had almost made him sober. Later, Molly woke up and was violently ill. Claire tended to her, while Billy paced up and down in an agitated state, muttering to himself.

"Why, Mum? Why?" Claire asked numbly the next morning, as her mother, pale as a ghost and nursing a ferocious hangover, sat at the breakfast table with her head in her hands and a piece of dry toast on the plate before her. Billy for once remained mute, utterly shocked by the events that were taking place.

"Why?" repeated Molly, still half drunk. "I wanted to see," she said slowly, her words slightly slurred. "I wanted to see what he gets out of it. I wanted to see what drink can give him that I can't! I wanted to forget all my troubles for once. Do you know, Claire, that man has given me nothing but worry and misery?" She pointed a shaking finger at her horrified husband. "Promise me that you'll never marry a man who drinks! Promise me, Claire."

"Ah, Mum!" Claire was crying now. Crying with pity for the thin worn woman at the table in front of her. Molly began to weep herself.

"Stop that now, stop that carrying-on the both of yez," Billy Doyle muttered. "I'll go down and get you a cure for your head, Molly. Stop that crying now." In all the years of their marriage, Billy had never seen his wife like this, broken, dishevelled. It was frightening. "Make her stop," he ordered his daughter.

"I hope you're satisfied now," Claire said furiously. Billy, who was about to retort, was silenced by the hatred and fury in his daughter's eyes. That Christmas, for the first time ever, he was home on time and relatively sober for the Christmas dinner that Claire had cooked. She insisted that Molly sit at the fire and relax and as she worked in the kitchen she swore that no man would inflict on her the misery that Billy Doyle had inflicted on his wife.

That evening Sean phoned from Drogheda to wish her a happy Christmas. "Are you all right?" he asked. "Is your mother all right? I've been terribly worried about you." She felt great warmth towards him for the first time. It was nice to have someone worry about her, nice to have someone share her great burden. She didn't feel quite so alone. He came back to Knockross a few days later with a gold chain for her and as she kissed him in thanks, to his surprised delight, she realised that in his own way, Sean Moran loved her. When he asked her to marry him she agreed, remembering her mother's words. He was a good man and at least she'd never have to worry about him coming home to her drunk. He was twice her age but at least she felt safe with Sean. He treated her with respect and kindness, something she had never experienced with her father.

Her mother was so pleased when she told her. "He's a good man, Claire. He'll look after you well." Billy just grunted something unintelligible. But Rosie had been terribly shocked to hear of her friend's engagement to the schoolmaster.

"He's much older than you, Claire. You've your whole life ahead of you. Why don't you leave here and come to Dublin with me? We could get a flat together and have such fun. You've plenty of time to settle down and get married. What's the rush? Marriage isn't the be-all and end-all of life, girl! I'm not going to get married until I'm at least twenty-five. Please, Claire, think about it! Don't rush into anything."

But Rosie was so different from Claire, so confident and self-assured. Claire was different. Having lacked security all her life she was greatly attracted by the prospect of marriage to a man who could give her a serene and secure life. Sean would never abuse her and he would protect her from the harsh world. The more she thought about it, the more marriage appealed to her. How lovely it would be to have her own home, to cook meals for someone who would arrive on time and appreciate them. To have someone to share her joys and pleasures with, someone who would appreciate her as Sean clearly did. Her whole life had been a struggle against hatred and terror of her father. Sean would rescue her from all that.

They were married six months later. Rosie was her bridesmaid. As she walked down the aisle on Sean's arm and saw her mother smiling at her, Claire knew that by marrying Sean, she had given her mother great peace of mind. The thought gave her added pleasure and as they emerged into the sunlight from the sombre shadow of St. Ibar's, Claire felt a moment of true happiness before she was enveloped in a flurry of hugs and kisses from Rosie and the girls. Lying beside her husband in the double bed, Claire smiled at the memory. Maybe happiness was in her grasp after all.

·Now, sailing into Dublin after her week's honeymoon,

Claire looked more happy and relaxed than she had ever done before. They had had a wonderful week. The weather had been good, the hotel they stayed in delightful. They had eaten out a few times and explored the small island. At night, sitting in the hotel lounge in Douglas, they would watch the lights come on and Claire had never seen anything so magical. Strings of fairy lights all along the promenade made the place look like something out of Disneyland. Claire never tired of looking at them. And the shops. She would have spent the whole day in the shops if she had got the chance. Claire grinned as she remembered the hundreds of naughty post-cards of big bosomy ladies and skinny men. Rosie and the girls would have howled laughing at them. Sean had not been impressed when he caught her giggling. They didn't appeal to his sense of humour one whit. He thought them vulgar and had forbidden her to send any of them. But she had kept the ones she bought. They were safely in her handbag and she would give them to Rosie and the girls personally and enjoy a laugh with them.

Sean did not like anything suggestive or vulgar—that much she had learned about her husband on their honey-moon. He had almost had a fit when she had dressed one morning in a pair of hot pants. They were a gorgeous shade of yellow and she had bought them in Waterford especially for her honeymoon but Sean had made her go and change into a skirt. "I don't want men looking at my wife's legs," he said firmly. She knew he didn't like her wearing a bikini either. In fact he had gone and bought her a swimsuit instead. But apart from that it had been a lovely week with little to trouble her and she was looking forward to going home to tell the girls all about it.

As the ship moved gracefully towards her berth, Sean, pasty faced and wan, joined her on deck. He was not a good sailor! "We're almost there," she said comfortingly.

"Thank goodness for that," he replied, brushing his sandy hair away from his glasses. "We're a bit late. I hope we'll make the train in time."

"Of course we will." Claire smiled reassuringly. Honestly, Sean was such a fusser! "Anyway, we can always stay in Dublin for the night and go down tomorrow."

Sean looked horrified. "We can't go over our budget, Claire. We'll have a lot of expense when we get home."

She gave a little sigh. Her husband was right of course. They were moving into a small cottage that had to be furnished and the rent paid for, but still, one night extra in Dublin wouldn't break them. It was a pity she had to give up her job but it wouldn't be practical to cycle all that distance to Waterford day in, day out. And besides, Sean told her he didn't want her to work after they were married. But the money would have come in handy all the same. Still she might be able to make a few bob doing hairdressing at home. Brightening at the thought she smiled at her husband and he smiled back at her.

## Sunday, April 16, 1972

Claire held her tiny week-old baby as she wriggled and squirmed on her knee. She was trying to dress her in her christening robes. She was absolutely terrified as she tried to insert one tiny arm into the satin-beribboned christening robe that had been her own.

This tiny being with a mind of her own had caused Claire intense anxiety since she brought her home from the hospital two days before. Every time she cried, she nearly had a heart attack. What was wrong with her? Was she getting enough food? Had she colic? Why did her face go so red when she roared? It was all most distressing and Sean was no help. "Sure you should know these things. You're a woman! These things come natural to a woman!" he said helplessly as he watched the bawling mite in dismay.

"Well, I don't know what's wrong with her. I don't think she's getting enough food." Claire was really worried as she unfastened her blouse and put the child to her breast.

Sean averted his eyes. "Why don't you do that in the bedroom?" he muttered awkwardly.

"Because I'm doing it here," Claire snapped, in un-characteristic bad temper. Lack of sleep and fear that she would never be a good mother were taking their toll.

"Very well," her husband retorted tightly, two pink spots on his cheeks. Claire knew she had annoyed him. He was so easily annoyed. She watched him retreat in a huff. Should she know what to do automatically because she was a woman? Should maternal knowledge come instinctively? Claire had never felt so helpless in her life.

From the moment when she discovered she was preg-nant, Claire had felt a sense of growing unease. As her body was taken over by the child inside her, she had a feeling of resentment that caused her great anxiety. She must be unnat-ural, she thought, as she waved away the early-morning cup of tea that Sean brought her. She had always loved her first cup of tea of the morning but, ever since she had become pregnant, she couldn't face it. She didn't think that was very fair really. Pregnancy was something you had no control over. It controlled you, changed your moods, changed your taste, gave you backache and heartburn and made you fat. Her boobs were huge! At night you couldn't sleep because of the kicking and if Sean said once more that it was a miracle of God she would swing for him. What distress did *he* have? None! Not one ounce of physical distress. He was going around as proud as a peacock telling all and sundry that he was going to be a father.

She must be odd. Her pregnancy had given her no joy. Not one bit. She was petrified at the thought of labour and what did she know about babies? Sean couldn't understand her! She couldn't understand herself! The only good thing about it was that she was spared the agony of her period for nine months.

Of course it was inevitable that she would get pregnant. She should have thought about it before. After all that was what marriage was all about. Sean wanted children and so did she but she would have preferred to wait a while. When she had suggested using contraceptives Sean was absolutely horrified. You would have thought he'd been asked to commit murder. "Claire, it's against the teachings of the church! I'm surprised at you!" he declared in dismay when she voiced the thought one day after a false alarm. "Don't you want children?"

"Yes . . . but not yet. I want to get used to being married first. I want to have them when I'm ready to have them."

"Tsk, Claire, that's no way to talk. I have no time for this modern stuff. God will bless us with children as he sees fit and that's the way it will be."

"That's all right for you to say," Claire protested heatedly. "*You* don't have to have them!"

"But you're a woman, Claire! It's the natural thing for a woman!" Sean had been amazed at her attitude. "Now don't be worrying yourself over it—there's a good girl."

Claire sighed. There were times when her husband treated her like a schoolgirl and she resented it. Still, maybe he was right. She was quite happy as she was, although having a baby would give her something to occupy herself with. Since she had left work she found the days long until Sean came home from school at three-thirty. He had been totally against the idea of her doing home hairdressing for a few extra bob. Didn't want the tax man after him, he said when she suggested the idea. Marriage was not quite what she expected. Sean was very thrifty and expected her to account for every penny that was spent. On Saturdays he took her to the supermarket in Waterford where they bought their weekly groceries. He signed the cheque that paid for them, Claire never handled the money. She had a small float to cover things like milk and bread from Griffin's shop but at the end of the week, she had to account for what she had spent. If she needed anything for herself like tights she had to ask him for the money to buy it.

Sean loved Saturday night when he would spend an hour going over his accounts. "We've saved ten pounds this week, love," he'd inform her cheerfully. Silas Marner couldn't have been happier than Sean at his accounts on a Saturday night, Claire thought fondly as' she observed him in the firelight, with his head bent over his account book, writing happily. There was always good food on the table and plenty of coal for the fire but there was no doubt that her husband was a very careful man with money. It was Sean who had selected the furniture for the house and he had a preference for brown that depressed her. Brown curtains! Brown suite of furniture! Brown carpets! She had been so looking forward to decorating her home. Some of the magazines in the hairdressing salon where she had worked had given her great ideas and she had been dying to try them out. Pink and grey, cream and apricot, lemon and white, she had furnished and decorated each room of their tiny cottage in her mind's eye many times, but the reality was always there. Dull Brown! "It's easy to keep clean and it will last, Claire!" her husband assured her. Still, at least she had a roof over her head and a loving husband—so she often told herself.

But confirmation of her pregnancy had left her with an awful feeling of dismay. So many things could go wrong. Her sessions at the maternity clinics only compounded this fear as other women swapped horror stories of things that could and did go wrong. Sean would never come with her, even when he was on holidays: "That's all women's business. I don't want to be interfering."

Molly was a great comfort to her. "Don't be fretting, child. I'll be with you," she'd reassure her poor upset daughter.

Claire was right to be worried. She'd had a terrible long and painful labour before the little red-faced bundle was placed in her arms. Then she'd had to learn to breast-feed! The baby wouldn't suck and the nurses said not to bother, it was much easier to give her the bottle but Claire had stuck to her guns. She wanted to breast-feed. It gave a good start in life to the child, at least that was what she had read. Not that bottle-feeding had caused her any harm but she wanted to breast-feed her baby and after a few tears and false starts she at least succeeded in that. She knew that Sean was disappointed that the baby wasn't a boy. He couldn't conceal it as he leaned over the cot and took a look at his daughter. "Never mind, we'll have a boy the next time," he assured her. That's what you think, Claire thought to herself. There never would be a next time if she had anything to do with it. Once was enough to go through that ordeal.

Having suckled her daughter five minutes on the right breast, five minutes on the left, Claire recommenced the struggle with the christening robe. The baby stared red-faced at her mother. She couldn't be! She had just been changed, for God's sake. Laying her tiny daughter on the sofa, Claire investigated and had her fears confirmed. She'd have to change her again! Was it natural to be having so many soiled nappies? Maybe she had the runs. She seemed healthy enough, and now that she had been fed again, quite contented. In fact she was falling asleep. Blast it! Claire would never get that bloody christening robe on. A beaming Molly entered the sitting room. Claire had never been so glad to see her mother as she was that minute. Catching sight of her harassed daughter's flustered face Molly said comfortingly, "Go on up and get ready and leave the babe to me." Claire obeyed with alacrity.

Watching the priest pour the holy oil over her sleeping daughter's forehead Claire felt a mixture of emotions. Pride, love, fear. This helpless little being was dependent on her now so she'd better get her act together and stop panicking because it was obvious that Sean was going to leave her to get on with it. She caught Rosie's eye and smiled. Rosie was the godmother and she was besotted with the baby. In fact for the first time in her life, Claire knew that Rosie envied her. As Rosie handed the baby back to her after the christening, she woke up. Claire gazed down at her tiny daughter, who stared right back at her with eyes unblinking. "Well, here we are," Claire whispered. "You and me. We'd better do the best we can."

# Lainey

*L*ainey Conroy stamped out ten Mills & Boon romances to the borrower standing at the desk in front of her. It was three-fifteen, and she was starving. It must be time for tea break soon, so she'd be able to have a sandwich. Lainey had worked her lunch to enable her to leave early to catch the train home that evening. By rights, she should have been off this afternoon and due to work until nine, but one of the other girls had wanted a swap and Lainey had been only too happy to oblige.

It was no joke, working in the public library service. The hours were dreadful. She worked late two nights a week and every second Saturday, having Thursday off instead. Big deal! What use was a Thursday to anybody? Everybody at home thought she must be making a mint on overtime. What a laugh! They weren't paid one measly penny for their unsocial hours. When Lainey started work six months before, she was told that her job was more important than her social life.

Because she was the most junior person on the staff, Lainey had to work late on Monday and Friday nights and this meant that on her weekend off she couldn't go home until Saturday, so getting off early was a real bonus. "Tea time!" Anne, one of the other girls, called out to Lainey and the two of them walked into the back workroom.

"If one more smart alec tells me it must be great to have nothing to do all day except read books, I'll split them!" exclaimed Lainey.

Anne chuckled. "You'll get used to it. How are you getting on in the flat? Do you like living in Dublin?"

"It's fine and I love Dublin," Lainey assured her. "You must come over some evening."

"Lovely," agreed Anne. "We could go to the pictures or something. Do you think you'll last in the libraries?"

Lainey shook her head. Although she really enjoyed the variety of the work and meeting the public, and though most of the people she worked with were extremely nice, a great bunch in fact, the hours were dire and the working conditions were tough. Already she had worked in three different branches, had her nights changed at a moment's notice, and knew she could be transferred from one library to the other according to "the exigencies of the service," as the higher echelons put it. What about *her* "exigencies"? She'd had to look up the dictionary to find out what the word meant! Lainey didn't intend to spend her life hopping and trotting across the city, spending hours waiting for buses. She knew one poor unfortunate who lived in Shankill and had been transferred to Phibsboro. Imagine doing that journey in the rush hour! She knew of another girl who had recently moved to a flat in Rathmines, to be near the branch she worked in. A week later, she was transferred to Baldoyle Library. "One must be flexible in this profession," she had been informed loftily when she complained. "I don't mind being flexible within reason but I'm not made of bleedin' India rubber!" she announced in disgust as she filled out her resignation form.

Remembering this, Lainey grinned at Anne. "I don't think so, somehow or another. I don't think I'm exactly what they are looking for. I might try and get into the general services, because the carrying-on couldn't be any worse than it is here."

"It's a pity because the work here is very interesting and you work with really nice people . . . like myself!" Anne laughed as she plonked herself down on a chair and poured out a cup of tea. "God, my feet are killing me! I didn't sit down once today—it was so busy at that desk! Of course, your woman"—she nodded towards the librarian's office—"is inside all day drawing a timetable for the children's summer project. You should see it, the writing is tiny but very fancy, all these curlicues and things—but the kids won't be able to read it. I'd have had it done on the typewriter in twenty minutes. This is her second day on it and wait until you see—she won't even go out to the desk to relieve us for the tea break. And that's what she was sent to college for, on ratepayers' money! It's disgusting. Here's you and me getting half the salary, running around like fools! While she's inside drawing!"

"Ah, but!" Lainey remonstrated, "as the higher-ups would put it, she's 'very artistic.'"

"Very artistic, my arse!" snorted Anne, tucking into a cream slice.

"Some of them take themselves *so* seriously," Lainey reflected. "I was told that we were here to disseminate information, not to entertain, so put that in your pipe and smoke it!"

"*Puke!* How did you keep a straight face?"

"I don't know," admitted Lainey, as the buzzer on the intercom went and the plaintive voice at the other end apologised for disturbing their tea break, but there were ten people at the desk, two dogs were fighting in the porch, a child had piddled on one of the chairs, someone was on the phone trying to find out the capital of Mongolia for a competition she was entering, and the librarian hadn't appeared to relieve Anne and Lainey.

It was a very tired Lainey who stood waiting for a bus into town later on that evening. There had been a big rush in the afternoon and they had been run off their feet. She was hot, tired, and very apprehensive about getting down to Amiens Street Station to catch her train. Three weeks ago to the day, three car bombs had gone off in the city, right in the middle of the Friday rush hour, killing twenty-three people and injuring more than a hundred. It had been one of the greatest days of horror in living memory. One of the bombs had gone off in Talbot Street, along which she must pass to get her train. Since the tragedy, she, like everyone else, had been nervous walking the streets of the capital. Each parked car was a potential threat and she found herself taking deep breaths and rushing past two cars parked illegally. Her family had been frantic with worry that Friday until she was able to phone to reassure them that she was all right. If only she was on the train. It would be nice to get down to Moncas Bay for the two days. She might go to the beach and have a swim if the weather remained fine. Anyway it would be terrific just to unwind for a while. She liked her life in Dublin, but there was no place like Moncas Bay for relaxing in the sun.

The traffic was brutal and she sat almost steaming with impatience on the bus ride into town. Finally reaching the city centre, she took off down Talbot Street as though all the devils in the universe were after her. Heart thumping loudly, she passed Guiney's where the bomb had exploded. Just keep going, she told herself, keeping the façade of Amiens Street Station in view. While she was passing under the railway bridge a train thundered overhead and for a moment she nearly jumped out of her skin. Fool! she cursed herself. She was breathless, perspiration trickling down between her breasts. She had never felt so hot and sticky in her life. Licking a bead of salty sweat from her upper lip, she groaned as she saw the queue at the ticket kiosk.

Crikey! She'd never make the train. The minutes seemed to stretch into an eternity as the queue shuffled slowly forward. A young guy in front of her tried to pass himself off as underage and there was an argument. Cursing bitterly, he paid full fare and finally she was able to purchase the precious ticket to Arklow. Another queue at the ticket checker's gate and then she was legging it down along platform four, which had never seemed so long before, to where the Rosslare train was almost ready to pull out. Hauling herself and her bag on to the last carriage, she stood gasping at the window as the porter slammed the doors shut. Then they were moving slowly out of the station.

The train was packed, she noticed in dismay. She'd probably be standing all the way to Arklow. Tripping over a student's rucksack she made her way along the swaying train, hoping against hope that there might be a seat at the front. Everybody else seemed to have the same idea and there was a lot of passing and excusing as they all tried to achieve the same goal. It was useless: the seats were all occupied and the passageways just as crowded. In a thoroughly bad humour and with the beginnings of a pounding headache, Lainey hunkered down in one of the corridors and prepared for an uncomfortable journey.

She had given up hope of a seat, when a group of four rose to depart at Dun Laoghaire and because she was nearest the entrance to the carriage, she was able to make a successful run for a seat. So did about half a dozen others, three of whom were successful. Lainey sank back into her window seat with a sigh of satisfaction. Apart from the few minutes on her tea break, it was the first time that she had sat down all day. They were passing Dalkey now and she settled down to enjoy the view.

The whole panorama of Dublin Bay spread before her. A big cargo ship was heading into port away over to the east, and above, she could see a jet making its descent towards Dublin Airport. As they headed towards Killiney, she could see strawberry-pink houses dotted along the overhanging cliff. Some of the houses and gardens out here were magnificent, but of course this was where the monied people lived, and what a beautiful place it was. The beach below, though stony, was fairly crowded still, and along its length she could see children dancing around, building sandcastles, while their mothers knitted and read and their fathers snoozed. Swimmers bobbed in the sea and the surging surf rushed in and carried them with it as they shrieked with delight. Spaced apart like sentinels, fishermen cast their lines into the sea in hopes of catching "the big one."

As the train sped by, young and old alike turned to wave. There was something about a train going by that made people wave. When Lainey was in her own home as a child, she had always waved at the train going past their garden and loved it when someone waved back at her. Now, feeling like the queen mother, she waved back to the smiling occupants of the beach. Others in the carriage did the same and for a few moments a sense of camaraderie spread through the carriage as its occupants smiled at the people below, and then a little foolishly at one another, before retiring back into their books, papers, and thoughts. Before long they were thundering through the Bray Tunnel, and she caught sight of a reflection of herself in the window.

She didn't look too bad, considering how hot and sweaty she felt. Her blond hair was in a French plait that one of the girls in work had shown her how to do, and it made her look so sophisticated. Her eyebrows had been plucked and shaped nicely last night, and her nails painted a delicate shade of lavender to match her lipstick and her lavender pants. The pants had been a good buy. She'd got them in a sale in Roche's, and they were linen, very cool and casual looking with just that little bit of class. She wore a white loose-knitted sleeveless top and white espadrilles and her large summer shoulder bag, for which she had searched the city, was exactly the same shade of lavender as the trousers. Colour coordination was so important—it always finished the look so well. All in all, she decided, she didn't look the way she felt. She looked dressy yet casual. Anne had told her she looked like something out of a magazine and she felt such a great sense of satisfaction. She was getting there! Lainey had learned a lot since she had come to Dublin, and she would go on learning. She'd be as good as that lot in Moncas Bay yet. Lainey Conroy would show them.

Rooting in her colour coordinated bag she withdrew a book and settled back to put in some serious study. *Etiquette For Every Occasion: A Guide To Good Manners* was the title. She had got it in the library that very morning. Honestly, the library was great for things like that; she could look for information on any subject under the sun and be sure of finding something. Scanning the chapter headings she came to "Dinners, Restaurants and Hotels." Lainey's lips tightened. Never ever again would she not know what cutlery to eat with and what side plate was hers, as had happened on a mortifying occasion when she had been invited to dinner by the Mangans. Lainey's cheeks flamed at the memory of her introduction to "the set." The Mangans lived in Sea View, a big eigh-teen-roomed Victorian house overlooking Moncas Bay. They were loaded and leaders of high society in the area. They had three daughters and one son, and every matron in Moncas Bay had their eye on the poor unfortunate youth as a potential wealthy spouse for their marriageable daughters. Unfortu-nately for them, although they did not know it, young Tony Mangan's taste did not run to women. It was to Lainey that he had confided this awful secret when she caught him trying to drown himself off the pier one early summer's evening during their Leaving Cert examination.

Her brain addled from study, she had decided to take a walk before going to bed to try and induce a good night's sleep. In the pearly light just after sunset, as the encroaching night was beginning to cast shadows, she walked briskly down the road that led to the pier. There was a slight breeze, enough to blow her hair from her face, and she sniffed its salty scent appreciatively. She felt better already! No one dis-turbed her solitude. The fishing boats were in, the nets lining the pier awaiting mending. Behind her, along the cliff's edge, house lights were starting to twinkle, delicate pinks and yel-lows and whites, depending on the colours of curtains and lampshades. Ahead of her the pier curved protectively around the bay, its high storm wall seeming almost impenetrable. Lainey had seen the winter sea exert its authority on the high solid wall, waves lashing over the top on wild and stormy nights.

But tonight the sea was flat calm and she climbed the steps of the pier to walk along the top. She thought she heard a noise. It must have been the gulls, but no, they were long gone. Maybe a seal then. Sometimes they fed on the small fish thrown overboard from the fishing boats. It came again, a faint cry, and peering out into the gloaming she saw someone struggling in the water.

"Jesus help me, someone's drowning!" she cried aloud, her hand going to her mouth. "Oh God . . ." She looked around frantically for a lifebelt but saw that it had been stolen off its hook and she cursed the scum who had stolen it. On their heads be the person's death if he or she drowned. Quickly, unthinkingly, she flung off her sandals, and without hesitation dived off the wall into the sea. She gasped as the icy water hit her, but she came out of her dive in a graceful curve and struck out to where the flailing swimmer was. Lainey was a strong swimmer, and had dived from the pier many times with the boys from the village, the only girl to dare to do it. Now she thanked the Lord that she had accepted their challenge because, had she not done it already, she doubted that she would have had the nerve to do it in the almost dark. She could see the swimmer's struggles getting weaker and more desperate as she fought to get near. She realised that it was a man and that he was fast reaching the end of his tether.

The current was strong but just as he was finally sinking under water she caught him. He had not the strength even to panic anymore and for that she was grateful, because she knew he could have drowned her. Catching him under the chin, she raised his head and began to make for the pier. Her arms seemed to be getting heavier and heavier but she bit her lip and forced herself to swim. It wasn't too far away but to her, the looming wall seemed unreachable. "Please, God!" she pleaded in desperation as she fought the current that swirled and eddied around the curve of the pier. If the weather had been stormy she knew they could have been battered against the rocks, but, as if in answer to her prayer, a wave lifted them along and deposited them within arm's reach of the big boulders that protected the pier. Treading water, she managed to grab one. Where she got the strength from she would never know, but she pushed and shoved until the youth was lying motionless across it. Hauling herself up alongside him, she knelt astride and began to squeeze the water out of his lungs. He seemed to have swallowed half of the Irish Sea and she was beginning to think she would have to give him the kiss of life when he gasped, spluttered and gagged. "Thank God! Thank God! Thank God!" she muttered over and over again as shock hit her and she started to shake.

"Ye bloody idiot, going swimming on your own at this hour of the night," she spluttered angrily.

Then, peering in the dark at the person she had rescued, she recognised with a shock that it was Tony Mangan. "What the hell are you swimming in the sea for? Haven't you got a swimming pool at home?" Then, looking down at the prone youth beside her, she said a little more calmly, "Do you think you could walk? We'll have to try and get up the steps over there to get you home."

"I don't want to go home! Just go away and leave me alone," Tony muttered, burying his head in his hands.

"You don't want to go home? Don't be daft! Why not? Nobody will say anything to you about ruining your clo—" A thought struck her. He was fully dressed. Why would anybody go swimming while fully dressed? Sacred Heart! He'd been trying to commit suicide!

"You tried to do yourself in, didn't you?" she demanded, totally baffled. "Why? Is it because of the Leaving Cert?" Lainey knew that Tony was taking the exams as well.

"You wouldn't understand so why don't you just fuck off and leave me alone!"

"Listen, Buster!" Lainey spat out, outraged, "I just saved your goddamn life. Don't be so bloody rude!" They glared at each other and then Tony started to laugh a little hysterically.

"This is pure crazy, you know."

"You can say that again!" Lainey replied indignantly. "Come on, let's get the hell out of here. I don't know about you but *I'm* freezing." She had started to shiver.

"Oh! . . . Oh! . . . I'm sorry," he said, and her heart melted as she saw him staring at her, water dribbling down his face from his soaking hair.

"I'm sorry I called you a bloody idiot," she apologised. "I just got such a fright."

"I'm sorry too. Come on, let's get out of here or you'll catch pneumonia and won't be able to finish the Leaving Cert," he muttered. They helped each other up and somehow managed to climb the steps of the storm wall. They made a sorry-looking pair squelching wetly along, but fortunately no one saw them and as they came to the fork in the road where their ways parted, Lainey asked anxiously, "Do you want me to go home with you?"

"Naw," he said gruffly.

"But will you be all right? I mean you won't do . . . you won't try to . . ."

"Look, I feel a bit of a fool standing here in wet clothes. I won't try to commit suicide again . . . well, not tonight anyway," he amended morosely. "Good night . . . and . . . er . . . thanks."

"Good night," she responded, troubled.

Lainey did not sleep well that night. She was worried about Tony Mangan. The next day after her exam, Lainey dawdled past the boys' school until, to her immense relief, she saw Tony appear.

"Hi," she said cheerfully.

"Hello," he responded sheepishly.

"How did you get on?"

"Okay. How about you?"

Lainey grimaced. "Just about passed, I'd say." They walked towards the bus stop in silence, but when the bus arrived, Tony sat beside her.

They bumped into each other several times during the exams, and his pale drawn face worried her. He looked as if he was under severe strain.

"Why did you try to commit suicide?" she asked him bluntly, one day as they were walking the last bit home. He had once again sat mute beside her on the bus for the entire journey.

"If I tell you you'll probably never speak to me again," he answered brusquely.

"Don't be a moron!" Lainey retorted. "Why did you do it? What could be so awful that you'd prefer to die than live?"

"You wouldn't understand."

"How do you know until you've told me?"

"I . . . I'm . . . I'm a homosexual!" he blurted out, his

face flushed, his hands clenched. "Do you know what that means? I'm gay . . . I'm a fruit. Imagine trying to tell that to my parents and all those silly schoolgirls who are always simpering around me trying to get me to invite them out so they can come up and swim in the pool and use the tennis courts. Imagine if the rest of the blokes found out, I'd . . . they'd batter the crap out of me." He was nearly crying now.

Lainey didn't know what to say. Of course she had heard about homosexuals and it all sounded vaguely disgusting, but this was the first time that she had ever spoken to one of them, and Tony wasn't the least bit disgusting. In fact she rather liked him in a maternal sort of way, feeling responsible for him because she had saved his life.

"Does anyone else know?" she asked hesitantly.

"Just . . . just P J . . . he's my . . . my friend," Tony explained, amazed that she hadn't gone running off.

"Well, I don't see what's so awful about it that you have to try and *kill* yourself!"

"Don't you?" His tone was incredulous.

"No! Sure when you start college, you'll be living up in Dublin, won't you," Lainey said logically, "and nobody will know anything about you. You can do what you like."

"That's another thing. My Dad wants me to be a doctor and I don't want to. I want to be an accountant. He just puts so much pressure on me to live up to his expectations. I can't cope."

"Just put your foot down and say that blood makes you faint or something," she urged.

"You make it sound so easy," he muttered.

"It is!" she said crisply. "Just try it once."

Two days later, she met him again. "I'm going to do Commerce," he said, grinning from ear to ear. "I just told Dad straight out that I didn't want to be a doctor, and that I'd probably end up killing people instead of curing them. I think the thought of the scandal was enough to change his mind." He paused and seemed rather agitated. "Lainey, I . . . was just wondering . . ." he stammered, red faced. "I was just wondering if you would come up to the house now and again. I could kinda pretend that you were my . . . my girlfriend," he said, all of a rush.

"Of course I would," she agreed kindly. "Only I've asked John Keegan to my debs. You won't mind if I'm two-timing you?" she teased.

"Not in the slightest!" Tony laughed, delighted with himself.

That was how she found herself one evening sitting at a dinner party in the Mangans' house, a bewildering array of cutlery and glasses on the table in front of her. When the soup was served she took her roll and began to butter it, only to hear with mortification the scornful reedy voice of Sheila, Tony's thirteen-year-old sister.

"Mummy, Lainey doesn't know what plate to use! She took the wrong roll."

Nettle stings of mortification wounded Lainey's heart and she wished the floor would open up and swallow her.

"Be quiet!" hissed Tony as Mrs. Mangan silently swapped Lainey's plate with her daughter's. It had been a nightmare of a meal but Lainey held her head up and got through it by watching Tony carefully. All the well-dressed women there in their posh frocks had made her feel so gauche and out of it. And she swore that one day she would show them. That's why she was sitting on a train reading a book on etiquette. As she read, "start from the outside in," the rhythmic clickety-clack-clickety-clack of the swaying train made her eyelids droop and before she knew it, she was asleep. Then a hand was shaking her gently.

"Elaine . . . Elaine!" A deep voice she did not know was calling her by her full name. Sleepily she opened her eyes. It was a man she didn't recognise at first, and then, with a sense of shock, she realised he was Steve McGrath from Moncas Bay. He was shaking her shoulder and smiling at her. "We're just arriving in Arklow," he said, laughing. "It's just as well I was on the train or you'd probably have slept all the way to Rosslare."

"Crikey!" she gasped, flustered. She could feel the train slowing down as they pulled into the picturesque station.

Steve reached up and pulled down her bag. "I wasn't sure if it was you or not," he grinned. "You sure have grown up, Elaine Conroy."

So have you, Steve McGrath, Lainey thought in appreciation. She hadn't seen him for about four years. He had been studying in Dublin at the College of Catering, and then he had gone to Switzerland to work and study in the hotel trade. He'd left Moncas Bay a skinny, lanky youth but the man striding up the train ahead of her was tall, dark and very very handsome. Thank God for her French plait and colour coordination. At least she didn't look like a hick little schoolgirl, which was, no doubt, how he remembered her. He had looked at her quite admiringly, his eyes moving up and down her lavender-and-white-clothed figure. A little glow of pleasure ignited in Lainey, as Steve McGrath turned to help her off the train.

## Friday, August 6, 1976

Not even the chaos of a bank holiday Friday's traffic could put Lainey in a bad humour as she sat in her blue Toyota, fingers tapping against the steering wheel, at the bridge in Ringsend. She had been stationary for the previous ten minutes.

A long weekend in Moncas Bay. Oh bliss! It had been a scorcher of a summer and there were no signs of the heat abating. In fact people were seriously worried about drought. She was going to go for a swim as soon as she got home, *if* she ever got home. The traffic inched forward and she got as far as Ringsend Library. She looked across at the squat little building sitting by itself in the middle of the road. She had worked there on relief a few times. It was one of her favourite libraries. Well, if things went to plan, she'd be handing in her notice to Dublin Public Libraries in the very near future. Lainey gave a broad grin. After two years, she was moving on to a new career. A career where she would be her own boss, more or less, and where all her hard work would be rewarded. She couldn't wait.

Two months ago when she had been transferred yet again, she couldn't believe it. There had been talk of a changes list for ages and out it finally came, but she hadn't expected to be moved. After all she had been on the Christmas transfer list, when she had gone in to Central, on relief. In one way she had been glad to be moved to a branch library again. Relief was a bit of a pain; you never knew from day to day what library you were going to. And it was impossible to make plans. She had gone to her new library on the day required and had had her interview with her new librarian.

"I don't like lates, I don't like laziness and I don't like cheekiness and if you remember that you'll do fine," Lainey had been informed by the stern-faced woman sitting behind her desk. She felt like a ten-year-old in front of the headmistress and it rankled. For crying out loud, she was an adult young woman supporting herself! *Where* did they come from? Her nights had been changed yet again and she had been forced to abandon a French language course she had been taking. It had thoroughly pissed Lainey off. She had been reading the newspaper during her lunch hour when she saw the advertisement for sales rep with a publishing company, car owner essential. She had her own car, her blue Toyota, Bluebell by name. It was Lainey's pride and joy. Hard saving had got her that car but it had been worth every penny for the freedom it gave her. No more standing waiting for hours for buses. No more waiting for taxis after a night out. No more depending on people for lifts. Buying the car had given Lainey a great sense of achievement and getting her driving test first go had made her feel like a million dollars. Now here was a job jumping out at her from the paper, a job that required a car owner with full licence and experience of the book trade. To hell with it! She'd give it a bash.

That night she did out a glowing CV and sent it off. The next day, at work, she got back issues of *The Bookseller* and

*Books Ireland* and read them from cover to cover to make herself conversant with the publishing world. Three weeks later she was summoned for an interview. It sounded a most attractive job, going around the bookshops keeping them supplied with books and taking orders for new titles. She'd be meeting wholesalers and retailers, she'd be travelling around the south of the country and she'd have to attend the Frankfurt and London book fairs. Lainey knew she'd love it. Mind, the salary was slightly lower than what she was currently earning. But a drop in salary would be worth the increased job satisfaction. At least she'd be treated as a person and not as a cog in a machine.

Lainey did an excellent interview. Her research had paid off and her library experience was of tremendous help. At least she was familiar with the current best sellers and the like. Articulate, well groomed, she knew she had made a good impression. She had worn her new Fiorucci pure wool suit and she had looked so elegant. That suit had been a great buy. It had cost her an arm and a leg, even though she had got it in the sale in Brown Thomas, but it had been worth it.

Since she had started working, Lainey had begun to accumulate an elegant and well-thought-out wardrobe. She didn't buy many clothes but what she bought she spent time looking for and spent money on. She would put aside so much every week for her clothes and then, twice a year in the January and July sales, she did her serious shopping. She bought two or three good items that she could match and mix to create different outfits. It paid off. Lainey always looked as though she had stepped from the pages of *Vogue*. She had an innate sense of style and elegance that was the envy of her flatmates and workmates and often they would come to her for advice when buying clothes or dressing to go out on a special date.

From the time that she had come to Dublin to work, Lainey had set out to improve herself. She took evening classes, she learned how to ride, took tennis lessons, and it was all paying off. Now she could mix with the Moncas Bay crowd and not be worried about making social gaffes. This poise and sophistication had certainly impressed her interviewers and although there had been hundreds of applicants for the job, just that very morning she had got the letter saying she had been selected to attend for a second interview. They had narrowed the numbers down to ten. She was one of them!

Lainey had hugged the letter to herself that morning before she set out for work. Just wait until Steve heard the news. He'd be delighted for her. She could feel in her bones that the job was hers.

Lainey smiled to herself as she drove in a bumper-to-bumper line of traffic towards the Merrion Gates. As she reached them, the lights flashed and the barrier went down. A train flashed by. Probably the Rosslare train, she mused, and a little glow enveloped her as she remembered that first lovely meeting with Steve. It must have been fate, she decided. She had been dating him ever since. Two years and two months practically to the day. She had never felt happier.

The barriers lifted and she continued her journey towards Blackrock. Tonight she would feel Steve's arms around her. They might even go for a midnight swim and make love in a secluded spot in the soft ferns that overlooked the beach. And afterwards, Steve would light a cigarette for each of them and with her head resting against his tanned muscular chest he would tell her how things had been going since she had seen him last. Lainey loved those special confiding times. Then he let down his guard and told her his fears and worries about the hotel. Not that he needed to worry much, she thought, as she nipped neatly into the inside lane and passed a lorry that was holding up traffic at a right turn.

Fourwinds had changed beyond all recognition since Steve had taken it over from his father. With the help of grants from Bord Fáilte, he had transformed it from a third-rate dingy hostelry into one of the smartest places on the east coast. True it was still small, but Steve had great plans for expansion. Not only that, but he had bought twenty acres to the south of Moncas Bay that he proposed turning into a trailer and camping holiday park. Steve was the most ambitious man Lainey had ever met. He reached towards his goals with a single-mindedness that awed her. Nothing and no one stopped Steve McGrath from getting what he wanted and he had stepped on quite a few toes in Moncas Bay since he had moved back home. Now he was a force to be reckoned with in the village and because Lainey was his girlfriend she was part of it all. The Lainey who had sat at Imelda Mangan's dinner party not knowing which cutlery to use no longer existed. In her place was a cool young woman who knew what she wanted and where she was going. In two years, Lainey had come a hell of a long way.

She smiled as she thought of the Mangans. Imelda Mangan had never forgiven her for dropping Tony in order to start dating Steve. Not that she cared! Tony and she were still the greatest of friends. He was having the time of his life in Dublin and loved the freedom that college gave him. Only two nights before, he had met her for dinner and taken her to a Greek restaurant to relive memories of his recent holiday. He was bronzed and glowing and she had never seen him looking better. "Lainey, they carried me onto the plane at Mykonos screaming! I didn't want to leave. I've never seen such beautiful men in my whole life. Lainey, I had a ball, literally."

"You're incorrigible, Tony Mangan," Lainey remonstrated, laughing. Tony was great. He had such *joie de vivre*. He was so different from the suicidal young man she had saved from drowning a few years ago. Now, he was living his own life in the anonymity of the capital under no pressure to date women. He would never, he told Lainey, go back to Moncas Bay to live.

"You're dating Tony Mangan?" Steve McGrath had asked, that first weekend two years ago, when she met him again at a barbecue the Mangans were holding. She had caught the flicker of interest in his eyes as he gave her an appreciative glance.

"We're just very good friends; it's nothing serious,"

Lainey said truthfully, hoping against hope he would ask her out.

"I see." His reply was noncommittal.

Blast it! thought Lainey. By pretending to be Tony's girl-friend she had most likely scuppered her chances with Steve. But she couldn't explain to Steve that Tony was gay and that she wasn't really his girlfriend in the conventional sense. It wouldn't be fair to Tony. She had promised to keep his secret. What a pickle! Just at that moment, Tony came over and gave her an affectionate hug. Oh, Tony, she moaned silently.

"Mother wants to introduce you to some of my aunts," he said with a grimace. "I've been getting hints about engage-ment rings. Wouldn't they just sicken you! Hi, Steve. How's it going?" He greeted the other man cheerfully while Lainey's heart sank to her boots. *Now* she'd never get anywhere with Steve.

"Excuse us," she said forlornly. What was wrong with her, anyway? She'd only met him for the few minutes on the train and here she was acting like a lovesick teenager. Cop on to yourself, Lainey Conroy, she told herself sternly, as Tony walked with her across the lawn to where his mother and aunts were waiting. Tony's aunts eyed her up and down as the introductions were made. Whoever Tony Mangan married would end up as a member of one of the wealthiest families in Wicklow and they wanted to make sure she was eminently suitable. Lainey almost laughed at the irony of it. Poor Tony! What a pressure to be under. There was no way he could admit to his homosexuality to his family. They would *never* understand. Too much was at stake! If Tony didn't provide a son and heir, there would be no continuation of their branch of the family line, or so he had confided to her. He was the only male Mangan left.

She chatted and laughed, pretending a gaiety she did not feel, very much aware that Steve McGrath was surrounded by half the females at the party. Occasionally their glances crossed, his cool and indifferent, hers pretending to be unim-pressed. Later, they all went swimming in the Mangan pool and she was glad that she had worked on her tan. In a brief white bikini, she looked stunning, and whenever Steve was swimming past he made a long cool study.

"So when's the engagement to be announced?" he enquired caustically as she took a breather at the edge of the aquamarine pool.

"There isn't going to be one," she replied levelly. "I told you we were just very good friends, nothing more, nothing less. It's no big deal, Steve!"

"But the talk in the village is that you're a strong item," he said sceptically.

"Really!" Lainey gave an amused laugh. "Typical of Moncas Bay. Don't believe all you hear. *I* never listen to gossip," she finished cuttingly, executing a graceful dive and swimming away. Just who did he think he was, interrogating her like that?

"Who was that hunk of a man you were flirting with?" Cecily Clarke, her brother's current girlfriend, asked in her breathless girly voice. Lainey gave an inward sigh. Simon, her brother, had dated some dames in his life but this one was something else. Tall, blond, model-thin, she looked good with her clothes on. In a pink one-piece that clung damply to her, Cecily had no bust, no hips and looked almost anorexic. Her motto, she had confided to Lainey soon after Simon had first introduced them, was the Duchess of Windsor's, "You can't be too rich or too thin." Cecily had come to Moncas Bay from Dublin, convinced of her superiority over the country hicks she was expecting to meet. Simon had pleaded with Lainey to secure them an invitation to the Mangans' barbecue and it had been an eye-opener for Cecily with its style and unmistakable air of affluence. Cecily eyed Lainey with a new respect. After all, she was dating the son of the owners of this fabulous pad. Suddenly she had become much more chummy but Lainey had seen through her immediately. Cecily Clarke was an unmistakable social climber. And as far as Lainey could see, her brother Simon was going to be her means of escape from her dead-end secretarial job and her two-up two-down parents' house off the North Circular Road. Unfortunately, Simon was completely smitten. She had never seen him so taken by a girl. All of a sudden he was smoking cigars, eating in all the right places, and going up to Dublin to shop for clothes. Where he was getting the money from, Lainey couldn't fathom. Just as well his young dentistry practice was starting to take off. If he planned on marrying Cecily Clarke he'd certainly need plenty of money to keep her in the style to which she planned to become accustomed.

"What will Tony have to say if he sees you chatting up gorgeous men?" Cecily was wagging a coy finger.

"*I* wasn't chatting him up, Cecily. *He* was chatting *me* up," Lainey drawled. Cecily could just go and get lost. The last time she had met her, when Simon had invited his sister to join them for a meal, Cecily had been in one of her moods and had hardly spoken two words to her all evening. Now she was being ever so friendly. Lainey just wasn't in the humour for it. All she wanted to do was to go home. She'd had enough of Cecily, the Mangans, and, most of all, Steve McGrath.

"Excuse me, Cecily, I'm going to dry off," she said politely, gracefully climbing out of the pool, unaware that Steve was observing her. Wrapping a pale peach towelling robe around her she headed towards the changing rooms, the sound of laughter and splashing following her. All the good had gone out of the party for her and she was disgusted with herself that Steve McGrath could have got to her so thoroughly. But there was something about him that had attracted her immediately. An animal magnetism, a sense of challenge. Lainey was used to men's company. She had a good social life in Dublin, was a regular nightclubber and had several admirers, all of whom she dated. None of them had ever had the impact Steve had on her and she found it most unsettling.

She heard footsteps behind her but didn't bother to turn around. "Had enough of the pool party?" an unmistakable voice inquired and her heart did a little somersault as she saw Steve outlined in the moonlight, rivulets of water trapped against the dark tangle of hair on his chest. He was a handsome man, there was no denying that, she thought, admiring the firmly chiselled mouth, the strong hard jaw, the grey glinting eyes ringed by dark lashes that would have made a woman weep with envy.

"Frankly, yes," she said coolly, damned if she was going to let him see what kind of an effect he had on her. His ego must be huge at this stage; every unmarried woman in the village was doing her best to get him to notice her since he had returned from his sojourn in Switzerland.

"How about coming up to Fourwinds for a drink and a bit of peace and quiet then?"

Their eyes met. It was as though he was challenging her.

Lainey smiled. "I don't think so, Steve. I'm rather tired. Good night," she said pleasantly. Steve McGrath wasn't going to pick her up just like that. Without a backward glance she walked through the swing doors of the changing cabin, leaving Steve staring after her, a disgruntled expression on his saturnine face.

Inside, she stared at herself in the mirror. Steve McGrath had asked her to go for a drink. And she had refused! Was she crazy? He obviously fancied her as much as she fancied him. But she was right, she decided. She wasn't going to fall into his arms just like that. She had her pride after all! She knew that Steve would ask her again. Lightheartedly, all bad humour gone, she started to towel herself dry, humming happily to herself.

The next day was the day of the Moncas Bay regatta, one of the highlights of the social calendar. And as Lainey sat on the bank, the breeze whipping her blond hair around her tanned face, she concentrated her gaze on the blue-and-white sailing boat that Steve had entered in the race. It was a beautiful day. Fluffy clouds scudded along in the azure sky. Small white-capped waves frothed against the sides of the boats that were bobbing up and down waiting for the start, their gaily coloured sails fluttering in the breeze. The top of the bank was lined with spectators, many of them having picnics, as below on the beach crews made last-minute preparations for the race. Near Lainey, her mother and her sister Joan, Cecily and Simon sat quaffing champagne on a checked car rug! "Edward and Mrs. Simpson," she murmured dryly to Joan, who went into a fit of giggles. Her mother gave her a reproving glance but the corners of her mouth quirked in amusement. Lainey should have been sailing in the regatta in Tony's boat. They had been practising any weekend they both got down to Moncas Bay and although she knew they didn't have much of a chance she would have enjoyed the race. It was so invigorating to be out on the waves with the sea spray and the wind against your face. Unfortunately a badly cracked mainmast had put paid to their plans. Still, Lainey was enjoying herself immensely, watching all the activity from the top of the bank. And the comments of some of the old seafarers from their vantage points amused her greatly.

When Daniel Flynn, a local businessman who was very conscious of his image and position in the village, went down the slope kitted out in a brand-new Aran jumper and thigh waders, old Dick Roberts, who had sailed around the world more times than Lainey had had hot dinners, said caustically, "Would ye look at Sir Walter Raleigh! Be janey, they go on about these regattas. I've been longer on the crest of a wave." There had been a guffaw that had travelled the length of the bank. Dick was not known for keeping his comments to himself.

Regatta Day in the Bay was a day for everyone. Boats from as far south as Rosslare entered and today there were about fifty. After the race there would be a buffet and dance in a big marquee on the village green. Lainey hoped she'd bump into Steve again. She lifted her binoculars and trained them on Steve's boat, the *Fourwinds Fancy*. She could see him in shorts and stripped to the waist, issuing instructions to his crew. A strange heat suffused her. She'd like to feel his hard muscled thighs against hers. He was the sexiest man she had ever laid eyes on. Lainey was still a virgin, despite her sophistication. She had not, in all her dating, met a man whom she felt sufficiently interested in, or attracted to, to sleep with.

She had grown up with the idea that sex was for marriage alone. Well, Lainey wasn't too sure about that. What about if you didn't want to get married ever? Did that mean you had to be celibate for the whole of your life? Was getting married just an excuse for some who wanted a sex life but were afraid they'd be sentenced to final damnation if they had sex outside marriage? If sex was supposed to be a gift from God and such a wondrous gift why was there so much guilt about it all? As far as she could see, all the church preached about was the sixth commandment. What about all the other commandments? Lainey rarely heard a sermon about treating people with dignity. About the rights of workers. About social justice. There were so many other things to life and yet it seemed that most of the time the emphasis was on the evils of sex, contraception, and divorce. Lainey didn't go to mass anymore except to please her mother when she was at home. There were too many rules and regulations in the Catholic church for her taste. What right had these men of the Vatican to decide that contraception was against the law of God? Surely having two or three children that you could provide for instead of eight or nine that you couldn't feed, couldn't be wrong? If any of those yokes had to go through ten pregnancies there would be a rapid about-face change of policy and no doubt about it. It seemed to Lainey that with all the concern about rules and regulations and dos and don'ts, the real loving merciful God had been lost sight of. Well, there were many paths to God and she'd find hers. And when she did lose her virginity she wasn't going to feel one bit guilty.

Neither did she when, a few months later, in the honeymoon suite of the Fourwinds Hotel, she gave herself utterly and completely to Steve McGrath. It was the most satisfying moment of her life, an affirmation of her womanhood, and she gloried in it. To be sure, Steve had been most surprised that she was a virgin and the first time had been sore and over too quickly but the night was long and she was eager to learn and Steve was a good teacher and she a willing pupil. It was a night of pleasure and revelation and she had fallen even deeper in love with Steve. From the night of the regatta when he had first kissed her, Lainey had known that Steve McGrath was the man for her. She hadn't meant to kiss him. She had meant to play it cool and keep him dangling a little, but when he strode into the marquee with the winner's cup in his hand, grinning broadly as he met her gaze, she had grinned back in spite of herself and fell in love with him there and then. "Drinks for everybody," he called out to shouts and cheers and then he was beside her saying softly, "Would you be too tired to have a drink with me this evening then, Lainey Conroy?"

"I've got to catch the train to Dublin," she demurred. "I've work in the morning." She was saving as hard as she could for a car. If only she had it now, she could stay as late as she liked.

"Couldn't you catch the early-morning bus?" He glinted at her.

"I'd have to be up at five-thirty!" she exclaimed.

"Be a devil!" he laughed.

She laughed back; she couldn't help it. "Well, maybe! I'll see."

"Go on," he coaxed. "There's going to be a hell of a party here tonight! And if you're not here to rescue me, some woman might get her claws in me and I won't be able to ask you out again."

"What a tragedy that would be for you!" she said pertly.

He laughed. "I like you, Lainey Conroy. I want to see more of you, if what you say about being just friends with Tony Mangan is true. How about it?"

"You're very sure of yourself, Steve McGrath, aren't you?"

"I know what I want. Nothing wrong with that. And I want to get to know you. You're an interesting woman. I like your style," he said frankly.

"I'll see you here at eight," Lainey replied calmly. "Excuse me. I'm supposed to be getting my mother a drink." She walked away from him, outwardly composed but inwardly in turmoil.

"You're an interesting woman. I like your style," he had said. And the way he said it, the way his eyes looked at her, had made her insides melt. She felt almost intoxicated. She saw a few envious glances coming her way and smiled. She'd be the envy of the village if she started dating Steve McGrath. Mind he didn't have as much money as the Mangans, not that she gave a hoot! But people would talk, and poor Tony would be fair game again for the young nubiles of the Bay . . . and their ambitious mothers.

"I'll pretend you've broken my heart and I'll never come back," Tony said with a laugh when she told him about the developments. "Lainey, it will be perfect," he assured her. "I can stay up in Dublin much more. It's a bit of a drag having to come home at weekends. There's so much to do with my friends up above, and I can't invite any of them down here, really."

"People will think I'm heartless," Lainey mused.

His face fell. "I never thought of that."

"Well, let them!" Lainey tossed her hair back. "You and I will know the truth and that's all that matters."

"Lainey, you're the best friend in the world." Tony hugged her. "Some day I'll repay you. Now go and slay Steve McGrath. You lucky thing. He's absolutely divine. Are you sure he's hetero? Did you ever see such legs?" Lainey laughed. Tony was irrepressible.

That night she didn't get to bed at all. She went home, had a bite to eat, packed her holdall and dressed in a simple white broderie anglaise dress that revealed her shoulders and showed off her glowing tan. Sweeping her blond hair from her face with two jewelled combs, she put on her makeup, the merest hint, liberally sprayed on her perfume and sallied forth looking fantastic. It was a marvellous night. She and Steve had danced the whole night long. He looked magnificent in a white jacket and black pants. He was most attentive and charming, making sure that she got what she required from the buffet, topping up her glass with champagne.

In the early hours when the dance was over, they went

walking on the deserted beach which was bathed in moonlight. He had put his jacket over her shoulders in case she felt chilled. Lainey loved the masculine musky scent of it, snuggling into its smoothly lined depths. He carried her sandals for her and they laughed and talked and when he kissed her, that first lovely long languorous kiss, she thought she was in paradise. He took her to the bus, and on the early-morning journey back to Dublin, Lainey watched the pastel rays of dawn light up the eastern sky with a smile on her face and a glow in her heart.

It was the first of many dates. On the weekends, when she was working and couldn't get home he would come up to Dublin for a couple of hours, unable to stay the night because the weekends were his busiest times in the hotel and business was booming. Several months after their first date she had quite happily decided that this was the man she wanted to make love to. With her there had been no holding back, no guilt, no demands, just honest ardent desire which had matched his. As they grew closer and he confided in her she had never felt so happy. Not even the uncertainties and irritations of her job could prick her bubble of happiness. Steve had thrown an elaborate twenty-first birthday party for her in Fourwinds and the gossips had a whale of a time when Tony Mangan arrived with a huge bouquet of roses and a gold chain for her, much to the consternation of his mother, Imelda, when she heard about it. From the moment Lainey had started dating Steve she cut her with a vengeance any time their paths crossed. Not that it bothered Lainey one whit. She was far too happy, and so was Tony up in Dublin, despite his mother thinking his heart was broken.

Steve had presented her with an emerald and diamond dress ring, the emerald to match her eyes, he told her, and it was her dearest possession.

In the two years that she had been dating him, she had become a happy and fulfilled woman. Now, with, she hoped, a new career ahead of her what more could she ask? Lainey stretched as much as she could in the car as a juggernaut whizzed past her on the other side of the road. She was stuck in Shankill and ahead of her she could see the bottleneck that was Bray absolutely chock-a-block. Once she got on to the dual carriageway ahead it wouldn't be too bad and apart from the delay she could expect in Newtownmountkennedy, she should be able to get up a bit of speed.

It was a tired Lainey who got to Moncas Bay two hours later. There had been no letup in the traffic, a bad accident at Lil Doyle's Pub had caused more delays, and Arklow had been a nightmare. Still, her mum had a delicious steak and kidney pie for her and she scoffed it down ravenously. It was too late to have a swim as she had planned, so, after a quick shower, she raced off to Fourwinds. Steve hugged her but he seemed preoccupied and barely commented on her news about the interview except to say that it was "great." He showed her where the builders had started to construct the new conservatory dining room and the extension with twenty *en suite* bedrooms. It was no wonder he was preoccupied. Lainey knew that he had borrowed more than half a million to refurbish the place. The hotel would be second to none on the east coast and she was proud of Steve, proud of the way he had built it up from nothing.

The Dwyers, a big land-owning and farming family, were hosting a twenty-first birthday party for their daughter in Fourwinds and naturally, Lainey and Steve had been invited. It was handy enough for Steve, as he could keep an eye on everything. Lainey had been looking forward to it for ages. She mingled happily. She wasn't the type that demanded that Steve stay by her side like glue and she always thought it pathetic of some of her girl friends who clung to their partners, unwilling to mix at a party. She chatted happily to acquaintances, catching Steve's eye as he left to check up on the dining room. Later, when the party was over, they would have a quiet drink in his suite, maybe go for a walk on the beach, make love and then he would see her to the car. It was such a nuisance having to go home, but she wouldn't upset her parents by staying out all night. Fair was fair after all—she was under their roof while at home. Still it would be nice to spend the full night with Steve. On the few occasions that they had managed it, it had been blissful to wake up in his arms.

He was back, head bent attentively to hear something that Helena Casey, Surgeon Casey's daughter, was saying. Helena looked most put out about something, Lainey noticed. A pale, insipid-looking girl, Helena always reminded Lainey of a Barbara Cartland heroine with her whispery voice and limpid blue eyes. Men were always very protective of Helena but Lainey knew that her delicate air was only a front. Helena Casey was as tough as nails. Just like her father, who was reputed to be filthy rich. Still, at fifty pounds a consultation, why wouldn't he be? He was also reputed to own a mining company in the West of Ireland. What Helena wanted, Helena got from her doting father. She even owned her own BMW and she was only two years older than Lainey. She hadn't, of course, gone to school in the area; it wasn't posh enough. She had gone to a private boarding school. Despite her genteel ladylike air, Helena was an utter snob who thought herself above everyone in the village. Heaven knows why she had condescended to grace Sally Dwyer's twenty-first. After all she had been overheard saying that the Dwyers were only "farmers," despite the fact that they were as wealthy as, if not more wealthy than, her father.

Poor Steve! She wondered if she should go over and rescue him from Helena's wishy-washy clutches. Both of them were looking in her direction, frowning. Steve turned away, said something to Helena which made her look annoyed, and walked towards Lainey. Unfortunately he was intercepted by his hotel manager and again she saw him leave the room. Lainey sighed. The joys of dating a hotelier! Still the party was good and she'd soon have him all to herself.

By one-thirty, it was nearly all over. Steve was supervising the counting of the night's takings and suggested she go up to his suite. He'd follow her shortly, he told her. Needing no second urgings, Lainey did as she was bid, had a quick shower, and slid into bed, naked.

Steve arrived about twenty minutes later. He looked tired and harassed and she held out her arms to him. "Come on to bed, darling, and let me get rid of all your worries." She smiled at him.

Steve didn't smile back. Removing his jacket and tie he sat on the bed and said quietly, "Lainey . . . we have to talk." She met his gaze and knew instinctively by the tone of his voice and the expression in his eyes that her world was about to be turned upside down.

## Friday, May 19, 1978

Lainey burned with hate, seethed with rage, was consumed by jealousy as she watched Steve McGrath and his bride posing for photographs after their wedding. It should have been she, not Helena Casey, standing under the delicate cherry blossom trees, with Steve's arm around her, laughing as the pink blossoms fell on to her braided hair and snowy veil.

A large tear plopped onto her hand.

"Bastard!" The cry was torn from the depths of her.

Tony Mangan reached out a concerned hand. "Will we go?" he asked gently, squeezing her fingers. "You shouldn't have come."

"I had to come! I had to see with my own eyes that he's married her. Now I know I'll never have him. Oh, Tony," she sobbed, "even after nearly two years the pain hasn't gone away. What am I going to do? How will I ever get over this? How could he have married her? I know he doesn't love her the way he loved me. I know it! I know it!" Lainey was bawling her eyes out, her mascara running down her cheeks, her shoulders heaving with great big sobs.

"Lainey, we're getting out of here now!" Tony said firmly, starting up the car they were sitting in and pulling slowly away from the crowded churchyard. He drove along the coast road and pulled into a little lay-by as Lainey sat crying beside him. Putting his arms around her, he let her cry away.

"He only married her for the money, you know. Look at the way he and Surgeon Casey have invested in that new estate." Lainey wept bitterly.

"I know, I know!" Tony said soothingly. He had heard all this a hundred times before.

"Oh, Tony, you're so good to me. Thanks for being such a mate," she sniffed, wiping her eyes with the back of her hand, a gesture that reminded Tony of his young niece. It made Lainey seem so vulnerable, someone totally different from the composed young woman that she appeared to be.

"You've always been my best mate. I'm only sorry this is how I can be a mate to you," Tony said, smiling.

Lainey managed to smile back. She was so lucky to have Tony. He really understood exactly how she felt and he was the first person she had turned to on that awful bank holiday weekend nearly two years ago when Steve told her he was ending their relationship. Even though it was a warm day, she shivered as she remembered the chill that had enveloped her heart when Steve told her that they had to talk. As she had sat naked in his bed, he had walked away from her to the window, and with his back to her, unable to meet her eyes, had told her that he was ending their relationship. The almost physical pain that she had experienced in her heart left her speechless for a minute or two and then she said quietly, "Why, Steve? Why, all of a sudden, out of the blue? What have I done wrong?"

"You haven't done anything wrong! It's just . . . well I need space. I need time. I feel crowded. You expect too much of me, Lainey! You should never depend totally on one person for your happiness, it's not fair on them or you." She sat numbed, listening to him. Had she been making demands? Did she depend on him too much for emotional sustenance. It wasn't as if she demanded that he marry her or anything like that. She was perfectly happy the way they were and when she wasn't with him in Moncas Bay she had a very good life in

Dublin. A *very* good life, and if she got the new job her career would really take off. Why wouldn't he look at her? There was another reason, the real reason, and he wasn't going to tell her. Another woman? But *who*? Frantically Lainey's thoughts ran around her head as she sat, the sheets pulled up to her chin, in Steve's big double bed.

"Lainey, I'm sorry. Hurting you is the last thing that I want but I just think it will be better if we cool it for a while."

Lainey was not, or never would be, the type to beg. But with Steve at that moment she almost did. Didn't he know how much she loved him? Didn't he realise that she was so crazy about him there was no room in her life for any other man? Couldn't he see what he was doing to her? Did it not matter to him? It was this thought that kept her from running to him, from pleading with him not to end it. He wasn't telling her the truth, instinctively she knew it. There was a reason, another reason, that he wanted to finish with her but he was trying to put the blame on her. That it was all her fault. Implying that she was clinging and demanding. And for how long did he want to cool it? A week, a fortnight, a month, six months? Why should he feel so different then? And what did he think she was? Did he think she was going to sit patiently waiting while he found his "space"? Anger and hurt ripped through her. Who did he think he was, anyway? She made more sacrifices than he did for their relationship. Coming down to Moncas Bay, waiting for him to finish in the hotel at night. Always fitting in with his plans. Socialising with his friends because he felt hers just weren't quite upmarket enough. How many nights had she been forced to listen to hours of pretentious garbage from the crowd that Steve mixed with because they were important to his hotel, because he was so anxious to attract the big spenders. And had she moaned? Never! And now he wanted space and time to himself and to feel less crowded. Well, let him have it, if that's what he wanted.

For a moment her resolve faltered. She'd never get through life without him. She needed him. She loved him. A lump came to her throat. Oh, God, she couldn't disgrace herself. He'd hate it if she started to cry. He wasn't good at coping with emotion and she wouldn't give it to him to cry in front of him, not after this, not after what she had just heard.

Swallowing hard, Lainey wrapped the sheet around her and got out of the bed. Before, her nakedness never bothered her, she had no inhibitions with Steve, but now, somehow, after what he had just said, she didn't want him to see her naked.

"That's fine, Steve," she said coolly, although inside she felt as though her heart was bleeding with pain. "If that's what you want. But I'd have preferred if you could at least have been honest with me."

"I am being honest with you!" Steve said angrily, a dull flush suffusing his handsome face. "I just need a little less pressure, a little time to think about us. I think we've been seeing too much of each other!"

Lainey almost laughed. Seeing too much of each other! Every second weekend and the occasional weekday when Steve came to Dublin, could hardly be constituted as living in each other's pockets. His excuses were pathetic. Whatever or whoever his reason was for finishing their affair, he obviously wasn't going to be honest and tell her, and it was this more than anything that killed her. If he had just come out and said, "Look, Lainey, there's another woman," she might have been able to take it, but this talk about needing space and time was just *not* Steve and she knew it.

"Look, Lainey, I'm doing this for the best, for both of us, believe me."

"That's crap, Steve! You know it and I know it. I'm not the demanding type and never will be. I've always been totally honest with you and you could at least have been honest with me. If we haven't got honesty, we've got nothing. That's not the kind of relationship I want with anybody. Now excuse me. I'm going to get dressed." Proudly, head held high, she gathered her clothes and walked into the bathroom. When she came out he was gone.

She would never ever forget that weekend. She drove home and sat shaking all night at her bedroom window overlooking the sea. Why? Who? What? A hundred thousand questions raced around her head. Why had he done it? Who was the other woman? Lainey knew there must be someone else involved. Steve was not the solitary type; he needed a woman on his arm. What was she going to do? She cried for hours, hating him, despising him . . . loving him. The following morning at seven she left for Dublin, telling her mother only that something had happened between her and Steve and that she had to get away.

Coward, coward, she accused herself as she sped towards the city she had been so glad to get out of only twelve hours before. There was no traffic on the roads, just she and the dawn chorus, and when banks of fog had come rolling in over Wicklow and she had to slow down, she cursed viciously, ranting and raving. It was a nightmare journey and when she finally drew up outside Tony's apartment she was a wreck.

He got the shock of his life when he saw the apparition at his door at eight-thirty on a bank holiday Saturday. He was horrified at the state of Lainey. Devastated was too weak a word to describe it. He had listened and hugged her and made her eat, and got her drunk, and done all the things that best friends do when a great crisis occurs. Lainey knew that without him she would have been lost. Tony was her greatest friend, he knew her better than anyone, and only with him could she show just how much Steve had hurt her.

"I'm never ever going back there again!" she sobbed a few weeks later on being told by Tony, who in turn had been told by his mother, that Steve McGrath had been seen at a function with Helena Casey.

*Helena Casey!* Steve had ditched her for little Miss wishy-washy Casey! How could he? What did Helena have that Lainey could not give him? she had demanded angrily of the helpless Tony.

"Money!" he answered succinctly.

And she stopped in mid tirade. "He couldn't, not Steve.

He's got too much integrity," she whispered forlornly as even more tears stung her eyes.

"We'll see," said Tony evenly.

Somehow she got through the weeks and months that followed. She had decided she wasn't going to bother going for the second interview for the job with the publishing firm. "I won't get it; there's nine others in for it as well as me," she said flatly to Tony.

He got really angry with her, and she had never seen him in a temper before. "You're going for that interview if I have to carry you in myself, Lainey," he thundered.

"I am not!" she snapped back.

"By God you are, and you're going to get it too, miss. You're going to show Steve McGrath that you don't need him, that you can get by without him and you're going to get that job because it's perfect for you. I won't let you bury yourself in the libraries forever and have to put up with your moans about your unsocial hours and your transfer lists! And for Christ's sake do me a favour and stop feeling so bloody sorry for yourself. You're not the only one who's ever been dumped. Look at me! Did I go around trying to sabotage my life when Jason dumped me? Did I?"

"No!" she shouted. "You just stayed drunk for six months!" They glared at each other angrily. And then, despite herself, Lainey started to laugh. "Sorry for being such a drip," she apologised.

"I don't mind you being a drip, but, Lainey, he's not worth throwing away the chance of a good job."

"I know, Tony." She sighed and it seemed to come from the depths of her being.

"You'll survive, Lainey, believe me." He grinned. "It will get easier as time goes by. I know . . . I've been there. Besides you'd never be happy, married to him and stuck in Moncas Bay, you know you wouldn't!"

I would, I would, she cried silently. With Steve, she would have been happy anywhere.

The day before the interview, Lainey visited a beauty salon and had the works done. Just because she was suffering from a broken heart there was no need to let her looks go, she decided. Tony's words echoed in her ears as she walked in to face the interview panel. "You're going to show Steve McGrath that you don't need him, that you can get by without him," she repeated to herself as she sat down and smiled. When they asked her why she was the right person for the job, she argued her case so passionately that the managing director had to smile. The next day he phoned her at work to say the position was hers. I'll show him, she vowed, as she asked her senior librarian for a resignation form. "Couldn't stick the pace?" asked the older woman with a supercilious smile.

"No. I couldn't stick you!" Lainey retorted coldly, getting immense satisfaction from the shocked expression on the librarian's face. "She almost swallowed her dentures," Lainey told her friend Anne, who was dying to hear what had happened.

"Good enough for her, the pretentious old bat! She really thinks she's above us, a superior being. It makes me sick."

"She is above us . . . in orbit. Anyone who goes around calling herself 'an officer of the corporation' has to be on a higher plane," laughed Lainey, pleased with herself that she'd only have to put up with her boss for another fortnight.

"Ssshh! Here she comes . . . on her broomstick," murmured the irreverent Anne.

Lainey found it surprisingly easy to settle into her new job, despite her fragile emotional state. It was just what she needed. She was constantly meeting people, she was given a lot of responsibility and she turned her energies to the job with a ferocity that surprised even Tony. When sales rose by 15 percent after her first three months with the firm, her boss called her in, congratulated her and raised her salary. Travelling around the country was what she enjoyed most. The beauty of Ireland astounded her. It was so varied: the lushness of Cork and Kerry, the barren beauty of Connemara, the diversity of the midlands. She enjoyed calling to the bookshops in the cities and small towns, always feeling a great personal satisfaction when she persuaded the wholesalers and retailers to order more books. She worked hard and kept herself busy and somehow succeeded in keeping her misery manageable. But back to Moncas Bay she would not go.

"You've got to go home for Christmas!" Tony insisted.

"I'm staying up here in Dublin. I'm just going to pretend Christmas isn't happening. The thought of it is making me depressed." She groaned. Christmas in Dublin without Steve would be bad. Christmas in Moncas Bay, watching him and Helena Casey together, would be unbearable.

"Look, Lainey, you can't go through the rest of your life not going home in case you bump into Steve McGrath," Tony said firmly. "You're coming home with me. People will think we've started dating again, that will give the gossips a field day and you can look at Steve McGrath and tell him to go to hell. Now go into town and treat yourself to something really exotic and get packed and be ready to leave for Moncas Bay tomorrow evening. We are going to waltz into Fourwinds, smiling, without a care in the world and to hell with the lot of them. Lainey Conroy is made of stern stuff and who knows better than me? Now go and get ready."

With mixed emotions Lainey did as she was told. She treated herself to a gorgeous Chantal Thomass slinky black dress that clung to every curve of her shapely body. If she was going socialising at home at Christmas, she was damned if she was going around looking like a shrinking violet. Deciding to go the whole hog while she was at it, she had a beauty treatment and a session on the sun bed to bring up her tan. To her surprise she actually felt a bit better. There was nothing like going on a spending spree to cheer a girl up!

She left her own car in Dublin and got a lift down to Moncas Bay in Tony's Volvo.

"Now I have it all planned," Tony reassured her. "You can have tonight and tomorrow at home. Boxing Day you start socialising. We'll be having the usual do up at the house. The Ryans and the Clearys will be having their bashes. And then we'll go to the New Year's Eve ball in Fourwinds as usual." He looked at her anxiously, as though expecting an argument, but she didn't have one to give him. Tony was right. She had to start living again and if she wanted to show Steve that she was over him what better way than by swanning around dressed up to the nines on Tony Mangan's arm. Besides, she had to show the rest of the village that there was life after Steve McGrath, and that she was living it to the hilt. Tony deposited her at her parents' house where she was greeted with hugs and kisses, and before long she was engrossed in the usual Christmas Eve preparations, making stuffing, trimming the turkey, cooking the ham, and she didn't even have time to feel depressed.

On Christmas morning, she took extra special care with her appearance. Lainey knew that it would be her first meeting with Steve McGrath since they had parted, and what was more, it would be a very public meeting. Practically everybody in the village went to Christmas mass at ten-thirty. Today, she had to pull out all the stops.

She wore her blond hair up in a sophisticated chignon. Her green eyes, outlined by eyeliner and mascara and a brown-gold eyeshadow, looked huge and mysterious. On her lips she wore hot pink lipstick that matched her nail varnish. In her royal blue David Clarke coat, with black trimmed sleeves and lapels, and patent high heels that made her legs go on forever she looked magnificent. Traditionally, the family walked together to Christmas mass, as did most families in the village. It was a crisp frosty morning that brought a colour to the cheeks and by the time they got to the church, Lainey was glowing. As she walked up the gravel path laughing and chatting to her sister, Lainey's heart gave a lurch. Coming up the other path were Steve and Helena. They reached the porch simultaneously. He looked so rugged and so handsome and so familiar that it took a supreme effort of will not to let it show how much she still loved him. The pale delicate girl with the steely eyes, standing with her arm possessively on his, helped Lainey to remain composed. She wouldn't give Helena Casey the satisfaction of knowing the pain she had caused her. Steve caught Lainey's eye. And she knew he was remembering how they had walked to church together last Christmas. "Morning, Lainey. How have you been?" the familiar voice was asking—that voice that had once murmured passionate endearments to her.

Lainey summoned all her reserves, aware that half the parish had found some excuse to remain in the church porch. She smiled. "I've been just fine, Steve. Busy, of course, but fine."

"You got the job then?"

"Of course!" she said coolly. "That's why I don't get home as much as I'd like. I have to do a lot of travelling—London, Frankfurt, it's all go!" She was delighted to have been able to slip that in. It was a bit of a fib to give the impression that she was constantly jetting abroad, but she had been to London twice, and the book fair in Frankfurt had been in October. At least he wouldn't know that *he* was the reason she hadn't been home since their breakup in August.

Steve's eyes widened a bit and he was looking at her very appreciatively. Then Helena gave a discreet tug at his arm. "Steve, if we want to get a seat, I suggest we go in." She smiled frostily at Lainey. "You know what it's like at Christmas."

"Oh, indeed," said Lainey with a frosty smile. "Everybody likes to get a good seat to show off their finery, don't they? Just as well it only happens once a year." Helena was dressed in a red suit with a white blouse that had a big fussy collar and which was a bit too little-girlish. Compared to Lainey, she looked overdressed. Helena was furious, as Lainey intended her to be.

Before she could respond, Tony arrived, kissed Lainey on the cheek and said, "Good morning, darling, Helena, Steve. We'd better get in or we'll be late." He took Lainey's arm and marched her through the crowd in the porch. "Hope you didn't mind me calling you darling. I thought it might give them something to think about," he whispered as they walked up the aisle to where her family was already seated.

Lainey gave Tony's arm a squeeze. He was such a brick.

So supportive. Although outwardly composed, inside she was in bits. The physical pain she had felt when she caught her former lover's eye had been intense. Suddenly she felt as though she wanted to run out of the church and go back to Dublin and never come home again. Iron will got her through the moment, and through mass, and through the visitors who called to her home afterwards, but she couldn't eat her dinner. It tasted like sawdust to her. Around nine, pleading a headache, she went to bed and cried herself to sleep.

She didn't see Steve again until the New Year's Eve ball. As he had promised, Tony kept her busy, whirling her from one party to the next, but when she tried to cry off going to the New Year's Eve party, he was firm. "You're going. Once you have this over you'll be fine."

"But it's in Fourwinds. I don't want to go there again," she protested. She hadn't been in the hotel since that awful night.

"Precisely!" Tony stated. "Once you've been there, you're over the worst of it. And besides, if you don't go everyone will have something to say. You know what they're like in the village for talk. Come on now, you did so well on Christmas Day," he cajoled. "Anyway, surely you don't want to be at home sobbing into your pillow when Cecily's there. You can't let her see you're miserable, now can you?" He added this wickedly, knowing *exactly* how to persuade Lainey. She certainly wouldn't let her soon to be sister-in-law divine how badly the breakup with Steve had affected her. Cecily was staying with them for the New Year.

On New Year's Eve, having listened to Cecily rabbiting on about her wedding plans, Lainey was fit to be tied. The other girl was deliberately needling her, saying how much she looked forward to being married and starting a family, and wasn't it time Lainey started making plans herself, and that she had always thought that she and Steve were the perfect couple, and how surprised she had been to hear the romance was all off and was it Steve's decision or Lainey's to end it.

"It was mutual," Lainey lied in as civil a tone as she could muster. "And no, I'm not interested in getting tied down just yet. I've a fascinating career and I want to travel, I just couldn't settle down without having done *something* with my life." That shut Cecily up and Lainey escaped to the bathroom to have a long soak. No doubt Cecily would be watching her and Steve very carefully. Well, she could watch. Tonight Lainey was going to put on an Oscar-winning performance. And she did.

She strolled into Fourwinds on Tony's arm and handed her coat to the porter. Then they entered the ballroom. A slight hush descended on the couples gathered there as they observed Lainey in her black off-the-shoulder dress that clung sexily to every curve, showing off her sun-bed tan, and looking sensational. Helena, dressed in virginal white which did nothing for her colouring, had gone a lighter shade of pale, Steve just stared, and Cecily gawped. "All in all," Tony whispered as they danced cheek to cheek for the benefit of the gossips, "everyone was gobsmacked!" Lainey laughed, causing Steve to flash her a grim stare. Let him stare, she thought as she entwined her arms around Tony's neck. "Just as well I'm gay," Tony said, grinning, "or I might end up ravishing you on the floor and that would *really* give them all something to talk about."

Lainey laughed again. Tony was such a tonic! If it hadn't been for him, she would never have faced Steve again.

As the night wore on, keeping up the façade got harder for Lainey as she observed Steve holding Helena in his arms as they danced around the ballroom floor. Once, he touched his lips to her cheek and Lainey just wanted to lie down and die. Tony, ever sensitive, decided that enough was enough. He didn't want Lainey to be there when the clock chimed midnight and "Auld Lang Syne" was sung and kisses were exchanged. Watching Steve kiss Helena would be too much, so around eleven-thirty he had told her they were leaving. Lainey did not argue. She had made her appearance, been the belle of the ball, been danced off her feet, kept a smile on her face and she had had enough. Tony took her home and they sat in the kitchen drinking hot chocolate and not talking much. After midnight, they hugged each other, went in and hugged her parents, and then he was telling her to go to bed and that he'd see her in the morning. It was the worst New Year's Eve of her life.

Lainey went back to Dublin and threw herself into her work. The next time she went home, two months later, she didn't see Steve at all and then she had heard that he and Helena were engaged. That had set her off into another depression and Tony was hard put to keep her going. When she eventually found out the date of the wedding, and heard all the talk in the village about it, Lainey thought she was going to go mad. Secretly she had cherished the hope that Steve would realise that Helena wasn't the woman for him despite her money, and that he would return to her. Many nights she had imagined their reunion—she imagined it so much that eventually she almost believed it. To hear that Steve was actually taking the irrevocable step and getting married to Helena left her utterly shocked.

"It's over. Face it!" Tony told her, over and over.

"I want to see them getting married. Then I'll know," Lainey said harshly.

"Don't put yourself through that. You won't be invited so don't let him see you in the church. Where's your pride, Lainey?" Tony snapped, at his wits' end.

"I have to go, Tony. I have to see for myself, then I'll put it behind me."

"Right!" declared Tony. "In that case you might as well say to his face, 'I still love you.' Because if you set foot in that church on his wedding day, it will be written all over your face."

"I won't let him see me."

"Don't be daft! Someone's going to see you. It will be all over the village."

"You're right, I suppose," she muttered miserably.

Tony thought for a moment and a gleam came into his blue eyes. "You could go in disguise!" He laughed and clapped his hands. "Perfect! Robert can get you a wig. Black!" Robert was Tony's partner and he owned his own hairdressing business.

"That's a good idea." Lainey agreed.

"Now this is what we'll do . . ." Tony was full of enthusiasm.

*"We'll* do?" echoed Lainey in surprise.

"Well, you don't think I'm letting you go by yourself, do you?" he demanded. "I'll see this through to the bitter end."

That was how Lainey found herself, in a short black wig, wearing sunglasses, seated in the car beside Tony outside the church in which Steve McGrath made Helena Casey his bride. Tony was wearing an auburn permed creation, with a false moustache for good measure. Although she had roared laughing at the sight of Tony as they drove down from Dublin, as they got nearer Moncas Bay she had become more subdued. How crazy could you get, putting on a wig to watch an ex get wed. It was pathetic. If anyone ever found out she'd die of embarrassment. This was the lowest point of her whole life. But she had to do it to try and end her obsession with Steve. This was it, she promised herself. Once today was over, it was time to get on with life. But she couldn't stop crying once she saw the newlyweds and as she sat with Tony overlooking the Bay, she cursed herself for being such a fool. As the cavalcade of cars, led by the white Rolls-Royce carrying Steve and his new bride, drove past where they were parked on the way to Fourwinds, she watched with bitterness in her heart. When the last car had gone, she took off her wig, put on her makeup and said grimly:

"Let's get the hell out of here. There's more to life than Steve McGrath and I'm going to prove it!"

# Dominic

**D**ominic Kent hated himself for the surge of resentment that enveloped him as he watched his wife Rita feed his three-month-old son. Outside in the smoky dusk of an autumn evening his three other children played amidst the gold and copper leaves that covered their back garden. He loved all his children. It was just that Rita never seemed to have time for him anymore. Once the babies came he had been pushed into the background and it rankled. It was all the baby this and the baby that! He never got a look-in. That's why he'd sprung this on her. "It's only for a weekend, Rita, I'm sure Mona would mind the kids, God knows you're always minding hers," he added a little sarcastically.

"Dominic, I couldn't leave the baby, I'm still breast-feeding," Rita said reproachfully.

Dominic tried to keep his temper. "You've been giving him the bottle as well. Surely one weekend on the bottle wouldn't do any harm."

He'd gone and arranged a weekend away for two at the beginning of November, thinking that his wife would appreciate the break away from the children. But she just wouldn't hear of it. He had spent the last twenty minutes trying to persuade her to go away with him.

"The children need me, love!" his wife said as she lifted her son to her shoulder and proceeded to pat him on the back.

"I need you too," Dominic said quietly but Rita wasn't listening to him. She was gooing at her son, who was chuckling with delight.

"Rita, I think we need a break away together," he reiterated.

"Sure, aren't we always together, love." She smiled affectionately at him.

"Ah, Rita! Think of it as a second honeymoon!" he urged. "No babies crying, no kids disturbing us. We could eat out and take in a few shows up in Dublin."

"Dublin!" Rita's eyebrows shot up, as the baby puked down her front. You'd think he'd asked her to go to outer Mongolia. "That's too far away if anything happened to the kids."

"What's going to happen?" He tried to keep his tone reasonable.

"Mam! Mam! Michael threw wet leaves on me and there were snails in them," wailed their six-year-old daughter Denise, erupting into the room like a mini hurricane.

"She started it!" Michael said, accusingly, hot on his sister's heels.

"Look what I found." Kimberly, his four-year-old, arrived, proudly holding aloft a dead bird. Rita and Denise shrieked simultaneously. The baby started to bawl and the phone rang.

Gently removing the dead bird from his daughter's grasp, Dominic told her older sister to bring her upstairs to wash her hands, warned his son not to throw leaves again and went to answer the phone.

"It's Mona for you," he informed his wife. "Ask her about the weekend," he reminded her. An hour and a half later, after he had buried the bird, changed the baby and put him in his cot, put the younger children to bed, helped Denise with her homework and tidied up the sitting room, Rita finished her conversation with Mona, her best friend. "Well, did Mona say she'd take the kids?" he inquired anxiously.

"Oh, Dom! Sure I couldn't go away that weekend anyhow. Just as well Mona reminded me. It's the annual general meeting of the women's guild and I'm up for treasurer. We'll have to go some other time. Maybe in the New Year, love."

"And pigs will fly!" her husband snapped. "I'm going out for a pint." Rita's jaw dropped. Dominic never went for a pint during the week. He always went after work on a Friday and that was all. Whatever had got into him?

When Dominic returned several hours later Rita was in next door and the neighbours' sixteen-year-old daughter was babysitting. And he'd been feeling guilty for going out midweek and leaving Rita on her own, he thought wryly. Paying the girl, he switched off the lights and went to bed. He was asleep before his wife came home.

## Wednesday, November 14, 1973

Dominic's heart sank as he turned into the driveway to find the house in darkness. Where the hell was she gone now? God, he was starving! He hoped Rita had left him some dinner at least. He cast an angry glance at his watch. Seven-fifteen. He'd been at work since six that morning, he was tired, hungry, and put out.

It was too bloody late to be keeping the children out, especially when they had school the next day. And the baby should be in bed! Slamming the car door Dominic let himself into the house with a face like a thunder cloud. In the kitchen a note from his wife told him that there was a pot of stew on the cooker and that she had taken the children over to her friend Mona's house to watch Princess Anne's wedding. "Princess Bloody Anne," muttered Dominic as he lifted the lid and gazed at the congealed mess in the saucepan. It would be all right when it was heated up, he supposed. Cutting himself a slice of bread, he buttered it thickly and spread some blackberry jam on it. You'd think that Mona would have her hands full with her own five kids without wanting their four as well. Honestly, Rita and she were like blasted Siamese twins. One couldn't go anywhere without the other. Still, he could have come home and had Mona and her gang here. They practically lived here, eating him out of house and home. No! they wouldn't have been able to watch that wedding on his TV— he didn't have the stations. Mona had a big aerial that received all the English channels. Surely the wedding wasn't still going on. No doubt his wife and children had been gone since early afternoon, maybe the whole day for all he knew. The fire wasn't cleaned out, and the house was cold. For Chrissake! It was the middle of winter and he'd been down on the quays since the crack of dawn this morning, waiting for ships to dock so that he could search them for contraband. Being a customs official was no joke in the middle of the winter.

In a foul humour, Dominic set about lighting the fire and tidying up the nappies and socks and toys that lay around the sitting room. It would match his wife better if she did a bit of housework instead of gallivanting over to Mona's all the time. The smell of burning sent him rushing out to the kitchen where he found, to his fury, the remains of his dinner stuck to the bottom of the saucepan. Cursing viciously, he got his coat, found his car keys and slammed the front door behind him. Fish and chips yet again for dinner! It just wasn't good enough! Heaven knows he gave his wife enough money for food if only she'd damn well cook some! As he got into the car, Mona's car arrived and his three children tumbled out, shrieking greetings. They were followed by his wife, who was carrying the sleeping baby.

"Daddy! Hello, Daddy. We saw the wedding!" Denise informed him.

"Load of crap!" said his nine-year-old son.

"I'm dancing in a competition Daddy." Five-year-old Kimberly beamed.

The baby woke and howled hungrily.

"Hello, love. Where are you off to?" his negligent spouse inquired.

"Hi gorgeous!" Mona exclaimed, setting his teeth on edge.

"I'm going to get chips for my dinner!" he gritted.

"Goody! Chips!" yelled the children.

"Get me a spice burger," instructed his wife.

"And I'll have a sausage in batter," Mona sang.

Shit! That meant she intended staying for the evening. He

couldn't even have a bit of peace in his own home. With wheels spinning and a screeching of brakes, a thoroughly exasperated Dominic Kent roared out of his driveway.

## Sunday, June 25, 1978

Dominic Kent closed the file he had been working on, refiled it in the cabinet in his secretary's office, gave a last look around and locked the door behind him. He whistled cheerfully as he ran down the stairs to his car. He hoped that Rita would have his dinner ready. His mouth watered. He was starving and a roast with Yorkshire pud would go down a treat. He loved the traditional Sunday lunch. Then he was going to settle down and thoroughly enjoy the World Cup final between Argentina and Holland. He deserved the break with all the hard work he was doing.

Not that he was complaining, he reflected, as he drove along the Cork docks. Business was booming and he didn't mind a bit coming into the office on a Sunday to do a bit of work. Mind, he had always hated working Sundays when he was with the customs. But when you were working for yourself it didn't seem to matter somehow. It had been a hell of a risk that he had taken, giving up the good permanent and pensionable job and setting up on his own—and he with a wife and four kids to support. But the gamble had paid off. He had done his background work thoroughly and his customs clearance business was doing terrifically well, so well in fact that he was seriously thinking of opening up an office in Dublin. That was next on his agenda. The only thing about it was that he would have to spend three days a week up in the capital. He'd have to leave Rita on her own with the children. The eldest was fourteen, the youngest nearly six, a big responsibility. Dominic sighed. They probably wouldn't even notice that he wasn't there. Rita was never in anyway. Most evenings he went home to find a note that she had gone to her ICA meeting, or a school committee meeting, or a feis, or her aerobics with Mona. He had thought that once they moved to

Montenotte on the other side of Cork from where they had lived, maybe his wife wouldn't see quite so much of her friend and that perhaps they would have more time together themselves, but that had been wishful thinking. Indeed, Mona and her five children were as much on the scene as they had ever been. It sometimes seemed to Dominic that she might as well move into the house; she practically lived there anyway. Of course Mona had terrible marital problems, his wife would explain, when he remonstrated with her. Mona's husband was a drinker and a gambler and Rita was her oldest friend. Dominic thought that perhaps if Mona had been at home a little more often, instead of over at his house with Rita, her husband might change his ways a little. Neglect could drive a man to drink and gambling, he thought, a little unkindly. It wasn't that he was an unkind man; it was just that he wished mightily for a little more peace and solitude in his own home, an existence a bit more ordered, so that he could come in from a hard day's work, sit down and have his dinner with his family and spend a couple of evenings with his wife, instead of the constant rushing around to this thing and that, the slapdash meals, the constant state of disruption that seemed to be his lot. Paddington Station was an oasis of peace compared to his house. Sighing again, he swung his car up the drive. His blood began to boil as he saw Mona's familiar station wagon parked outside the door.

"For fuck's sake!" he cursed viciously. She and the gang couldn't be here again! Christ Almighty, a man could only take so much! One day in the week! He couldn't even have his Sunday dinner in peace. And what about the match, he thought in horror. The kids would have the stereo on full blast in the next room, Mona and Rita would be nattering away. The World Cup final only happened once every four years and he couldn't even watch that in peace. Well, damn it to hell, he *was* going to enjoy his match in a bit of peace! Reversing down the drive, he headed back the way he had come until he arrived at the Country Club Hotel. He parked the car, checked into a room and walked into the dining room. After a feed of roast beef, Yorkshire pudding, roast potatoes, creamed potatoes, carrots and Brussels sprouts, and a half bottle of wine, he walked along the corridor to his room, kicked off his shoes, lay down on the bed, arranged the pillows comfortably behind him, switched on the television and in the featureless solitude of a hotel bedroom, prepared to enjoy the World Cup final.

# Cecily and Simon

## Monday, November 24, 1975

Cecily Clarke curled up in a tight ball beneath the bed covers. She was trying not to move from the warm patch in the sagging middle of her bed. Outside the blankets her nose was cold and she could feel the icy fingers of winter on her face. She thumped the alarm clock with a vicious wallop. "Oh, shut up, you!" If there was one thing she truly hated in this life it was her alarm clock, its loud insistent ringing waking her from her precious slumber to face another cold dark miserable Monday morning.

Groaning, she buried her head under the pillows. She just couldn't face getting up for work today. She could hear the rain pelting relentlessly against the rattling windows. It was a horrible day.

If only she were rich! She would leave this Godforsaken island to go and live in the Bahamas or some other exotic place where the sun shone and it never rained and the temperatures never dropped lower than the eighties. She gave an experimental little cough. Yes! She could definitely feel a tickle in her throat and she was a bit chesty. If she went out in that weather she'd be in danger of getting pleurisy or even pneumonia! Again she coughed, quite pleased with the result.

Definitely bronchial. Snuggling down in her comforting co-
coon of heat, Cecily decided that she was definitely not going
to work that day. Old hatchet-face Muir could go and take a
running jump for himself. He'd just have to manage without
her. He could answer his own phones and tell his own lies,
she decided self-righteously. How many times had she sat in
that dingy outer office saying to telephone callers, "I'm afraid
Mr. Muir is unavailable today; he's in court," while he sat, not
twenty feet away from her, unwilling to take the call. It fascinated Cecily that he actually *had* any clients. He never returned their calls and frequently the cases he was involved in
took years to get to court. Law was a noble profession, he
often told her in his dry, humourless way. Ha! There was
nothing noble about Alfred Muir, BCL. He was the greatest
crook going, making a fortune in interest on clients' money.
As soon as she possibly could she was getting out of his
clutches.

Cecily smiled beneath the bedclothes. She knew just who
was going to rescue her from her life of drudgery. Simon
Conroy, dashing young dental surgeon, certainly knew how
to treat a lady! She had been dating him for a good while now
and things were getting better and better. Last night before he
drove back to Moncas Bay, he brought her for an exquisite
meal in the Burlington, then they had gone dancing in An-
nabel's nightclub. It had been so . . . sophisticated . . .
and Simon had such a charming manner. He asked her what
she would like for Christmas and he hadn't batted an eyelid
when she had told him she would like some heated rollers,
even though they were expensive enough. She'd lay a bet he'd
give her some jewellery as well—he was extremely generous!
She'd met the family too, which was a step in the right direction. The parents were all right, she supposed. A bit countri-
fied but what else could one expect. Joan, the elder sister, was
a bit drab but nice. She hadn't really taken to Lainey, the
younger sister. A bit of a consequence, but surprisingly glamorous for a country girl. She had been wearing a most elegant
Italian knit suit, and she really thought she was somebody.

"Cecily!" her mother called from the doorway. "You'll be late for work."

"I'm not going in today, Mummy." (Cecily always called her mother Mummy; it sounded much posher.) "I don't feel well." She made her tone sound as pathetic as possible. "Just ring in and say I'm sick."

"Oh, dear, is it your chest again, love? Well, you stay there and I'll bring you up some toast and honey and I'll heat up a hot-water bottle for you," her mother said comfortingly.

"Thanks, Mummy." Cecily gave a theatrical wheeze and settled down for a nice little nap while she awaited breakfast.

Simon Conroy gave a mighty yawn and let himself into his dentist's surgery. Even though it was eight-thirty it was still very dark. The main street of Moncas Bay looked deserted and forlorn, with just a few Coke tins rolling around in the wind—and what a wind! It was a howling gale. He bet the waves would be lashing in over the pier wall today. He yawned again. He'd better drink some good hot coffee to wake himself up; he had a busy day ahead. He had appointments all morning and he had to see his accountant in the afternoon.

Of course it had been all hours when he got home from Dublin last night. It had been a most enjoyable evening, though, and Cecily was in sparkling form. And she had been so thrilled with the gold brooch he gave her. He'd been lucky to get it in a sale in Arklow. Cecily was a very classy woman who really knew how to listen to a man. It was the first thing that had attracted him to her that night they met in the Horseshoe Bar in the Shelbourne. He'd been up in Dublin for a dentists' convention and he and a few of the others had gone for a quiet drink in the renowned hotel. Cecily and some of her friends had been there and they had all got talking. Cecily had seemed really fascinated by him and wanted to hear all about his practice and all about Moncas Bay, which she said sounded like a paradise. She had told him that she was a personal assistant to a high-powered lawyer and her own job sounded mighty interesting too. She might even take up law as a career herself, she told him. It was a very nice evening and he was delighted when she agreed to see him again.

They had been dating for quite a while now, and though going up and down to Dublin was an expensive enough business, he didn't mind too much. It was just that the late Sunday nights were a killer. But Cecily wouldn't hear of him going home early. "I'll be here all on my lonesome," she'd pout prettily and what could he do but stay. He hated the Monday mornings but then you can't have your cake and eat it, as the saying went. Talking of cake, he was hungry. He'd send the nurse out for a couple of coffee slices when she came in. Bad for the teeth, he knew, but he had a terrible sweet tooth despite the fact that sugar was a killer. Dentist, practise what you preach, he ordered himself. A nice juicy apple would be much better for him. After all he was starting ever so slightly to lose his hair. He'd better make sure he didn't lose his teeth too! Cecily wouldn't be too impressed with a balding toothless man, now would she?

## Saturday, August 20, 1977

As the wedding band slid easily along her left finger, Cecily Clarke felt a warm glow of satisfaction. At last! Simon had married her. Cecily Clarke-Conroy sounded so imposing —she intended keeping her maiden name as well. And oh, how she was looking forward to living in Moncas Bay.

It was the happiest day of her life when she gave in her notice to the hated Alfred Muir, BCL. He was really furious at the thought of having to go and recruit a new secretary because he'd have to pay her more money than the pittance that he was paying Cecily. No one would come and work for him otherwise. He hadn't even given her a wedding present, the tight old bastard! When she had seen that one wasn't forthcoming, and when she had her reference safely in her handbag, and her last week's wages, she had risen languidly from her desk, strolled into his office as he prepared to close, torn out from her pad ten pages of shorthand letters (he was too mean to buy a dictaphone) that she hadn't bothered to transcribe or write up, ripped them neatly in four and said coldly:

"You can take these and stuff them you know where," (Cecily was too much of a lady to say arse) "as far as they can go. You are the meanest, most dishonest creep that any girl has ever had to work for. It has not been a delight to work for you, Muir" (she felt so *powerful* calling him just Muir), "but it certainly is a delight to know that I'll never set foot in this dump or see your ugly mush again. Good evening!" Then she turned on her heel as Alfred Muir, almost apoplectic, watched her exit from his life forever.

Cecily marched out without a backwards glance at her untidy desk. She had left two days' filing to be done; in fact she had left the place in a right mess and she didn't care. Let him sort it out before his new secretary came on Monday. On Monday, she'd be lying on a sun bed getting a tan in preparation for her wedding. After all, you couldn't wear an off-the-shoulder creation without a tan. And after that, Cecily knew that she was never ever going to have to work to earn her living again. Simon was going to take care of her and she could lie in bed in the morning reading magazines, eating chocolates, and watching TV as long as she wished. Simon's wedding presents to her were going to be a portable TV for the bedroom and a gold bracelet! Cecily practically danced down the stairs of the office at the thought of her fantastic new life as Mrs. Simon Clarke-Conroy.

As she firmly placed the ring on the finger of the man standing by her side and heard the priest pronounce them man and wife, Cecily smiled happily at her new husband. Everything was going perfectly. She'd deliberately chosen St. Peter's Church in Phibsboro because of the long aisle. She was really looking forward to swanning down it as Mrs. Conroy. They had booked the reception in the Burlington and that should really impress the Moncas Bay in-laws, although her father had had to take out a second mortgage, and her mother had taken up part-time work in the factory down the road.

"We want to give you a good send-off and we don't want to let the side down," her mother had assured her. Outside the church a white Rolls-Royce awaited her. And Simon, in his top hat and tails, looked absolutely divine. Rather Clark Gableish actually! Lainey would never outdo this wedding—*if* she ever got married, Cecily thought smugly. She wasn't dating Steve McGrath anymore and he was squiring Helena Casey around. Imagine losing a catch like Steve McGrath! Good enough for her, she was just too big for her boots! Well, she might have her prestigious new job, and her new car, and her designer clothes, but she hadn't got Steve McGrath and she was still single. Thus thought the new Mrs. Conroy as she knelt for the priest's blessing.

The smile froze on her face as she glided down the aisle on Simon's arm and saw her new sister-in-law looking absolutely stunning in a white silk suit, a mouthwatering pink pillbox hat, complete with a little veil, matching pink shoes, and a bag that was unmistakably Chanel with its trademark gold chain. She was laughing heartily at something Tony Mangan was whispering to her.

The *bitch*! Wearing white on Cecily's wedding day. Everybody knows you never wear white at a wedding to outshine the bride. And where did she get that tan? Cecily replaced her smile, remembering the video camera that was recording her progress down the aisle. There was always one fly in the ointment and La Lainey was hers. But not for long. Cecily intended taking Moncas Bay by storm when she went to live there and Lainey would only be trotting after her! Cecily smiled at the photographer who was waiting in the church porch.

Simon's shoes were absolutely killing him and the collar of his shirt was too tight as he sat beside his new bride and listened to the priest telling them to be kind and loving towards each other for all of their married life. He was wondering should he tell the band at the reception not to play any Elvis songs, seeing as the great singer had died earlier in the week. Simon wondered if it would be in bad taste to play his songs. He'd ask Cecily her opinion after the mass. He thought she looked stunning in her white wedding dress. Although she had taken out a credit union loan to pay for it, and ultimately it was he who would be paying the bills now that Cecily was no longer working, he didn't mind. He was glad Cecily was not going to work after their marriage. He liked the idea of being the breadwinner, the protector. It made him feel good about himself. Cecily could just go and take life easy. After all she was a bit delicate healthwise, with that troublesome chest of hers, and the sea air of Moncas Bay would be just the thing for her. He squeezed his new wife's hand and she squeezed his back, smiling radiantly at him.

Simon was so glad that Cecily was looking forward to living in Moncas Bay. Not many women would be happy to give up the cosmopolitan delights of Dublin to settle in a backwater like Moncas Bay. But Cecily had assured him that she would make the sacrifice for him, and anyway wouldn't they occasionally be able to go shopping and nightclubbing in Dublin for a treat? Mind they'd have to go easy for a while. Getting married and building a bungalow was an expensive old business and he'd had to get a substitute in to replace him while he was away on his honeymoon. But business was good and with a new housing estate going up about two miles from the village, it was bound to get better.

That Steve McGrath was really starting to do well and was getting things moving in the village! It was he and Surgeon Casey who had put up the money for the housing estate, and if what Simon had heard was true, all the houses were sold from the plans only. Moncas Bay was certainly changing, and for the better, although the village was divided on the issue, with one side saying there were too many cars driving through to get to Fourwinds, McGrath's hotel, and that the new trailer and camping site would bring in undesirables. But the shop owners were all for it and were rubbing their hands with delight. Only the other day, Lorna O'Shea had opened a souvenir shop for the tourists and she was almost cleaned out after the first week with the hordes that descended. Josie Molloy had opened a burger and chip take-away and was making a mint.

Mind, Josie was a patient of his and her personal hygiene wasn't the best. He wouldn't buy food from Josie's café if he was to starve to death. Still, the doctor might get a few extra patients! There was a lot of arguing going on about it all but Simon didn't really mind. His surgery was away from the main street, and he was all for progress, if it brought him business. It was a pity Lainey had stopped dating Steve McGrath all the same. It made things just a little awkward when Simon took Cecily up to Fourwinds for a drink, but that would ease. Simon intended staying friendly with Steve. He was a force to be reckoned with in Moncas Bay. He was the man to get the money rolling into the place and Simon Conroy intended being part and parcel of it all with his new bride Cecily at his side.

His wedding ceremony complete, Simon placed his top hat on his head, took his wife's arm and smiled a white-toothed smile for the video operator. Things were going great, and they were going to get better—he just knew it.

Monday, February 6, 1978

"I'll kill you if I'm pregnant, Simon Conroy!" Cecily Clarke-Conroy glared at her husband as he entered their bedroom, bearing his wife's breakfast tray.

"Maybe you have your dates wrong," he said helpfully, depositing the tray carefully on his wife's lap.

"I'm never late, you know that as well as I do, and now I'm five days over!" Cecily snapped as she examined the tray in front of her. "Simon, you know I don't like the chunky bits of the marmalade!" Her husband, raising his eyes to heaven, took the offending plate of toast downstairs, scraped off the chunky bits and marched upstairs again. He hoped to heaven that his wife was not pregnant. His life would be hell for the next nine months if she were. He banished this disloyal thought and smiled at his beloved.

"There you are, pet, not a chunk in sight." His wife ignored him and began to eat her toast. Simon's heart sank. If Cecily got into one of her moods she wouldn't speak to him for a week. The best thing he could do was to go to work and let her get out of it. "I'm off," he said as cheerfully as he could manage.

"That's right! Off you go. *You* don't have to worry about getting fat and losing your figure and having morning sickness," Cecily sniffed, feeling extremely sorry for herself. This had not been the plan at all. Getting pregnant! She was a bride of only six months. Life was just so unbelievably pleasant now that she didn't have to work for a living, now that she had someone to take care of her and worry about her and give her everything her little heart desired. It was blissful. Simon treated her like a queen. He brought her breakfast in bed every morning before he went to work. After that she would snuggle back down under the bedclothes and snooze until about eleven. Then she would have a leisurely bath, reading a couple of magazines and eating chocolates as she lay in the warm water. Simon would have the fire set, so all she would have to do was to put a match to it. Cecily loved lying on the sofa in front of the fire, reading Mills & Boons. Poor Simon, he wasn't exactly a Mills & Boon hero, but he was an excellent husband. If it wasn't for Simon, she'd still be slaving for that lazy old sod of a tyrant, Muir.

Simon spent two days a week doing operations and the other three at his practice. The days he was at his practice he came home for lunch so she would have to prepare something, but the other two days he ate at the hospital. If it was absolutely awful weather, she might stay in bed reading until four in the afternoon. Cecily adored the bed. Now if she was going to have a baby, she'd have to look after it and her blissful lazy days would be over. Babies were such messy, demanding little creatures. Mummy would just have to come down to Moncas Bay if she was going to have one.

Cecily raised her grey-blue eyes to her husband's and said in a tone that brooked no argument: "Simon, I want you to take my car and give me the Audi. I want to buy a few things in Dublin."

Of course he should have known that it was coming. Ever since she heard that Lainey was coming home on a visit, Cecily had been edgy. Only a trip to Grafton Street would assuage the edginess. Blast Lainey anyway! What the hell did she want to be coming home for, upsetting everyone? Why couldn't she stay in Dublin and parade her fashions up there? It was really awkward now that things were over between her and Steve McGrath. Why couldn't she just marry Tony Mangan and settle down and not be swanning around the place doing the career girl.

"All right!" he growled as he left the bedroom, knowing that his wallet would be a couple of hundred pounds lighter by evening time. Just as well his dentist's practice was doing extremely well. Otherwise his wife would have him bankrupt.

Cecily finished her breakfast, had a leisurely shower, then strolled into the village to have her hair done. One couldn't go shopping in Grafton Street uncoiffed after all, nor could one drive to Dublin in a ten-year-old Ford Escort. Her husband's Audi was much more her style. What would she buy today? If only she could get something that would really show that Lainey one that she wasn't the only woman who could show off in designer labels.

It would have to be Brown Thomas today, she decided. Helena Casey had gone on a spree in French Connection last week. Yes, decided Cecily, it was definitely time for a little serious buying. She wondered who did designer maternity dresses. If she was pregnant, that was it, there wasn't much she could do about it now. If she wasn't, Simon would just have to abstain until after the midsummer ball. She wanted to create a sensation at that. Last year Madam Lainey had stolen her thunder but this year, with any luck, she wouldn't be at it.

She wasn't coming home half as much these days, claiming that it was because of her new high-powered career. Cecily didn't believe a word of it. It was because of the breakup with Steve. She was sure of it. There was much more to that than met the eye, despite Lainey's claims that the decision to part was mutual. It had taken her sister-in-law down a peg or two. Good enough for her, the superior know-all. It would be just like her to marry that Tony Mangan and come back to Moncas Bay to lord it over all of them with his masses of money. It was such a pity having her for a sister-in-law, it ruined everything.

Deep down, Cecily acknowledged that Lainey impressed the hell out of her with her looks, her style, and her supreme self-confidence. Lainey was the kind of woman Cecily had always imagined herself to be. Being outshone was not easy to take, and Lainey outshone her every time. Well things were going to change. After all she was Mrs. Cecily Clarke-Conroy; her husband was a highly respected dental surgeon who was looked up to in the village. It behooved her to be expensively dressed and if she was pregnant, by heavens she was going to buy only the best. She was certainly not going to look like a sack of potatoes. While she was treating herself to a few outfits today she'd cast an eye on the maternity wear on display. Her mind made up, Cecily settled into the Audi for the drive to the capital.

# THE EIGHTIES

# *Liz*

It was the third anniversary of Matt's death and as Liz stood on the balcony watching the dawn rise over the low hills that surrounded Santa Ponsa, she couldn't believe that she had been widowed for three years. The terrible frantic numbing grief was gone but the sadness remained. Where was Matt now? Did anything of him still exist? Was his spirit serene and contented in another world? If only she knew. If only she could believe that there was an afterlife and that they would meet again, she would be comforted. Death was such a final thing. One minute her husband had been alive, breathing, warm. And then he was gone and there was nothing. She had never felt so powerless as she had done at the moment of her husband's death. Even the most powerful people in the world had no control over the moment of their death or of anyone else's. Death was the great leveller of human arrogance.

Sighing, she watched the fishing boats slipping in and out of an early-morning fog as they returned from a night's fishing. She loved this hour of the morning, watching the sun's rays dapple the sky with pale pinks and lilacs. The light was much softer than the harsh intensity of brightness that caused the eyes to squint later in the day. Still, she loved Majorca, loved the vivid blue of the Mediterranean sky and the whitewashed, orange-roofed villas surrounded by an abundance of bougainvillea and jasmine and many other beautiful flowering shrubs she didn't know the names of. It was an artist's paradise and she had done so much work the last two weeks.

How lucky she had been to meet Incarna. Liz smiled as she slipped into a towelling robe and walked down the white-washed steps that led from her balcony to a flower-filled courtyard. In the distance a dog barked, the only sound in the still morning. A jet flew overhead, making its descent towards Palma Airport. The tourist season was beginning to get into its swing, Liz thought regretfully. There was such a difference between the place in early spring and autumn and in the high season.

"Go! Take the girls with you and have a rest for yourself," Incarna had insisted, generous to a fault. She was the most amazing woman really. Liz never knew what she would surprise her with next. From their first meeting, it was apparent that Incarna Fitzgerald was a woman who got things done.

Liz had first encountered her at the official launch of her first mural, some months after Matt's death. It had been a glamorous glitzy night. Liz had spoken to celebrities, politicians, the rich and famous whose names she had only ever seen in the society columns. As regards the launching of her career, she could not have been luckier than to have all these monied people ooohing and aaahing over her masterpiece. Much to Christine's amusement. Christine was doing her best to keep her entertained with a string of dry witty asides and indeed Liz did try to enter into the spirit of the occasion but as the night wore on, in spite of her best efforts to make the most of it, it seemed to her that the evening had turned flat, like champagne without its bubbles. Liz knew exactly why. Matt wasn't here to share it with her. He would have been so proud of her and her achievement. Liz knew so well how they would have celebrated her success. They would have left the party early and taken a bottle of champagne with them and they would have gone to Burdock's for a fish and chips, as they did that first magical evening they had spent together. Then they would have gone home to their snug flat and made love until the early hours before falling asleep contentedly, curled up close together. Matt had been such a supportive husband, so loving and considerate. For all of their short married life, Liz had felt cherished and loved and exquisitely happy as never before. Marriage had given her such a sense of freedom because Matt had been there to share her joys and her troubles. Now, alone, she was trapped in the bondage of grief. She doubted that she would ever experience such happiness again.

She was standing, lost for a moment in thoughts of Matt, a heartbreaking sadness in her eyes, unaware that a pair of vivacious black eyes were observing her with more than a little understanding. The next minute, the owner of the black eyes was sweeping across the room towards her and Liz came back to earth to find her hand being very enthusiastically pumped by a small raven-haired, foreign-looking woman who spoke with the most marvellously musical, accented English.

"My dear, I have longed to meet wiz you. It ees such a pleasure to finally meet such a wonderfully artistic person as you are. I am Incarna Fitzgerald, a director of thees company, and, my dear, I wish to know if perhaps you are not too busy you might consider to do a mural for me?" the woman exclaimed breathlessly.

"Oh!" Liz was taken aback by the impetuous stream of words.

"I realise that you must be very booked up but I have decided you and you alone can do what I wish to be done and I will wait until you are free!" Incarna exclaimed dramatically.

"What is it exactly that you want me to do?" asked Liz, intrigued.

Incarna smiled, showing pearly teeth. "I want you to paint me a mural. I want you to paint the *catedral de* Palma de Mallorca on the wall that encloses my swimming pool! It would make me very happy and remind me of my home."

This was unusual, Liz decided, but there was something warm and friendly about Incarna that she liked. Some of the people she had met this evening had been rather superficial, to say the least, with their murmurs of "charming" and "delightful" as they surveyed her work and the limp handshakes as they were introduced, their eyes constantly surveying the room in search of photographers and journalists and other important personages as they spoke to her. Incarna's interest was quite genuine—of that there was no doubt.

"The cathedral in Palma," she mused. "Have you any sketches or photographs that I could work from? I would need those if you have them—and I'm afraid it will be a few weeks before I could start on it as I have work in hand already."

"A few weeks!" Incarna laughed, a low throaty chuckle that seemed to come from her toes. "My dear, I expected it to be months. This ees wonderful."

As they spoke, a tanned man in a business suit strode up to them. "Incarna, stop hogging the guest of honour." He turned and spoke to Liz, shaking her hand for rather longer than was necessary. "I really must congratulate you, Mrs. Lacey." He was in his mid-forties and everything about him spoke of success and affluence: his tan, his gold Rolex, his made-to-measure suit. He was looking at Liz and his gaze was frankly admiring.

"Allow me to introduce myself, seeing that Incarna won't do the honours. Marcus Kennedy and I'm delighted to meet you." He smiled a charming smile. The name sounded vaguely familiar to Liz but she couldn't remember where she had heard it.

"How do you do, Mr. Kennedy," she responded politely.

"Oh, Marcus, for heaven's sake! Mister makes me sound so old." He smiled again.

She thought she heard Incarna make a noise suspiciously like a snort. "Marcus," she amended politely.

"Mrs. Lacey and I were discussing business," Incarna said coolly and Liz felt from her tone that Mr. Marcus Kennedy was not one of her favourite people. "Mrs. Lacey is going to do a mural for me." The Spanish woman smiled sweetly.

Marcus's neatly trimmed eyebrows rose a fraction. "You

don't waste much time, do you, Incarna?" He turned again to Liz. "A mural. That's very interesting. Very interesting indeed. I own a couple of restaurants," he said smoothly. "Perhaps you might consider doing some work for me—when you're finished with Incarna, of course."

So that's why his name was familiar. Marcus Kennedy owned some of the most exclusive restaurants in the city as well as several lucrative nightclubs. Really, this evening was doing wonders for her career. For that she had to be thankful.

"Certainly," Liz smiled. "It may be some months, though. As I explained to Mrs. Fitzgerald I already have work in hand and of course I'm not yet sure how long her mural will take to execute."

"I quite understand. I'll give you my business card and you can phone me at your convenience." Marcus smiled, his grey-eyed appraisal making her feel a little uncomfortable. She wasn't sure whether she liked him or not. He was a bit too arrogant and self-assured for her taste, despite his suave charm. Handing her an elegant pale blue business card with gold lettering, he said pleasantly, "I'll look forward to your call." Then he turned and was lost in the crowds that eddied around.

"My dear. One word of advice," said Incarna seriously. "Be careful of that man. He ees unprincipled and makes his wife most unhappy with his philandering."

"Oh! I see," said Liz, in some surprise. She had often seen photographs in the papers of Marcus and his glamorous wife Angela as they attended various functions. They were a high-profile couple in the jet-set life of the capital city. She supposed Incarna knew what she was talking about. After all, she did mix in those circles, and it was clear to Liz, even from their brief acquaintance, that Incarna was extremely well known. All the time they were talking, people had passed by and saluted her by name. Well, it didn't matter if it was Marcus Kennedy or Harrison Ford, Liz wasn't the slightest bit interested. No man would ever take the place of Matt so Incarna had no need to worry about her succumbing to the charms of the suave restaurateur.

"Let's forget about him and return to our discussion," Incarna urged, catching a waiter's eye and appropriating two glasses of champagne. "Would you care to come out to my house to see where I wish to place thees mural?"

"I'd love to," Liz responded warmly. This was going to be an interesting assignment and very unusual. Imagine wanting a mural of a cathedral on one of your swimming-pool walls. Imagine having an indoor swimming pool, she thought enviously. She'd have to go for a swim in it to see what the best position would be for viewing the mural from the pool. That would be a treat. To her surprise she found herself looking forward to it. Meeting Incarna had lifted her spirits to a surprising degree. She wondered what the vivacious Spanish woman's husband was like. Incarna lived on Vico Road in Killiney and it was obvious from the elegant black silk jersey cocktail dress that moulded her ample curves, the glitter of gold at her throat, and the diamonds sparkling on her fingers, that she was not short of a penny or two. Like a lot of the people at this reception.

"Can I be your assistant? I'll hold your paintbrushes and things," Christine said with a grin when Liz told her of her encounter with Incarna. Privately Christine was delighted to hear about it. It was something just like this that her sister needed to give her a little boost. Christine knew that Liz was still grieving deeply for Matt although she put a brave face on things.

Three weeks later, having knuckled down and finished the rest of her commissioned work, Liz was ready to start Incarna's mural. She and Christine drove to the house one weekend at Incarna's invitation, so that she could make her plans. The house had been an eye-opener. A dormer bungalow set in an acre of ground, Vista del Mar was a plush modern residence commanding magnificent views of Dalkey Island and Killiney Bay. The emerald lawns that surrounded the house were immaculate and there was a profusion of daffodils and multi-coloured crocuses heralding the arrival of spring. The house was beautifully decorated and Incarna's Spanish heritage was much in evidence. Tiled floors covered with expensive rugs, heavy oak furniture whose wood gleamed with polishing, archways leading to rooms and balconies all gave the impression of Spain. Brightly coloured scatter cushions dotted the pastel sofas and chairs and there was a bright airy feel to the house that was at the same time relaxing and homely.

"Wow!" murmured Christine, as Incarna, chattering gaily, led them to the indoor heated swimming pool where Liz was to execute the mural. All one wall of the room was glass with big patio doors leading onto a veranda from where could be seen the beautiful vista from Dalkey to Wicklow with the purple-hued Sugar Loaf dominating the skyline. It would be no hardship, thought Liz, to spend lazy hours lolling about in that pool with a view like that to survey.

"It ees nice, ees it not?" Incarna smiled, delighted by the girls' reaction. "My late husband decided we would settle here. The view reminded him of Naples. He was a sailor, you know."

So Incarna was widowed too, thought Liz sadly. Another bond. Liz wondered how long she had been widowed but didn't like to ask. Later, over tea and delicious pastries, they discussed the mural. It was a big wall and although Incarna had photographs of the magnificent and imposing cathedral, they just were not detailed enough or focused enough for Liz to do it justice.

"Would you be able to get a professional photographer in Spain to take some shots from different angles for me, Mrs. Fitzgerald?" Liz asked as she examined the photos in front of her.

"Oh, please call me Incarna, it ees much more friendly," the older woman insisted in her warm, breathless manner. "Yes, I can get the photographs that you require. You just tell me what you want and I will organise it."

Liz looked at the photo in her hand, took out her notepad and wrote down a series of instructions. "Usually I would take the photos myself and make a study of the building, but if the photographer takes these shots it should do fine."

The following day, Liz received a phone call from In-carna. "Liz, I was thinking, would it not be much better for you to see the cathedral yourself? Then you can study the angles and get a good impression of what it ees really like instead of having to try and get an idea from photographs."

"Well, it would be the ideal thing. But I'll manage from the photos, don't worry," Liz assured her cheerfully.

"Can you be ready to travel with me to Majorca as my guest the day after tomorrow?" Incarna queried, and Liz could tell that she was smiling. A paid trip to Majorca in the spring! How lucky could she get. Just wait until Christine heard about it. It was just what she needed, really. She hadn't done much travelling abroad: a trip to Paris with the school, an Inter-rail trip across Europe during her student days, and her honeymoon in Greece. She had never been to Spain and the artist in her looked forward to it with pleasure. New cultures and experiences always gave her great inspiration and she felt that she badly needed something new to challenge her. Her work would be the big thing in her life now that Matt was gone and so with some of her old vigour she packed her paintbrushes and sketch pads in preparation for her first trip to Majorca.

The flight left Dublin Airport at eight-thirty in the morn-ing and by ten forty-five they were circling Palma Airport. Below her, Liz could see the coastline caressed by a sparkling blue sea and forests of green pine trees interspersed with fields and villages. It looked absolutely beautiful. She had really enjoyed the flight with Incarna who had told her all about herself and how she had met and married Gerald Fitz-gerald, the most dashing Irishman in the world.

He had sailed into Montevideo one day on a cargo ship and, as the captain, had hosted a party for various ships' agents and chandlers. Incarna had been on an extended holi-day with her mother's family who came from Montevideo and had accompanied her aunt, uncle, and cousins to the party in a state of great excitement. Since she had come to Montevideo she had attended so many balls and parties, much more than her strict father in Majorca would have liked, had he known. She had never been on a ship and this was going to be a new experience. Climbing the steep gangplank she had caught her heel in a ridge at the top and fallen into the arms of the captain, who was standing on the deck to greet his guests.

He was dressed in his tropical whites, with a flaming red beard and a head of red hair. Incarna had never seen anyone like him. She had recovered her composure, thanked him, met his twinkling blue eyes and fallen head over heels in love. For the two weeks they were in port Captain Fitzgerald called upon her, much to the dismay of her aunt, who was certain that Incarna's father would not approve. Incarna, too, knew very well that if her father knew that she was seeing Geraldo, as she called him, he would most certainly forbid her ever to see him again. Wasn't a match arranged for her at home with Jose Del Montoya, the son of a prestigious landowner in Majorca. For her father's only daughter only the best was good enough. And the Montoya family was allied to Spanish nobility. For this, Incarna did not care a fig. Comparing Jose to Geraldo, Incarna knew she would never be happy married to her countryman.

Although she had only known Gerald Fitzgerald for two short weeks, their souls had touched and she felt as though she had known him a lifetime. That he was as enamoured of her as she was of him was evident. They both had a sense of humour that was to be a great bond through their lives. And Incarna's memories of her first weeks with the flame-haired Irishman were of laughter and giggles. Captain Fitzgerald was a strong, tough, muscular seaman and Incarna saw a side that few others saw. To her he was kindness and gentleness itself, treating her like a precious jewel. The night before they were to part, she clung to him, weeping. To think she would never see him again was worse than death. He tried to comfort her, promising that he would write, but she knew her father would never permit her to see his letters. Gerald was almost as distraught as she. Her elder cousin, who was acting as a discreet chaperone, was in tears as well, thoroughly enjoying the romantic drama being enacted in front of her very eyes.

"Incarna, will you marry me?"

Incarna, her black eyes glittering at the memory, reminisced to Liz as they winged their way down along the French coast. "I did not have to think twice, Liz. I said yes yes yes, Geraldo, I will marry you!" Liz could just imagine Incarna throwing caution to the winds in her impetuous fashion. Naturally, her family was horrified and forbade the match but Incarna, strong willed and deeply in love, tried to persuade them that Gerald was the man for her. When they remained adamant that she give him up, she packed her bags and eloped with him. Her father disowned her but she was with her Geraldo and they sailed the world over before settling on a ranch in Brazil. The discovery of an emerald mine on their land made them wealthy and they returned to Ireland to live. In time, Incarna's father became reconciled to his daughter's marriage and they visited him at home in Majorca. Before long her parents came to appreciate their affable son-in-law, and Incarna's happiness was almost complete. The only sadness of their marriage was that she could not have children.

"But we loved each other deeply. Our love grew stronger over the years and no woman was ever loved by a man as I was loved by my Geraldo. Throughout the years of my marriage I was forever smiling. He was my soul mate," Incarna said with a distant look in her eyes.

Liz nodded in empathy. She knew exactly what Incarna meant. She too had spent most of her brief marriage smiling. It had been ridiculous, really. Sitting on a bus, walking through the park, engrossed in her painting, she only had to think of Matt for a smile to come to her lips and light up her eyes. She could quite happily spend five minutes daydreaming about her husband, smiling to herself and oblivious of everyone. Or else when they were together Matt and she would catch one another's eye and share a special little smile that always brought a glow to Liz's heart. Christine was always chiding her good-naturedly. "You're worse than a love-sick teenager. Everybody in the universe knows when you're thinking of Matt—which is most of the time. Girl, you'd better grow out of it or you'll get terrible crow's-feet before you're thirty!" But she hadn't grown out of it and when she looked back on the photographs of their wedding the happiness in her smile was almost tangible to her. Liz knew that if Matt had lived they would have had an exceptionally happy marriage.

She sighed deeply and Incarna took her hand. "My dear, I know just how you feel. When Geraldo died of a heart attack I was as devastated as you are now. I wanted to die myself; my grief seemed almost too much to bear. It took many years before the pain of it left me. But you will survive it even if you never quite get over it. I was luckier than you, my dear, I had my husband for thirty-five years, but what I will say to you ees thees. Just say to yourself every day, 'I was lucky to have known such a love.' Because it ees something given to very few people."

Liz nodded, unable to speak, tears streaming down her face. This woman knew what she was going through. Christine, Eve, her mother, although they tried to comfort her, couldn't understand how she felt or comprehend her enormous sense of loss because they hadn't experienced it. But Incarna, who had, could. And it comforted Liz more than anything had done in the months of her mourning. Incarna was by now in tears herself and the two of them sat on the plane with tears sliding down their cheeks. A passenger who had partaken very freely of the duty-free passed by on his way to the loo, did a double take at the sight of them, gave a horrified hiccup and ambled on. Liz and Incarna caught one another's eye and they got a fit of the giggles which lasted a good five minutes and left them feeling quite cheerful.

The days Liz spent in Majorca brought a balm to her wounded soul. From the minute the plane doors opened and she breathed the warm flower-scented air of the island, she knew that Majorca was going to be special to her. Driving through Palma, looking at the green-shuttered terra-cotta houses with the waving palms dotted here and there, Liz was entranced. Passing the huge picturesque marina she could see fabulous yachts, sleek and graceful and gleaming white. Seeing her interest, Incarna told the driver to slow down. "There ees King Juan Carlos's yacht." They drove slowly by and Liz could see beautiful women and handsome men sitting on the decks of their vessels, sipping champagne and watching the world go by.

"Oh, for the life of the idle rich," she laughed.

"My dear, with your talent you may yet enjoy the life of the idle rich," Incarna smiled. "Which is something else we must talk about. The price you quoted me for the mural ees outrageously low. No, don't argue with me," she said firmly as she saw Liz about to protest. "You must market yourself, my dear. I know what I am talking about. I am a businesswoman too, you must remember. If people get something cheap, shall we say, they will put no value upon it. But if it is expensive and they have to suffer a little to get it, they will treasure it all the more and others will see what pride is taken in it and they will want one for themselves. Then if *they* have to pay more they will feel that they have got something more valuable than their friends—and so it goes. You must never undervalue what you have to offer."

She gave a twinkling black-eyed glance at Liz. "I think I should be your agent, hmm? You would make a lousy businesswoman. You are much too soft." She rubbed her hands with glee. "I shall be your agent and we shall charge Marcus Kennedy an outrageous amount for his mural. Ha! Ha!" She chuckled devilishly. "And he will pay it too, because now that he knows that I'm getting a mural painted by you he will not rest until he has one also. Ooooh, this ees going to be the greatest fun! We will be a team, you and I, and Liz, my dear, if in twenty years' time you can't afford a yacht like so"—she waved a beringed hand at the yachts berthed in the marina they had just left behind—"it will surely not be my fault. Now feast your eyes on thees."

She pointed ahead and Liz caught her first glimpse of the stunning cathedral outlined against a deep blue Mediterranean sky and overlooking the highway they were driving on. Majestic, classical, its beauty took Liz's breath away. What would it be like in the dawn? In a sunset? Or was this the way to paint it. In the bright blue heat of almost noon, with the palm trees swaying in the scented breeze and not a cloud in the sky.

"Tomorrow, Antonio will drive you in. Today we will unpack and relax," Incarna said firmly as the car picked up speed and they began to leave the city behind them and head towards open country. Liz was amazed by how green the island was. Now it was verdant and beautiful although no doubt after a long hot summer it would get quite parched.

"We used to live in Palma in an old house with a view of the cathedral and overlooking Parc de la Mar, but I sold the house when my parents died and moved to a villa in Santa Ponsa. When I bought the villa, twenty years ago, Santa Ponsa was a small undeveloped village with a beautiful bay. Now unfortunately it has become somewhat built up. But not too much where I am, up in the hills, and it ees still very beautiful. You can see right over the bay to Paguera from my villa. It ees magnificent in the sunset. You will love it."

Before long they were driving along Avenida Rey Jaime I, heading into the centre of Santa Ponsa with its open-air restaurants, shops, bars, apartments, and hotels. Liz couldn't wait to explore. They drove past the white plaza, past the beach, along the main street and then they were climbing up into the wooded hills past beautiful villas. Finally they came to a pair of ornate gates which opened to reveal a delightfully secluded villa set amidst rolling lawns and a myriad flowering shrubs that outdid each other in colour. Liz's fingers itched for her paintbrush. Her eyes widened as she caught sight of the turquoise kidney-shaped pool glittering like a blue diamond in a beautiful patio. Loungers covered with fluffy cushions and shaded by matching umbrellas lay around the pool waiting for bodies. Beneath them Liz could see the town of Santa Ponsa and the bay that stretched across to Paguera, ringed by low hills. It was breathtaking. And pure luxury.

Incarna smiled at the expression on Liz's face. "You see, I told you it ees beautiful. Now, my dear, Maria will show you to your room, where you can freshen up and we will have lunch and a little siesta and then tonight I will take you out to dinner. Tomorrow you may start work if you wish." Maria, a plump, smiling woman, showed Liz to her room which over-looked the pool. Decorated in shades of blue and white, it was a cool haven from the heat of the noonday sun. With a sigh of pleasure Liz stripped off her clothes and walked into her *en suite* cool, tiled bathroom where she had a refreshing shower. This was the life, she thought. Christine would really enjoy it here.

The next day she began her studies of the cathedral. Antonio, Maria's husband, drove her to Palma where she took photos of the imposing structure from every angle. She then began to do some preliminary sketches. She went at dawn, she went at dusk and marvelled at the different lights and how the whole image changed according to the time of day. Her favourite moment was on the day she arrived to find the cathedral wreathed in an early-morning fog. It looked almost ethereal. After much consideration, though, Incarna and she decided that the cathedral in the hot blue-skied noonday sun was the quintessential Spanish image and the one Incarna wanted painted on her wall. It was the one that would most remind her of home.

Once she got back to Dublin, Liz set to work on the mural with skill and infinite care, preparing the wall to receive it, enlarging the design she was going to use, chalking the image on, before finally beginning the painting process. The result was breathtaking. Colouring in the last swaying palm tree, Liz knew without conceit that she had done a superb job. Incarna was thrilled with the mural and immedi-

tely set about organising a huge party to celebrate its com-
pletion.

It was the start of a friendship and partnership that had a
lasting influence on Liz's career. True to her word, Incarna
began to secure commissions for Liz. She dealt with the financial side, causing Liz slightly shocked dismay at the huge
sums she demanded. But people were more than willing to
pay and Liz began to get a name for herself as the up-and-
coming talent in the Irish art world.

Marcus Kennedy, the restaurateur, contacted her again
and she agreed to do a mural for him in his most prized
restaurant, the Plaza, jewel of the jet set and ladies who lunch.
The Plaza was way beyond Liz's price range and all she knew
of it was what she read in the gossip columns. Incarna told
her of an unfortunate who, in an effort to impress his girlfriend, took her for a meal and told her to order what she
wished. The menu was varied and exotic and of course there
was no mention of price. The delighted girlfriend ordered
with gay abandon, the waiters danced attendance, the chef
came from the kitchen to see that all was well, and the couple
thoroughly enjoyed their meal. Upon being discreetly presented with the bill, the young man blanched and fainted
clean away. "So be careful," said Incarna with a grin. Her
voice took on a more serious tone. "And be careful of that
Marcus. He's not a nice man," she added darkly.

"You don't like him, do you?" Liz asked, a little puzzled.

"I can't stand him, my dear," Incarna replied, her usually
pleasant features stern.

"Why not?" queried Liz, agog.

"If I tell you, it ees to go no further, Liz. I have never told
anyone else."

"Oh, if you'd prefer not to, Incarna . . . I didn't mean
to be nosy," apologised Liz hastily.

"No, no, Liz, it ees quite all right. I know you will be
discreet and perhaps it will be of some help to you when he
turns on the charm—for he can charm the birds off the trees,
as they say. That man"—her eyes darkened with anger—"that

man used to be a guest in my house at many soirées and
parties. I introduced him to many valuable contacts and do
you know how he repaid me?"

Liz shook her head, mystified.

"Maria's daughter was working here as my maid and he
got her pregnant. And then he arranged for her to go and
have an abortion and I never knew anything about it until it
was all over. I only discovered it when I found the child half
dead from sleeping tablets one night. She had tried to commit
suicide because of the guilt. I wanted to kill him with my bare
hands. Naturally I confronted him and do you know what
that bastard said?" Incarna's black eyes flashed with fury. "He
told me that I could prove nothing and if I was not careful he
would sue me for slander." She sighed. "And do you know
something? He would. I tell you all thees so you will know
what he ees like."

"I don't think he is the kind of person I want to work
for," Liz murmured doubtfully.

"It ees too late, you are committed and, besides, it ees
very good business for you. We will charge him an arm and a
leg and hope he chokes on it," her mentor said with grim
determination.

And so, Liz found herself having lunch in the Plaza with
its owner in order to discuss his idea for his mural. "This is a
place for lovers," Marcus said smoothly, motioning to the
waiter to pour the Dom Perignon. "As I'm sure you've noticed." He smiled conspiratorially, his eyes coming to rest on a
well-known politician who was gazing adoringly into the eyes
of a young blonde half his age who most definitely wasn't his
wife. Marcus returned his grey-eyed appraising gaze to her.
"What I was thinking of was a mural showing some famous
lovers in history, dining together almost as though they were
in the restaurant itself? What would you think?" From anyone
else Liz would have thought it was a fantastically original idea
but from him somehow it seemed tacky. Perhaps because his
smile was a shade too warm, his eyes lingering on her mouth,

and because of what she knew about him. It was a pity she didn't like him because the idea itself was a real challenge.

"Who do you see as the lovers?" Liz said evenly before biting into a delicious mouthful of crab in filo pastry. Whatever else about Marcus, she couldn't fault the food served in his restaurant; it was mouthwateringly superb. She felt slightly guilty for enjoying it so much. Incarna would be disgusted if she knew.

"Oh, I don't know." He smiled. "Napoleon and Josephine. Abelard and Héloise. Romeo and Juliet. Edward and Mrs. Simpson. Burton and Taylor. Himself and yer one." He grinned, nodding in the direction of the enamoured politician. Liz could quite understand how Marcus could charm a woman. As a host he was faultless. He was intelligent, well read, extremely cosmopolitan, and witty. It was quite a shock to discover that their lunch had lasted almost two hours.

"You'll take the commission, then?" he enquired as he politely held her coat for her.

"I'll send you a quotation. You might prefer to engage someone else when you see the price," Liz responded firmly.

"I think not." His eyes met hers squarely in challenge. That he found her attractive was more than obvious. You haven't a hope, buster, she thought to herself as she walked down the marble steps of the poshest restaurant in Dublin.

"Charge him a million, the smug geek," Christine urged when she heard the latest.

Liz laughed. "I'll see what Incarna says. She knows all about these things."

"You're not serious!" Liz exclaimed, when Incarna told her the amount she should charge.

"I am—very serious. Don't worry, he will write that off to tax and boast about it to his friends. My dear, that amount will cost him little sleep. He is a wealthy man and he is getting something unique. A Liz Lacey original. He would be disappointed if you were to charge less. Believe me, I know." She sniffed. "The lovers' mural will be a most talked-about thing. It will draw the diners to his restaurant. He will have one up

on all his competitors and that is what he wants. So charge
away and don't feel one bit bad. That's the way it's done with
these people. Outdoing each other ees the name of the game.
I have seen so much of it." She chuckled. "Some of them take
it so seriously it ees so entertaining."

Liz enjoyed painting the mural and in spite of her antipathy towards her employer, she found the work utterly re-
warding. In the end, she used all the couples he had suggested, seating them in various poses at tables that matched
exactly the ones in the restaurant. She worked behind a specially rigged-up screen and she knew from the staff and Marcus himself that the anticipation was rife among the clientele.
It became a talking point in the gossip columns, with people
trying to identify the subject of the mural. Someone even
attempted to bribe the staff to get them to reveal what exactly
was behind the screen, but to no avail. The literati and glitterati, the politicians and poseurs, the ladies who lunch and the
men who punch all had to wait for the great unveiling. Marcus was rubbing his hands at the furore. Business was booming. He couldn't put a price on the advertising he was getting
free. Incarna was torn between her delight for Liz and her
dislike of Marcus.

Once, he asked her out. "I don't go out with married
men," she said, unable to hide the contempt in her voice.

"You don't quite understand," he said, hurt. "Ours is now
only a marriage of convenience. My wife leads her life and I
lead mine. You've been here long enough, you've seen how
many broken marriages there are in this city. Look at the
number of couples you've seen in here who aren't married. It's
a fact of life now, Liz. You shouldn't be insulted because I
asked you out. I meant it as a compliment."

Of course you did! she thought wryly. "The answer is no,
nevertheless," she responded coolly.

"I see," was his only comment and he did not press the
issue further.

The first anniversary of Matt's death passed and she told
Marcus she wouldn't be working for a week. She got into the

Mini she had bought with the money from Incarna's mural and drove to the West to see Mrs. Lacey. It was so hard to believe a year had passed since she had been widowed. "I survived it," she murmured as she drove along, the characteristic low stone walls of the West beginning to appear once she crossed the Shannon. "But at what cost?" The sight of Mrs. Lacey waiting for her brought back all the old heartache and visiting Matt's grave she broke down and cried her eyes out. Had she made a mistake in coming? She didn't know. Did the grief ever go away? Would she ever be able to think of her husband and not feel pain?

"Yes, believe me, yes. One day only the happy thoughts will be with you." Incarna comforted her on her return, recognising what the young woman was suffering.

Christine and Eve, always supportive, hatched a plan to take her away for a few days. This was how she found herself one sunny Friday evening, her Mini packed to the gills, driving down to Roscarberry in Cork. "We hired a cottage. All you have to do is drive us there," her smirking companions informed her.

"I don't think Buttercup will make it!" Liz protested that afternoon as they packed the little yellow car for the journey.

"More like an epic voyage," muttered Christine, grinning as she placed three tennis racquets and three sun mats along a backseat that was already crowded with a box of groceries and goodies bought because the shops would be shut when they arrived. Eve came out with a ghetto blaster. "In case we have a party!" she informed her sister-in-law innocently.

Christine emerged from the boot she had been packing. "I hope to God we don't get a puncture because I'm not unpacking that lot on the side of the road." Liz raised her eyes to heaven and gave up.

It was a hilarious journey. Liz could barely see out the back window because of the stuff piled on the seat. She really thought they weren't going to make it at one stage as the poor little car struggled manfully up a steep hill.

"There's a huge traffic jam behind us," Christine informed her helpfully.

"I can't go any faster! My foot's on the ground," wailed Liz, beginning to panic. They were coming near the crest of the hill and she had an awful feeling they weren't going to make it to the top. She broke out in a cold sweat. What would she do if they started rolling backwards. "Come on, Buttercup, you can do it. Come on!" she urged. Christine started to giggle in spite of herself and the drama of their predicament as the little car chugged up the hill.

"Maybe if Chris and I got out and walked up the hill, the car would be lighter and she'd go faster," suggested Eve.

"I'm not stopping as long as we're moving forwards!" Liz exclaimed. "Imagine trying to do a hill start here!" They inched forward and Liz, glancing in her rearview mirror at the train of cars behind them, felt quite under pressure.

"Your man at the back isn't as close as he was. I think he realises your predicament." Eve cheerfully continued her running commentary from the backseat. Buttercup gave a little wheeze of protest, chugged dramatically and then they were gloriously on the flat and power returned to their little chariot.

"Good girl, Butsie!" Christine patted Buttercup's gleaming dashboard. "By God, that's some car you've got!" she remarked admiringly as they were overtaken by every car behind them, getting some irate glares in the process.

"Up yours, too!" Eve snorted as a Mercedes sped past with a derisory beep.

They journeyed onwards, stopping to have a picnic near the Rock of Cashel. Liz took a big bite out of her tuna and salad roll. She was starving. Driving always made her hungry and after the trauma of the hill she was a little drained, to say the least. It was a beautiful summer's evening and the sun was sinking slightly in the west, behind the outline of the Rock, tinting the sky with pale pink and purple hues. She would have loved to have done a quick watercolour but had to be content with a charcoal sketch. They ate their picnic with pleasure. There was something about flasks of tea and eating in the open that really whetted the appetite. Munching on a Crunchie, Christine stretched long limbs, much to the appreciation of a passing motorist, and sighed. "Girls, this is the life!"

They made good time to Cork with nothing untoward happening but had just left the outskirts of the city and were heading towards the airport when a malevolent fog descended from out of nowhere. To her right Liz could make out the runway and control-tower lights in the distance. She vaguely remembered passing a signpost, but before long they were well and truly lost.

"For crying out loud!" she swore about twenty miles later as they hit upon a signpost.

"Crikey!" exclaimed Christine. "We're in Ballinspittle! For God's sake, *what* are we doing in Ballinspittle?" Surrounded by swirling fog they booted out of Ballinspittle in search of their holiday cottage in Roscarberry. By the time they got there and unpacked the Mini, the sisters' tempers were slightly frayed.

"Never mind," comforted the ever-placid Eve, producing a bottle from her overnight case. "A few vodkas will put us all to rights. Don brought home this bottle the other night. Someone gave it to him as a present, so I thought I'd appropriate it."

Liz and Christine grinned. Things could only get better.

It was a strong-tasting vodka, Liz thought as she accepted another one a little later, watching Christine lowering hers with gusto. By heavens it was strong! she realised woozily after her third. She giggled as Eve said, slurring her words slightly, "God lads, I feel a bit fluthered!"

Christine snorted as she poured herself another measure. "Sure the smell of it makes you fluthered. Look at the pair of you, tiddly already." She sipped away confidently, feeling immensely superior because she could at least hold her drink. That last glass was the rock she perished on for when she went to stand up she began to weave and, with a look of comical dismay, she sat down heavily. "I . . . I . . . I feel a bit peculiar," she confessed and the other pair began to giggle again. Unsteadily they helped each other up and giggling and laughing and as drunk as skunks they managed to make their way to bed.

A sorry-looking trio emerged to meet around the breakfast table the following morning. Pale and red eyed and suffering monumental hangovers they sat with their heads in their hands, feeling very very sorry for themselves. Fortunately it was lashing rain outside so they crawled back to bed and slept it off to emerge again at noon feeling more human. "What in the name of God was that you gave us to drink last night?" Christine grimaced at Eve as she drank a glass of cold water to try to allay her dehydration.

"I've never felt like that after a few vodkas before," Liz said, slightly mystified. "It must be old age or something."

"That's what I get for stealing my husband's vodka," Eve muttered, holding her head. "I'd better give him a ring to tell him we got here. Come on with me. Why don't we all go? The fresh air will do us good." The rain had stopped and it was wild and blustery as they walked along the road to the phone in the village. As Eve dialled, the girls looked around with interest. Roscarberry was a quaint little village, immaculately kept, and the tangy sea breeze was a bracing tonic. A shriek from the phone box caused them to look in at their sister-in-law with dismay.

"What the hell's wrong with her?" Christine wondered aloud to Liz.

A minute later Eve stood looking at them, her face a study. "You'll never guess what we were drinking last night!" she exclaimed.

"What?" the others demanded.

"It wasn't vodka that was in that bottle; it was moonshine!" she informed them, half amused, half horrified.

"We drank a bottle of poitín between us?" Liz exclaimed, quite shocked. "No wonder we were fluthered."

"Pity it's all gone." The incorrigible Christine grinned.

"We could have put some in Buttercup's petrol tank, and she'd scorch home to Dublin, no trouble." They burst out laughing and headed down the village, chuckling at the idea of their innocently lowering the poitín in the belief that it was vodka. They had a lovely long walk and, feeling famished and much refreshed, went back to the cottage, cooked a slap-up feed, got out their books and lounged contentedly for the rest of the afternoon.

It was such a pleasure to come away with the girls, Liz thought to herself as she watched Eve nodding off over her Jackie Collins blockbuster and Christine deeply engrossed in an Inspector Morse mystery. It was great to be with people you felt utterly comfortable and relaxed with and the three of them got on so well it was a joy. They were really lucky with their sister-in-law. Eve was one in a million and their brother was a lucky man. He was great too, Liz mused. He was all for Eve getting away for a weekend with the girls. Matt would have been the same. He realised how important friendship was and had never felt threatened by the relationships she had with her friends. Liz had seen so many of her friends become utterly consumed by their boyfriends and husbands, letting their girlhood friends fall by the wayside. It was something that appalled her. Matt had never smothered her like that. She would have gone crazy if he had. Just as she had never smothered him.

Matt had loved fishing and had occasionally gone away for a weekend with his fishing buddies. They had feared that once he got married he would no longer be able to spend time with them as before. Liz was horrified when Matt had mentioned this notion to her. "You go whenever you want to go," she insisted, and smiled like a Cheshire cat when he nuzzled her earlobe and murmured, "I'd much rather stay with you." But both of them had kept their friends and their interests after marriage; it was no threat to their relationship ever, and now that he was gone Liz at least had the comfort and companionship of the girls. Matt would have roared laughing at the tale of the poitín, she thought with a pang, and gave a little sigh.

"You okay there?" Christine peered across the room at her sister. Eve opened a concerned eye.

"I'm fine," Liz assured them, warmed by their care. It was a lovely lazy few days that they spent together and it was just what Liz needed to help regain her equilibrium. She hadn't laughed so much in ages.

The weather turned good for them and they spent a lot of time exploring the beauty spots of Cork. They treated themselves to dinner in a small but exclusive restaurant in Kinsale one night and en route to their holiday cottage had to stop for petrol. It was a do-it-yourself station, which Liz hated. She always went over the amount required by a penny or two if the pumps weren't automatic. It was infuriating but this time she was going to get it right, she thought determinedly. She waited patiently for the motorist ahead of her to finish. She guessed, from his Bermuda shorts and the thick cigar clenched between his teeth, that he was American.

"There ya go, honey!" he said with a smile, replacing the pump. Liz smiled back politely. "Gee!" he said in amusement. "That's a mighty small car. I ain't never seen such a small car before. If a dawg pissed into your petrol tank he'd fill it. Haw! Haw!" He guffawed, much entertained by his own wit.

Liz was not the slightest bit amused to have her little Mini so insulted. "We've got very big dogs in Ireland," she said shortly, turning her back on the Bermuda-shorted man as she proceeded to fill her car with petrol.

Christine was doubled up with laughter in the backseat. "You told him, girl! We've got very big dogs in Ireland—that's the best I ever heard!"

"Shut up, you." Liz grinned, her good humour beginning to reassert itself.

They returned to the capital much refreshed and Liz prepared to put the finishing details to the mural, making sure that the tablecloths and cutlery and fixtures and fittings matched exactly those in the restaurant. It was a very demanding piece of work and Liz was able to become engrossed in it, the hours and days flying by as she painted away. It was such a relief to her that she was able to forget about everything and just concentrate on her work. For a while after Matt's death she felt sure she had lost that ability. No matter what she did, her thoughts constantly returned to her husband and she could not concentrate. But as time passed she found that she was able to concentrate with greater intensity and she drew a great comfort from the satisfaction her work gave her.

Marcus was delighted with the progress of the mural and complimented her profusely. "Liz, it's superb! Just what this place needed. And it's so different from anything I've seen anywhere else. It's unique!" He smiled warmly at her as she sat cross-legged on the floor painting in a detail of the hem of a tablecloth. "Come on, let's have lunch. Leave that for a while."

Liz shook her head. Couldn't the man ever take no for an answer? If he wasn't inviting her to lunch he was inviting her to dinner and she just wasn't interested. All she wanted to do was get the mural finished. She wanted to keep their relationship strictly business but he was so insistent it was beginning to get her down. He was obviously so used to women falling at his feet it must be a new experience for him to have someone turn him down outright. "Come on." He grinned disarmingly. "I insist on treating you to lunch. Let's go over to the new place off Grafton Street that everyone is raving about and see what all the fuss is about. I like to see what the opposition is up to every now and again."

"Thanks, Marcus, but I really must get this finished. Incarna has a load of other commissions for me and besides, I'm sure you want to be able to unveil this soon."

Marcus sighed in exasperation. "An hour for lunch won't make much difference. Come on, Liz, stop playing hard to get."

Liz's jaw dropped open at that. "Are you serious, Marcus

Kennedy? Just who do you think you are?" She was furious. "If you were the last man on this planet I wouldn't be interested in you!"

"I'm sorry!" he said, taken aback at her vehemence. "I was only kidding."

"Not funny," she snapped.

"Well, I apologise then," he said stiffly. "Excuse me."

Liz sat there, fuming. Honestly, some men just thought they were God's gift to women. Playing hard to get. The cheek of him! She worked like a demon, not even bothering to have anything for lunch. The sooner she was finished with his damned mural the better. Why was it that now that she was widowed some men seemed to think that she was fair game for anything. Only a couple of weeks before, she had been at a dinner party in a friend's house and her friend's husband had been so attentive and overfriendly that it had been embarrassing. Norma had been very cool with her when they met later that week and had cancelled an evening of bowling that they had planned. Liz was disgusted. And hurt. Didn't Norma know her better than to think that she would play around with a friend's husband. Didn't her friend realise that the only man who occupied her thoughts was Matt? Obviously not! Obviously she felt threatened by the fact that Liz was single and available again. She had encountered it a few times, in fact. At first she thought she was imagining it but then she had seen another friend swiftly fly to the side of her husband who was making Liz laugh at the saga of his disastrous attempts to take up golf and heard her say, sweetly but firmly, "Darling, stop boring Liz. Mick wants to talk to you. Excuse us, Liz, won't you?"

"Of course," Liz said, a little puzzled. Surely Mick could have come over and joined them—after all, he knew Liz well. But Maria had taken her husband possessively by the elbow and steered him across the room to Mick, leaving Liz alone. Then it struck her! Maria didn't want her talking to her husband alone! How absolutely pathetic and ridiculous. But obviously she was seen as some kind of a threat now that she was no longer part of a couple.

"That Maria one was always a jealous bitch anyway!" Christine remarked when Liz told her of the incident. "Remember the shenanigans of her when Marcy Nolan, who was supposed to be her best friend, got a bouquet of roses one Valentine's Day and she only got chocolates. She was raging. The next year she made sure she got a basketful of roses from Tommy, the fool. And boy did she go on about them. She was always like that. I remember getting a lift from her and Tommy once, before I started going with Liam. Well the two of us were getting out of the car and she started kissing Tommy as though she was never going to see him again. He was mortified. But she was just doing it for my benefit. Letting me know she had a man and I hadn't. She's a real pain and very immature. Ignore her," Christine instructed her briskly.

Painting in a delicate single rose on Romeo and Juliet's table Liz felt a moment of self-doubt. Was she unconsciously sending out some sort of vibes or something? No, that was absolutely ridiculous, she told herself firmly. If there was one thing she wasn't, it was a *femme fatale*. And besides, she just couldn't see herself starting a relationship with anyone else. Maybe in five or ten years' time, she didn't know; right now though all she needed to keep her going was her work. And if Marcus Kennedy didn't like that he could lump it. He kept out of her way for the next week, for which she was truly grateful, and it was with a sigh of great relief that she painted in the last brush stroke.

"You'll come to the unveiling, won't you?" he queried as he stood beside her viewing the finished work.

"It would look a bit odd if I didn't," she remarked drily.

"Thanks, Liz. We'll have a great night. This is going to be a party to beat all parties," he promised her.

In that, he did not lie. She had never seen so many well-known faces. People flew in from London and the States just to be there and Marcus had spared no expense. It was the social event of the year and if you weren't on Marcus Kennedy's guest list, your social standing wasn't worth tuppence, as Liz overheard one well-known gossip columnist say nastily to a well-known lawyer when he inquired about the whereabouts of a mutual acquaintance who hadn't been invited.

Liz spent the evening being photographed for papers and magazines and her head was in a whirl from being introduced to so many people. Marcus paid a glowing tribute to her as he formally unveiled the mural to gasps of appreciation, and in spite of her antipathy towards him she had to admit that he had done her proud with the party. Her career was set to ascend into orbit, Incarna informed her, thrilled for her protégée. She had come as Liz's personal guest but had to leave early to meet a relative at the airport.

As Incarna left, a soft voice at Liz's shoulder caught her attention. "Hello, I'm Angela Kennedy. We've never been introduced." A petite blond woman was speaking to her and with a faint sense of shock Liz recognised Marcus's wife. She was elegant and expensively dressed, with diamonds at her neck and in her ears. But despite her flawless makeup she looked tired and unhappy, as if she didn't sleep well at night. Liz had read somewhere that she had met Marcus when she was working as a receptionist in a hotel and Marcus was running the restaurant. Together they had built up his business into a successful chain of restaurants and nightclubs. They were wealthy and successful beyond their dreams but Marcus played around and it was rumoured that Angela had suffered several nervous breakdowns. Liz's heart went out to her: it was obvious from the way her eyes followed her husband's progress around the room that she was still in love with him.

"Your mural is beautiful," Angela was saying with genuine admiration in her voice.

"Thank you very much," Liz responded warily. Did this woman realise that her husband was trying to start a relationship with her? She seemed very pleasant though.

"What are you going to do next?" Angela inquired.

Liz laughed. "I've a list of commissions as long as your arm. I might surface around 1990 with them all completed!"

"That's marvellous. It's great to see talent getting a chance. I'd love to be able to do something like what you do. Or to have my own business. I'd love to do something on my own." There was a faint trace of bitterness in the older woman's tone. It was obvious the life of a social butterfly left Angela Kennedy completely unfulfilled.

"What do you like to do?" Liz asked.

"Ooh, I like . . ." She thought for a while and laughed. "I like painting and wallpapering actually. Not that I get much of a chance anymore. Marcus gets the decorators in when we're getting anything done."

"You could always do an interior design and decorating course," Liz suggested. "There are some good ones around. I could get you the details if you like," she added helpfully.

"Would you? Would you really? How kind!" Angela smiled and her eyes lit up. "Yes, I could really go for that. That would give me something to get my teeth into. These charity things that I'm involved in are all the same. I'd like to do something different now that the children are in secondary school. They don't seem to need me as much."

"That's the way of it with children, isn't it? We all have to grow up," Liz said comfortingly. She liked Angela. She deserved better than Marcus Kennedy, that was for sure.

"Oh, excuse me, Liz, would you? There's that awful woman who writes a gossip column full of malice. I don't want to have to talk to her. She's so vulgar. Will you send me on that information?"

"I will, of course," Liz assured her. Appearances were so misleading, she mused, as Angela slipped discreetly away. She appeared so soignée and self-assured and yet, speaking to her, Liz had found her self-effacing and shy. Seeing the dreaded chronicler of trivia bearing down on her in turn, Liz decided to follow Angela's example. She slipped away to Marcus's private office where she had left her coat and bag. It was very late and she was tired. It was time to go home, she decided.

She was just reaching for her coat when she heard Marcus's suave tones. "Allow me." He had followed her in. "Going so soon? Won't you come and join us in Angie's?" he murmured as he held her coat for her. Liz shook her head. She didn't feel like nightclubbing in the jewel of his nightclub empire.

"I want to see you again. You must know I'm very interested in you."

Liz stared at him. He was incredible. His wife was outside and he was asking to see her. "Marcus, I'm not interested. Let's leave it at that, okay?"

"But you've always enjoyed my company. We get on well. Why?" he demanded almost angrily.

"For one thing, your wife who is outside waiting for you to take her home. And for another, no one could step into my husband's shoes." Liz's eyes glittered angrily. Just what kind of a woman did he think she was?

"Oh, Angela! She's so bloody boring, Liz. I've tried, but it's over between us. And you can't go around being the grieving widow all your life. You're young! You're desirable. Face it, Liz. Men are going to want you and you're going to want them sooner or later. So why not me?"

"I think this conversation has gone far enough. Excuse me." Liz's tone was icy. She brushed past him but he caught her by the shoulders and swung her around to face him.

"Let me remind you what you're missing in life," he said, bending his head to kiss her passionately.

Liz was so shocked by his behaviour that it was as if a bucket of ice had been poured over her. "Let go of me!" She struggled out of his embrace and stood staring at him. Blind fury took over and in an almost instinctive response she raised her hand and walloped him hard across the face. "You're pathetic," she said contemptuously.

Marcus rubbed his jaw. "You should try being a little more sophisticated," he said cynically.

"If you consider your behavior sophisticated, well, you can keep sophistication. I think you must be the most uncouth, insensitive man I ever met!" That hurt, she could see by the expression on his face. Head held high, Liz strode out the door into the babble of the by now well-lubricated glitterati. Pushing through the throng, she escaped out into the welcome night air. Needless to say there wasn't a taxi to be had on Stephen's Green. Marcus had sent a limo to collect her and she had expected to be going home in it. But if she had to walk across the Sahara she'd do it rather than ask him for transport.

Her anger kept her going down Grafton Street and past Trinity until she was across the Liffey and walking the length of O'Connell Street. It was a fine starry night but she never noticed, she was so angry. Why did Marcus Kennedy think he could treat her like that? "Because that's the way he treats all women. Like dirt!" she muttered to herself, causing a passing couple to give her a wide berth. By now her feet were killing her. Stiletto heels were not the footwear for a long trek home. She half considered taking them off and going barefoot. There wasn't a taxi to be seen. What would you expect on Friday night? she mused, beginning to feel mighty weary. She was just standing at the traffic lights by the Rotunda waiting to cross the street when a car passed her, slowed down and then reversed. Her heart sank. This was all she needed, a kerb crawler!

"Where are you off to at this hour of the night?" a deep voice said from the rolled-down window.

"Hi, Liz!" came two more male voices. She gave a sigh of relief, it was Brendan Fagan, a friend of Matt's, and two other detectives in an unmarked garda car.

"You lot!" she said, grinning.

"Do you want a lift?" Brendan asked.

"I thought that was against regulations," she said primly, knowing full well that there was no way they were going to leave her there.

"So it is. You're under arrest," Brendan riposted promptly, getting out and holding the door open for her. Liz climbed gratefully into the back of the car.

"What's the charge?" she said, laughing, sinking into the comfort of the seat and easing her feet out of her shoes. "Hi, James, Hi, Philip!" She acknowledged the two other men as the car picked up speed and sped off.

"Section 108 against the state—and I must caution you that anything you say can and will be used against you," Brendan said in his most official voice.

"Section 108! Never heard of it," she scoffed, wriggling her toes with pleasure. She was never going to wear high heels again, she swore.

"Of course you haven't—it's just been invented," Brendan informed her. "Heels over an inch high are not permitted after midnight on a Friday night if the wearer is unable to procure a taxi." He grinned and Liz felt her bad humour lift. There she was, giving out about men and the way they treat women and along had come three lovely blokes who treated her like a queen and always had. Marcus Kennedy was just a rotten apple, here was the rest of the barrel. The trio had been good friends of Matt's and when he had died they had kept in touch and kept an eye out for her.

"Where did you have to walk from?" James, the driver, inquired.

"Stephen's Green." She grimaced.

"In those yokes!" Philip leaned down and held up one of her stilettos. "Brave woman! They could be constituted as a dangerous weapon. Tell you what, though?"

"What?"

"We could be persuaded to drop the charges."

Liz laughed. "All right. You can come in and have a toasted cheese sandwich when we get home." She knew them of old. She sighed happily. Instead of being a disaster, her night, or rather early morning, had turned into a pleasure. The lads came in and tucked into one of her toasted specialities and gave her all the news before taking their leave of her. Then, running a bath, she poured in a generous amount of Radox, wiped her makeup off with passion fruit cleansing gel and sank back against the foaming suds, massaging her poor put-upon feet. To hell with Marcus, she decided. She wasn't going to let their encounter get her down. There were far too many nice people in her world for her to waste her time getting upset over that delinquent.

She lay back and began to relax, sipping a mug of hot chocolate. Liz always believed in making a production out of a bath. Not a quick five-minute dip for her; she liked to linger. Have a little read, drink a mug of hot chocolate, give herself a face mask. It was one of life's little luxuries that she treated herself to. It was a great way to unwind, especially if she had been painting all day. Her green-and-peach bathroom was her haven.

Don and Eve had made such a comfortable home for her in their flat. It was great really, she had her own privacy to come and go as she pleased, to have who she liked stay with her, and yet she had the comfort of knowing they were just beside her. Eve often came in to her for a couple of hours if she was there on her own at night. She really was one of the kindest human beings Liz had ever met. She was totally un-selfish, unmaterialistic and had such a sunny nature that she made Liz feel ashamed of her moanings. Eve was the perfect optimist and Liz was going to take a leaf out of her beloved sister-in-law's book, she decided, luxuriating in the comfort of the bath. She would take life as it came, she promised herself, beginning to feel a little bit sleepy. She got out of the bath, wrapped a fluffy peach bath towel around her, tidied up and went into her bedroom. Liberally pouring moisturising cream into her palms she rubbed it all over her body, loving the silky feeling it gave her skin. Matt had loved that little chore, she remembered a little sadly. "No sad thoughts, think positive," she told herself, remembering her new resolution. She pulled a clean silk nightdress over her head and slipped between cool sheets and soon felt her eyes grow heavy. Yes, she was definitely going to think more positively and take life as it came, she thought drowsily. After all, as Scarlett O'Hara would say tremulously, "tomorrow is another day." That night Liz slept like a baby.

Thinking back as she stood on Incarna's patio looking out over the deep blue Mediterranean, Liz smiled to herself. Boy, had life changed after that night. She could safely say that the lovers' mural had been the launchpad of her career. And now she was about to take another big step. The biggest step she had ever taken. Eyes sparkling, Liz contemplated the future.

## Sunday, July 15, 1984

She had spent the day painting in Tijuana and Ensenada, contrasting the gaudy commercial city with the quieter, more authentically Mexican fishing port. Ensenada was beautiful and restful and she had got some great material but Tijuana, with its numerous bars, open-air restaurants and shops was a colourful bustling contrast which had translated into some great pictures on canvas. It was Liz's last full day of painting before her return home to Ireland. She had been away for over a year and a half and she had enough material for her own one-woman exhibition—which was one of the reasons she had gone abroad in the first place.

Liz had been living and painting in La Jolla, just north of San Diego, California, for the previous six months and had enjoyed every minute of it. Before that she had spent six months with friends up the coast in Los Angeles. She had come there from Washington. She couldn't believe that the time had gone so fast but now she was looking forward to going home. It hadn't been easy putting her hugely successful career at home on slow burn. Liz had thought long and hard about it and decided that her decision was the right one for her as an artist. "Polly O'Rourke, you did me a bigger favour than you know," she said to herself, remembering the fat little untidy woman who had interviewed her once. What she had written in her article had been one of the spurs for Liz to reflect on her career and radically alter course for a year and a half.

Liz poured herself a Bacardi and Coke, added a few ice

cubes from the freezer and went out onto the deck to watch her last sunset in the Pacific. Sitting in a cane chair stuffed with plump cushions, Liz stretched out her tanned bare legs, feeling the heat of the sun on the wooden floorboards beneath her feet. A cooling breeze blew in from the ocean, lifting the hair from her forehead. Today's watercolour sketches lay at her feet. She would do them in oils at home in Ireland. Her "Tijuana Trolly" caught her eye. She had enjoyed that experience. She had made the short journey to the Mexican border town in a bright red trolly car and from the international crossing gate she had taken a Mexican taxi for the mile ride into town. It was a great way of seeing the countryside and she couldn't resist painting the jolly red trolly car. Looking at the painting made her smile, and she decided she might keep it for herself. She was hopeless really—growing attached to her paintings. The thought of selling them in her exhibition dismayed her. Maybe she'd do a few duplicates of her favourite ones. But which ones were her favourites? The "Moonlight over the Potomac" that she had done in Washington? Or the "Desert Rose" that she had painted in Palm Springs? Or "New England Autumn?" Then there were her Irish ones. "Temple Bar!" She loved that one and her Mediterranean ones. "The Fishermen!" That was another favourite.

"Stop it, Liz!" she instructed herself, taking a sip of Bacardi. The setting sun was putting on a magnificent display. The size of it never failed to fascinate her. One minute it was there, the next, sliding silently into oblivion on the horizon, its dying rays slashing a violent farewell across the southern Californian sky. A thought crossed her mind. Maybe no one would be interested enough in her paintings to buy them. After all this would be her first ever exhibition. She was so lucky to have been asked to exhibit. Many artists spent half a lifetime trying to get a gallery interested in their work and often ended up sharing an exhibition whereas she had been approached by a prestigious Baggot Street gallery owner and invited to hold a one-woman exhibition. It was a fantastic opportunity and all because of the way her career had taken off with her two murals.

Liz grinned, sinking her teeth into a juicy peach. Boy, had her career taken off after the lovers' mural party. The phone had been hopping all the next day with journalists and feature writers wishing to interview her for their papers and magazines. "Major New Art Talent Discovered" screamed one of the tabloid papers. "Liz Lauds Love" proclaimed another. Photographers were hastily sent to snap this new young discovery who was making the headlines. "Seduce the camera, dear," one excitable young man told her as he danced around with his Nikon. He caused her to succumb to a fit of the giggles, much to his annoyance. She was invited on radio and television programmes and much to her surprise had become something of a celebrity. The work poured in. Incarna was in the seventh heaven of delight as she sifted through the offers. Watching Liz writing little notes on the back of an envelope to remind herself to keep appointments, she had thrown her eyes up to heaven and gone into Eason's and bought her a Filofax.

That Filofax made her the butt of much teasing from Christine, who informed her sister that she was turning into a yuppie, but it was soon bulging with appointments. Prospective clients, journalists, and media people, it was all go, she decided, as she sat one morning about a year later, in the Kilkenny Design Centre, waiting to do yet another interview.

It had been a year packed solid with work. In fact she was having to turn down commissions. She had worked for publishers, illustrating book covers. She had been invited by an author to do the artwork for a new book about Dublin. She had even done set design for the theatre, which had been a whole new experience and which once again caused her to be hailed as a major talent, as the play was a success and her work was praised by the critics. Liz had worked nonstop and although she was enjoying each fresh challenge, she was looking forward to her little trip to Majorca with the girls. It was just what she needed. Liz was glad that she had had such a wide variety of work. At one stage she had been beginning to think that she would spend the rest of her life painting murals. But now she was really being stretched as an artist.

She was also socialising a lot more than before, which she supposed was a good thing. She was being invited to so many functions, exhibition openings, and the like, as a result of her celebrity status. Inevitably she had run into Marcus again but, much to his annoyance, she had played it very cool and acted as though nothing had happened between them. She made sure never to be in his company alone and if Angela was at the gathering, Liz made it a point to seek her out. She had forwarded the various college prospectuses to the older woman and had been delighted when Angela told her that she was working on a recognised interior design course. Angela was so enthusiastic about it all that Liz was delighted for her.

Slowly Liz was growing accustomed to life without Matt. The periods of loneliness became less intense although she could still cry over the silliest things. One day she was in a supermarket doing her shopping when the familiar voice of Gene Pitney came from the piped music system singing "Something's gotten hold of my heart, keeping my soul and my senses apart . . ." Liz stood stock-still as a stab of grief pierced her heart and tears welled in her eyes. Oh, God! That had been one of their favourite songs of all time. She tried to compose herself, feeling such a fool standing in a busy supermarket with tears running down her cheeks, but she couldn't stay. She couldn't bear to listen to the song, so abandoning her half-full basket she had left as quickly as she could and sat in her little Mini crying her eyes out. It was at such unexpected moments that it would all come back to her and she would feel her loss deeply.

Christine and Liam got married and she had been her sister's bridesmaid. That had been a tough day as memories of her own wedding came flooding back and she hated herself for the deep envy she had felt when she watched the look in her sister's eyes as Liam slid the ring along her finger. Please let it all go well for her, she prayed swiftly, ashamed of herself.

"You're only human, Liz. Stop trying to be perfect!" Eve scolded her that night as she burst into tears on the way home from the wedding.

"I felt so mean . . . my own sister . . . and I was thinking, why couldn't I have been allowed to stay as happy as she is now, and for a moment I felt such resentment. There are times I hate myself. Am I always going to be like this? Crying for the least thing? I'm sick of it!"

"Of course you are," Eve said consolingly. "But you can't expect to get over Matt just like that. It's going to take time. So stop pushing yourself so hard and give in to yourself now and again. These little upsets are only natural. Just look at what you've achieved this last year with your painting, in spite of your bereavement. Isn't that something to be proud of?"

"I suppose so," Liz sniffed, wiping her eyes. Her sister-in-law made her outburst seem so reasonable. Maybe she *was* being hard on herself. That was the thing about being a perfectionist. Well there was nothing she could do, just plough on. She gave Eve a watery smile. "Who needs a psychiatrist when they've got an Eve around?"

"My bill will be in the post!" came the smiling rejoinder.

Sitting at a round table and gazing over at Trinity, Liz smiled at the memory as she waited for the tardy journalist. She conceded that she had worked through the very worst of her grief. The ache was still there but the future did not appear so fearful as it had once done.

Where *was* this woman, she wondered. Liz had got used to people ringing her up to arrange for interviews. Sometimes they came to her place or sometimes, if it was handier, they met in town. "How about the Kilkenny Design Centre at ten o'clock?" Polly O'Rourke had suggested, and Liz had agreed, despite the fact that she had a million and one things to do. It was now ten-thirty. Polly had assured her that she knew what she looked like from her photographs. Polly was a freelance journalist who contributed to a wide variety of papers and magazines. Liz had read some of her articles and been a bit wary as Polly could be extremely judgemental sometimes. The restaurant, as usual, was buzzing: elegant women having morning coffee, grey-suited men deep in discussion, couples with eyes only for each other, singles like herself observing all that was going on around them. Liz thought about the beautiful pink lamp that had caught her eye as she walked through the shop to get to the restaurant. It would suit Eve and Don's sitting room perfectly. Maybe she'd run down and buy it for them as a little treat.

"So sorry to keep you waiting!" a breathless voice said beside her and Liz saw with surprise a stout little middle-aged woman, with dyed red hair streaming down her back, slump into a chair beside her. Polly was dressed in a low-cut black dress that revealed more than it concealed and that clung to each generous curve, and she was the most ungroomed person Liz had ever encountered. She waved imperiously towards the waitress, then held out her hand and gave Liz a brief limp handshake. Limp handshakes always put Liz off and the fact that the other woman was nearly three quarters of an hour late for their appointment didn't help.

"I was at my aerobics class. I can barely walk!" Polly said breathlessly as she dived into an untidy-looking sack of a shoulder bag and began rooting for a pen.

You'd *need* an aerobics class, Liz thought with uncharacteristic nastiness as she watched fat fingers tighten their grip on the ballpoint in preparation for the interview. It just annoyed her to think that she had gone to the trouble of being on time only to be left twiddling her thumbs for three quarters of an hour while madame had been at her aerobics.

"Tell me about yourself," Polly instructed her in a clipped accent, trying to catch the waitress's eye.

"You have to queue," Liz said helpfully.

"Drat!" muttered Polly. "Well, never mind. Carry on," she ordered crossly. She was something else, thought Liz with amusement.

"I was born and reared in Dublin. I have a brother and sister. I went to Dominican College, Eccles Street."

"Ah ha . . . a convent-educated girl," Polly said, seizing on this piece of information as if it were a particularly juicy nugget, her small beady eyes lighting up. Liz vaguely remembered from some of her articles that she had a thing about convent educations. Obviously Edna O'Brien's stories had made a great impression on her. "Did you find it repressive?" she queried eagerly.

"Not at all!" Liz responded, surprised. "I found the Dominican nuns extremely enlightened and very forward thinking. They urged all of us to aim for our full potential and were open to all kinds of discussion and argument. There were very few rules in the school and the few they had they expected us to keep. We were treated as adults and given a good all-round education with as much emphasis on physical education as intellectual. I thoroughly enjoyed myself at school," Liz finished firmly. Nun knockers annoyed her.

Polly looked extremely disappointed. The interview proceeded. "Will you marry again?" she asked finally after a gruelling hour.

"I don't think so," Liz murmured, wishing she wouldn't be so intrusive.

"Don't you want a man to take care of you?" Polly asked, round eyed.

"I can take care of myself. I can provide for myself. I'm earning a good living from my art," Liz assured her, amazed at her attitude. But then she was of a different generation. She came from a generation in which it was the norm for men to marry women and provide for them. The independent-minded career woman was obviously still a novelty to Polly O'Rourke.

"Well, may I say that you are an inspiration to us all and that will be the theme of my article," the older woman gushed as she shoved her notepad into her bag and threw a grey shawl around her shoulders.

"Well, that's nice. Thank you very much," responded Liz,

glad that the interview was over. It had been an experience,
she mused, as she watched Polly waddle through the restaurant. Not one that she had particularly enjoyed when she
compared it to some of the interviews she had done with very
approachable and genuine people. With Polly she had felt like
a specimen that was being dissected. She glanced at her
watch. It was almost midday. The whole morning was gone,
she thought ruefully. Well, she might as well have lunch. She
decided to have the carrot soup, cod Provençale, and fresh
fruit salad and she thoroughly enjoyed her meal. Not being in
the humour for work, she dawdled in the shop, bought the
pink lamp and two gorgeous soft cashmere scarfs for her
mother and Incarna and spent a few relaxing hours meander-
ing in and out of the shops on Grafton Street. She made up
for her sloth the next day.

A few weeks later, as she lolled around after lunch one
Sunday, she heard Eve give a horrified gasp.

"The *bitch*!"

"What's wrong?" asked Liz, startled.

"That O'Rourke one! Her interview with you is in this
paper."

Liz had forgotten all about it. "Well, what does she say,
then?" she yawned lazily, not too put out. Eve had cooked a
feast of roast beef and Yorkshire pud and roast spuds and veg
and all Liz wanted to do was have a snooze.

"Here, read it yourself," Eve said, disgusted.

Liz took the paper. "Well, the photo is nice." She grinned
at the sight of herself with paintbrush and palette in hand.
"Rather artisty!" She began to read and her eyes widened in
amazement.

*Liz Lacey, one of the Filofax brigade, has recently emerged
into the limelight of Dublin's arty set. Applauded as a rising
new star in the world of "Art" she undoubtedly has a talent
for what many would see as "chocolate-box art." Liz comes
from a middle-class family and had a happy childhood and
girlhood. Her biggest trauma was the tragic death of a*

*young husband. She has weathered the storm well. Pretty in a gamine sort of way, she is very offhand about her new-found fame. She was dressed in a cool summer dress that she confessed to buying in Roche's Stores and she has obviously not spent her loot in any of the capital's posh clothes spots!*

" 'Chocolate-box art!' 'Confessed to buying . . . !' Well, the old bag—the cheek of her! And the state of her, I've seen better-dressed scarecrows! And I was supposed to be an inspiration! Huh!" Liz finished the rest of the article and threw down the paper. She couldn't believe it. Polly had been so smarmy about the mural and the rest of her work and here she was calling it chocolate-box art. Why hadn't she been straight about it at the interview? Liz didn't mind criticism at all. She had the common sense to know that her work would appeal to some while others could take it or leave it. If Polly had said that her art wasn't to her taste Liz would have much preferred it. At least she would have been prepared. There wasn't a mention of forward-thinking nuns either!

Eve had a face like a thundercloud and was muttering about getting her hands on that bloody woman. Liz caught her eye and started to laugh. "Wait until Incarna sees this. I wouldn't be in Polly O'Rourke's shoes for anything! Eve, imagine going in to confession and saying, 'Bless me, Father, for I have sinned. I bought a dress in Roche's, Father.' "

Eve laughed. "Pretentious snob! I'd be ashamed to earn money like that."

"Don't worry about it, Eve. Stop getting upset. That article will be wrapping somebody's chips tomorrow."

"I'd like to wrap it around her neck," her sister-in-law expostulated, not to be placated. The phone rang. It was Christine.

"Did you see that article? Liz, I won't be able to hold my head up at work tomorrow. You're a major embarrassment to the family!"

Liz could picture her sister grinning at the other end of the phone.

"I warned you about that Filofax," she teased her.

"Well, if poison pen had been on time I wouldn't have been reduced to doodling in it. Don't worry, I'll take the next flight out of the country," Liz said cheerfully, rather amused at this stage.

An hour later the phone rang again. Both Eve and she were snoring peacefully, the papers in glorious disarray around them. Don had gone over to visit their parents—he was great like that for doing a bit for them or dropping in to see if they were all right—and the girls had settled down with the rest of the papers and fallen asleep. "I'll get it," Eve murmured, giving such a yawn she nearly dislocated her jaw.

Liz struggled into a sitting position. "It's all right. It's probably someone else to commiserate. Stay where you are." Ooh, she had enjoyed that little siesta. There was something so luxuriously decadent about reading the papers and going for a snooze after lunch on Sunday.

It was Incarna on the phone. "Liz, I have just read that . . . that tripe! My dear, take no notice. I know that one of old. You are young and slim and very pretty and very very talented. And she is just a jealous old hackette of no talent who is reduced to writing smart-assed cheap jibes. So ignore it, I beg you!"

Liz laughed at Incarna's fury and assured her Spanish friend that she wasn't in the slightest bit upset. "I'm not that sensitive, honestly. I'll get over it," she assured her outraged friend.

"Well, I'm ringing the editor to complain. He ees a friend of mine," Incarna grumbled.

"Now, Incarna, stop taking this so seriously. The woman is perfectly entitled to her opinions and I have been really treated well by the media here so let's forget all about it. Right?" Liz said firmly. Knowing Incarna she'd probably order the editor to sack Polly or something.

"Ha!" said Incarna. "This I will not forget. An enemy of my friend ees my enemy also. My forbears had great ways of dealing with the likes of her."

It was fortunate for Polly O'Rourke that the Spanish Inquisition no longer existed.

"Liz, let me treat you to lunch some day next week to get over this shock. Let's say Tuesday. Would that suit?"

"Lovely," agreed Liz. Anything to pacify Incarna.

"Would the Burlington do? I'll be in that area on business. Oh, and I've an interesting commission for you. You should enjoy it. I'll tell you all about it when I see you."

"Fine," Liz agreed.

"One-thirty then on Tuesday. I look forward very much to it, my dear."

"Me too. 'Bye, Incarna," Liz said, smiling.

That night as she lay in bed she wondered what the new commission was. Well, whatever it was, she was first going to Majorca with the girls for a fortnight's holiday in Incarna's villa. Don and Liam were coming out for the first week, the second week they would have on their own. She really needed a holiday; she had done Trojan work. Her mother was always at her to slow down. But when the work was there it was a shame to turn it down and, besides, it kept her occupied. She wondered if Polly's article would affect her career. The term chocolate-box art was so condescending and insulting that it might put people off.

Oh, to hell with her, she thought, snuggling down and wishing Matt had his arms around her.

"What's the new commission?" she asked Incarna, tucking into chicken Kiev the following Tuesday.

Incarna smiled triumphantly. "How are you at portraiture?"

Liz's eyes widened. "Well I'm no Edward Maguire, but I'd be willing to have a go."

"Ah yes, Edward Maguire. A genius! I love his portrait of Seamus Heaney," Incarna enthused. "Well, I was speaking to Arthur Wallace the other day and your name came up in the conversation and he was wondering how would you feel about doing a family portrait?"

"Arthur Wallace! He owns the Wallace chain of furniture shops, doesn't he?" Liz reflected.

Incarna nodded. "Among other things. It is a very good opportunity. He has many many contacts here and abroad and many will see the portrait."

"Well certainly, I'll speak to him about it."

"Henry Kohler charges from thirty thousand dollars upwards. Bear that in mind when the price is being discussed," advised her mentor.

"Of course I will," Liz said fondly, having no intention of charging anything like that amount. Although it was true, she mused, wealthy people expected the price to be high and were prepared to pay. Well, she was no rip-off artist and she'd charge what she thought was fair.

Incarna and she were enjoying coffee and petits fours when a man approached their table and smiled at Liz.

"Excuse me for interrupting your lunch, but aren't you Liz Lacey?"

Liz nodded. She was beginning to get used to being recognised in public.

He held out his hand. "I'm Bryan Ross. I own the Ross Gallery on Baggot Street and I've been thinking about you. I admire your work very much and was wondering if you had ever exhibited anywhere?"

Liz laughed. "Except at the end-of-year exhibition at college and the people's art exhibition in the green I'm afraid I've never had the opportunity."

Bryan Ross smiled. He was a middle-aged cuddly sort of man and instinctively she liked him. She knew of the Ross Gallery. It was very prestigious indeed and many renowned artists held exhibitions there. She also knew that Ross had a reputation for helping young artists. Liz felt a frisson of excitement. Maybe he was going to ask her to exhibit one or two paintings.

Ross turned to Incarna and said courteously, "Again I apologise for intruding but I have been anxious to get in touch with this young lady and when I saw her I decided to strike while the iron is hot."

"Exactly what I would do," approved Incarna as Liz made the introductions.

"I was wondering, Mrs. Lacey," he continued, "if you would like to consider holding an exhibition of your work in the gallery at some future date?"

Liz swallowed, unable to believe her ears. Not one or two paintings but an exhibition! What an opportunity. She began to have a palpitation with excitement. Ross smiled at the expression on her face.

"Don't look so shocked, Mrs. Lacey. With your talent I'm surprised you haven't been approached already."

"Thanks very much, Mr. Ross," she murmured, wondering if he could hear the thunderous beating of her heart.

"Look, I'll tell you what: here's my card. Ring me and we'll make an appointment and discuss it at length. How does that sound?"

"That sounds pretty good to me," she said, beaming.

"Excellent. I'll look forward to it. Once again excuse me for interrupting your lunch."

"Not at all," Liz murmured starry-eyed. Her own exhibition! Oh happy day!

Incarna was pleased. "That man was delightful. And such nice manners. I always say no matter who or what you are, if you have not got manners you have got nothing. The breeding shows with the manners! Oh, Liz, this ees wonderful." Her black eyes flashed. "And so much for chocolate-box art! Ha ha! Eat your words, Ms. Polly O'Rourke."

"I wonder if he saw that," Liz mused, coming down from cloud nine.

"You can bet he did," Incarna said firmly, "and it means nothing. You heard what the man said—you are extremely talented. Do you think for one minute that you would be invited to exhibit in such an influential and well-regarded gallery if he thought otherwise?"

"You're right, absolutely right! I *am* talented and now I have a chance to prove it. Oh, Incarna, isn't this exciting?"

"Darling, it ees no more than you deserve," the Spanish woman said warmly, leaning across the table and planting a red-lipsticked kiss on Liz's cheek.

The meeting with Bryan Ross was one of the turning points in Liz's life. She rang and arranged to meet him in his gallery, expecting the meeting to last for an hour or so. It lasted for five. She spent a full afternoon with him and found him to be one of the nicest people she had ever encountered. His enthusiasm for art matched her own and after five minutes in his company she felt as though she had known him all her life. She found herself telling him about Matt and how she was just beginning to get her life together and all about her blossoming career.

"Have you done much painting, as in canvas, lately?" he queried.

Liz shook her head ruefully. "I just don't have the time. But I'll *make* time now. That's for sure."

Bryan shook his head. "No, Liz. I don't want you to feel under pressure. I want fifty paintings from you."

"*Fifty!*" she almost shrieked.

Bryan smiled. "I want a good representation of your work. Fifty is a decent number to give the customers a choice."

She smiled back, delighted.

"Liz, what do you say if we plan this exhibition for two years' time? That will give you a chance to work on your paintings. You know how important a first exhibition is. We want to make sure everything is just right." He winked. "With art critics like Polly O'Rourke around, everything has to be perfect."

Liz laughed. She liked Bryan more and more. He had a sense of humour rather like Matt's.

"Have you travelled much?" he asked, as his secretary brought in yet more tea and cakes.

"Not really." She told him of her globe-trottings and he smiled.

"If you could afford it, a period of travelling might do you all the good in the world. Fifty empty canvases might be a bit daunting and I think you should get away from here for a time while you are working. Travelling is a great way to invigorate the muse. That's just a thought, of course. Don't think I'm telling you what to do," he finished hastily.

"Actually, I think it's a brilliant idea. I've been toying with it for a little while. I just didn't have the nerve to make the break. I've been clinging very much to my roots," she confessed.

"Well, that's very understandable. Do whatever is comfortable for you and whatever helps you to paint," Bryan advised her kindly. "Why don't you have the holiday you were planning and think about all of this."

This was precisely what Liz did. She had a beautiful relaxing two weeks in Incarna's villa and made up her mind not to take on any more work apart from the Wallace family portrait. When she finished her work in hand, she decided, she was going to take a year off to travel and work for her exhibition. She'd show Polly O'Rourke that she was a force to be reckoned with, chocolate-box art or no! Liz had made a substantial amount of money from her commissions and then the money from Matt's insurance policies and from the accident insurance had given her financial security. Financial reasons wouldn't stop her going travelling and painting for a year. Would she be able to stand on her own two feet without the backup of her family and Incarna? She'd never done anything like this before and it was a bit nerve-wracking, she decided, when her holiday visa for the States arrived. But when she started looking up addresses, she discovered that she had as many friends living all over the United States as she had in Dublin. In the end she stayed away a year and a half and ended up with enough material for a dozen exhibitions.

Sitting in the twilight as dusk deepened to inky blackness and the twinkling lights of La Jolla shimmered in the sea's reflection, Liz acknowledged that she was a far more confident person than she had been eighteen months ago. She had really done it; she had stood on her own two feet and made her way around the States, ending up by renting this little dream of a beach house and living in it alone for six months while she painted as she had never painted before. She had enjoyed herself though at times the loneliness had been hard to bear. When it got really bad she made herself go out and socialise. Now she was looking forward to seeing her family again. She had spoken to them all on the phone last night and they were in a tizzy of excitement at the thought of her homecoming. The intrepid Incarna had come to visit her a few months back and they had had a ball. They wrote regularly to each other and Liz could tell that her friend had sorely missed her company.

"Hey, Liz, are you coming over for supper?" Brett Ryder, her neighbour, was calling from next door.

"Sure thing!" Liz yelled back. She was really speaking the lingo. Wait until Christine heard her! She'd tease her unmercifully. She slipped her feet into flipflops, went inside, washed her face, brushed her hair and changed into a fresh pair of shorts and T-shirt. Everything was so delightfully casual and laid-back on the West coast. She'd made some nice friends, especially here along the beach. Brett and his wife Rachel had introduced themselves soon after she arrived and had taken her under their wing and gradually she had got to know the rest of her neighbours. She often had supper with them and the kids, sitting out on the veranda shooting the breeze, as they were fond of saying here. She caught sight of herself in the mirror grinning away. She could imagine Christine's reaction if she asked her to come over to shoot the breeze.

Well, she certainly looked a hell of a lot better from the thin pale-faced girl who had arrived in America. The big dark circles under her eyes had vanished and she sported a healthy tan. She had also put on a stone in weight, which really suited her. Her curves were back. When Matt died she had gone down to skin and bone. It was strange, but her time with Matt was becoming a little unreal to her, almost like some beautiful dream she had once had. Time was a healer. She could think of him now and smile a little instead of weeping. She had even dated men here in America. Well, not dated exactly. She had gone to dinner a few times and gone to see some exhibitions in Washington. She hadn't had a relationship as such. But they had been pleasant occasions and slowly she was easing herself back into a social life.

Brett's brother Dean was a very nice bloke and they had started going around together. A recently divorced man, he was still getting over the trauma of the separation and he quite understood Liz's reluctance to get into a close relationship. But they became good friends and he took her around a lot. She enjoyed his companionship very much. Liz had always liked men and enjoyed their company and Dean's undemanding friendship was just what she needed at that point in her life. The last six months in particular had been very good for her. She liked La Jolla, pronounced La Hoy-a, perched on its promontory which thrust into the pounding Pacific. Seven miles of rocky shore and cliffs interspersed by golden sandy beaches. Water-skiers, hang gliders, snorkelers abounded and there was always something happening on the beach. Liz thoroughly enjoyed the life of a beach bum. And there were enough art galleries, shops, and restaurants in the town to keep her occupied when she felt like a change.

She enjoyed the six months she had spent in La Jolla much more than the six months spent further up the coast in Los Angeles. Despite its laid-back image there was an undercurrent of violence about the smoggy sprawling metropolis that one could never quite ignore. And the traffic jams! And those nightmare freeways that encircled the city. If you missed your exit, as she had done several times, boy were you in trouble. Still that, too, had been an experience.

She had stayed with an old college friend and her husband. He was an architect, she a freelance photographer and both of them doing extremely well in their chosen careers. That was the great thing about California—opportunities abounded if you were prepared to take them. The hacienda-type bungalow that they lived in was the last word in luxury and Liz knew she'd never forget luxuriating under a starry Californian sky in a jacuzzi on the open-air deck that surrounded the house, watching the twinkling lights of Beverly Hills below her. Liz had her own small self-contained guest apartment which they told her to stay in as long as she wanted. Trish, her friend, had taken her shopping on the famous Rodeo Drive one day. It was really something.

They had browsed enthusiastically in beautifully laid out boutiques with everything a customer could desire, the crème de la crème being 273 North Rodeo Drive, home of Giorgio, the landmark store that was the basis of the Judith Krantz novel *Scruples.* Liz had seen the TV series. In real life the 9000 square feet of pure luxury was even more impressive and Liz gawped like a tourist when she saw Zsa Zsa Gabor sweep in with her chauffeur. "I saw Liz Taylor here once. She's gorgeous! Those eyes!" Trish murmured, as they sat down at the beautifully polished cappuccino bar and had a cocktail.

"I could get used to this," Liz confided, sipping the delicious concoction.

"No problem if you're earning a couple of million green ones a year." Trish grinned. "Wait until you see the clothes."

Liz didn't buy a dress, not even a T-shirt, but she left clutching the unmistakable yellow-and-white striped bag containing several bottles of Giorgio perfume to take home as presents.

The affluence of California had to be seen to be believed —magnificent houses with perfect lawns and huge swimming pools. Limousines were ten a penny and nobody walked. Liz rented a car for the duration of her stay. Her friends took her to the theatre, opera, museums, and art galleries; and they ate out most nights, it was so cheap and the range of food so varied.

It was Trish who told her about a friend who was subletting the beach house further down the coast in La Jolla for six months. Liz had been half thinking of going home. She already had a lot of material and she had seen and done so much. But the idea of six months living on the beach appealed to her and the rent was quite cheap as the man who was subletting wanted a recommended tenant. Liz sounded perfect to him and after a lunch meeting he quoted her a very reasonable figure so she decided to stay. Liz really loved the sun and the fact that it would have still been winter at home was a major factor in her decision.

She had thoroughly enjoyed living on the beach, painting morning noon and night, taking little trips across the border into Mexico with Dean, having Trish and her husband down at weekends, cooking barbecues for Brett, Rachel, Dean, and the kids. It had been like living on a permanent holiday. But the six months passed and it was time to pack up and go home. She had an exhibition to mount, the biggest challenge of her career, but she'd always look back on her stay in California as a healing happy time in her life.

## Wednesday, July 18, 1984

L iz flew out of LAX with a few pangs of regret, but by the time she got to Washington she was excited at the thought of getting home. She was spending a few days with the same friends she had stayed with on her arrival eighteen months ago. They met her at the airport, exclaiming in delight at the change in her. "You look fantastic!" Antoinette hugged her as Bobby, her husband, whistled in approval. Shrugging off her jet lag she sat with them until the early hours, telling them of her adventures.

"We've arranged a little farewell party for you," Antoinette informed her as she showed Liz to her room. "Nikki and Hugh and Marty and Jo and Ken are coming. And a few others."

"That sounds great." Liz was delighted at the thought of seeing her old friends once more before she left, and stretching like a cat in the bed, cramped after hours of flying across the continent, she yawned hugely and fell asleep.

Friday, July 20, 1984

Antoinette and Bobby went to so much trouble with the party. They hired caterers and flower arrangers and the whole thing was really swinging along. Liz was enjoying herself immensely. She looked like a million dollars with her California tan, her black, soft curly hair cut short, emphasising her darkly lashed vivid blue eyes. Men were falling over themselves to get her a drink and talk to her. She was laughing at something someone said when she heard Antoinette. "Liz, I'd like to introduce you to someone. Hugh Cassidy, this is Liz Lacey. Liz . . . Hugh." She felt her hand taken into a firm grip and found herself staring at a vaguely familiar and very handsome man.

Monday, June 30, 1986

"It's nice, isn't it?" Liz murmured to Hugh as two other viewers also stepped out on to the balcony of Apartment 3B. "And the light is superb. I could turn the second bedroom into a studio. I suppose it would be ideal, really."

"No supposing about it. It's perfect for you," Hugh assured her.

"I like my little flat, though, and now that Eve has the baby, I'm not sure I want to move," Liz said doubtfully.

"Well, you know what the accountant told you. You're going to be hammered for tax unless you go and do something like buying property," Hugh pointed out. "And besides, that baby is interfering with your painting. As far as I can see, you spend most of your time gooing and gaaing at her."

"Oh, but Hugh, she's *beautiful*! I've never seen such a beautiful baby. Oh, you should hear her!" Liz enthused. "She's learning to talk and she's making the most comical sounds. You'd die laughing." She caught his eye. "I'm doing it again, aren't I?"

"Yes, you are! I've heard of adoring mothers—but adoring aunts! Just as well you only have one niece, otherwise you'd

go bankrupt with all those presents you buy," he teased her.
"Mind, if you'd goo and gaa over me as much, I wouldn't
object at all."

"Now, now!" Liz reproved. "Aren't I cooking dinner for
you tonight? Who cooked dinner for you yesterday so you
could watch Maradona and his gang dance around a little
football?" Hugh had been bitterly disappointed when Argentina won the World Cup.

"You know what I mean." Hugh's tone was serious.
"We've been seeing each other well over a year now. Don't
you think things should progress? You've no idea how my ego
is suffering." He spoke lightly but Liz knew he was serious.
She sighed deeply, staring out at the view of the purple-green
Dublin Mountains in the distance. That would be a nice view
to paint, she thought idly.

"What are you thinking about?" Hugh enquired.

Liz jumped.

"What were you thinking about? It wasn't about us!" he
grumbled. Honestly, he was getting nowhere with this
woman.

"I was just thinking this would be a nice view to paint,"
Liz answered mildly.

Hugh raised his eyes to heaven. "I give up."

"Thank God!" teased Liz, and he burst out laughing.

"Well, are you going to buy this place or not. Don't forget, I haven't got all day. I've to go home and pack and fly to
Manchester first thing in the morning to see what's happening
with this Stalker thing," he moaned. "We're doing a programme on it."

"Aw, poor Mr. TV personality." Liz grinned. She knew he
loved getting his teeth into a job.

He had apologised when they met to view Apartment 3B.
They had made plans to go to the theatre, but as often happened with their plans, something would come up and Hugh
would find himself off on an assignment. Liz was used to it at
this stage. "Definitely something fishy is going on. John
Stalker was suspended from duty pending an investigation of

his alleged association with 'known criminals.' I'm sure it's a setup to discredit him. He was getting too close to the bone in his investigation of the Royal Ulster Constabulary 'shoot to kill' policy. Well I'm going to leave no stone unturned to get to the bottom of this. This is corruption at the highest level, Liz, and we're going to try and prove it. Sorry about tomorrow."

"Well, what do you think?" Eve asked as she and Don emerged onto the balcony to join them.

"It's a good buy, I'll tell you that for nothing, and you're buying at an ideal time—the property market is in an awful slump," her brother remarked.

Eve caught Liz's eye. "Well, at least it's only down the road from us. Isn't the kitchen something else?"

Liz nodded. The kitchen was fabulous. Fully fitted with all modern conveniences, it was a dream. Liz decided to have one last look around. There were several other interested parties and she realised that she could be bidding against any of them.

She had liked the apartment from the moment she had entered it. It was bright and airy, a most important consideration. A flower-filled balcony ran the length of the apartment with access from the sitting room and master bedroom. The second bedroom which she envisaged turning into a studio also had its own little balcony facing west. So she'd always have sun. Well, whatever sun was to be had! Liz liked the master bedroom with its enormous closets and its *en suite* tiled bathroom. It was all very luxurious, just the thing for a successful artist. Christine would really give her a teasing if she bought Apartment 3B. But of all the places she had looked at, it was the place she felt most at home in and besides, as Eve pointed out, it was only down the road from her house, and only ten minutes away from her parents. And after all, she was twenty-nine, successful and independent. It was time she had a place of her own. Not that she wasn't happy in the flat she had lived in since Matt had died seven years ago. It was comfortable and cosy and she would have been quite content to stay there. Eve and Don were also perfectly happy for her to continue living there but her accountant had advised her to buy property for tax purposes and if she bought somewhere, she might as well live in it.

Liz had looked at a good few places, houses, town houses, and apartments, and, so far, Apartment 3B, Mountain View, Glasnevin, was the place that was ideally suited to her needs. It was a small classy complex with superb amenities: swimming pool, floodlit tennis court, laundry. What more could a person ask for? And the price was well within her means. Property prices had never been so low, as her brother said, so it was the time to buy. And Hugh liked it.

Hugh. He had become important to her, she acknowledged. Little did she think that their first meeting in Washington would have any effect on her life. But it had. She had liked him from the very start when he had stood smiling at her. Once Antoinette said his name she recognised him immediately. Hugh Cassidy was a big media star in Ireland and a journalist of renown. He was pretty good-looking too, in a Cary Grantish sort of a way, she conceded—square of jaw, lean and muscular, of medium height. She could understand why women fell at his feet at home.

"I don't believe it. Liz Lacey!" he was saying, his eyes smiling into hers. "You'll never believe this, but before I left home I was thinking that I'd like to interview you some time. You're one of my favourite artists."

Liz smiled politely. "Thank you," she murmured.

"No honestly—you are!" he assured her. "I bought your works before you became famous. I've a watercolour of Killiney Bay and the Sugar Loaf at home. I bought it from you in Stephen's Green. Don't you remember?"

Liz grinned. "Well I don't actually remember you but I remember selling the painting. It kept me in paints for six months. That's a long time ago."

"It is," he agreed, "but I've got a lot of pleasure out of that painting. I'd like to buy another one some time." Liz sensed that his interest was genuine. Lots of people assured her they'd like to buy one of her paintings but they were only flattering her. They moved along the buffet together. "Are you on holidays?" he asked, popping a stuffed mushroom into his mouth. "Here, try these, they're gorgeous," he urged handing her the plate. They were too.

"I'm just going home actually. I've been in the States for eighteen months preparing for an exhibition."

"An exhibition! That's great!" he said enthusiastically between mushrooms. "Where are you holding it?"

"The Ross Gallery on Baggot Street."

Hugh let out a low whistle. "The Ross Gallery no less! You couldn't do better."

"I know. It's a great opportunity."

"And richly deserved, if I may say so," he said, munching on a smoked salmon savoury. "Here, try these. Melt in the mouth. The food here has me ruined. I always put on weight in the States. What are those things? They look interesting."

Liz laughed, handing him a plate of seafood savouries. "Here, take the plate and try them all." They had a most enjoyable time sampling everything and they chatted away easily, having a lot of mutual acquaintances in the society set in Dublin. Hugh brought her up to date on the gossip.

"And did you know that Angela Kennedy left Marcus? You did a magnificent job on that mural of his, I must say."

"Angela left Marcus!" Liz was astounded.

"Yep. Seemingly he'd been having an affair with this gorgeous French model, and it had been going on for years. And she had a child by him that no one knew about. Angela found out and told him she'd had enough. She walked out on him, took nothing from him and has set up her own interior design business. She's doing well too, I heard. Ken Healy asked her to refurbish the Majestic Hotel for him, and she's doing a lovely job by all accounts."

Liz was stunned. That bastard Marcus. All the time he'd been trying to seduce her he'd had a mistress on the side as well as his wife. He was something else. She was delighted for Angela. The only way she could go was up.

Liz enjoyed the evening with Hugh and the rest of her friends but when he asked her out to dinner the following evening she told him that she had made plans she couldn't break, and that she was returning home the following day. He was doing a programme on Geraldine Ferraro, the Democratic vice-presidential nominee, and then he was taking some holidays before heading west to do an item on the opening of the Olympic games in Los Angeles.

"Maybe when I get home?" he suggested.

"Maybe," Liz agreed noncommittally. She knew that when she got home she was going to be up to her eyes with her exhibition. Incarna had phoned her a week before to say that she had several commissions lined up if she was interested and the publishing firm that she had worked for previously had written to her asking if she would do several covers for them. Her holiday was well and truly over.

The excitement of arriving home was wonderful. The entire family greeted her at the airport and hugged the daylights out of her. Her mother was delighted at how well she looked and Christine and Eve pretended great disgust at her glowing tan. Then they all went back to her parents and tucked into a banquet of a breakfast.

"Oh, the taste of Irish rashers and sausages!" Liz exclaimed, starving after the flight. She took a bite out of her mother's homemade brown bread, savouring every delicious mouthful. "This is the life," she smiled at her family, delighted to be with them again. Then it was time for giving out the presents and for talking and catching up on all the news. She stayed a few days with her parents and then headed across the road to her little flat.

Before she settled down to work, Liz made a trip to Connemara to see Mrs. Lacey and to visit Matt's grave. Her mother-in-law, older and frailer, had welcomed her warmly and they had both gone to visit the lovingly kept grave. Liz was so glad she had had her husband buried in Connemara rather than Dublin. It was his place—the wild beautiful West of Ireland. It was home for Matt and Liz had always recognised that.

She stood for a long time with her hand on his headstone, thinking about him. How her life had changed after his death. She had reached undreamed-of pinnacles of success. She was successful and independent, the epitome of the eighties career woman and yet deep down Liz knew that she would trade every bit of it to be Matt's wife and the mother to his children. "That's not the way things turned out, my darling. I love you. I always will," she murmured in farewell before going to join Mrs. Lacey in the little church. The resentment she had once felt about Matt's death had passed and for the first time in many years Liz sat in a church and felt a serenity envelope her. Much to her poor mother's dismay, she had stopped going to mass, hating God for taking her husband from her. Now, sitting in that little country church with ribbons of multicoloured light streaming through the arched stained glass windows, Liz reflected that Incarna was right. She had been lucky to meet and love a man like Matt, even if it was only for so short a time. He had been a gift from God to her and she would always have her memories to sustain her. Liz returned to Dublin more at peace with herself than she had been for many years.

Immersed in preparing for the exhibition, she had been surprised one day to get a phone call from Hugh Cassidy. She heard a smiling voice on the other end of the receiver. "Hi! Remember me? We shared some magic food together."

"How did you get my number?" she asked, knowing that she hadn't given it to him.

"Well I am an investigative journalist of the highest calibre, who retains information long after it's been given to him, and I just rang Bryan Ross and told him I was interested in doing a documentary about you and your forthcoming exhibition," he informed her calmly.

"Oh!" She exclaimed at his coolness. "And are you going to do a documentary, Mr. Cassidy?"

Hugh laughed. "I do *happen* to have my own company,

which does *happen* to produce documentaries and I just *happened* to be looking for some new subjects, when who should appear on my horizon but a certain extremely talented artist who just *happens* to be mounting her first exhibition. How could I resist?"

"Are you serious?"

"If you're interested. It would be good for you publicitywise and good for me workwise. How about discussing it over lunch?"

"I'm awfully busy."

Hugh was not to be put off. "I could come to your studio. We could discuss it as you work if you prefer."

"Why not!" Liz laughed. He had an answer for everything.

"Leave lunch to me," he said cheerfully as she gave him the address.

Hugh arrived the following day with a picnic hamper and a bottle of champagne. "Don't let me stop you working," he said matter-of-factly as he laid a rug on the floor and proceeded to set two places. Liz stood open-mouthed as she watched him arrange two beautifully pink salmon fillets in a bed of lettuce, radishes, and chives. He had dishes of potato salad, Waldorf salad, coleslaw, and Russian salad as well as French bread and a variety of cheeses. "Tuck in," he invited her, handing her a linen napkin.

"You don't do things by halves, do you?" Liz said in amusement.

He smiled at her, his brown eyes twinkling. "I have business lunches like this all the time."

Hugh's public persona gave the impression of someone rather serious but in reality he had a boyishness that was rather endearing. He wasn't a bit affected by his celebrity status and Liz liked his direct manner. To her surprise, she enjoyed her lunch very much and in fact it was he who rose to leave, saying he had an engagement in the city. The terms he offered to do the documentary about her were more than reasonable and he asked her if she would have any objection to a camera crew arriving the next day.

"No problem," she replied calmly.

As she stepped around cables and sat under bright lights while the young director posed her for a close-up, she began to have second thoughts. But eventually she got used to the crew and continued painting away as they filmed her.

"I'm raging I didn't take a few shots of you while you were in the States," Hugh remarked one day as he supervised the filming of her painting the Halfpenny Bridge. "Never mind, we're getting great stuff. This will sell all over the place." He was the eternal optimist, Liz was learning, as she got to know him. Mostly he left the filming to the director, but if he had free time he joined them all on "the set," as he laughingly called it, to see how they were getting on. The next big thing was the opening of the exhibition itself. Hugh had the camera crew all lined up for it, and they knew exactly what he and the director were looking for.

Incarna was ecstatic about it all. She was delighted that Liz was back home and that her career was zooming off in all directions again. "Now, my dear, you will have to look so glamorous on your opening night. Tomorrow, you are taking a day off to go shopping for a dress," she said over the phone.

Liz threw her eyes up to heaven. If she had her way, she'd go in her 501's.

"Great idea!" exclaimed Brendan, the director, when she told him she was going shopping the next day. "We'll go too, it'll be a new angle!"

Liz stared at the eager young man, saw that he was quite serious, threw her arms in the air and said, laughing, "I give up!"

Her exhibition was a great personal triumph for Liz, with more than thirty of the fifty exhibited paintings sporting the little red "Sold" sticker before the end of the launch. Bryan, who had been so supportive and who had given her such useful advice, was delighted for her. "A lot of people like chocolate-box art, it seems!" he murmured, eyes twinkling, as he gave her a great bear hug.

"So it seems," Liz responded. "How mean of you not to invite Ms. O'Rourke."

"Didn't you hear? She's busy writing a novel. No doubt it will win the Nobel prize for literature!" Bryan chuckled.

Liz gave him a dig in the ribs. "Don't be nasty!"

"Well, it will be good for a laugh anyway. Maybe they could ask you to review it. That would be sauce for the goose. 'Polly pens purple prose!' "

The idea tickled Liz's sense of humour and she roared laughing, really beginning to enjoy herself now that the effort and strain of preparing for the exhibition were over and the evening was going so well. She could see Brendan and his camera crew conducting interviews with various guests as they examined her work. Incarna appeared at her elbow. "This ees a marvellous evening, Liz. People are really enjoying themselves, not just standing around making polite conversation. Congratulations, my dear."

"Ah, thanks, Incarna!" Liz hugged her friend. It was true what she was saying. There was a great buzz in the gallery. She had been to a few such functions herself, where people quaffed their champagne, ate whatever was to eat, and, surreptitiously looking at their watches, made fast exits. Well, tonight, no one was in a hurry to leave and the atmosphere was getting more animated by the minute.

"I suppose there'll be no living with you after this?" Christine remarked as she passed her sister on the trail of another oyster.

"All this excitement isn't good for a pregnant woman," Eve joked, patting her tummy. "Those scampi things are gorgeous. I'm developing cravings!" Her sister-in-law had confided to her a few days before that she was in the early weeks of pregnancy and Liz was over the moon about it. This was even more exciting than the exhibition.

"For God's sake, take things easy! Why don't you sit down for a while?" Liz urged.

Eve guffawed. "Lord, you're worse than Don. I'm ready for anything. When this is over I'm going boppin' in Leeson Street," she teased.

Brendan and crew arrived, pointing the camera at Liz. Then Hugh appeared. "Smile! You're on *Candid Camera*! You look great, Liz. Congratulations on a terrific opening." He smiled at her. The expression in his attractive heavy-lidded brown eyes was unmistakably admiring.

"Thanks," she murmured. She was wearing a simple but chic white linen Paul Costello suit which showed off her tan and her curves to perfection. Strangely, she found Hugh's admiration hard to handle. For the first time since Matt, she found herself somewhat attracted to a man and she wasn't sure she liked the feeling. It made her feel a little guilty, almost as if she was being unfaithful to her dead husband. She buried the thought, as she had been doing for the past few days in Hugh's company. Tonight was the night of her opening and she was going to enjoy it. These disturbing thoughts were not for now.

Perhaps sensing her reserve, Hugh said lightly, "I bet you haven't had time to eat yet. Let's see what goodies are on offer?"

Taking her cue from him, Liz joked, "It's just as well you don't film cookery programmes. You'd be like the Michelin man."

Hugh patted his lean midriff. "I'm a growing lad. I need my grub and if we don't hurry on there won't be any left." He took her arm and led her in the direction of a waitress who was carrying a platter of nibbles.

The evening passed in a blur of congratulations as people complimented her and wished her well. Afterwards Christine and Liam invited Liz, the family, and anyone else who wanted to go back to a buffet supper and party in their house which went on to the early hours. Liz got to bed just before dawn, delighted with the success of her first exhibition.

Gradually she began to see more of Hugh. They began to socialise together, discovering that they had many mutual interests, like tennis. Liz loved playing tennis. She had always liked to keep fit and found tennis a great way to relax after a day spent in concentration on her painting or artwork. Although he was, naturally, the more powerful player, she was the more skilful and their games were fairly evenly matched. No quarter was given by either of them and she found their hard-fought marathons invigorating. They also shared a love of swimming and went to the pool several times a week. The healthy life-style suited Liz. For so long she hadn't bothered with any of her hobbies, immersing herself in her work. Now with Hugh she was rediscovering the enjoyment these sports gave her and she began to feel much better both physically and mentally. Whereas before she would do her work and spend much of her time at home, reading and watching TV, unwilling to make the effort to get dressed up and go out, now she found herself looking forward to whatever activity they had planned together.

Hugh was exciting to be with. He was always on the go but she found, behind the brisk and sometimes brash manner, a sensitive man who understood her reluctance to enter into a new relationship and who nevertheless was happy to be in her company. He was very supportive of her career, being very career-minded himself, and he took great interest in whatever commission she happened to be working on. His documentary turned out to be extremely interesting and once she had got over the shock of seeing herself on film, Liz had to admit that she was more than pleased with it.

Of course food played a great part in their budding relationship. Hugh loved eating out. It was part and parcel of his life-style. See and be seen was important in his job, he told her, and eating out in posh hostelries was an ideal way of keeping a high profile. The only place Liz would not go to was the Plaza, being unwilling to risk a meeting with Marcus Kennedy.

The first time Hugh kissed her she felt very mixed emotions. It was a cold winter's day and after two days of blizzard the snow was still thick on the ground. They were larking around throwing snowballs at each other on their way home to Liz's after attending a reception. Liz had got in a particularly lucky strike and Hugh in retaliation had an arm lock around her and was threatening to deposit some snow down her neck. "Say you're sorry!" he demanded.

"Never!" she protested, her eyes sparkling, cheeks red from the cold, snowflakes white against the shining blackness of her hair.

Hugh drew her closer, a big snowball in his hand. Liz squealed and he started to laugh and dropped the snowball. "You're lucky I'm such a softie." He was smiling down at her, his face almost touching hers. Their eyes met and then, softly cupping her face in his hands, Hugh kissed her, very gently at first and then, when she did not draw away, with a passion that left them both breathless.

"Hugh . . . I . . . I don't know . . ." Liz drew away, confused.

"I'm sorry." He rubbed a hand over his jaw. "I didn't mean to be quite so . . . so . . . enthusiastic," he said ruefully. "I don't want to rush you, Liz, but you must know I've been wanting to do that for a long time."

"I know that," she admitted, feeling pretty shaken.

"And did you want me to do it?" He held her gaze.

"I . . . Hugh . . . Oh, let's go in!" She refused to answer the question.

"Liz, don't run away from it, please. It's important to me, to us. Have you thought about our relationship?" he said urgently, taking both her hands in his, his breath frosty on the cold night air.

Her eyes in the moonlight were big and troubled. She knew it had to come to this. Hugh was a very attractive man and he was seriously interested in her. He had told her a little of his past relationships, but he hadn't been seeing anyone since before he had started spending time with her. When he kissed her, she had felt herself responding, felt herself wanting more. Liz was a normal young woman with normal sexual needs. Hugh was the first man she had felt this response to since Matt, but she felt so confused over the emotions that were in conflict inside her. Predominant was a feeling of terrible guilt, as if she was betraying her dead husband in some way. It was stupid, she knew, and Matt would have been the first to tell her so.

"Have you thought about us?" Hugh persisted.

"I'm confused Hugh . . . I need time. Please don't push," she pleaded.

He shook his head and sighed. "I've been remarkably restrained. After all, we've been seeing each other for four months." His tone was a little wry.

"I know," Liz murmured. Seeing her distress, he put his arm around her.

"Ah, cheer up. I won't try and seduce you tonight, if you'll give me some of that cherry pie that's in your freezer."

Liz couldn't help smiling at him. "You're a nice man, Hugh. Thanks for being so understanding."

"Sshhh! Don't tell anyone! My reputation will be ruined. Government ministers have to take Valium before confronting me!"

They went in to partake of cherry pie.

"Incarna, did you ever get involved with anyone after Gerald died?" Liz inquired of her friend as they met for lunch one day several weeks later. Incarna's black eyes darkened with understanding. "I was in a different position from you, my dear. I was widowed late in life after many many years of happy marriage. Like you, I could not contemplate life without my husband. I threw myself into looking after our affairs. I became more of a businesswoman than previously and each night I cried myself to sleep. But like you, I lived through my grief and learned to control it rather than letting it control me. And in time I too began to go out and take an interest in life again. I've had men friends, but for me, at my age, I am happy as I am."

She smiled at Liz and reached over and took her hand. "My dear, you are a young woman, your life ees ahead of you.

Matt would want very much for you to be happy. Eees this not true?"

Liz toyed with her chocolate profiterole. "Yes," she murmured.

"Well, then if you think you could be happy with Hugh . . ." She smiled. "It ees Hugh we are not discussing, ees it not?"

Liz laughed. Incarna was extremely shrewd.

"My dear, you must grasp the chance for happiness with both hands. Do not live in the past. Think of the good times of course, but you must move forward or there ees no point to life." Incarna lit an Yves Saint Laurent menthol cigarette and inhaled deeply. "Of course the first time I kissed a man after my husband died I felt as though I had betrayed him. I felt so guilty." She grimaced at the memory. "I think it ees an emotion common to widows. This man was a kind and patient man. We talked, we became good friends before we became lovers. He was and ees a pillar of support in my life and what I feel for him in no way diminishes my great love for Geraldo. So, my darling, do not feel bad about Hugh. He ees a nice man, he ees good for you, you have been alone for too long," Incarna comforted her.

Liz squeezed her friend's hand. "Thank you, Incarna, for being so frank with me. I did not mean to pry. But you understand so well what it is like and Hugh wants more from me."

"Of course he does. A beautiful-natured woman like yourself is very hard to resist and that Hugh, he ees very red-blooded, I would say." Incarna's eyes twinkled. "But, my dear, only when you are ready. Do not allow him to pressurise you. When it ees right for you you will know, believe me. And I would never think of you as prying. Now, if you don't eat up that profiterole, I will!"

Standing on the balcony of Apartment 3B, Liz smiled as she remembered that conversation.

Inside, Hugh was talking to the estate agent, and Don and Eve were taking a stroll around the magnificent grounds.

She took a deep breath and walked into the carpeted sitting room, with its magnificent marble fireplace. "I'm interested in buying," she told the estate agent.

"Let's talk business then," he smiled.

"You made up your mind very quickly," Hugh remarked as they relaxed together after dinner.

"I tend to do that." Liz smiled.

He sighed and rubbed a hand wearily over his face. "I'd better go home," he said, getting up from the sofa.

Liz stood up with him, put her arms around his neck, drew his mouth down on hers and kissed him long and deeply. "You don't have to go home if you don't want to."

Hugh's arms tightened around her and he lowered his head and kissed her hotly, leaving her in no doubt as to his desires as his hands slid down to her waist and he drew her close against him. "Oh, Liz!" he murmured huskily against the side of her neck as he caressed her. "Are you sure?" He sounded almost anxious, concerned for her. He had been very patient with her and for that she loved him.

Her arms tightened around him. She inhaled the male musky scent of him, felt the hardness of his body against hers. "I think so!" she whispered against his lips.

He lifted his head and stared down into her eyes. "Liz, you have to be sure. I don't want you to have regrets or to feel bad." His voice was not quite steady.

She met his eyes. "I'll have no regrets, Hugh, I promise," she murmured and her lips sought his to prove it.

Saturday, December 10, 1988

"Do you want to feed her?" Eve smiled at Liz as she drooled over her baby niece.

"Oh, Eve you're the best sister-in-law in the world," said Liz, holding out her arms for the precious bundle. Big blue eyes stared solemnly up at her. "Hello, my darling. Hello, Caitriona," Liz cooed, utterly entranced.

The baby smiled, a smile that went from one ear to the other, showing a gorgeous little dimple. "You are beautiful! The most beautiful baby in the universe," Liz informed her five-month-old niece. Caitriona gurgled in appreciation as she made an assault on the thick gold chain that dangled around Liz's neck, the chain Hugh had given her for her thirty-second birthday.

"'Allo, Auntie Liz!" Her three-year-old niece Fiona flew into the room like a little whirlwind. "I've packed for my holiday and I'm bwinging my zigsie saw," the little girl informed her as she clambered up on the sofa beside her and planted a big kiss on her cheek. "Your zigsie saw! Brilliant!" exclaimed Liz, hiding a grin. Fiona came out with the most wonderful expressions. A few days before she had informed her aunt grandly that when she grew up she was going to be a "skate icer." She was coming to stay with Liz for the night, a treat for Fiona, but an even bigger treat for her doting aunt who loved being with the child. "Caitweena can't come. She's only a baby an' I'm a big girl now," Fiona informed Liz importantly.

"Of course you are and we're going to have great fun. We're going to go into town, first to buy you a treat and then we're going to go to McDonald's and then I was wondering if you would help me wrap some Christmas presents?"

"Am I in chawge?" Fiona asked, laying down the ground rules.

"Oh, yes, you're in charge," Liz promised. She took the bottle from her sister-in-law as Caitriona went into an ecstasy of excitement at the sight of it. Liz held the baby close to her, fascinated by her perfection: the tiny little fingers that were learning to hold on to the bottle and the softness of the dark fine hair that was in such contrast to her flame-haired little sister. Liz ran her palm over the downy head. She loved holding the baby, loved the feel of her in her arms, and each day she called in to visit and have a "go" of her. If it was feeding time Eve always let her give Caitriona her bottle and the thrill of it never wore off. From the moment she had felt her niece kick lustily in Eve's womb Liz had started to feel dreadfully broody. All through the pregnancy, as Eve's shape changed and she bloomed—she was one of those people whom pregnancy suited—Liz had wistfully looked on, wishing that she was in the same position. Fiona had of course told her where she was going wrong.

"We're on the waiting list for a baby. We're this many to go!" her young niece informed her out of the blue one day, holding up five little fingers. "Would you like a baby, Auntie Liz? Do you weelly weelly wish you were me?" she enquired, snuggling against Liz for a cuddle.

"Oh, I really really wish I was you. I'd love to be getting a baby." Liz smiled. She adored the way her niece could not pronounce her r's.

Fiona paused and took Liz's face in her little hands, her blue eyes round and solemn. "I'll tell you why you're not getting a baby like us. Because you're not saying enough payers. I said loads and loads of payers to Holy God and now we're on the waiting list," Fiona exclaimed triumphantly.

Eve was doubled up on the other side of the room. Hugh's face was a study and Christine, who was also on a visit, grinned. "Put that in your pipe and smoke it then, Liz!"

Liz had moved in with Eve and Don the week before the baby was due so that she would be on hand to look after Fiona when her sister-in-law went into labour. "What will I tell Fiona if she wants to know how the baby got out of your stomach?" Liz enquired anxiously. Fiona had been informed by her cousin that the baby was in her mammy's tummy. Put there by Holy God! That had been easy enough to assimilate so there hadn't been too many questions but Liz decided that, like the scouts, she would be prepared.

Eve laughed. "Don't worry, Liz. She'll be so excited about the baby that that won't even cross her mind."

"Well, it's the first thing *I'd* want to know," Liz said doubtfully.

"I'm telling you, Liz, wait and see."

Eve went into labour one morning in the early hours. Liz

was woken by a gentle shake. "I'm away," Eve said, grimacing as she sat on the bed and did her breathing to get through a contraction. Liz felt a pang of sympathy for her sister-in-law. Having babies was no fun. Labour didn't even begin to describe it. Whoever invented childbirth must have had sadistic tendencies. Standing in her dressing gown waving Eve and Don off, Liz reflected that if *she* were heading off to Holles Street Hospital to face the ordeal of childbirth, she'd be absolutely petrified. It was awful, really, to have to go through nine months knowing that at the end you were faced with a painful labour about which you could do very little, whether you liked it or not. It was all out of your control, and Liz found herself feeling quite resentful of the idea. Maybe she was unnatural, she thought, as she made herself a cup of tea and watched the sun rise.

At ten-thirty, the phone rang. She nearly fell down the stairs in her haste to answer it, with Fiona hot on her heels. "It's a girl! Nine pounds six ounces! Eve's a bit shattered but she's fine!" Don was elated on the other end of the phone. "Let *me* tell Fiona!"

Liz put her arm around the little girl and handed her the phone. "Daddy wants to talk to you."

She heard Don say, "You've got a little sister."

She watched her niece's blue eyes grow wide with wonder and felt a lump come to her throat. Idiot! she reprimanded herself, blinking the tears from her eyes. Hugh was always teasing her about crying at sad films.

"I've got a new baby," Fiona said, beaming.

"I know, it's great, isn't it? It's so exciting." Liz hugged the little girl as they did a little dance of happiness in the hall.

They decided to finish the washing-up after the breakfast. Fiona was putting away the cutlery. "Liz, did the baby come out of Mammy's bottom?" The three-year-old fixed her aunt with a piercing stare.

Liz's jaw dropped. "Aah . . . mmm . . ." she stuttered inadequately.

Fiona gazed at her expectantly.

"Well . . . ah . . . I don't know, actually, I've never had a baby," she fibbed. "We'll have to ask Mammy this afternoon. Why did you think that?" Liz was curious to ascertain exactly what her niece knew, courtesy of her older, better-informed cousin.

"I saw something on the telly." Fiona neatly laid the spoons one on top of the other.

Sacred Heart, thought Liz in horror, she's seen a baby being born on the telly. And she's only three! "What did you see?" she asked, trying to be casual.

"Me an' John were watching the telly and we saw a baby cow being born and it came out of its mammy's bottom," Fiona told her matter-of-factly. She worked industriously, her little red pigtails swinging cheerfully.

"Oh, I see," Liz murmured. "Well, we'll ask Mammy this afternoon."

"Can I go out on my swing now?" the little girl said, quite happy to ask her mother, who, in her eyes, knew everything.

That afternoon they went in to visit Eve. Her sister-in-law looked exhausted and could hardly move. "Three stitches!" she groaned, but her expression was so proud and tender as she glanced at the cot beside her.

Liz leaned over and held her breath. A tiny little face with eyes tightly closed and a head of soft dark hair was all that she could see. The lump came to her throat again and she met Eve's eyes. Her sister-in-law's eyes were moist as they hugged each other. "Oh, Eve, she's beautiful!" Liz whispered.

Fiona stood speechless, staring down at her new sister. Finding her voice she turned to her mother. "Oh, Mammy, she's brilliant!" The question of how the new baby had arrived was completely forgotten in the excitement.

"It was so moving!" Liz told Hugh later that night as she lay with her head resting on his chest.

"You surprise me! You really do," he replied, caressing her cheek. "You're such a maternal soul. I thought artists only had time for the muse. Sometimes I feel that if you had children you'd never paint again."

"Well, I'd paint them," Liz laughed. "But you're probably right. If I had children I'd spend most of my time rearing them. And what's wrong with that?" she asked defensively.

"It would be a bit of a waste of your talent," he pointed out.

"Don't you think raising children and giving them as happy and carefree a childhood as possible is a talent?" Liz retorted. "It really annoys me the way housewives and mothers are downgraded. It's the hardest thing in the world to rear children, for all the thanks mothers get."

"Don't get on your high horse," Hugh responded calmly. "I was merely noticing that your maternal feelings are so totally at odds with your media image."

"Well, I didn't create my media image and frankly I couldn't care less what people think. I think motherhood is as demanding a career as any and if ever I'm lucky enough to have children the media can go and whistle," Liz said grumpily. Hugh wasn't the slightest bit interested in children. He had told her many times that he wouldn't dream of settling down to have a family until he was at the top of his career. He'd always been very straight about that, she couldn't deny it. Neither could she deny that more than anything she longed for a child.

Hugh and she had been together for several years now. And mostly it had been good. Both maintained their own establishments. Liz had settled into Apartment 3B. Hugh had his mews in Donnybrook. It was a system that suited them. Hugh was often away making programmes and Liz liked the freedom living on her own gave her. She could paint when she liked and come and go as she pleased and still have the comfort of a steady relationship. Because she had been on her own for so long she felt that she had become a little selfish and used to doing as she liked. Her relationship with Hugh was nothing like her marriage to Matt. But then Hugh was nothing like Matt either. Hugh's career was everything to him, and Liz, whom he did love, realised this more than any other woman he had been with. He often told her so. It was something she could not quite understand. Liz loved her own work and was as ambitious as the next person, but to her, family and friends were far more important than any success she could ever achieve from her painting. She would never be as driven to succeed as Hugh was and this was the greatest difference between them. They often argued bitterly when he had to break plans they had made because of the demands of his job.

One night she cooked a special dinner for him. It was his birthday and she had gone to a lot of trouble to have everything just so. He arrived three hours late, and the minute he walked in the door, she knew he was high on something. Liz knew he snorted coke. Hugh had taken her to a party in Ballsbridge once and everybody was nipping into the bathroom to do a line. She had seen enough of it in America to know what was going on. "Just try a little bit. It's really something. You'll be on a high for the rest of the evening," Hugh urged. Liz wouldn't touch the stuff and she hated to see him using it. No matter how much he tried to convince her that he could give it up anytime and that he only took it because of the stressful demands of his job, Liz was not happy about his habit and she let him know it. That night when he arrived as high as a kite and full of the joys of spring she had let fly, accusing him of being totally irresponsible for driving in that state in the first place and warning him that if he ever came to her like that again it was over between them.

"You're overreacting, Liz!" he snapped. "I'm totally in control. And don't start doing your nagging housewife bit. That I can do without!"

"Well, if you had an ounce of good manners I wouldn't have to," she yelled furiously. "And don't think for one moment that you're in control because you're not! How can you even begin to fool yourself that you are? You're as bad, if not worse, than any drunken driver."

"Ah, for Christ's sake, Liz. You're paranoid about drunken drivers," he retorted angrily.

"Matt was killed by a drunken driver!" Liz's voice shook with fury.

"Oh, for God's sake, spare me the Saint Matt bit!" Hugh snorted. "Have you any idea what it's like trying to live up to a paragon of virtue? *He'd* never take a little whiff of coke! Oh, perish the thought!"

"Get out! Get out, Hugh. Now!" Liz was white with anger.

"I'm going, Liz." He flung the bottle of wine he was carrying onto the sofa and slammed the door behind him.

Liz was sorely tempted to pick it up and fling it after him but restrained herself. No doubt the whole apartment block had heard their row. She'd be the subject of a few curious looks the next day. Blowing out the romantic candles on the table with vicious gusto she marched into her studio and began to paint with a vengeance, slashing on the colours until the fury had drained out of her. How dare he talk about Matt like that! Just who did he think he was! Well, he could get out of her life if that was the way he felt.

Sleep would not come that night. Did she want Hugh out of her life? Had she canonised her late husband so much that Hugh felt defensive about it. She hadn't done it intentionally. She and Matt had never argued like she argued with Hugh. But then she had only been with Matt a year. The rosy bloom of newly wedded bliss had not yet worn off when he was killed and they hadn't begun to irritate each other about little things as most couples did after spending a long time together. She and Matt had not had to make the huge adjustments that she and Hugh had to make in their relationship—a relationship that was strong and supportive despite their occasional differences. She supposed it wasn't that easy for him to have to live with the ghost of her dead husband. Liz sighed. Hugh could be so bullheaded sometimes, but then she wasn't perfect and God knows he put up with her. She decided she'd ring him first thing in the morning to talk things over and by then his anger might have died down. At least they could always talk about things. It was one of the things she liked about him. He was always willing to see the other person's argument. No doubt this trait had been developed by the job he was in.

In fact, she slept late and it was Hugh's phone call that woke her. "Hello," she murmured groggily, struggling to come to a state of wakefulness.

"Hi. It's me and I'm sorry. I was out of order!" Hugh's deep voice penetrated her muzziness and she came instantly awake.

"Well, it was a bit below the belt . . ." She wasn't letting him get off that lightly.

She heard a deep sigh at the other end of the phone. "I know. I apologise."

"Apology accepted," Liz said evenly, never one to hold a grudge. "I salvaged the dinner if you want to come over tonight."

"I'd like that." She could sense that he was smiling. They talked into the early hours that night and he assured her that his cocaine habit was nothing to be concerned about. Nevertheless, despite his assurances that his drug-taking was merely occasional and recreational, Liz worried about it.

She was still up to her eyes in work. After the success of her exhibition, offers continued to pour in. She had settled very nicely into her new apartment. Once she moved in, she decorated it to her own taste in light airy pastel colours that always had a calming effect upon her. She had turned the second bedroom into a studio where she spent many hours painting happily. In the mornings, early, she would use the pool and she and Hugh frequently played tennis on the complex's court. The facilities were excellent and, having settled in, Liz felt she had made the right decision.

It took a while before she got to know her neighbours. Usually she would meet them in the lift or in the foyer. Directly underneath her were the two sisters, Muriel and Maud. They had given her a few strange looks at first, obviously wondering if this high-profile artist was going to cause trouble by throwing outrageous parties. Gradually the coolness thawed and Liz got to know them better at the management committee meetings that were held every so often to discuss the running of the building. Muriel was a lovely homely woman who confided in Liz one day that she should never have left her little cottage when her husband died in order to move in with her sister. Maud, the sister, was extremely elegant and refined but before long it dawned on Liz that the poor woman had a liking for the bottle. It was obvious that the two sisters did not get on, which must have been hell since they had to live together.

A couple and their two children lived on the second floor. Al and Detta were obviously striving to out-yuppy even the most yuppyish of yuppies. Al was an information scientist, a fact of which his wife had proudly informed Liz at the first meeting she had attended in their apartment. Their rooms were colour coordinated and furnished like something out of *Good Housekeeping*. The children, Tralee, so named because the little girl had been born prematurely and unexpectedly in Tralee General Hospital, and Candine, her younger sister, had behaved outrageously, crying and whining, when in Liz's opinion they should have been long gone to bed. "Don't do that, Lee darling!" Detta murmured as Tralee kicked the leg of the cream O'Hagan Design sofa in a tantrum. She might as well have been talking to the moon. "Oh, dear!" sighed Detta helplessly as her husband carried the screaming child into a bedroom.

"I usually spend some quality time with them at night when I get home from work, but tonight I was preparing for the meeting. Perhaps I should have got Tina to stay, but I think she was going horse-riding or swimming or something." Tina was the nanny! Liz noticed the dismay on Al and Detta's faces when it was decided at the meeting to have the foyer and landings repainted for a not inconsiderable sum. Obviously, money was not all that plentiful, despite the image. She felt sorry for them. Al always looked utterly harassed and Detta could not cope with her children.

Dominic Kent was the neighbour she liked best. He lived

on the ground floor in one of the smaller apartments and was only there part of the week. He told her that he had a business in Cork and one in the capital and that he spent his time commuting. They often met in the swimming pool and she liked his sense of humour and the wry comments he would make about their neighbours. He often had a beautiful blond girl staying who was many years younger than him and they seemed very happy in each other's company. He had introduced her as Lainey Conroy and Liz had to admit she had never seen anyone so elegant and glamorous as the blond air hostess. Despite her soignée aura, Lainey was extremely down-to-earth and good fun, and Liz always enjoyed meeting her when she was staying over.

The last person in the building was Derek, a young broker who obviously felt he was going somewhere. In his smart suits and carrying his executive briefcase he cut an impressive business image. He was, as Maud said snootily one day after being kept awake by one of his parties, "only a rented"—renting the apartment from a property speculator-owner whom Liz had never met. Derek fancied her like mad, much to her amusement, and he was always going out of his way to impress her with his man-of-the-world ways. All in all it was a very mixed bunch that lived in her block but by and large they got on well enough except when Derek gave one of his parties and Maud and Muriel would complain for days on end, trying to get up a petition to have a formal complaint made to the landlord. Dominic would promise to take his next-door neighbour aside and talk to him man-to-man, and the ladies would be mollified . . . until the next time.

Hugh, who had once had to help Maud operate the lift when she was more than a little under the weather, was fascinated by them all and teased Liz that he was going to do a documentary about them. She wouldn't put it past him!

"Where's Hugh?" Eve was asking as Liz expertly burped her niece and laid her down to change her.

"He's gone to do a programme about the changes taking place in the Eastern-bloc countries. He's doing an interview with the prime minister of Czechoslovakia, tomorrow, no less," she explained as she patted Sudocrem on the baby's bottom.

"He certainly gets around!" Eve exclaimed, thoroughly enjoying her hour or so of freedom as the doting aunt took over.

"Mmm," murmured Liz absently. Caitriona was trying to eat her toes and it was fascinating to watch. "He's off to the States next week. He's taken two months off work here to try and get some project off the ground over there. That's why I'm going over for Christmas and that's why I've done my shopping early. You know Hugh: now you see him, now you don't!"

"Are we going on our holidays?" Fiona was getting impatient. Sometimes her aunt spent too much time with the baby.

"Of course we are. Are you ready?" Liz responded, drawing the little girl close for a cuddle, aware that her attention must be shared out fairly. Not that Fiona was jealous. She was delighted with the baby, but nevertheless, Liz was extremely careful to divide her attention equally.

With great excitement they set off. "Is she going on a cruise or what?" Liz enquired when she saw her small niece's luggage.

"Well, don't forget the zigsie saw. And I think My Little Pony and her tea set and Barbie are going on holidays as well." Eve chuckled as she waved them off.

That night, after a super sudsy bubble bath, with lashings of talc afterwards, Fiona sat on Liz's knee as she brushed the little girl's beautiful red hair. "Now this is what we'll do," her niece was explaining, seeing that she was in charge. "We'll put all the bungles of pwesents in the miggle of the woom first. Wight?"

"Right!" agreed Liz.

"I've a new song," Fiona informed her aunt happily.

"Have you? Will you sing it for me?"

Fiona nodded. "Yep. It's called 'Ankle Doogle'!"

" 'Ankle Doogle'! That sounds nice," Liz murmured, mystified, only to hide a grin as she recognised the tune, if not the words, of "Yankee Doodle." Holding Fiona on her knee as she sang away to her heart's content, Liz reflected on the great joy her two nieces had brought to her life and wished heartily that she had a child of her own.

## Hugh

Friday, July 13, 1984

"Do you admit that the government should have acted more swiftly in this matter, Minister?" Hugh Cassidy cut through the minister's blustering response like a knife.

"Well now, Mr. Cassidy," the minister smiled ingratiatingly.

"I'd like you to answer the question, Minister, as we only have a few seconds left," persisted Hugh, who was enjoying himself immensely. The gorgeous redhead in the front row of the audience was more than impressed, he could tell.

"The Government acted as responsibly and quickly as was required," snarled the minister.

"Which wasn't quick or responsible enough in the eyes of many," retorted Hugh triumphantly. "And there we have to leave it."

He addressed the audience and camera one as the theme music began to play and the credits started to roll and the minister, furious, tried to respond. "Good night from this week's edition of News Review."

The lights in the studio darkened, the audience clapped and Hugh leaned back in his chair, elated. He loved it when an interview really came together.

"You're a bastard, Cassidy. I'll make damn sure you don't get to interview me again." The outraged minister fumed.

"Just doing my job!" Hugh smiled. "Here's the girl from hospitality to take care of you," he said briskly, rising from his chair. "Good night, Minister." Hugh didn't have the time or the inclination to stay and soothe the ruffled feathers of his eminent guest. He had to attend the post-programme discussion and then go home and finish his packing. He was moving house the following day. After that he had to get ready to fly to the States on Monday morning to put together a programme on New York Congresswoman Geraldine Ferraro, the first-ever woman chosen to run for vice-president by either the Democrats or the Republicans. In Hugh's opinion, presidential candidate Walter Mondale had made an inspired choice. Geraldine Ferraro was a brisk, no-nonsense, highly intelligent woman, adept at using the media. "She's a woman, she's ethnic, she's a Catholic." So one of Mondale's advisers explained the calculation that had led to her choice. That whole issue would give Hugh plenty of material for the programme. He hoped she would halt the gallop of Reagan.

Hugh was really looking forward to getting back to the States. He had done several documentaries about the thousands of Irish emigrants working there and his ultimate goal was to make it on network TV in America. This trip on Monday would be another step towards that goal.

"You really got the needle in tonight, Hugh," his producer grinned as they walked towards his office.

"Well, he's a sneaky scum at the best of times, despite the charm," Hugh observed. "I enjoyed watching him squirm."

"And no one better to make a politician squirm! The programme is still at the top of the TV ratings and looks like staying there if the feedback is anything to go by."

"That's what I like to hear," said Hugh.

By the time he got home to the house in Inchicore it was much later than he had anticipated. He'd run into a journalist friend and by the time he had caught up on all the gossip over a pint in Kiely's in Donnybrook, it was after eleven. Reluctantly he departed. He was not in the humour to empty the contents of his wardrobe into cardboard cartons. Moving house was a real pain but still, he had made a profit on his terraced two-up two-down. Five years ago he wouldn't have been able to consider moving to a semi-detached house in the suburbs, let alone into the plush designer mews in Donnybrook which was to be his new abode. He had done well for himself, very well. But he had worked damned hard for it.

Getting a burst of energy he started to pack. He had done most of it earlier in the week. As ever he was organised and the cardboard boxes packed with all his belongings lay stacked in the hall, neatly labelled. With his system, he reckoned that he should be unpacked and settled in his new house in a day. All he had to do now was clear his wardrobe and take down his pictures. Hugh sighed. Karen, his ex-girlfriend, would have been a whiz at organising his wardrobe but their relationship had ended a few years ago and she was now happily married and expecting her first baby. In fact she was glowing. He had met her recently and had been quite taken aback at how well she looked. Obviously marriage and impending motherhood suited her. He hadn't got into another relationship. He just hadn't the time, and social dating suited him just fine these days. Within the hour, his wardrobe was cleared. He had been ruthless. Anything he had not worn over the previous two years was neatly packed to be delivered to the St. Vincent de Paul Society. The rest lay ready to be transported to Donnybrook. Hugh sat on the end of his bed. All he had to do now was take down his pictures. He had only one in the bedroom, a Liz Lacey original. It was a lovely watercolour of Killiney Bay and the Sugar Loaf Mountain that had attracted him the first moment he had seen it on exhibition in Stephen's Green several years ago. He had bought it when she was unknown but it had more than quadrupled in value now that she was becoming the "in" artist with the rich and famous. A thought struck him. He must do an interview with Liz Lacey. Now that would be interesting. But first things first. He'd better start preparing for the Ferraro programme. Research was everything. Lighting a cheroot he lay back against his pillows, picked up his notes and began to read.

Thursday, August 21, 1986

"Damn! Damn! Damn!" muttered Hugh as he tried to ring Liz to tell her he would be delayed getting over to see her later that evening and that the game of tennis they had planned was off. For the first time in his career Hugh was annoyed because something big had come up and he had to work on it. The IRA suspect, Gerard O'Reilly, had been freed due to an error in his extradition warrant and they were getting a programme together about it. Normally it was something Hugh would love to get his teeth into but he hadn't seen Liz for three days and he was missing her like crazy.

He'd really fallen this time and fallen hard. No woman had ever affected him like Liz Lacey. From the minute he had been introduced to her at Antoinette's party in Washington, he had been intrigued. Hooked. Oh, she had recognised him all right, and Hugh was used to that reaction by now, but she hadn't been the slightest bit interested. He'd really had to make an effort there—a new experience for him. But then when he found out about her dead husband he had quite understood. It had changed things.

Normally, if he was interested in a girl, Hugh would pull out all the stops. He would wine her, dine her and bring her to all the glamorous events that he was invited to as a celebrity. Usually this was more than enough to get a woman seriously interested, but with Liz it had been different. She was a success herself. That kind of thing didn't interest her. And anyway Hugh didn't want that kind of relationship. There was something about Liz Lacey that was very special and if he could get her to like him for himself and not because of who he was, that would more than please him. Mind, he'd kind of bulldozed his way into her life, arriving at her place with a picnic lunch and persuading her to let him do a documentary about her. But she had been amused at his cheek and from then on they had begun to see each other. To his great delight she was as much a fresh-air fiend as he was and a sports lover

to boot. He really enjoyed their tennis matches. Liz was no
pushover; she was an extremely skillful player.

Hugh could see Liz fighting her own attraction to him
and it had driven him crazy sometimes. But he'd let her make
all the moves at her own pace, realising that the ghost of a
dead and much-loved husband was no easy thing to cope
with. Sometimes he wanted to shake her hard and shout
"Forget him; he's dead and I'm here and I'm alive." But it was
only in moments of extreme frustration and it was a matter of
pride to Hugh that he could say he had exerted no pressure
on Liz to become his lover. The decision had been all hers
and because of this, he treasured that beautiful night all the
more. When Liz looked at him with those smiling, incredibly
blue eyes Hugh knew that he was the luckiest man in the
world. Women like Liz were rare and he was blessed to have
found her. What fascinated him about her was her warmth
towards her friends and family. Hugh had a brother and sister
that he rarely saw. Not because he didn't want to, merely
because he didn't have the time. He went to visit his mother
once or twice a week and always made sure she had enough
money and plenty of coal and logs and stuff. But Liz called on
her family because she actually enjoyed being with them and
she would go out of her way to make sure she saw them. And
as for her niece! Hugh could take or leave children, although
he had to admit that Fiona was a beautiful little girl, but Liz
was besotted by her. It fascinated him to watch it. A very
loving woman was Liz and he, lucky man that he was, was on
the receiving end of a lot of it. Damn that bloody extradition
warrant anyway! He probably wouldn't get to see her tonight
at all, he fumed, as he waited for her to answer her phone.

### Tuesday, January 31, 1989

"I'm going to the airport with you," Hugh insisted.

Liz glared at him. "Not in that condition, you're not."

"What condition?" he snapped. Liz could be so bloody
stubborn.

"Hugh, you've been snorting coke and you know I hate it. I want to go in a taxi on my own."

"Oh, for Chrissakes, Liz, everybody does it here. It's like smoking a cigarette. Stop getting so het up about it." She was really annoying him going on about it all the time. Right now he was glad she was going home. She had flown out to join him in New York where he was working his ass off trying to get the biggest contract of his career, and at the beginning it had been great. Hugh had missed her so much and they had had a wonderful few days of reunion. The great thing about Liz was that she was well able to entertain herself, which was just as well because he hadn't a spare minute. It was all go go go in the Big Apple and Hugh loved it. He was born to work here, he told himself, striding down Fifth Avenue to this meeting and that meeting. And things were going well too. NBC-TV had been extremely interested in signing a contract with him but CNN were the ones he was after and so far they hadn't turned him down flat. Mind, he had a very impressive portfolio and list of credits at his back. All his hard work at home had more than paid off. It was a tough city, though, the city that never sleeps, the city of dog eat dog. It was no wonder that people turned to something like coke to get them through. Cocaine made him feel as if nothing or no one could get the better of him. It made him feel more alert and alive than anything else he had ever experienced. If Liz would only try it once she'd understand. But she wouldn't touch the stuff. And he wouldn't force her but he wished she'd lay off moaning about it when she didn't know what she was talking about. She was terribly restless lately, for some reason he could not fathom. Hugh wished more than anything that she would come out to the States and live with him when he finally made the move, but if her attitude the last month she had been here was anything to go by, he was going to have an awful lot of persuading to do.

Looking at her troubled blue eyes as she stared at him across the living-room floor, his heart melted. "Look I'm sorry, Liz. I was at a meeting until three this morning and then I had to go to another one at ten-fifteen. I just took a little snort so I wouldn't fall asleep on you. I can get by without it. No problem, believe me. It's just that everything is coming together right now and I need my wits about me."

"You won't have any wits if you keep taking that stuff," she said gently, unable to hide her concern.

"Don't be daft, Liz. It's a social habit, nothing else. I can give it up anytime I want to. Now, are you going to let me go with you to the airport or not?"

"Okay," she said flatly and he felt like shaking her.

"Don't sound too enthusiastic, for God's sake!" he snapped and then felt like a heel. "I'm sorry," he said contritely.

"So am I," Liz sighed as she walked into his outstretched arms.

Sitting in the taxi, with his arm around her as they sped towards JFK, Hugh reflected that they always seemed to be saying "I'm sorry" lately.

# *Claire*

Saturday, May 10, 1980

Claire struggled against a wave of nausea, praying she wouldn't have to leave the church. She'd hate to miss watching her son receive his First Holy Communion. Beside her, Suzy, her eight-year-old daughter, fidgeted restlessly. She earned a stern look from her father. "Say your prayers!" Sean growled.

"I'm saying them!" Suzy muttered defiantly, never one to take a rebuke lying down. Their son, David, on the other hand, would have meekly done as he was bid. Claire sighed. Chalk and cheese her two children were, though David was only one year younger than Suzy. Her daughter was spirited, full of life, her son, gentle and quiet. And this new baby that she was carrying? What would it be? Boy or girl?

She sighed again. Maybe it was a sin but she had cursed when her period hadn't arrived and she noticed the unmistakable signs of pregnancy. Even at this early stage—she was only a few weeks gone—her breasts felt tight and sore and were already too big for her bra.

If only she hadn't had to come off the pill in order to have that operation she would have been fine. Maybe it was God's revenge for deceiving her husband for the last six years. She cast a sidelong glance at Sean, who knelt beside her mother, watching two of his pupils with a gimlet eye. The boys were messing around and laughing and they'd be in trouble when her husband got his hands on them. Honestly, he made no allowance for the fact that they were children. Some of their fiercest arguments were caused by his sternness. Sean had an iron will and an inflexible way of thinking that got worse the longer he taught. He liked the position of power his job conferred on him but he couldn't leave it behind him once school was over. Sometimes Claire felt as though he saw her as another one of his pupils to be moulded and shaped as he saw fit. As he got older, he became more set in his ways and more difficult to live with. He'd be forty-five in two weeks, and she was twenty-seven. Being passed over for promotion at work hadn't helped. He had been so set for so long on getting the position of principal that since they went over his head and took in a new, younger, more forward-thinking headmaster, he ranted and raved and made life at home a misery.

"Bloody whippersnapper! What bloody experience has he got? I've been teaching for twenty-five bloody years, Claire. It's just not good enough. Damn that parish priest!" She had felt for him, felt his deep disappointment at being passed over but in truth she could understand why he had not impressed the interviewers. Rigid, deeply conservative, he had no time for the more modern teaching methods. "Bloody nonsense," he called it. She had lived with the word "bloody" for the last nine years and she was tired of it. Marriage was not the idyll she had envisaged.

Now, as well as being pregnant, she was going to have to uproot herself from all that was familiar in Knockross and move to Dublin with her husband. His unmarried Aunt Tess had died and left him her house in the city. At first he was going to sell the property, so sure was he that he would be made principal of the local school, but when the job went to someone else he was so embittered he had immediately started looking for a position in the capital. "Well, you can't expect me to work under that young upstart?" was his gruff response to Claire when he told her of his plans and saw her face falling.

"But the children are settled at school. All their friends are here!" she protested.

"Claire, my mind is made up. We're going to Dublin and that's final," he said in his "I know what's best" tone of voice.

"Well, I don't want to go!" Claire replied heatedly.

"Dear, we all have to do things we don't like. I thought you'd be much more supportive."

"I am being supportive. I just think it's such a drastic step. Couldn't you look for a teaching job in Waterford!"

"But sure, they'd be wondering why the parish priest couldn't see his way to making me principal here. I'm telling you, Claire, it's the kiss of death for my career if I stay in this area. I've got to go to Dublin or Cork or one of the big cities if I'm going to get anywhere at my age. I might be lucky in a school in one of those new suburbs that are supposed to be mushrooming all over the place. Dublin is the ideal place now that Tess has left me the house, God bless her!" He smiled comfortingly at Claire. "It's a great opportunity to start afresh and sure, won't you have Rosie to visit? Isn't she living in Dublin? Come on now, Claire! It will be for the best. We'll drive up to Dublin at the weekend and have a day out and have a look at the house."

They'd driven up to Dublin the following weekend, the children in the back of the car, wildly excited. Sean had told them that when they moved to the city they'd be able to go to the zoo and the botanic gardens and other interesting places. This promise had helped ease their dismay at the thoughts of leaving their pals. As they neared the capital, Claire found herself getting almost as excited as the children. Maybe the move *would* be good for them all. She had loved Dublin the few times she had stayed in it. All the shops! The huge supermarkets. Not that Sean would let her go wild but at least she'd be able to look at the things.

He was *so* careful with money. The previous year when it was time for Suzy's Holy Communion she had had an awful job trying to prise the money for the child's dress out of him. He didn't believe in such nonsense, he had informed her. There was far too much emphasis on the dresses and veils and the money they'd get from neighbours and relations. Of course he was right in a way but Claire didn't want *her* little daughter to have anything less than her classmates. The prices of dresses was outrageous. Heaven above, she hadn't spent as much on her wedding dress, she thought in shock when she saw the price of one flouncy creation. She knew her husband would never shell out the amount she would need. After all shoes had to be bought, a white bag, and a cardigan in case it was cold on the day. All she had in her own cache was twenty pounds. Twenty pounds hard got through appropriating the odd tenpence piece off the dressing table at night. There her husband neatly piled his loose change before getting in to bed. She'd never risk taking fifty pence—he'd know he was missing that amount—but the occasional tenpence he didn't miss. It was just like her mother with her father. The only difference was that her father drank all their money whereas Sean saved his for a rainy day. Holy Communions did not constitute a rainy day in his opinion.

Her mother had come to her rescue. "Buy me the material and I'll make her dress for her," Molly offered when Claire told her of the price of clothes. The price of material was almost as bad. Obviously, when the First Communion was coming up, the prices were increased. But she managed to buy a piece of white material that didn't cost the earth, and by the time her mother had added a few lacy frills it looked as expensive as any model in the shops. Claire had knitted the cardigan herself. The shoes were the main difficulty.

"Can't you dye a pair white?" Sean demanded when she asked him for the money for the shoes.

"For heaven's sake, Sean, it's the child's Holy Communion!" she snapped in exasperation and he stared at her in surprise. Claire rarely went against his wishes.

"Oh, all right!" he said grudgingly, taking some notes out of his wallet. "I suppose you'd better go and get something for yourself as well. It can do as your birthday present."

This was a surprise and she was mightily relieved. Suzy had come home from school full of tales about whose mother was buying what and that Valerie Reilly's mother was going to buy a hat for the communion. "Are you going to get something new?" she asked her mother anxiously. Claire had expected to wear her lemon going-away suit that she had first worn at her wedding eight years previously. By dint of changing the buttons and adding some black trim and shortening the skirt, she had managed to update it and it was her "good" outfit, worn many times. Suzy obviously hoped that her mother would buy something new for the communion.

Taking the notes that her husband gave her and with the eight pounds left out of her own cache, she bought the communion shoes and a lovely mint-green summery suit in Dunnes. She even had enough to buy a cheap pair of white shoes for herself, which nearly killed her on the day. But at least she had looked well and Suzy was thrilled with herself in her finery.

Claire knew it was hard on her children sometimes. They didn't get the treats and toys that their friends got because Sean didn't like to spend money on frivolities. She remembered Suzy, with her innocent little face, asking her was her Daddy too poor to buy her a pair of roller skates, because all her friends had them and she hadn't and she really wished she could have a pair.

"Santa will bring you some for Christmas," Claire had promised, but it grieved her. Sean earned a good salary. He could have given her the money to go and buy a pair but he wouldn't.

"You spoil the children, Claire. They've got to realise that they can't have *everything* they want in life."

"Ah, Sean, you were a child once. They don't ask for much and a couple of pounds isn't much to give to make Suzy happy."

"Yes," he agreed patiently. "But it's skates now, the next time it will be a bike or some such like. You've got to draw a line somewhere."

Claire's heart bled for her daughter. She knew what it was like. There had never been much money when she was a child, only what Molly could scrimp and save from the measly allowance that Billy gave her. But it was even worse with Sean. He *had* the money but he wouldn't give it to her. Fortunately, Rosie was a very generous godmother and always gave her godchild a decent present. She had rung from Dublin some time later wondering what to buy Suzy for her birthday and Claire had been able to say with delight that a pair of skates would go down a treat. But it galled her that she hadn't the means to buy them herself.

David, her quiet gentle little son, rarely asked for anything. He was such a good little boy. Even as a baby he had been so good. Claire had been devastated to find herself pregnant again three months after Suzy was born. She hadn't even got used to her new baby when she was off again. The pain of childbirth was still fresh in her mind and the thought of going through the ordeal again had petrified her. But her second pregnancy was completely different. She hadn't been as sick with David and even his kicking had been gentle, not like the lusty movements of his sister. She hadn't been as big either and because she had so much on her hands with the new baby, changing nappies, mixing feedings, bathing, housekeeping, and looking after her husband, she hadn't the time to worry about herself as much as she had done during her first pregnancy.

Suzy's arrival had completely changed her life. No longer did she sit waiting patiently for her husband to come home from school. Now she prayed that he would be a bit late so she could catch up with herself. Every time her daughter cried she would watch her anxiously, wondering what was wrong. Each dirty nappy was scrutinised to make sure that there was nothing unusual in the colour. Every time the child's cheeks got a bit flushed Claire would stick a thermometer in her mouth. If she didn't sleep, Claire fretted. If she slept too long she worried about cot death. The first year of her daughter's life, Claire was a nervous wreck, and knowing that she would have to go through the whole saga again with her next child made matters even worse.

But when David was placed in her arms after a painful but mercifully short labour and she gazed at the little mite sleeping so peacefully, with his beautiful head of black hair and the little dimple in his cheek, she experienced the greatest moment of happiness in her life. There was something about him that calmed her. She studied his perfection for hours: the tiny perfectly formed little hands and feet, the long curling eyelashes, the big eyes that looked at her so trustingly.

She took him home to his father and sister and Sean had puffed up as proud as a peacock when he held his son, the heir and carrier of the Moran name. Suzy had been utterly put out and her tantrums at feeding time caused Claire to smack her harder than she intended on one or two occasions. She always regretted it bitterly and both she and Claire would be bawling as David lay placidly, waiting to be fed. Her loss of control worried her. She'd want to be careful. Suzy was still a baby herself and she could so easily hurt her. It was just that she always seemed to know instinctively when Claire was at her lowest ebb and then she would start misbehaving.

David never cried. He just lay waiting patiently for her to pick him up and feed him and then he would fall asleep until it was time for his next feed. As he grew older, Claire began to enjoy him much more than she had enjoyed Suzy as a baby. It lifted her spirits like nothing else to go into his room and peer into his cot, to be greeted with a gurgle and a smile. Those few moments that she spent alone with her son were something that she always treasured.

To her dismay, Sean told her that she was spoiling him. And she was thinking she was doing so well this time! It was only years later that she recognised that her husband was jealous of the attention she gave David. She had hoped to breast-feed for a year—at least that might help prevent her getting pregnant so soon again—but as with Suzy she got mastitis and after three months was unable to continue. When Sean turned to her in bed ten weeks after David's birth, she refused him for the first time in their married life. He had been most taken aback.

"I don't want to get pregnant again. I want us to use contraceptives," Claire pleaded.

He was shocked. "No, Claire, it's against our religion."

"I don't care," she was nearly in tears, "I just can't go through another pregnancy. I can just about cope with the two babies I've got!"

"But Claire! It's against God's law," her husband muttered as his erection began to subside.

"God doesn't have to have babies. If he did his laws might be different," Claire replied wearily, turning away from him.

"Claire! That's sacrilege!" Sean was aghast.

"Oh, Sean, go to sleep!"

From that night on, she began to dread sex. She couldn't relax. As her husband took his pleasure she feared the invasion of sperm, knowing that one of them could take control of her life and that there was nothing she could do about it. Between her worry and her periods, which had got really heavy and irregular, she was a wreck.

"For heaven's sake!" Rosie exclaimed in disgust, when Claire confided in her one weekend that she was visiting her family in Knockross. Rosie couldn't stand Sean and he couldn't stand her. Rosie couldn't fathom why Claire had ever married him.

Once, when he was still single, Rosie and some of her friends had been at a dance. She had had a few jars and was feeling nicely tiddly when she espied Sean, dressed in a green shirt and brown jacket and trousers. "Oh, lordy!" she giggled, "He looks like a mint choc-ice on legs!" The others exploded in mirth. Rosie had no cause to change her poor opinion of Sean the more she got to know him. For Claire's sake, they made an effort to be polite to each other, but it was only a façade and they knew it.

"Claire, I know a real nice doctor in Waterford. You've got to get yourself seen to and you've got to get some sort of protection. Otherwise you could end up having a baby a year!"

This horrific thought made Claire decide to do something about her situation. She couldn't go to old Dr. Harris in the village. He was a crony of Sean's and, besides, when she had consulted him before she was married about painful periods, he had brusquely told her to go and have a few babies and that she'd be fine. He wouldn't be a bit sympathetic. She made an appointment with the doctor Rosie knew in Waterford and found him to be most understanding.

"I think, Mrs. Moran, that you should start to take the contraceptive pill."

"Oh, I couldn't! Sean, my husband, wouldn't let me. He doesn't agree with contraception!" she said miserably.

"I see!" The doctor's tone was dry. "Well, I wasn't only suggesting it as a contraceptive. I am also recommending it for medical reasons, to regulate your cycle and lighten your menstrual flow. Do you understand?"

"I still don't think my husband would be too happy," she murmured.

"*He* doesn't have to suffer painful periods. Believe me if he did, he'd want a double dose." The doctor smiled while writing the prescription.

"Now get this in the chemist's, go home and take it as directed and come back to me in three months. All right?"

"All right!" she agreed.

The first time she took the little white tablet her hand was actually shaking. If Sean ever copped on he'd have a fit. But she had to take some control over her life; she couldn't carry on the way she was going. To be sure, she put on a half stone, and found that she retained fluid and got a few spots, but it was better than being terrified about getting pregnant and suffering excruciating periods.

She felt terribly guilty about deceiving her husband, never thinking that it was his selfishness that had placed her in such a position. In time, she got over her guilt, took her pill, pleased her husband in bed and at least knew that she was safe from another pregnancy for the time being.

For six years she kept her little secret to herself. When Sean queried the money for the monthly prescription she told him that she was deficient in iron and had to have a supplement. He never dreamt that she would lie to him and took her at her word.

She watched her children grow from toddlers to children as her husband became stricter and more intense. She seemed to be living day after day in a vacuum. Then, a cyst on one of her ovaries had started to cause trouble and necessitated an operation. Her doctor instructed her to come off the pill six weeks beforehand and between the time she came home from hospital and the time she was able to go back on the pill, her husband had once again successfully implanted a sperm in her womb. He hadn't given her a chance even to get over the operation. Where sex was concerned, Sean was totally selfish, demanding his husbandly rights, and she, her mother's daughter, rarely denied him.

Well, she should have denied him, should have made sure she was protected. Now it was too late. Still, she couldn't really complain, she thought, as she fought down the nausea. She'd had a break of seven years. Thousands of women weren't so lucky. It was just the thought of moving into that old-fashioned house in Dublin and having to shift all their worldly goods that depressed her. It was a fine house, she had to admit, big and roomy, although it would be expensive to heat, Sean had warned. It was on the northside of Dublin, between Ballymun and Glasnevin, in a parish called Ballygall. There were fields to the rear of the house, a rarity in Dublin, she imagined, and in the distance she could see the purples, blues, and greens of the Dublin Mountains. Claire had rather liked it, once she was able to see beyond the old-fashioned wallpaper with the cabbage roses, the yellowing antimacassars on the lumpy old chairs and sofa, the valances with the ornaments on top, and the kitchen with the big cast-iron gas cooker. These would all have to go, she told her husband, and he agreed hastily, relieved that she seemed to like the house. The jungle at the back would keep him occupied. If there was one thing that Sean had a passion for, apart from sex, it was his garden. Cost was never a consideration when it came to his garden. Well, he'd have plenty here to keep him occupied for the long days of his summer holidays. Claire had noticed a few children playing on the street and that had cheered her up. At least Suzy and David would be able to make a few friends.

If only they could move into the house after it was decorated. But Sean wouldn't dream of *paying* to have the place done, so she knew better than even to ask. Well, she was going to get the house ready before the new baby was born. Sean didn't know how lucky he was to have inherited a house. People were paying huge chunks out of their salaries for their mortgages. Sean wouldn't have that worry and they'd save the money that they were paying on rent in Knockross. He could damn well spare a couple of thousand to get the house straight—otherwise she wasn't moving! She'd make that clear tonight after the children were in bed; she didn't want to spoil David's big day with a row.

She watched her precious son walk with his classmates up the aisle to receive the host. He was so anxious to make sure he swallowed it. "What will I do if it sticks, Mam?" he asked worriedly.

"It won't," she assured him. "I'll tell you what! We'll practise with the ice-cream wafers on Sunday." Sunday was a big treat for the children, Sean allowed her to buy a small block of ice cream to go with whatever tart she baked. The wafers tasted similar to the communion wafer and they had had great fun practising, she and Suzy and David. Suzy, of course, was an expert, having made her communion the year before.

"Do it like this, David," she instructed, sticking her tongue out to its full extent as Claire placed a piece of the wafer on it. Claire had made sure that her husband was safely ensconced in the armchair beside the radio in the sitting room, listening to his favourite programme. Sean wouldn't have been impressed by her idea of practising for Holy Communion with wafers.

Watching her son walk proudly down the aisle, cheeks working as he swallowed his wafer, Claire was so glad she had practised with him and taken the fear and anxiety out of his day. Catching her eye as he passed her seat, he gave her a big gap-toothed grin and she grinned back, resisting the urge to give him a big kiss and a hug there and then. With his unmanageable cowlick and his huge brown eyes smiling happily and his front tooth missing, he looked adorable. And in his new Holy Communion suit, he was so proud. She was wearing the same mint-green outfit she had worn the previous year. "Not much point in getting a new suit if you are going to be wearing maternity clothes," Sean told her cheerfully. He was delighted she was pregnant. Why, exactly, she did not know. He couldn't really relate well to his son and daughter; there was always the element of the strict teacher in the relationship no matter how much she pointed it out to him. It was probably the fact that his manhood was proven again, she thought glumly, giving a discreet burp.

At last the mass was over and they were outside and Molly was making a fuss of her grandson, who was so chuffed with himself. Suzy was talking to her friends and Sean was telling Mrs. O'Toole that he'd got a position in Dublin and that they would be leaving Knockross soon. She'd miss Knockross. It was home. She'd worry about Molly. Her father's health was bad. He had cirrhosis of the liver and life was not easy for her mother. At least until now she'd had Claire. The only small comfort was the fact that her father wasn't drinking as much, simply because he wasn't able to. He spent most of his day in bed moaning and groaning. Claire wouldn't miss *him* a bit and at least she'd have Rosie up in Dublin.

Rosie was thrilled that she was moving. Her friend had done very nicely for herself. She had opened a small boutique which had done so well that she had opened another. Now, seven years later, she had five boutiques in Dublin and the suburbs and was pregnant with her first child. She had married an airline pilot she had met on holidays in New York and they lived in Howth. Claire had the greatest admiration for Rosie. She had always done exactly what she wanted with the intention of succeeding. Rosie never limited her vision nor did she let anyone else limit it for her. Her baby had been planned and was much wanted. If only Claire had had the nerve to go to Dublin with Rosie that time instead of marrying Sean, how different her life would be. Well, there was no use complaining about it now. It wasn't that she was dreadfully unhappy or anything. Sean was a good provider and he loved her. Her children loved her and depended on her. It was just that she had this vague feeling of restlessness. Her life was passing her by and she had not yet made her mark on it. Maybe the move to Dublin would change all this. She'd make it change. She didn't want to be stuck for much longer in the rut she had carved for herself. Watching Mrs. McNulty give David a pound, she smiled to herself. She'd make sure that her son spent that pound on whatever his little heart desired. They were going to Waterford to the pictures and then to have tea in a café as a special treat.

The two children couldn't contain themselves. "Can I

have chips, Mam?" Suzy danced along beside her as she walked towards her husband.

"An' me, an' me?" David piped up.

"Of course you can! And you can have a banana boat each for dessert," Claire said cheerfully. She saw her husband's eyebrows go into orbit at the mention of this extravagance but her children squealed with delight.

## Monday, June 24, 1985

Watching her father's coffin being lowered into the grave, Claire's overwhelming feeling was one of relief. It was more for her mother than for herself; after all, she hadn't lived at home for years now. In fact, since she moved to Dublin five years before, she had had very little to do with her father, a state of affairs that had suited her just fine. No doubt many would think that she was an unnatural daughter to have no feelings of regret or sorrow at the passing of her father, but then, they hadn't had to suffer as her mother and she had done.

Beside her, Molly, white-faced, watched the priest scatter a few lumps of soil on the coffin. Then the undertakers were covering the grave with the green cloth that would remain until the gravediggers filled it in after the mourners had gone. It was hard to believe her father was no more, she reflected. Death was such a final thing. Like yesterday, when the Air India Jumbo had crashed into the sea off the Irish coast. One minute 329 people had been alive, sitting on a plane making plans, looking forward to reunions with their loved ones. Then they were blown up out of the sky, their lives over. The thought depressed her. She could die tomorrow and what could she say she had achieved? Very little, she decided glumly.

"We'd better go, Claire. The neighbours will be calling in," Molly whispered.

"Okay." Claire gave her mother's arm a reassuring squeeze and turned to Sean. "We're going to go back to the house now. Are you going to go straight to Dublin or will you come back for a while?"

"Hmm," mused Sean. Claire knew that Sean hated taking time off school during term. He had wanted David to go back with him so that he wouldn't miss the last week of primary school. But Claire had put her foot down. Suzy, in her first year at secondary, had had holidays since the beginning of the month but David still had a week to go. As if a week was going to make a huge amount of difference, she had argued with Sean. It was not as if he was always missing school.

"That's not the attitude to have, Claire," Sean lectured. "We're preparing our children for life—they've got to learn responsibility. After all, when he's working he won't be able to take days off to suit himself. And besides he has two months of holidays ahead of him."

"Look, Sean, Mum's going to be on her own long enough. I want to stay with her for a while. Suzy's going to be here. I want David here as well. God knows, Mum couldn't have them to stay when Da was alive. I think they'd be good company for her just now."

"And what about me?" Sean said plaintively, surprised by Claire's vehemence. "I'll be up there all by myself."

"You'll be fine," his wife said dryly. "Weren't you looking after yourself for a long time before you married me? And anyway it's only for a week or two."

"Or two!" he echoed, horrified.

"Sean, my mother needs me and that's final!" Claire retorted sharply.

"Well, I know that. I'm not *that* insensitive! I just didn't think you were going to stay for two weeks—that's all. I suppose you'll be wanting money."

"I suppose I will."

Sean had been huffy ever since and drove them down to the funeral like a demon. He was a dreadful driver. Most aggressive. It was as if he was in competition with every other driver on the road once he got behind the wheel. He changed gears like a rally driver and, in spite of Claire's remonstrations, loved to put the boot down whenever he got the chance. He wouldn't let her have the car so there was no point in her learning to drive.

"We couldn't afford the insurance for two and besides, I need the car for work," he objected when she broached the subject. "Sure what do you want to learn to drive for, anyway? Don't I drive you anywhere you want to go? And aren't there buses all over the place?" He said this airily with the ignorance of one who had never, as she had done, stood in O'Connell Street on a cold wet day waiting for a bus.

"If you don't drive a bit more slowly we won't get to the funeral alive," she remarked to her husband as he sped past a long lorry. He had spent the previous ten minutes fuming behind it on a winding bit of the road.

"Bloody lorries! Should be banned!" he retorted, slowing down only very slightly. He had been very cool towards her and David since she had asked that her son be allowed to stay with her for the week and had told Claire that he would be leaving for Dublin immediately after the funeral. Hence her question at the graveyard.

"Are you going straight home?" she repeated patiently.

"I'll come back for a quick cup of tea," Sean decided. Claire smiled to herself. She knew Sean would never be able to resist coming back to see their former neighbours and showing off his children to them. Hadn't she heard him telling Mrs. Fitzpatrick outside the church that he held an important post of responsibility in the big school in Dublin in which he was now teaching. Mrs. Fitzpatrick had been deeply impressed. But then Sean had made it seem as though he were a principal or something, instead of just an ordinary teacher with the extra responsibility of running the library.

They walked out of the graveyard towards the waiting cars and out of the corner of her eye, she caught sight of Rosie and her two children. Claire's heart lifted. Rosie really was the best in the world, driving all the way down from Dublin for the funeral even though she was so busy combining mother-hood with her career. If it wasn't for Rosie she would have gone mad up in Dublin, not knowing a soul. But then if it wasn't for Rosie, she wouldn't be comparing her marriage to her friend's and finding so much lacking in her own.

"Are you coming back to the house, Rosie?" she called over. Sean marched straight on. His attitude towards Rosie had not improved over the years, nor hers towards him.

"I'll just leave the children over at Ma's and then I'll call in," Rosie promised. By the time she did arrive, the house was full of neighbours and friends come to convey their condolences, and Claire was up to her eyes making pots of tea, passing round plates of sandwiches and brack and fruitcake and meeting people she hadn't seen for years. Molly accepted the condolences, sitting with back ramrod-straight in her rocking chair, and Claire had the feeling that in a strange sort of way she was enjoying herself. The relief of knowing that Billy wouldn't come staggering in disrupting the gathering was so liberating for her mother that Claire could sense the tension that she had lived with for so long was lifting already. She was glad. It's about time she had a bit of peace in her life, she mused, as she waited for yet another kettle to boil.

There had never before been so many people in the house. When Billy was alive they had rarely had visitors. On the Friday night that Claire and Sean arrived after hearing of Billy's death in Árdkeen Hospital, Molly had set to with a vengeance and scrubbed and polished every piece of furniture, every ornament, everything. Claire had washed the net curtains for her mother on the Saturday morning and she got the strangest impression that Molly was scrubbing and cleaning Billy out of her life. Her mother's pride wouldn't allow the neighbours to come into anything but a spotless house. Despite the fact, as Claire had protested upon seeing her mother engaged in all this work, that you could already eat your dinner off the floor of the cottage. Then they had had to prepare for the hospitality after the funeral. Molly had made tea-bracks and tarts and of course some kind neighbours, in the old country tradition, had sent cakes and scones and the like.

Claire and Suzy had got up at the crack of dawn to make plates and plates of ham, egg, and salad sandwiches. Claire smiled to herself as she buttered another plate of tea-brack. Her thirteen-year-old daughter was great in a crisis, even to the extent of telling her mother how to make the sandwiches. "It's the way we do it in home economics," she informed her mother grandly and with an air of supreme self-assurance, slicing the crusts off the sandwiches, cutting them neatly in four and arranging them on the plate in a nice design. Claire hid a smile of amusement. Suzy was enjoying secondary school and the start of her teens immensely. She swanned off each morning in her navy uniform. She adored the uniform and Claire was delighted she had to wear it, as Sean was not exactly generous when it came to buying his daughter the latest fashions. Clutching her leather schoolbag to her budding bosom, Suzy would stride off to school, humming her favourite Bruce Springsteen song.

Sean had almost had a fit when he heard the words of the song on *Top of the Pops* one Thursday evening and saw his son and daughter singing enthusiastically as they watched The Boss gyrate sexily on TV. "Oooh, oooh, oooh, I'm on fire." Stony-faced, he switched off the TV, to howls of protest from his children, and informed them that in his opinion *Top of the Pops* was not a suitable programme for children and that in future it would not be allowed in the Moran household.

Claire was furious and there had been an almighty row. "Oh, yes! Take their side as usual!" Sean flung the accusation at her angrily.

"Someone has to," she raged. "You're being totally unreasonable!"

"Excuse me," her husband said coldly, "but some of that . . . that filth that is played on that programme is almost pornographic and you don't seem to care that your children's minds are being corrupted."

"Ah, for God's sake, Sean! They said the same thing about Elvis when you were growing up, and the Beatles and the

Rolling Stones when I was growing up. And we weren't cor
rupted!"

"I never looked at such rubbish," he said loftily.

"Well, maybe you should have!" Claire angrily left the
room, slamming the door after her. Her husband was out
raged at her rudeness. Ever since she had started knocking
around with that Rosie one again, she was getting these no
tions. Wanting to have her own cheque-book and a joint ac
count, wanting to learn to drive. Wanting this that and the
other for the children. Sure they'd never have a penny if there
was that sort of carrying-on. In a foul humour, Sean began to
correct exercise copies, scoring the pages with his red
ballpoint and muttering angrily to himself.

Suzy had overcome the ban on *Top of the Pops* by going to
her friend's house on the pretext of doing a project, but
David, who was still at primary school, had no such excuse
and his father, knowing of his son's weakness in maths, un
dertook to give him extra tuition every Thursday night.

"Mam?" Her daughter interrupted her musings. "Is there
any more of that tea-brack. Those two funny oul' fellas in the
Wellingtons are after eating nearly a whole plate of it between
them. One of them even put a slice in his jacket pocket
Imagine being so greedy!" Suzy exclaimed. Claire knew ex
actly the men to whom her daughter was referring. She had
seen Mickey Hayes and Paudi Leary standing at the back of
the church and knew as sure as eggs were eggs that they
would arrive back at the house. There wasn't a funeral within
a radius of fifty miles that they didn't attend. It was a great
way of socialising and there was always great eating and
drinking at funerals. Claire had had no doubts at all that
Mickey and Paudi would put in an appearance.

"Is there anything I can do?" a familiar voice inquired
Rosie appeared at the kitchen door.

"Hi, Rosie. Thanks for coming." Claire hugged her friend
warmly.

"Hi, goddaughter!"

"Hi, godmother!" Suzy grinned at Rosie who was, in her eyes, nothing short of perfect.

"Here's the brack, and don't give that pair another bite," Claire warned. "They've eaten a banquet already."

Rosie grimaced. "Paudi and Mickey?"

Claire nodded, raising her eyes to heaven.

Rosie gave a snort. "Do you know what that old goat Paudi said to me when I came in just now? 'You're the one that got away on me. I could have given ye the life of a lady.' He had the nerve to tell me that!" They stared at each other and then Rosie was giving that familiar chortle and Claire and Suzy started giggling. The more they tried to stop, the worse they got, with tears streaming down their cheeks. They buried their faces in tea towels to try to muffle their unseemly mirth.

Then Claire had told Rosie the story Cis Maguire had told her about Mickey. During the mushroom season of the previous year, he went out one morning and found a fine crop of mushrooms and took them home. That night, after a few pints, he had invited Paudi to partake of some of his mushrooms and the pair of them had staggered home, cooked and eaten the mushrooms, started to laugh, and couldn't stop. A neighbour called in on hearing the racket and found the two oul' fellas sitting on Mickey's bed as high as two kites, roaring with laughter, unable to stop. "Up ye boya!" they yelled between guffaws, "How's she cuttin?" They had laughed the night through, quite unaware that they were under the influence of more than drink. Mickey, who had got shortsighted in his old age, had picked up quite a few magic mushrooms in his early-morning foray. By all accounts magic mushrooms were better than pot and the lads were enjoying the effects mightily. The neighbour told the whole story in Griffin's shop the next morning.

Sean walked into the kitchen with his empty plate and tea cup and stopped short at the sight of his wife and daughter and Rosie convulsed with laughter. Disgusted, he turned on his heel and walked out. Claire met Suzy's eye and then Rosie's and they looked at each other for a moment and then they were off again even worse than before. It was the best laugh Claire had had in ages, she thought a little guiltily. After all, she had just buried her father.

Lying in bed in the pink-painted room of her childhood Claire smiled at the memory. Across the room from her Paul Newman's twinkling eyes had not dimmed with the passage of time. Suzy had been most impressed. Claire knew she had risen notches in her daughter's opinion because she had a poster of a film star in her bedroom, even if he was aging. Sean wouldn't allow the children to stick anything to the walls so Suzy had to be content with sticking her posters of Mel Gibson and Bruce Springsteen on to the inside of her wardrobe. Claire had had a row with Sean about that too. In fact, lately they seemed to do nothing else but row. She felt that the children's bedrooms were their own, their one small part of the world where they could relax and be private. As long as they kept them reasonably tidy, Claire didn't mind how they arranged the furniture, or what they put on the walls. Her own bedroom in Knockross had been her little haven. Billy had never crossed the threshold and it was there that she could escape to dream of Paul Newman rescuing her from countless imaginary disasters.

Sean did not agree. It was his house, the upkeep of which was paid for by his hard-earned money and he was not having wallpaper ruined by posters and tape. Claire had been so angry. Typical of Sean! Everything they had he considered to be his and he magnanimously shared it with her and the children. He did not subscribe to the theory that wives had equal rights in a marriage. He was the provider and he provided very well in his own eyes. It was not necessary for Claire to know what his salary was. He would give her what she needed. All she had to do was ask. For as long as they had been married, he had given her anything she asked for, for herself and the children and the house—if he deemed it necessary. He couldn't understand how she was prepared to risk the good wallpaper in the bedrooms by allowing the children to mutilate it with tape.

Claire snorted in the bed as she remembered his argument. "Good wallpaper, my hat," she muttered angrily, forgetting that Suzy was asleep on a camp bed beside her. The girl didn't stir as her mother lay crossly in bed visualising the "good wallpaper."

They had bought it to replace some of the cabbage roses in the house after they had moved in. Claire had not succeeded in persuading Sean to have the house decorated before they moved. "We can do each room as we go along," he decided. When he got tinned corned beef for his dinner three days in a row because Claire refused to cook on the old cast-iron cooker he decided that maybe they did need a new cooker. She told him that she wasn't unpacking one thing until she got new cupboards and new lino in the kitchen. With a deep sigh, he agreed to her suggestion that they go to the huge MFI store in Santry. Claire had spent a wonderful afternoon going around looking at all the furniture, the fitted kitchens, the bedrooms, the suites. Of course in the end Sean rejected most of her choices and they ended up with the cheapest items, but still Claire was happy enough. She got cupboards for her kitchen and new beds with a wardrobe and desk ensemble for the children. These she persuaded her husband to buy by emphasising how advantageous it would be for the children to have a desk in their bedroom for the purposes of study. Suzy and David had been thrilled with themselves. Compared to the Spartan decor of their bedrooms in Knockross, this was paradise.

Claire also managed to persuade Sean to buy a new sitting-room suite, but he was adamant that they did not need a new dining suite, so Aunt Tess's antique one would have to do. Still Claire felt that she had got something reasonable for the house. Sean felt so too because that was the only leeway he allowed her. He wouldn't allow her to pick the more expensive washable wallpaper and the paper they bought had been a nightmare to put up. She had lost the baby because of that damned wallpaper.

She hadn't been feeling too good the particular Saturday.

They had been papering the landing. Standing on a small table placed in the curve of the stairs, she had stretched up to stick the roll of paper that Sean had pasted for her onto the wall. A wave of dizziness had hit her and she lost her balance, fell off the table and halfway down the stairs. The next day she lost the baby.

It took her a long time to get over that miscarriage. Instead of being relieved, she felt terribly guilty. That's what she got for not wanting the child in the first place. It was God's punishment. "Sure we can have another baby," Sean had assured her, dismayed by his wife's grief and depression.

"If you'd got the house decorated before we moved in this wouldn't have happened," she accused him bitterly. Let him share her guilt!

"Claire! Haven't I spent a fortune on the place for you?"

"It's not for me!" she snapped. "It's for *us,* the family. Stop going around as if you had done something wonderful by buying the few bits and pieces for the house. It's the least you could do!"

"You're not yourself," her husband assured her after this uncharacteristic outburst. "I'll bring you up a cup of tea."

It was Rosie who got her through those first few months in Dublin after the miscarriage, listening patiently as Claire spoke incessantly about her unborn child. "I wonder did it sense that I didn't want it?" she would weep. "Did it feel any pain when I fell down the stairs? Oh, Rosie, I feel so bad about it. The poor little baby."

"Stop tormenting yourself, Claire. You'll only make yourself ill. What happened happened. It was the will of God and you had no control over it. And you *did* love that baby. Look at the way you're grieving now." Rosie was so positive about everything. Claire always felt so much better after one of her visits. Sean usually went out into the garden when she arrived so they were able to natter away to their hearts' content. In time Claire's depression lifted but she always felt a sense of guilt whenever she thought about the baby she had lost. Rosie was very kind to her and she knew she was so lucky to have a friend like her who was always there for her in good times and in bad. Rosie was as solid as a rock and during that hard time after the miscarriage Claire drew great strength from her friend.

Rosie and her husband Shane lived in a beautiful bungalow in Howth and Claire had been really impressed by the luxurious decor. "It's gorgeous, Rosie! You've got great taste," she said warmly after her tour of the house. The bedroom with its *en suite* bathroom had been most impressive, with its elegant tinted Sliderobes, its luxurious deep-pile carpet, and the huge satin-quilted double bed.

"Well, we worked hard for it, Claire, and we knew what we wanted. But I love decorating and I'll give you any help you need with the house," her friend offered generously.

Sean looked most alarmed at her offer. "Claire, we can't afford that type of life-style so don't start hankering after mirrored closets and dishwashers and the like," her husband warned her as they drove home after the visit.

"Well, when the children get a bit older I could always go back to work to buy the few luxuries."

"Indeed and you will not," Sean said rather sharply. "I'm quite capable of providing for my family and your place is at home looking after them and not out as some type of career woman while your children are left in public nurseries to be looked after by strangers." This was a snide dig at Rosie's life-style.

"I *said*, when the children are older," Claire quietly corrected her husband.

"Well, God willing, we will be blessed with another baby or two so that won't be for many years yet," Sean said cheerfully, overtaking a Saab at eighty miles an hour as they drove up the Ballymun Road dual carriageway.

Claire sat silently in the front seat, his words searing into her brain like a brand. "Another baby or two." Was that why he wanted her to be pregnant? Because being pregnant and having young children made her even more dependent on him, with the prospects of going back to work even more remote. Once he had married her, he had given up coaching her for her Leaving Certificate. She had planned to resume her studies as the children grew older and needed her less but Sean never seemed as anxious to help her as he had been when she had been single. It struck her then that Sean didn't want her to better herself by resuming her education and he certainly didn't want her ever to return to work.

It was only as a result of going shopping with Rosie and comparing her situation with her friend's that Claire truly began to comprehend how little control she had over her own life.

One day when they went into town together Rosie was horrified to discover that Claire did not possess a cheque book. They had been thoroughly enjoying themselves wandering through Arnott's. Claire saw a lovely boxed set of towels and said, "Oh, aren't they lovely. We've to get a wedding present for Sean's niece and they'd be ideal."

"You should buy them now. They're in a sale and they'll probably be snapped up," Rosie advised.

"I don't have the money now. I'll have to get Sean to come in at the weekend."

"Can't you write a cheque?" Rosie urged.

"I don't have a cheque-book," Claire said, not attaching too much importance to it. It was something she had never thought much about. After all, her mother had never had a cheque-book either. She too had been dependent on her husband. Wasn't that the way of it with most wives?

"Oh, have you Visa or Access then?"

Claire laughed. Sure they were only for people who were loaded. She shook her head.

"That's a bit of a nuisance. Do you have to go to the bank and draw out money every time you need it?" Rosie enquired as she held up a pair of midnight blue silk sheets.

"God, no!" Claire laughed. "Sean would have a fit if I did that."

"Well, what do you do when you need money, then?" Rosie asked, perplexed.

"I ask Sean for it," Claire said simply.

Rosie paused in her examination of the sheets and turned to face her friend.

"You *ask* for money?"

Claire nodded.

"For *everything* you need?"

"Yep, but I usually wait until he's in a good humour. You know Sean."

"Oh, Claire!"

"Well, we don't all have boutiques and careers," Claire said, a little defensively.

"That's not the point, Claire," Rosie said gently. "Come on, let's go and get a cup of tea and have a chat."

Now, sitting in the car with Sean as they drew up outside the house, Claire could still remember the icy fingers of embarrassment that had touched her at that moment. It had been a spur-of-the-moment decision to go into town with Rosie and she hadn't asked Sean for any extra money. All she had in her purse was seventy-five pence. And besides, even if she *had* asked, Sean wouldn't have been too impressed at her squandering money on tea and cakes in town.

It was the first time she had ever felt so acutely the fact that she had no money of her own, and she didn't like it.

Rosie, seeing the expression on her face, had instantly divined the reason for it.

"Well, maybe we haven't time for tea. Won't David be home from school soon? I'll tell you what, I'll get a few cream cakes in the Kylemore and we can have a cup in your house." Rosie had a live-in nanny and didn't have to worry about being home in time for her children's arrival from school.

As they sat drinking tea and eating the lovely gooey éclairs that Rosie had bought, Rosie said quietly, "You should discuss opening a joint account with Sean. After all marriage is a partnership—you contribute as much to it as he does and you're entitled to your share. I hope the house is in joint names."

"Well, it's not, actually," Claire murmured uncomfortably. "Sean feels he should look after the money. He doesn't want me to be worrying about paying bills and things."

"Bullshit!" Rosie retorted succinctly. "Do you know how much he earns?"

Claire shook her head.

"Listen to me, girl, it's about time you copped on and started asserting yourself," Rosie said grimly. "This is the nineteen eighties we're living in, not the middle ages. And if I were you I'd think about going back to work even part-time now that the children are both at school."

David's arrival cut short any further discussion but Claire pondered her friend's words and that weekend as Sean sat doing his Saturday-night calculations, asking her to account for what she had spent her float on, Claire raised the matter of a cheque-book and joint account with him.

Sean nearly blew a gasket. "I knew it! That's that Rosie giving you ideas. Haven't you managed perfectly well up until now without a cheque-book? Don't I give you money when you ask for it? Such bloody nonsense. We'd be bankrupt within a week. You'd give those children everything they asked for. You'd have this that and the other in the house and we'd be broke!"

"We would not!" Claire said hotly. "And how dare you even suggest it, Sean Moran! I was so embarrassed today when I couldn't even go for a cup of tea. Have you any idea what it's like always having to ask for money, money that's as much mine as it is yours."

"I don't know what's got into you, Claire!" Sean said, shaking his head. "I'll tell you what," he continued reluctantly. "I'll give you a personal allowance every week so that if you want to go and have a cup of tea with that one you can, but I'm looking after the money. It's my responsibility as a husband and I think I've fulfilled my role more than adequately."

After that he would hand her a fiver for herself each Friday and you would think by him that he was handing her a million. But a joint account he would not countenance and as time went on, Claire became more determined in her resolve to start working again and earn her own money. When she heard him mentioning her having more children and staying at home to look after them, Claire decided to go back on the pill. She had not gone back on it after the miscarriage, out of guilt. But she was going to now, after what she had just heard. Sean wasn't going to trap her with babies, she vowed. She *would* go back to work. She'd make sure it didn't adversely affect Suzy and David but she had come to Dublin with the intention of doing something with her life and by God she was going to do it.

Lying in bed in Knockross, after her father's funeral, Claire felt adrenaline surge through her. She was going to stay in Knockross with her mother for at least two weeks, maybe three, and then she was going to go back to Dublin and start looking for part-time work in a hairdressing salon. And with her first week's wages she was going to treat David and Suzy and her mother and Rosie to a super meal somewhere. Now that she no longer had Billy to worry and fret over, Molly would be able to come up to Dublin and they'd have great times going shopping and exploring the city. Just wait until Molly saw Dublin at Christmas. It was beautiful to behold: the trees decked with fairy lights, the streets aglow with decorations and lights strung between the shops, the store windows a child's delight with Christmassy scenes. Oh, Molly would love it! Next Christmas, she could come and stay with them and with any luck Claire would be working and have her own money and they'd have a ball. Snuggling down into the soft mattress, Claire fell asleep, smiling at her plans.

Friday, October 16, 1987

It had been one of the worst storms in living memory. In fact in England they were calling it the storm of the century. Claire thought that they might not be too busy at work today, even though it was Friday. People might be afraid to venture out for fear of terrible weather. Listening to the accounts of the storm on the news, she shivered as she stirred Sean's porridge. She had been up for the past hour, bringing Sean his cup of early-morning tea and preparing his breakfast and lunch. It was cold down in the kitchen. Now that she was working every day, Sean didn't allow the heating to be switched on until late afternoon. "No point wasting good money when there's nobody here to waste it on!" he pronounced.

He had been absolutely furious when she announced one day about two months after her father's funeral that she was starting to retrain as a beginner at a big hairdressing salon in Finglas. Claire had been elated. They couldn't have been nicer when she approached them. She had tried a few places and some of them had told her quite bluntly that she was too old. Indeed, when she met the other juniors that she was training with, she did feel old. Some of them were only two years older than Suzy, who was fifteen since April. It had been a bit nerve-wracking even going in to the salons looking for a job in the first place. Even the fact that she had hairdressing experience hadn't made a difference. She had been put off after her first rejection but Rosie had kept at her and so had Suzy, who thought it was a great idea for her mother to go back to work. Now that Suzy was maturing and coming into contact with the world through her secondary education, she was beginning to realise that Claire was not treated the same by her father as many of her friends' mothers were treated by their husbands. Lots of her friends' mothers drove cars and some of them worked. Most of them had cheque-books. They didn't have to ask their husbands for everything that they required.

As she grew older, Suzy grew closer to her mother, the bond between them deepening and strengthening. It was a joy for Claire to watch her daughter growing up. But she was growing up so fast. She was a child no longer but a strong-minded teenager growing from girlhood into womanhood almost before Claire realised it.

Claire felt a stab of regret the day her daughter got her first period but Suzy had been thrilled. That was the real farewell to childhood. She was one of the first in the class to get her periods and her friends had been most impressed. She revelled in her new status as a woman and she confided in her mother that buying her first bra was one of the most exciting things that she had ever done. Claire smiled into the innocent trusting face of her daughter and hugged her hard. She would have loved to have taken Suzy somewhere posh, to treat her to a grown-up meal and then maybe go to the pictures but most of her money had gone on clothes for Suzy and David and all she could afford out of her paltry allowance was a Big Mac each and fries and a milkshake between them. Suzy wolfed down the treat, enjoying the noisy din that surrounded them in McDonald's. She gazed down at the traffic flowing past them in O'Connell Street, grinned at her mother and said cheerfully, "Isn't this the life! I'm going to get a summer job and I'll treat you the next time and we'll get a taxi home so we won't be waiting for hours. Look at the queue for the thirteen bus!"

One thing about her children, Claire thought with pleasure, they hadn't inherited their father's meanness. She had instilled in them over and over the concept of sharing their toys, treats, or whatever, and it was automatic for them now to share whatever they had between them. If David got a bar of chocolate or crisps or something Claire was always the first person to whom he offered some.

He was such a lovable son, so gentle and placid with his ready good-natured smile. She worried so much over him. Sean was always pushing him much harder than he should. David was not good at maths and science subjects and no matter how hard he studied and no matter what coaching his father gave him, it was always a struggle. But her son was a genius with his hands. He loved woodwork and was always carving pieces of wood. He was fascinated by nature and would sit in the kitchen with his binoculars and notepad, while she was getting the dinner, and watch birds to his heart's content. There were plenty of trees at the back of their house and David knew every variety of bird that nested there and appeared in their garden. He carved robins and magpies and squirrels and rabbits and spent hours amusing himself. When Claire noticed his talent and saw how hard he was finding his science studies in secondary school she asked Sean to consider sending him to the Ballymun Comprehensive, one of the most progressive comprehensive schools in the country. There, he'd be able to study woodwork and metalwork as well as taking his Leaving Certificate in the subjects he was most competent in.

Sean had nearly had a seizure. "A comprehensive! Good Lord, Claire! Indeed I'm not sending him to a comprehensive. He's in a top-class secondary, with the best of teachers. He'll just have to apply himself more instead of wasting his time with those carvings. In fact, if he doesn't improve his grades in his Christmas report, I'm going to stop him going to the Boy Scouts."

Over my dead body, Claire thought furiously, knowing there was no point in arguing with her husband. David loved the scouts, loved going camping, and it was a great way for him to mix with other lads of his own age. He had no other social outlet, unlike his extrovert sister who was off out with her friends as often as her father allowed her. That was another problem. Sean didn't want her going to dances in the local youth club. Her time should be spent studying, he informed her. But Suzy, unlike her brother, had a mind of her own and was quite capable of arguing with her father. Claire often had to intervene but Sean would always get his own back by stopping his daughter's pocket-money for the week— a severe blow to the young teenager. Claire had insisted that Sean give Suzy and David some pocket-money once they started secondary school. He had moaned and protested and given them a Scroogelike sum but once she started working herself she was able to supplement the meagre amount herself. Not that her wages were anything fantastic; they weren't. But Claire didn't care; the money was her own to do with what she liked.

When Sean found out that she was serious about going

back to work, he told her that he would be discontinuing her five-pound-a-week allowance and furthermore that he expected her to contribute towards the shopping bills. He wanted her to start doing this when she finally succeeded in getting a position.

"You really can't take the fact that I went out and got a job, sure you can't?" Claire said. "Well, I'll tell you one thing, Sean Moran. My money is going to be spent on buying clothes for myself and the children. And—if I've any left over—for giving them little treats like the odd cassette or book or even a trip to McDonald's. Little things that most parents give to their children but that you are too mean to. And if you think for one minute that I'm going to start paying for groceries and things and that you're going to pocket the difference, you can think again, mister!"

"Claire!" Sean was shocked by her vehemence.

"Don't *Claire* me." She was deeply hurt by his attitude. Instead of being supportive and delighted that she had got herself a job, and pleased because she was so happy about it, her husband was being huffy and cold.

"I just don't think women should work if they don't have to," her husband fumed. "A mother's place is in the home, not taking the jobs from young school-leavers. You know the state of the economy! You know that kids in their thousands are emigrating and yet you go looking for a job just because you're a bored housewife. Why don't you take up voluntary work and make a contribution to society that way? There are several old people's homes in the parish. Why don't you go visiting them or do meals on wheels or something?"

He was really angry with her. She had never seen him so angry in all their married life. She couldn't believe his attitude. Did he think he was going to be neglected, did he think she wouldn't be there for the children when they came home from school? That they would be latchkey kids? Hadn't she explained that she was working from eight-thirty until four with only a half hour for lunch so that she would be back to have their meal on the table when they came home from school. Both of them were at secondary school and they usually weren't home until four-thirty. A lot of the time Sean was home before them. Since both children had started secondary school, they now had dinner around five. Claire saw no reason that she couldn't carry on as before with careful planning, despite Sean's protests that something would have to give. The last straw was him trying to make her feel guilty about going back to work and taking jobs from school-leavers. Surely she had as much right as any other individual to fulfil her potential to the best of her ability. Under the constitution of the state all citizens were to be treated equally. Well, she was a citizen and she had rights, the same rights as her husband. She angrily told him so.

"Don't be ridiculous, Claire! That's a childish argument," he sneered.

A flash of temper ignited in her. How dare he try to minimise her achievement! How dare he ridicule her! Her normally serene brown eyes glittered with temper that made them appear almost black. Standing up from the kitchen table where she had been drinking a cup of tea before Suzy and David arrived home, Claire turned on her husband.

"You know what you can do, Sean Moran? Go sit on a red-hot poker and then you can go fuck yourself." Her voice was shaking, she was so angry. She hated confrontations and rarely had them, instead letting Sean get his own way. But this was different. This was very important to her and she had put up with enough for long enough. The worm had turned, and it was about time.

Sean turned pale. "May God forgive you," he said, utterly shocked by her outburst.

Claire walked out of the room, sick to her stomach. She had never spoken to her husband like that before. She had never spoken to anybody like that except for the time she had cursed her father so many years ago the night he had whipped her with his belt. It wasn't in her nature to be abusive and she felt quite ill after the scene with Sean.

He didn't speak to her for two weeks after, until in the

end, unable to put up with his air of martyrdom, she apologised.

"I was extremely hurt by your remarks, Claire, I can't deny that," he told her coolly, his eyes behind his horn-rimmed glasses cold and unfriendly. "But I accept your apology and we'll let bygones be bygones."

How bloody magnanimous of you! Claire thought resentfully. He couldn't even be a bit graceful about it. But her first pay packet had made it all worthwhile. It had been a nerve-wracking week: learning where everything was in the salon, getting to know her workmates, realising with a sinking heart as she watched one of the girls scrunch-drying a client that techniques had changed so much since her day. Still, she thought briskly, wielding her brush, hair still had to be swept up off the floor, that hadn't changed, and then there were two customers waiting to be shampooed. It was an extremely busy salon with about ten stylists, and on Fridays and Saturdays she didn't have a minute to call her own. Sean bitterly resented her working on Saturdays. But she managed to ignore his moans and persevered, with Suzy's and Rosie's encouragement.

Claire began to get to know the clients and as she settled down in the job, really began to enjoy herself after so many years of stagnating. She had enjoyed rearing her children when they were small but they needed her less and less now and until she went back to work, she didn't realise how heavy time had hung on her hands, or how deep a rut she had been stuck in.

On her Saturday off she would take David and Suzy into town and they would have a great time going through the shops looking at this and that, buying something nice for her fashion-conscious daughter, and a book on birds and wildlife for her son, who had no interest whatsoever in clothes. Then they would go to McDonald's, their favourite haunt, where they would enjoy burgers and fries and the delicious ice cream with caramel on top. She enjoyed these outings with her children so much, delighting in the fact that she could buy little treats for them after so many years of having no money. Once or twice she bought some shrubs and bedding plants home for Sean, but they were always the wrong variety or the wrong shade for his immaculate regimented garden and so after a while she didn't bother—he was always so ungracious. She knew that it really irked him that she had her own money and he was always making remarks about working women that made her blood boil. When she and Suzy joined an aerobics class in the local school hall he informed his wife that she had lost her mind paying out good money for exercises she could do at home for nothing.

"It's my money. Thank God I can do what I like with it," she retorted, utterly fed up with his attitude.

She had hoped things would improve after a while when he got used to the idea of her working and he saw that her housework and his meals weren't being affected by her job. But the longer she worked and the better she appeared to enjoy it, and the more he saw evidence of her new sense of independence, the further he drew away from her. He had never got any further in his own teaching career and he had become more bitter about it over the years. He had turned into a rigid, morose man who seemed to get no joy out of life except for his precious garden where he spent most of his free time. Every plant was placed with military precision, unlike the riotous abundance next door which grew in a profusion of colour with no shape or plan but which looked beautiful and untamed. Sean had no time for such extravagance of nature. His garden was precise and neat, every flower in its place and a place for every flower. His bedding plants were neatly arranged in serried rows and each blade of grass was of uniform height. No weed ever dared make an appearance in Sean Moran's garden and autumn was the bane of his life.

"Such an untidy season," was his response one day when she commented with delight upon the colour of the leaves on the trees at the bottom of their garden. The children had never been allowed to play on the lawns when he was there, although Claire ignored the rule when she was alone with them. And he wouldn't hear of putting a swing up for them. "'Tis far from swings they were reared, let them go over to the park beyond," was his response to her request.

That first Christmas she had been working, she had had her mother up to stay with her. Molly, looking ten years younger, all the lines of stress and strain erased from her face, was very smart in the new wool coat that Claire had sent her down a few months previously. Stepping out of the train, her face was wreathed in smiles as David and Suzy launched themselves upon her with hugs and kisses and Claire couldn't contain the guilty thought that it was such a relief her father was no longer alive. Molly had thoroughly enjoyed her few days with them. Claire had pampered and spoilt her, bringing her breakfast and the paper in bed and not letting her do any housework, and Molly had sat by the fire contentedly knitting a mohair sweater for Suzy. She rarely bought daily papers, she confided in her daughter, they were just too expensive, and it was such a treat to stay in bed to read Claire's. Claire had felt terribly sad. Imagine not being able to buy a miserable old paper after a lifetime of hard work. Claire knew her mother was not unique. Many of the elderly ladies who came to the salon were living a life with no frills or luxuries. They just existed, watching every penny, and things like the papers or a magazine or dessert after dinner were rarities. She wished heartily that she could win a million pounds so that she could give her mother the life-style she deserved after all her years of hardship with Billy.

She saved up enough money to take the children down to Waterford on the train with Molly as a special treat. Although they were in their teens, David and Suzy had never been on a train and they had thoroughly enjoyed the journey and the weekend they spent with their grandmother. Molly loved having them around her and for the first time in her life Claire could say that her mother was happy. They went for long brisk walks around the country lanes and David was in his element pointing out different species of birds and commenting on the various aspects of nature that he was familiar with.

Sean had stayed at home, nursing a cold. To tell the truth Claire was guiltily relieved. Free from pressure, she had enjoyed herself in her mother's house, and Suzy and David had been thrilled with themselves when Claire suggested that they go to the Saturday-night dance in the village if they wanted to. They could stay out until one, she told them. Suzy was ecstatic. At Claire's old dressing table, she carefully made up her face from her little cache of makeup, taking at least two hours to get ready, before she was finally satisfied with her appearance. David was more diffident about going. It wasn't really his scene, he told his mother. But Claire whispered to him, telling a little white lie, that she would like him to go so that Suzy would not be alone. Amenable as always, he agreed to go to look after his sister.

David and Suzy had had a ball, they told her over breakfast after mass the next morning. This too was a rare treat, as Sean did not believe in fry-ups for breakfast. Tucking into a slice of crisply fried bread at Molly's urging—although he had eaten three slices already—David grinned at his mother. "I met a real nice girl, Mum. Is it okay if I meet her after breakfast? She's going to show me a beaver's den."

Claire was delighted. This was the first time ever that her son had taken an interest in a girl, being as shy as she herself had been in her youth. "Of course," she assured him, "and if you're not back in time, I'll put your dinner in the oven."

"Thanks, Mum, you're brill!" her son responded, giving her a hug as he left the kitchen, mouth still full of crispy fried bread. Ten minutes later he was out the door on his way to meet his new friend and Claire and Suzy were left grinning at each other.

"It was great, Mam. I knew he was feeling a bit awkward. You know David!" said his sibling, who wouldn't know what it was like to feel awkward, so outgoing was she. "Well, anyway, I saw this girl of about fourteen standing by herself and she didn't look as though she was having a great time and I said to David—why don't you ask her to dance. He wouldn't at first. He was really nervous, but I kept at him and he did, and she got all red and said yes, and they danced around without talking for a while and then they started to yak and they were yakking all night. She's into nature too and she paints. She's going to show her paintings to David. It's great, isn't it? She's real pretty, too," Suzy enthused, delighted for her brother. She was always very protective.

"Did *you* meet anyone nice?" Claire queried, smiling broadly.

"Hmm!" Suzy grinned back. "I met this real dish called Nick. He's studying in the regional technical college but I told him I was committed. So it won't develop into anything," Suzy continued airily.

Claire hid a smile. Suzy had a boyfriend in Dublin, although her father didn't realise it. He always walked her home from school and was part of the gang she went around with. Sean was very strict. Suzy always had to be in by eleven on the one night a week that she was allowed out. And Colin, the boyfriend, was very good about making sure she got home. This impressed Claire, who had met him in her daughter's company several times, although Suzy had never brought him home, knowing that her father would put a stop to her going out. It was enough for Suzy to know that she had her mother's tacit approval. Claire, knowing from her own youth the importance of having a boyfriend, was glad that her daughter was much more sure of herself and outgoing than she had ever been, despite Sean's sternness. Suzy had got six Valentine cards the previous Valentine's Day, six more than her mother ever had, Claire reflected ruefully. Sean didn't go in for such nonsense.

Next Valentine's Day, David got one from Audrey, the girl in Knockross. They had kept in touch by post. He was so chuffed with himself that you'd think he'd won a fortune. Claire knew that that Valentine card was his most treasured possession. Each week without fail, a fat white envelope would come through the letter box and David would retire to his room to read his correspondence in private before setting off to school with a jaunty walk. Having a girlfriend, even if their only contact was through the post, had given *such* a boost to his confidence, Claire reflected, as she poured Sean's porridge into a dish and buttered his toast. She could hear her husband moving around upstairs, calling the children as he passed their rooms. He had to travel across the city to his school so he left much earlier than they did. As soon as he had eaten breakfast and left she would turn on all the rings on the cooker and heat the place up, so that the three of them could have a bit of comfort as they had breakfast together. She shivered again. The kitchen was really cold because it was north-facing. And it was still only October. It would be like a fridge in December. She'd just have to insist on putting the heating on for an hour in the morning. Of course that would cause another row. Life was a succession of rows lately, it seemed. Still today was payday, and she had made quite a bit in tips this week. She had a surprise for David. She was going to send him off to Knockross to Molly next weekend. Molly would be delighted, as they were very close, and he'd get a chance to be with Audrey, his girlfriend. Sean of course would be most disapproving but she'd say that Molly needed sticks chopped and her yards cleaned for the winter. That might shut him up. Sean was very strong on the young helping the elderly. Well, he could just let David practise what his father was always preaching and Molly, Audrey, and David would be very happy. Yes, that was a great idea, a brain wave. She'd buy his train ticket today. Sighing, she began to peel potatoes for the dinner. She'd want to get a move on. She had to run around with the Hoover before she went to work as the next day was her Saturday to work and she didn't want Sean moaning about the state of the place.

"Is my breakfast ready?" her husband enquired, giving a mournful sniffle. Claire's heart sank. Not another cold. He'd be sneezing and spluttering and feeling sorry for himself and peeling lemons to make hot drinks; and life would not be a bowl of cherries. If he'd have a bit of heat in the house he might not be so susceptible to cold, she thought. "I spilt my tea on the sheets. You'll have to change them," he continued glumly. Frustration surged through her. *He* spilt the tea—why couldn't *he* change the sheets. She'd be late for work at this rate. She restrained herself from snapping. It would only lead to a row and he'd be able to throw her work back in her face. Then they'd end up not speaking and he'd never allow David to go away next weekend.

"I'll change them before I go to work," she said calmly, swallowing her resentment.

"It's on the duvet cover as well," Sean said cracking open his egg with precision.

Oh, shit! thought Claire angrily. It would take her at least ten minutes to get a blasted clean duvet cover on to their quilt.

"I'm going straight to bed when I come home," Sean added, eating a piece of buttered toast. "I have a migraine so I hope you won't be Hoovering." Claire knew he was waiting for her to explode. He was enjoying putting her under pressure. Ever since she started working he had been exerting a sly and subtle pressure on her. Maybe she could persuade Suzy to do the Hoovering and David would help her with the duvet. She'd buy tinned carrots today and that would save her peeling and chopping fresh carrots now, and once they were in the casserole, Sean wouldn't know the difference.

"This toast is cold," her husband informed her primly. "Would you do two more rounds for me, please, Claire?"

Bastard! Claire swore to herself as she silently did her husband's bidding.

## Wednesday, October 25, 1989

The heat in the hospital waiting room was stifling. All around people fidgeted, some staring at the sickly green tiles on the walls, some reading newspapers, others deep in conversations with their neighbours as they tried to outdo each other in horror stories about their operations and complaints. Claire sighed deeply. She had been here for two hours and it seemed as though the queue was getting bigger, not smaller.

Nurses rushed around calling people's names from lists, but her physician had been delayed and Claire resigned herself to being in the ugly crowded waiting room for at least another two hours, her precious day off wasted.

She was bursting to go to the loo but the thought of using the toilets nearly made her sick. They were filthy. It was disgraceful what public patients had to put up with. If it was anywhere else but a hospital, the place would be closed down by health officials. She really felt sorry for the nurses having to work in such conditions. They were there day in, day out. She only had to put up with it for a few hours. It was positively insanitary. "You'd think Sean would have you in the Voluntary Health Insurance," Rosie had said, disgusted, one day, when Claire was telling her about her experiences while going to see a gastroenterologist. Again she had been waiting for two hours before she was finally called into the inner sanctum. She had had the shock of her life.

Two physicians were seeing patients. She found herself sitting on a bench beside five other people. A name was called out and one of the people on the bench went over to the physician's table about twelve feet away. There he had to tell his tale of woe. He was trying to keep his voice down but it made no difference. Claire and all the others could hear everything. The consultant had a loud booming voice which reverberated around the room. "And have you tried eating bran for this constipation?" he inquired briskly of the timid little man in front of him. Claire had been mortified for him. It was like listening to someone's confession. She was tempted to stick her hands in her ears. A horrific thought had struck her then. Everybody else on the bench was going to be able to hear her tell the consultant about the awful bloating that lasted for two weeks of her cycle and the terrible diarrhea that was getting worse and worse every time she had her period. So much for privacy and confidentiality between doctor and patient! At another table a resident was speaking into a dictaphone. She could hear the patient's name and address quite clearly, and realised that it was someone who lived in a street not too far from her. The poor woman had a carcinoma in her small intestine and Claire was shocked that the doctor didn't bother to lower his voice, but dictated imperiously, unperturbed by the fact that this woman's private business could be heard by complete strangers. So much for the Hippocratic oath, Claire had thought in disgust.

Rosie was horrified when Claire told her the saga. She usually went to the Bons in Glasnevin whenever she had to have any little jobs done, although the last time, she'd had to go to the Blackrock Clinic, as her physician only saw patients there. The gulf between the super luxury clinics and the public hospitals was mind-boggling. "Mind you, the last time I went, despite the fact that I had an appointment, there were ten others in front of me and we all had to wait in this poky little waiting room," Rosie said disgustedly. "You'd think, for the amount you have to shell out you could at least be seen on time! A client of mine was telling me about this physician she went to who wears a watch with a timer that goes off every five minutes. Imagine how comfortable you'd feel with him." Rosie laughed. "I'd tell him where to stick his timer. Anyway this woman was having none of his nonsense and she really let him have it. She told him he could stick his private clinic the same place he could stick his timer and marched out the door in disgust to its sound."

"I'd loved to have seen his face. Honestly, but you would think some of them were God Almighty with the carrying-on of them," said Claire, amused by Rosie's story.

Rosie grinned back. "Ashes to ashes and dust to dust, I always say. They have to piss and fart like the rest of us."

Claire suppressed a smile as she shifted on the wooden bench. Her bum was gone numb from sitting in the same position for so long. Typical of Rosie to come out with something like that. Despite her affluence and success there wasn't a pretentious bone in her body. It was Rosie who had kept at her and at her to go back to the gynecologist to see if anything could be done for her. The last year had been a bit of a nightmare for her. Although she loved her job and had com-

pleted her training successfully and was now a qualified stylist, she was finding the going tough. If Sean had given her
even the smallest bit of support she might be able to cope a
bit better. But even after all this time he was still implacable in
his resentment of her working. If Suzy and David had not
been so good around the house she would never have managed. Not once had Sean ever been put out by her working.
She had been determined that she would never give him any
ammunition to throw at her. But there were times lately when
she felt like chucking it all up. Only the knowledge that she
would once again be dependent on him for money kept her
working.

It wasn't that she didn't enjoy her job, she did. She always got a great sense of satisfaction when she saw the end
result of styling someone's hair. She had lots of clients of her
own now and that too was a great source of pride to her. It
was just she felt so tired and lethargic these days. She'd give
anything to spend a week in bed doing nothing. It was her
periods, of course. She had always suffered with them, ever
since she was in her late teens. "Have a baby and you'll be
fine!" she'd been told by a gynecologist when she was seventeen. That's easy for you to say, she had thought resentfully.
What was she to do, go and become an unmarried mother?
What if no one ever asked her to marry them? She could
hardly put an ad in the paper saying—man wanted to marry
nice girl—so that she could have a baby to cure her painful
periods. Well, she had gone and had a baby, and then another, and still things had not improved.

After David's birth she had gone again to try and get
something done but after the indignity of the treatment she
got, she had sworn that she would never again set foot in a
hospital. After she had whispered an account of her symp-
toms, the physician of the booming voice had told her that
she was probably suffering from an irritable bowel brought on
by stress: he'd get his gynecological colleague to have a look
at her and for her to go and make an appointment. Another
half day wasted in the waiting room and then she had been

called in to one of the cubicles and told to undress. She was wrapped in a gown and brought in to the examining room. Perched in a big high chair with her feet in stirrups she had been examined by the physician who was accompanied by three students. Her permission had not been asked and as they investigated her vagina, discussing a rugby match that had been played the previous day, she had felt like a piece of meat. It had been excruciatingly painful and when it was over, Claire, who was sore, humiliated, and feeling utterly violated, had sworn that she would never, ever, go back there again. The gynecologist had told her brusquely that she was too young for a hysterectomy and to go and have another baby. At least then she'd be period-free for nine months. Maybe then he might consider removing her womb. I wouldn't let you remove a splinter, let alone my womb, she wanted to shriek at him but she was well and truly cowed by her experience. But for a long time afterwards she was sorry that she hadn't let fly at him.

Now, years later, she was sitting waiting to go through another ordeal. At least now she knew that she could refuse permission to have students witness her examination. What would she do if he said she should have a hysterectomy? She'd be out of work for ages and Sean, who had no time for women's complaints, wouldn't give her much sympathy. Sighing deeply, she could hear the woman next to her telling her neighbour. "I'm lucky to be alive, I am, luv. Nearly died on the table I did. He had opened me up when I started to hemorrhage. Lost five pints of blood, luv, as well as me womb." Claire swallowed. She really didn't feel so good. She'd give anything to have this over and done with. Her palms started to sweat and her heart began to beat faster. She felt sick with tension. She'd better go to the loo before she went in to be examined. "The last time I was here the nurse had the cheek to expect me to go to his understudy," the other old dear took up her own story indignantly, referring to the resident. "I told her I'd wait until Judgement Day to see himself and not to be pawnin' me off with no understudy." Leaving her lucky-to-be-alive neighbour to mind her seat, and the other one determined to see "himself," Claire went off in search of the loo.

All in all it wasn't too bad, she decided an hour later as she sat in Arnott's having a reviving cup of coffee. "You're not the world's slimmest woman," the gynecologist had told her as he examined her, leaving her slack jawed at his cheek. He was no Twiggy himself with his affluent little potbelly that spoke of good food and wines. He changed her pill, told her she was stressed, told her to lose weight and to come back in three months and see how things were going. "If this doesn't work I'll try you on something else," he said cheerfully, quite oblivious of the fact that she had hoped against hope that he'd be able to solve her problems there and then. Didn't he realise that she had a job to hold down and a house to run. It was all very well to say he'd try something else after three months: *he* didn't have to suffer her periods.

She bit glumly into a coffee slice. She'd start her diet next Monday. She *had* got heavy, she thought ruefully. She was at least a stone overweight but it wasn't that she ate loads of rubbish; she was a good eater really. It was just that she seemed to be so bloated lately. All around, the noisy chatter of people having a snack, the girls clearing the tables, the clatter of crockery and cutlery seemed somehow comforting. She didn't feel like queueing for a bus and going home to get the dinner, she felt like staying here. She should have arranged for Suzy and David to come into town and meet her after school and she could have bought them a meal. For once, Sean could have looked after himself.

She was really angry with her husband. David had failed maths in his Inter Cert and her husband had been furious. Despite the fact that the rest of David's grades were good, Sean had ranted and raved like a madman. He had put his son under such pressure that Claire had accused him of being a bully and a tyrant and there had been nothing but rows since the results had come out a few weeks previously. It wasn't that David didn't study, he did. He spent many hard hours at it and it had been a long slog for him. He just did not have an aptitude for maths. It didn't mean that he was any the less intelligent, Claire stormed at Sean, who told her that she was too bloody soft on him and always had been. Poor old David had planned to go to Knockross for the October weekend to bring Audrey to a school dance and he had been looking forward to it for ages, but Sean had put his foot down and forbidden it. He damn well was not going gallivanting down the country with his disgraceful result in maths. He could bloody well stay at home and let his father give him some extra tuition. Otherwise he'd never get to university.

"I don't want to go to university. I want to be a carpenter. And I can't let Audrey down!" her son protested in dismay.

"A carpenter! You'll be no such thing. I'm giving you the opportunity to go to university and make something of yourself. I'm working myself to the bone. And, by God, son, to university you will go. You ungrateful monkey!"

"But Sean, that's not fair!" Claire protested. "If David doesn't wan—"

"*Shut up!*" roared her husband, his face red with temper.

Knowing that David would only get the raw end of the stick if she persisted, Claire remained furiously silent. Later, while Sean was out viciously raking the leaves out of his precious garden, she told her son to go and ring Audrey while she kept watch. If Sean thought that David was making long-distance calls to his girlfriend he'd be incensed and there'd be another row. "Don't stay on too long," she advised her forlorn son gently. Five minutes later he was back and she could see the glitter of tears in his eyes. "What did she say?"

"She was mad. She hung up," he said miserably. "I don't want any dinner, Mum. I'm just going upstairs to my room." Claire watched him walk dejectedly from the room and her heart bled for him. She felt like crying herself. She cursed Sean.

That night she put on her sexiest nightgown, dabbed some eau de cologne that he had given her for her birthday behind her ears and waited for her husband to come to bed. It had been ages since they had had sex. She was too tired these days and he had lost his old drive since she had started working and undermined his manliness. He didn't even notice, so busy was he giving out about the fact that the principal expected him to perform miracles in the school library despite the fact that the budget had been slashed yet again and that the school library section of the corporation that they so depended on had been decimated by savage cutbacks. "Forget about it for tonight," she murmured, putting her arms around his bony body as he got into bed. She slid her hand under his brown pyjama jacket and gently caressed his chest. Sean gave a sigh of satisfaction and turned to her with pleasure. "This is a nice surprise," he smiled. "Usually you're asleep." Claire fought to suppress a yawn. She was really exhausted. Leaning over, her husband kissed her and slid the nightgown from her shoulders, kissing her creamy soft breasts as he did so. Claire observed that the bald patch on the top of his head was getting bigger, no matter how hard he tried to disguise it by covering it with strands of hair. He was lying on top of her now, his breathing harsh and ragged. She closed her eyes. There was this gorgeous man who came to the salon every month to have his hair cut by her and she really fancied him. He had a great sense of humour, beautiful blue eyes, and a body hard and lean that would tempt any woman, married or single. As Sean unbuttoned his pyjamas and slid her nightdress above her waist, Claire thought of that body.

Later as they lay together, Claire murmured, "Sean, I was thinking. We could all do with a bit of a break. We haven't been anywhere together for ages."

"That's because you're working," he said sanctimoniously.

"Yes, I know," she said soothingly, hiding her irritation. "Why don't we all go down to Mum's for the long weekend? I'll take a few days off." It would cost her a fortune but it would be worth it to remove the misery from her son's face. "You could give David his tuition down there, and I'd get to see Mum."

Sean grunted, half asleep now. "I'm afraid I told Peggy and James I'd call and see them on Saturday afternoon. It wouldn't be worth it to go down on Sunday and you know I don't like driving in the dark." Peggy and James were his sister and brother-in-law.

"Sure, can't you go and see them another time?" Claire said in desperation.

"I can't break the arrangement, Claire," Sean said smugly. "If I'd known you wanted to go away for the weekend I'd have been delighted to go but you told me you were working on the Saturday so I'm afraid I made other arrangements."

"*Please* let David go to Knockross this weekend," she pleaded.

"Absolutely not. It's out of the question. It's for his own good that he should stay here," her husband replied firmly. "Good night, Claire."

Hours later, Claire lay wide-eyed listening to her husband snoring, thinking about her son and wishing she had never married Sean Moran.

"Can I clear here?" A young girl smiled down at her. Claire smiled back. She had been lost in thought; now she'd better get a move on. Putting on her coat and gathering her few purchases, she left the cafeteria and walked out into the cold October day. She was waiting ages for a bus. Still, Suzy would be late. She was taking extra French classes and doing really well. She had a flair for languages and had spent a month in France last year on a student exchange trip and really enjoyed it. She confided in Claire that when she was finished her Leaving Cert she was going to go to France au pairing for a year and get a job there. Claire said nothing to Sean because he would forbid such a course of action. But Suzy would do as she wished anyway. She had never knuckled down under her father's thumb and couldn't wait to be independent. Although Claire would worry about her and miss her she would certainly not stand in her daughter's way and she'd give her every encouragement despite her husband's displeasure. Sean would be late because he had a staff meeting so only David would be in before her.

Rushing up the garden path she rooted in her handbag for her keys. Through the glass panel on the front door a movement caught her eye. David was home. Good! She'd bought him a little treat, a lovely illustrated bird encyclopedia she had chanced upon in Eason's bargain bookshop.

What was that shadow? Opening the door she felt as though she had been hit by a sledgehammer. Her heart began to pound as though it was going to burst. She tried to move forward but couldn't move. "David! David!" She thought she screamed but no sound came out as she stared in terrified disbelieving horror at the sight that met her eyes.

## *Lainey*

Friday, August 1, 1980

What a terrible tragedy! And to think she had so nearly been on that train. Lainey shuddered as she watched the news in her comfortable hotel bedroom. They were showing horrific scenes at the site of the crash of the Dublin to Cork express in which seventeen people had been killed and many others injured. She could very well be dead but for the fact that she had decided to take the car after all, even though it was still giving her some trouble. Life was so strange sometimes. Sighing, she switched off the news, unpacked her holdall, hung up her smart ice-pink linen suit that she was wearing the following day and decided to have a shower before going down to eat in the hotel dining room.

She was tired. She had driven down from Dublin very early and had made some calls en route. Not that she hadn't enjoyed it, she had. Lainey had got to know the bookshop owners and managers well over the previous two years and she loved the challenge of bringing in the new covers of books that were to be published and getting orders for them. She was very charming, very positive, and she usually ended up persuading them to order twice the amount they had intended to originally. Her publishing firm, Verdon, was doing extremely well, thanks in no small measure to her own contribution as sales and marketing manager, the job she had been promoted to in the past year.

Lainey loved her job. It was so different from working for the corporation. There, she had been a cog in a machine, an anonymous pay number. She got no thanks or recognition for initiative or hard work. She hadn't been a bit sorry to leave her permanent and pensionable job. The only regret she had was leaving the people she had worked with. A nicer, more dedicated group couldn't be found—for all the thanks they got!

Lainey had thrown herself into her new career. At night, if her thoughts were inclined to linger on Steve she would banish him from her mind with grim determination, and concentrate instead on her marketing strategy. It soon began to reap dividends. Publicity was the thing! The hype! The glitz and glamour! If Verdon wanted to compete with international publishing houses then they would have to take the bull by the horns and spend much more money on their marketing.

At an invigorating thought-provoking meeting attended by the managing director, the accountant, the editorial director, and herself, Lainey had given her assessment of the company's requirements for the eighties. She had spent hours working on her presentation and in a confident and articulate manner had convinced the other heads of department to increase her budget by 50 percent. In return, she told them, she would increase sales and turnover substantially. By hiring a PR firm to work on behalf of authors and the company, she would help make Verdon a force to be reckoned with in the Irish publishing world. It was no empty promise! Lainey had studied her English and American counterparts, seen their highly aggressive marketing strategies and taken a leaf out of their book. Patrick Nolan, the owner and managing director of the publishing company, and a man of great enthusiasm and get-up-and-go, was delighted with Lainey's contribution and where the accountant was inclined to be conservative, Patrick supported her arguments.

Lainey loved the excitement and challenge of her new job. It invigorated her, stimulated her and exhausted her and was just the remedy for a broken heart. She was so busy she didn't have time to visit Moncas Bay as much. At least that was what she told herself. She would go down maybe one weekend in six, usually in the company of Tony doing what he termed his "duty visit." She had such mixed feelings about going home. Lainey was trying her best to put the past behind her, to get on with her life, a life without Steve. It pained her deeply to see him with Helena, married and apparently very happy. Several times she had bumped into Helena in the village supermarket and the other girl had given her such a smug cat-got-the-cream look that Lainey had had to curl her fingers into her palms, so tempted was she to slap Miss Wishy Washy's pasty little face. Her pride always carried her through. Not for anything would she ever let Helena know how much Steve meant to her.

It was bad enough having to listen to Cecily rubbing it in. She did it deliberately every time Lainey came home for the weekend. "I saw Steve and Helena the other night. Simon and I had drinks with them. Marriage *really* suits them. They look so happy. You and Tony should try it and give us all a day out." She laughed gaily with a pretended artlessness.

"Don't hold your breath, dear," Lainey said coolly, trying hard to hide her irritation. She knew full well what her sister-in-law was up to. She was trying to rub salt in the wound. Cecily had a malicious streak that seemed to surface when she was around. What Simon saw in his wife, Lainey would never understand—she had never met a more selfish and self-centred individual. The carrying-on of her when she got pregnant a few months after her marriage! It was obviously a miscalculation but one for which her brother had suffered dearly.

After his day's work he would have to come home and turn around and cook a dinner, while Cecily sat with her feet up, plump cushions behind her back, resting, reading magazines and stuffing herself with chocolates. Not any old chocolates either but handmade chocolates. Cecily had told Lainey that she had such cravings and such terrible backache and heartburn and she couldn't possibly think of cooking a dinner. It would make her sick. So either Simon cooked it or else they ate out. Lainey never ceased to be amazed at her sister-in-law's utter selfishness. One weekend Lainey was visiting and Cecily was really playing the old soldier, complaining about not sleeping a wink because of the baby's kicking. Simon was looking absolutely wretched and exhausted and, listening to the other girl's moans, Lainey pitied him from the bottom of her heart. Cecily was so disloyal to him, always giving out about him in front of his family.

"Honestly, the house is like a pigsty. I've been asking him for months to paint the windows and they're still there waiting. Men!" Cecily sighed, throwing her eyes up to heaven and giving her husband a filthy look. If anyone was suffering nine months of misery it was Simon. Lainey forbore to make any comment. Putting in a day's hard work and coming home to cook and housekeep hardly left him any time for painting, she would have thought. "Don't ever get pregnant," moaned Cecily. "Simon, rub my back." Her husband dutifully complied. "I think I'd like a cup of hot milk," she said five minutes later. Simon, the fool, rushed out to the kitchen to get the hot milk.

"Is your gynecologist worried about you?" Lainey asked sweetly.

Cecily looked surprised. "No, not that I know of. Why do you ask?"

"Oh it's just . . . it seems unnatural the way you seem to be . . . suffering. After all, pregnancy isn't an *illness*, Cecily, it's the most natural thing in the world. I have a friend in Washington who's seven months pregnant. She gets up at

five-thirty every morning, leaves for work at six, arrives a
seven, works until five, doesn't get home until six and you'o
never hear a word out of her. She's really terrific, totally ir
control of the situation. Isn't it amazing how pregnancies dif
fer?"

Cecily was furious, absolutely ripping. Lainey, unable to
take any more, stood up to leave. But her little speech had the
desired effect; Cecily never again carried on like that ir
Lainey's company. In fact she had been extremely cool with
Lainey, who couldn't give a hoot. The less she had to do with
dear Cecily the better, as far as she was concerned.

"Is she booking into the Portland Hospital?" Joan
Lainey's sister, wondered, as they sat discussing the preg
nancy of pregnancies one evening after she had come up to
Dublin to spend the weekend with Lainey.

"The *where*?" Lainey was confused.

"You know! Where the Royals go to give birth in Lon
don."

"Bitch!" laughed Lainey.

"Well, I have to put up with it all the time, you only have
to endure it on your flying visits," retorted Joan with a gri
mace. "You should see herself and Helena McGrath trying to
outdo each other in designer maternity wear." She caught
Lainey's eye. "Oops! Sorry!"

"Don't be silly," sighed Lainey. "Steve married Helena
and not me and I've got over it. I had to, and if they have two
dozen children that's their business and nothing to do with
me." She said this firmly although it had cut her to the quick
when she had heard that Helena was expecting a honeymoor
baby.

"He's a self-seeking bastard anyway and you're better of
without him," Joan declared loyally. "If Helena hadn't any
money you can be damned sure he wouldn't have looked
twice at her."

"Well, she had and he did," Lainey said miserably, wish
ing that Joan would change the topic of conversation.

"Let's go to a nightclub!" Joan said eagerly. "What you need is a new man in your life!"

"That's the last thing I need, believe me!" Lainey assured Joan as she began to get ready to go out. She meant it. She had no interest whatsoever in dating, despite the fact that she was constantly being invited out. Lainey was perfectly happy to socialise with Tony occasionally but mostly she devoted herself to her career. Besides, much of her work was socially oriented anyway. She was forever organising and attending book launches, trying to make each one different and more newsworthy than the last. Then there were the book fairs and trade conferences to be attended and she was spending an awful lot of time in London, publicising and selling Verdon's books there. She rarely had time to dwell on her manless state or the fact that her heart had been broken by Steve McGrath. It was all go and she thrived on it.

She moved from her Rathmines flat to an apartment in Monkstown. Patrick insisted she be given a generous increase in salary on her promotion and she decided to treat herself to a bit of comfort. The apartment was small and compact and a nice change from the cold old-fashioned flat that she had lived in for so long. Everything was new. It was the first time the owner had let it and it was in perfect condition. Lainey could even see the sea from her balcony. She had been saving hard herself, with a view towards getting a place of her own and in time, she promised herself, she too would be a property owner with her own home. After all rent paid was money down the drain really, when you could be paying a mortgage, but for the time being the apartment in Monkstown suited her needs very well.

She now drove a company car which was marvellous as she hadn't to worry about tax and insurance costs or petrol expenses. But then of course she did a hell of a lot of driving around: bringing authors around the country for book-signing sessions; visiting the wholesalers and retailers; meeting artists who were designing the book covers. Lainey loved that part of the job. From the time she spent working in the library service, she knew the types of covers that appealed to people in the different markets. It was fascinating to discuss her ideas with an artist and a few weeks later to see the result of discussions. As far as Lainey was concerned the cover was as important as the contents of the book. It was the cover that first attracted the buyer and she had always been fascinated when she worked in the libraries to observe what books people went for in the new book displays. Invariably a glitzy glamorous cover meant that the book was never on the shelf for long.

Now Verdon's book covers were as glitzy and as glamorous as their competitors' and it was paying off in sales. Their last blockbuster had been on the best-seller list for thirty weeks and the cover had been much admired and commented upon. The literati might sneer at mass-market fiction but it was commercial successes like these that made the profits and kept publishers in jobs and the public happy. But then it was great having a boss like Patrick who was so amenable to suggestion and who was so supportive. Once he had seen that she could perform her job well he let her get on with it and that suited Lainey perfectly; she had always felt so constrained in the library. At Verdon she could develop and use her talents to the full.

As the water streamed down her back, Lainey stretched contentedly in the shower. She liked Cork and she liked staying in the Country Club Hotel. There was nothing she enjoyed more after a hard day doing the rounds than to sit, after dinner, in the beautiful big-windowed lounge and watch the lights of the city glittering below her. She had a busy day ahead of her tomorrow. She was collecting an author from the airport and then they were doing a signing session in Eason's bookshop as well as visiting the smaller ones around the city. Then there was a radio interview to be conducted as well as newspaper interviews that the PR firm had lined up. After that the author had to be wined and dined before being put back on a plane to London. So tonight, Lainey was going to take things easy and relax.

She dressed in a pair of black tailored trousers and a soft pink angora batwing sweater, wound her hair in a topknot, put on some lipstick and Chanel No. 5 and headed for the dining room. It was busy enough but the waiter, who knew her well, placed her at a window table and after ordering she sat back to enjoy the view. She didn't see anyone she recognised. Sometimes she would meet reps that she had got to know and have dinner with them but tonight there was no one that she knew. Of course it was bank holiday Friday. Who else would be working on a bank holiday? But tomorrow there would be more people in town than normal, all the better for the signing and book sales. Across at another table from her, a well-built man with greying hair worked on papers from a briefcase as he ate. Someone else working, she mused. He caught her eye and smiled. Lainey smiled back and then the waiter was beside her with her egg mayonnaise and, starving, she tucked in.

After dinner she went for a brisk walk. It always helped to clear her mind for sleep. Then as the dusk started to fall she headed back to the hotel for a drink before bed. Settling into a comfy window chair, she sipped her spritzer and glanced in a desultory way through her folder of covers for forthcoming books. There was a great selection of titles for the autumn/winter list and she was very pleased with them.

"I think you dropped this," a pleasant male voice was saying and looking up she saw the man who had been working at dinner smiling down at her as he handed her one of her book covers.

"Thank you very much." Lainey smiled back, taking the cover from him.

"You're in the book trade then?" He smiled at her and she liked the way his eyes crinkled up at the sides.

"Yes I am. For my sins."

"I'm sure the recession doesn't help," he observed.

"Well, it's not too bad now. In fact we weathered it well and business is picking up. Are you staying over yourself?"

she asked. She had never seen him before; he wasn't a rep that she recognised.

The man laughed. "I live in Cork, actually. I was supposed to be having a business meeting with someone from Dublin but because of the train crash there was a hitch and he phoned to say he can't make it until tomorrow, so I just decided to have dinner anyway and do a bit of work. It's quieter than at home," he said a little wryly.

"That was a terrible crash," Lainey remarked soberly. "I was supposed to be on the train."

"You had a lucky escape then." He smiled at her. She smiled back. He was nice. "Dominic Kent," he said holding out his hand.

"Lainey Conroy," she reciprocated, and her hand was firmly shaken.

"I was just going to have a coffee before I left. Would you like one?" he enquired casually.

It was too early to go to bed, she had nothing better to do and it was nice to have a bit of company. "Why not?" Lainey smiled.

"Why not indeed," Dominic said as he motioned to a waiter to come and take their order.

Tuesday, June 22, 1982

Lainey gasped with pleasure as Dominic slid the silky blouse from her shoulders and gently cupped her breasts. Her nipples hardened with desire. It was so long since she had made love to a man and she was hungry for him. Lowering his mouth to her breast Dominic's tongue caressed her, as his hands slid down to her waist and drew her even closer to him. He was as aroused as she and the heat from his body and the hardness of him made her ache with longing.

"Lainey! Lainey!" He was muttering her name, his breath coming harshly as he bent his head to hers and kissed her passionately. Frantically she unbuttoned his shirt, wanting to feel the roughness of his skin against her own. Her fingers gently caressed the tangle of dark hair at his throat, and then moved down his broad chest and over the lean flatness of his belly, to where the dark line disappeared inside the waistband of his trousers. "You're beautiful, Lainey," he said drawing her down on the bed beside him as she slowly unfastened his belt and unzipped his pants.

"Make love to me, Dominic," she whispered huskily. Drawing her close to him, he did as she asked.

Later, much later, as he slept with his head resting on her breast, his heavy-muscled thigh hard against her own, Lainey lay watching the moonlit sky through the window. It was a warm night and they had just a sheet thrown over them. The last time she lay in bed with a man, her body tingling and invigorated after passionate lovemaking, had been with Steve. It was so long ago she had almost forgotten the pleasures of making love. Maybe it was a good thing that her memories of Steve's lovemaking weren't strong enough to compare with what she had just experienced with Dominic. And what she had experienced with Dominic was pure unmitigated pleasure. After years of celibacy her body was celebrating and she smiled to herself in the moonlight. Dominic had been a generous and thoughtful lover, making sure that it was as good for her as it had been for him. It had not been Steve's way. If it had been good for him, he assumed it had been good for her. Dominic had made sure.

She had thought she would never get involved with a man again and she had certainly never envisaged herself making love to a married man. Lainey sighed in the dark. She felt a little guilty and yet from what Dominic had told her of his relationship with his wife and what she had observed in the almost two years that she knew him she could understand why the dark-haired man sleeping so peacefully beside her would eventually give up on the relationship and seek to find happiness elsewhere. Rita Kent was a fool! Her husband was a good man and until now had been a faithful husband. She had not seen the emptiness and loneliness that had over the years become part of his life as unthinkingly she had relegated him to the background of her life, and children and friends and social life had assumed a greater importance. When Lainey met Dominic Kent he was ripe for an affair, taken for granted, neglected emotionally, if it wasn't she, it would have been some other woman and Rita deserved a lot of the blame, Lainey decided. She had copped out of a lot of her responsibilities as a wife and she could take the consequences.

Lainey hadn't rushed into an affair with Dominic. There had been a lot of soul-searching and talking before they became intimate and only as she got to know and trust him and saw how genuine a man he was, had she slowly fallen in love with him. Two wounded souls searching for happiness, they had found in each other what Rita and Steve had taken from them. She would never have believed that night in Cork when she had first met him, just what an impact Dominic Kent would have on her life.

She had completely forgotten about him that Saturday as she had rushed around Cork with her author. It was a hectic but successful day and it was a relief to get back to the Country Club Hotel where a table was reserved for them for dinner. They had enjoyed the meal but hadn't lingered as the writer had a flight to catch and Lainey was bringing her to Cork Airport. When they were leaving the hotel she noticed Dominic and another man coming out behind them. They must have been in the bar as she hadn't seen them in the dining room. Giving a brief wave she opened the car door for her passenger and then got in herself. When Lainey turned on the ignition, she couldn't believe her ears! A pitiful sound emanated from under the bonnet. Silently using every curse in her fairly varied repertoire, she tried again, and again. Then she gave up, got out of the car and stuck her head hopefully under the bonnet. Frankly she hadn't a clue about the ins and outs of a car engine. Her talents lay elsewhere. She gave the distributor cap a twist, poked at her battery leads and offered up a silent prayer. Getting back in, she smiled confidently at her author, who was getting slightly agitated, and turned the key. This time the noise was infinitely more ominous.

"What's the trouble?" Dominic was tapping at her window.

She rolled it down and grimaced. "I think it's the battery. I've been having trouble but the mechanic recharged it and assured me it was okay for the journey."

"I'll try the jump leads on her," Dominic offered kindly.

"Thanks a million," Lainey said gratefully, trying to ignore the deep sighs emanating from the author.

"It's as dead as a dodo, I'm afraid," Dominic informed her five minutes later after fruitless efforts to revive the deceased battery. "It's not holding the charge."

Lainey got out to join him. "Oh shit!" she muttered glumly, forgetting where she was. Dominic's mouth quirked in amusement. "I beg your pardon!" she apologised hastily. "It's just that I've got an author in the car who's got to get a flight back to London and she's a bit of a prima donna. I'll never hear the end of it if she misses her plane, and by the time I call a taxi and it comes out here and then back to the airport, she just might miss it. We left things a bit tight, I think." Lainey wondered what the hell she was going to do now. Her charge was insistent on getting back to London that night and if she missed the flight Lainey did not relish the thoughts of spending the rest of the evening in her company.

"I'll drive you. It won't take that long." Dominic's voice intruded on her thoughts.

Lainey stared at him. "That's very kind of you. Are you sure?" she asked doubtfully. It was a big favour for a complete stranger.

"No problem," he said briskly. "Tell Prima Donna to hop in!" Lainey grinned at him and he grinned back. They made the flight comfortably and as Lainey watched the back of her author as she passed through the boarding gate she sighed with relief. That was one problem solved. Now she'd have to see about getting her car fixed as it was imperative that she get back to Dublin the next day. She was flying to Paris to represent Verdon at a trade fair and her flight was leaving at four the next afternoon. Turning to the man beside her she smiled. "Thanks very much, Dominic; that was a lifesaver. I think I'll give the AA a ring and see what they can do with the car. I'll get a taxi back to the hotel from here."

"I'll run you back," he offered.

"Not at all!" Lainey exclaimed. "I've taken up more than enough of your time."

"It's no trouble at all," he said affably. "I'm heading back in that direction anyway and I'm in no rush to get home. My wife's having a Tupperware party." He made a face and she laughed. "Come on and let's see what's the story about your car."

The story about her car was not good! It was a garage job, she was told, and it definitely wouldn't be on the road the following day. Lainey watched in dismay as the car was towed out of the hotel car-park to a garage in the city. She'd have to get the train in the morning and that was all there was about it.

"Come on. Let's go and have a drink in the lounge," Dominic suggested, seeing her crestfallen expression. "Cork's a nice city. Surely one day more here won't be too much of a penance," he teased her as he ordered drinks for them.

"Oh, it's not that," Lainey assured him. "It's just I'm flying to Paris tomorrow so I've got to get back. I'll just have to go on the early train. It's a bit of a nuisance and it won't leave me much time to organise myself before getting to the airport."

"You're a busy woman, aren't you?" he observed taking a draught of light ale.

"That's me!" she agreed, starting to relax. There was nothing she could do about the car so there was no point in worrying about it. She was tired after her hectic day and she might as well relax, have her drink and have an early night. Dominic and she talked about this and that and she found him easy to talk to. It was a shock to her to look at her watch some time later and find that they had spent almost three hours in conversation.

"Lord, is that the time!" Dominic looked equally surprised. "Well, the Tupperware party should be just about winding down." He smiled and held out his hand. Lainey took it.

"Thanks very much for the lift to the airport. I really appreciate it."

"You're welcome, Lainey, and thanks for your company." Dominic shook her hand. She watched him leave and thought, there's a nice man.

Preparing to check out early the following morning she heard her bedroom telephone ring and assumed that it was reception confirming her taxi. It was reception all right, with a message. "Miss Conroy, a Mr. Dominic Kent is waiting for you in the foyer."

"Oh!" Lainey said in surprise. "Tell him I'll be right down."

"Morning!" Dominic smiled as he watched her walk down the blue-green carpeted stairs.

"Morning yourself. You're up early."

"The early bird catches the worm, or so they say. Could I interest you in a trip to the capital?"

"You're going to Dublin?" Lainey managed to suppress a yawn. It was an unearthly hour and there wasn't another soul to be seen in the hotel.

"A little earlier than I had planned," Dominic admitted. "I had planned to leave early Monday morning until I went home and my wife told me she was having her best friend and her five kids over for a Sunday barbecue. So I decided to bring forward my departure by a day and get an extra day's work done. I thought you might prefer a lift rather than getting the train. You'll get to Dublin more quickly."

"Great!" Lainey said enthusiastically. Things weren't turning out too bad after all. She'd get to Dublin with a couple of hours to spare before leaving for Paris and she wouldn't be wrecked from having to drive the long journey herself. Dominic must be a real workaholic, she decided, as she ran back up to her room to get her luggage. He had told her last night that he had his own customs clearance business, with an office in Cork and one in Dublin. He spent up to three days a

week in the capital. How lucky for her that he decided to
leave a day early. Mind a barbecue with a load of kids
wouldn't exactly be her favourite way to spend a Sunday either. They made good time to Dublin. There was no traffic on
the roads and she couldn't believe that they were driving into
the city less than three hours later. Dominic drove fast but
carefully, obviously well used to the journey. Pulling up outside her apartment in Monkstown, he gratefully accepted her
offer of coffee. Before he left, he told her he would be in the
city until Wednesday and that if she was home from Paris and
wished to drive back down to Cork with him in order to
collect her car, she was more than welcome. Lainey cheerfully
accepted his offer. He gave her his number, told her to contact him on her return and left Lainey feeling very relieved to
have solved the problem of collecting her car.

In the following months, she met him several times in
Cork, always in the Country Club, where he conducted much
of his business, treating clients to dinner and drinks. It was,
he told her, almost his second home. She found him so easy
to talk to, he was genuinely interested in her career. And she
was fascinated by how he had given up his secure job with
the customs, despite the fact that he had a wife and four
children, to start his own business. In that respect they were
kindred spirits, risk takers, hard workers and haters of red
tape and bureaucracy. They used to try and outdo each other
in horror tales of officialdom that they had encountered in
their previous careers.

When they found out that they would both be in London
on business around the same time, they made arrangements
to meet for dinner. He had taken her to the Savoy Grill and
she had spent a most enjoyable evening with him. Much better than spending an evening alone in her hotel bedroom. It
seemed the polite and reasonable thing to do to invite him out
to the apartment in Monkstown for dinner the next time he
was due to be in Dublin.

From then on, he rang her when he was in the city and if
she was free they would meet for dinner and a drink. Lainey

never analysed their relationship. She just enjoyed him and his company, subconsciously reasoning that because he was married, she was not interested in having a serious relationship with him and therefore she could not be hurt as she had been in her relationship with Steve. Dominic was safe, a friend to spend an occasional evening with, nothing more, nothing less. Unfortunately, despite the excellent logic of her analysis, things did not work out quite the way she had planned.

Dominic rang her one Monday evening to find her uncharacteristically subdued and definitely not her confident self. "Do you feel like coming out for a drink?" he asked, surprised by her lack of energy. Usually Lainey was game for anything.

"Not tonight, Dominic. I'm a bit tired. But thanks for asking."

"Is anything wrong?" he asked, concerned.

Lainey felt a lump come to her throat. "Not a thing," she managed to say. "Good night, Dominic. Thanks for ringing. I'll be in touch." Hanging up the receiver, Lainey promptly burst into tears. It was something she had wanted to do, but she had restrained herself thus far since she came back from Moncas Bay early that morning.

She had gone down to attend her parents' fortieth wedding anniversary celebrations, something she had enjoyed very much. It was nice to have the family together. If only Cecily could have disappeared into thin air for the duration of the meal, it would have been perfect. Cecily's voice was music to her own ears but unfortunately to no one else's. She had been in one of her animated humours as distinct from her moody Great Garbo act and when she started rabbiting on about the new leather jacket that Simon had spent a fortune on for her wedding anniversary, Lainey switched off. The girl was *so* boring. Obviously leather was the "in" thing to be seen in in Moncas Bay this season, Lainey surmised in amusement. She had seen Helena McGrath swanning around the foyer of Fourwinds in a brown leather skirt with a chocolate-coloured

sweater with leather and beaded appliqué that had obviously
cost a fortune but that looked positively woeful. Helena was
certainly relishing her role as lady of the manor. She positively
gushed as she ushered them to seats by the roaring log fire in
the lounge and said that their aperitifs were on the house. As
they waited for their table, Lainey surveyed the hotel. Steve
really had the place beautifully decorated. It was rumoured
that he had hired an interior designer from London who had
charged an astronomical amount. Still, it was money well
spent, Lainey thought approvingly. The hotel, though plush,
had an understated air of elegant affluence. But then Steve
had always had good taste . . . until he married Helena. She
couldn't help the bitchy thought and sighed, annoyed with
herself. What did she care! She was doing extremely well
without him, thank you very much.

It was Simon and Cecily who had insisted on having the
meal in Fourwinds. Lainey's parents would have been quite
happy to go to the Arklow Bay Hotel had it been left to them,
but Simon had pooh-poohed the idea. If they were having a
celebration it had to be done in style. Lainey had made no
objection, knowing that this was exactly what Cecily wanted
her to do. She was never quite sure whether Steve had broken
Lainey's heart or vice versa and was determined to find out.
Lainey was equally determined that she could go to her death-
bed wondering! The prying little madame. "Any news?" she'd
always ask coyly whenever Lainey arrived home on a visit.
Neither could Cecily fathom Lainey's relationship with Tony.
And Tony, who was an extremely handsome guy in the Tom
Selleck mould, would always lavish attention on Lainey when
he was in Cecily's company. This always infuriated Cecily as
she liked to be the centre of attention.

"She'd turn any man gay!" Tony had groaned one evening
after two hours of Cecily blowing her trumpet about the great
career in law she had given up to marry Simon and live in
Moncas Bay. Tony had immediately launched into a glowing
description of Lainey's high-powered career and how she was
the talk of the publishing trade. Cecily, slit eyed with jeal-

ousy, had been raging while Lainey, knowing perfectly well that Tony was only winding her sister-in-law up, struggled to hide her amusement. It was a pity Tony couldn't have made it tonight—he would have enjoyed himself immensely. Especially now that her sister-in-law had started on about darling Andrew, the baby son who had nearly killed her trying to come into the world.

Fortunately Lainey had been nowhere near her sister-in-law during her confinement. From what Joan had told her it was high drama and trauma all the way. "She started screaming with the first twinge of labour; I unfortunately happened to be there," Joan informed her sister. " 'Mummy! Mummy! Mummy!' It was hilarious. Mummy was down from Dublin, and had been for the previous two months. No wonder Cecily is the way she is. Mummy thinks the sun, moon, and stars shine out of Cecily's arse and she wouldn't allow her to lift a finger. Not, mind, that she had been doing much beforehand. Anyway Mummy started getting hysterical herself and then Simon started panicking so I just piled them all into the car and drove to the hospital because Cecily was holding Simon's hand on one side and her mother's on the other and wouldn't let go, so he couldn't drive even if he had been capable of it. But he was totally rattled at this stage. He's not going to live to fifty, I'm telling you. It's a wonder he hasn't had a heart attack yet." Lainey felt a twinge of sympathy for her elder brother. What on earth had possessed him to marry Cecily. She was such a demanding person that he rarely got a word in. As long as he did what Cecily wanted, everything was fine. Otherwise forget it. Simon didn't smile much any more. Life always seemed one big hassle and he was only thirty-five!

"She's something else!" Lainey agreed. "I'm glad I missed it all."

"She could be heard screeching all over the hospital. It was mortifying," Joan said in disgust. "Then Mummy fainted!" The two of them burst out laughing. "They got caterers in for the christening, you know!"

"You're not serious!" Lainey had missed the event because

she had to go to a sales conference. "That's one up on Helena and Steve."

"Exactly," smirked Joan doing a good impression of her sister-in-law.

"I was so worried that we wouldn't bond after the trauma I had been through . . ." Cecily was explaining to one of the aunts and Lainey, catching her mother's eye, hid a smile. Her parents were in great form, enjoying having the family around them and Lainey was enjoying herself until she saw Steve appear in her line of vision. He strode over to their table.

"Good evening, Mr. and Mrs. Conroy. Are you enjoying your meal? Is everything all right for you?" he inquired suavely. Lainey, aware that Cecily was watching her closely, tried to keep her face expressionless. He looked so handsome! He got better looking as he got older. Then he was looking at her with those dark-lashed heavy-lidded eyes, smiling at her the way he used to.

"Lainey, it's good to see you."

"Hello, Steve," she said calmly. He had no business smiling at her intimately like that, damn him! With perfect poise, she extracted an Yves Saint Laurent menthol cigarette from its distinctive black box and lit up. Sitting back in her chair she exhaled the smoke in a long thin stream as her former lover looked at her admiringly.

"You look terrific. Is the job going well?" he asked.

"Marvellous, thank you. I travel a lot," Lainey said coolly. What the hell was he annoying her for in front of her entire family. Couldn't he just go and let them have their meal in peace?

"We're lucky she could manage to squeeze us in this weekend," Cecily remarked acidly. "She couldn't manage to get to Andrew's christening last year," she added. She had been furious at Lainey's not showing up at the event of events. Lainey drew on her long elegant cigarette and smiled serenely at her sister-in-law.

"That was unfortunate," she conceded. "But you have to admit I do make an effort to come home for the really important occasions." Ha ha, she thought as she watched Cecily fume. If the other girl was going to be a bitch, Lainey could be just as bitchy. No better woman. She wasn't going to sit there and take Madame's impudence.

"Well, any time you get home it's always nice to see you. Enjoy your meal," Steve said smoothly, as he smiled down at Lainey in amusement.

"Thank you. We will." She did not smile back. Let him go and be charming to someone else. She was damned if she was going to give him any encouragement. If he thought she was going to be all palsy-walsy after all this time he could think again. He had made his choice and she was not it. Forgive and forget was just not Lainey. No Christian martyr she to turn the other cheek. Steve had done the dirty on her and that was that as far as she was concerned. He'd never get the chance to do it again. It might not be the best attitude to have in life, but it was the best she could do.

The following day, she decided to go for a walk along the beach. It was just what she needed to blow away the cobwebs. Meeting Steve had unsettled her and she was annoyed with herself. You'd think after all this time she would be well and truly over him. How irritating to be reminded that he still held an attraction for her. "Come on, Max," she yelled at the mongrel who came yapping down the stairs in an ecstasy of delight as he saw his mistress wrapping herself up in a pale pink anorak and a grey cashmere scarf to match her grey cords. It was a wild blustery day and the waves pounded along the shore. Lainey inhaled deeply with pleasure. The tang of salty seaweed hung strong on the breeze. It was the smell of home and she loved it. The beach was almost deserted apart from a few hardy souls like herself. Well, she'd make the most of this Sunday afternoon walk because she probably wouldn't get back to Moncas Bay for a while. Life was going to be busy in the next few months. Verdon had a lot of new books coming out and she had a lot of marketing to do. Loosening her blond hair from its chignon she let it loose, enjoying the feel of the wind blowing through it. It had been nice to get home for the few days' break and her mother had been fussing over her, cooking her favourite steak and kidney pie and treating her like a queen. Her dad, extremely proud of how well she was doing in her job, had told her with pride that two of Verdon's books were currently riding high in the best-seller lists. He always kept an eye on them, he assured her. Apart from darling Cecily and Steve, it had been a lovely few days. She hadn't gone out socialising as she would have if Tony had been there. She had just stayed at home and enjoyed her family.

"Max, you idiot!" she laughed at the dog who was dragging a piece of driftwood nearly as big as himself towards her.

They walked a couple of miles before she decided to turn back. The sun was beginning to set and she was starving and she knew that her mother had made a cheese and bacon pie for the tea. Lainey always ate like a horse when she came home. As the pier got nearer and nearer she saw a car drive up and a man and a dog get out. Lainey smiled to herself. She had taken her walk, Max had been well exercised and now she was going home to tuck into her tea. She kept on walking and as the man got nearer to her in the twilight, her heart sank as she recognised Steve. Why him, of all people?

"Hi, Lainey!" He stopped to acknowledge her as their two dogs sniffed around each other. His was a purebred cocker spaniel.

"Hello, Steve," she said politely.

"Great minds think alike!" he observed as the two dogs ran up into the dunes and back down again.

"Fools seldom differ," Lainey retorted. If she got her hands on Max she'd kill him for consorting with the enemy like that.

Steve frowned at her tone. "Don't be so brittle, Lainey. It doesn't suit you," he reproved her with a hint of anger. "Can't we at least be friends?"

*Friends!* she wanted to shriek. You don't know the meaning of the word. But she restrained herself. She'd die before she let him know how she felt. How the sight of him in his cream trenchcoat had set her heart and pulse racing.

"Sure," she said in a cool offhand tone. "Let's be friends by all means. Max! Max!" she called the dog to heel. If he felt like standing chitchatting on the beach, she didn't.

"Bye, Steve," she said crisply, beginning to walk away.

"Lainey!" Steve caught her arm and turned her back to face him.

"Let go of my arm, Steve," she snapped icily.

"There's still something there! Isn't there?" he demanded. "I can feel it, sense it!"

Lainey stared up into his hard angry eyes. "What I felt for you died a long time ago, Steve, so don't kid yourself," she said scornfully.

"Liar! I know you better than you know yourself, Lainey. Why haven't you married Tony Mangan yet?"

"That is none of your business, Steve McGrath, but I *will* tell you one thing, you'll never be half the man Tony is. Now let go of my arm."

Steve glared down at her. The last rays of sunlight had disappeared and dusk enfolded them. Before she realised what he was doing he had bent his head and was kissing her hotly, passionately. "Now tell me there's nothing there," he said grimly as they stared at each other in the dark. "Because I can't get you out of my mind. I want you, damn it, more than I've ever wanted you and every time I see you it gets worse."

"Are you proposing we have an affair?" Lainey asked, stunned.

"Yes! If you want one," Steve said eagerly bending his head towards her again. Lainey pushed him away angrily.

"You're a beauty, Steve, a real beauty. You really want to have your cake and eat it! What's wrong? Is Helena making you keep to your own side of the bed? All you want is sex! That's all you ever wanted from me but I loved you too much to see it. Well I don't love you anymore, so tough fromage, Steve. You can buy sex any night you like down on the quays, that's if any of those unfortunate ladies would touch a creep like you!" She left him standing staring after her as she walked, head held high, towards the steps leading to the pier.

What a bastard! An arrogant selfish bastard! she raged. Did he think she would come running when he snapped his fingers. Just because he said he wanted her? Big deal! Well, he didn't know her half as well as he thought he did. If he went down on his bended knees and begged her, if he offered to divorce Helena to marry her, she wouldn't have him back. Helena had got what she deserved in Steve McGrath, she thought bitterly.

The encounter disturbed her and ruined her little holiday and she drove back to Dublin the next morning totally pissed off. When she got to work and found that Patrick Nolan had suffered a serious stroke the previous night she was utterly shocked. Then Dominic rang and asked her to go for a drink that night but she couldn't face the thought of going out. After she put the phone down and burst into tears she decided to have a bath and an early night. God knows what was going to happen at work. She'd need her wits about her, she reasoned. She was just pouring herself a cup of coffee before she went to bed when the doorbell rang and she heard Dominic's deep voice on the intercom.

"I was a bit worried!" he explained as she opened the door a few minutes later to find him standing smiling at her. "You didn't sound a bit like yourself. Is anything the matter?"

"No . . . yes . . . I don't know." To her dismay two big tears rolled down her cheeks.

"Ah, now!" he exclaimed putting a comforting arm around her as he closed the door behind him. "What's the problem?" he asked as she sobbed into his black overcoat.

"Everything!" she wept. "Every damn bloody thing!"

"Tell me about it then," he said comfortingly as he put his arms around her and let her cry.

She told him then about Steve and how confused she was and, as if that wasn't enough, about Patrick's stroke and the problems that was going to cause. He didn't say much, just asked a few pertinent questions and let her pour it all out of her.

"I'm awfully sorry, Dominic. I don't usually go around bawling my eyes out and telling all my deep dark secrets," she apologised a little later. "It must be PMS."

"I'm an expert on PMS," he said lightly. "My wife suffers from it, and so, therefore, do I."

Lainey laughed. Dominic was terribly nice and she felt quite at ease in his company. He made her fresh coffee and talked with her a while and promised when he was leaving to ring her the next day to see how she was and how things were. It was a promise he kept. He rang her often after that and they began to see each other much more regularly, at least once a week when he was up in Dublin. They found great companionship in each other. And as he confided in her more, Lainey realised that he was quite a lonely man despite having a wife and four children. As the situation at work deteriorated and more pressure was put on her because of Patrick's stroke, she began to depend upon him much more. He was always there for her and it was only when she hadn't seen him for six weeks that she realised just how much Dominic Kent was coming to mean to her. She had been in England, Scotland, and Wales for three weeks, doing a marketing blitz and when she got back, he was on holidays in the West with his family.

When he rang her to tell her he was back in Dublin for a few days she was delighted. She had so much to tell him, all about what was going on in Verdon, and she was really looking forward to seeing him. They arranged to meet at the gates of Stephen's Green before going somewhere for dinner. His whole face lit up when he saw her and she hugged him warmly. "It's good to see you," he said.

"I missed you," Lainey confessed. And it was true! She had missed him. They smiled at each other in the late afternoon sun and then as though it was the most natural thing in the world they kissed, a warm companionable loving kiss that made her feel utterly cherished. It was then that Lainey fell in love with Dominic Kent and he with her.

They agonised over whether they should part. They tried it for a while but they missed each other so much that it was impossible. They tried to keep the relationship platonic, the way it had been. But it had changed and they had to face it. How ironic, thought Lainey, as she wrestled with her conscience. She had felt nothing but disgust for Steve when he had told her he wanted to have an affair with her and here she was contemplating taking such a step herself. Still there was a hell of a lot more to the relationship she had with Dominic than sex.

"Everybody deserves some happiness, Lainey. Take what's on offer," Tony advised nonjudgmentally. Tony liked Dominic. They got on well, and the older man had no problems with the fact that he was gay. It was obvious to Tony that Lainey and Dominic cared deeply about each other.

If she had thought for one moment that Dominic was deceiving her about his relationship with his wife, she would have finished with him long before this. But in all the time she had known him, and even before they had fallen in love, it was obvious that Rita Kent's priorities did not include her husband, whether intentionally or unintentionally. It was this more than anything that made Lainey decide to continue the relationship with Dominic. And as she lay watching him sleeping after the first time they made love, she did not regret it. With Dominic it had been much much more than sex. Lainey had felt truly loved. As he pulled her close and sleepily kissed her she felt a lovely moment of happiness before she, too, fell asleep.

Wednesday, May 8, 1985

"Peter, I've had enough. I quit! If I had a thing dangling between my legs I'd never have been treated like this. You just can't stomach a woman telling you where you're going wrong. Well, let Damien do the job and make a balls of it. I couldn't care less. I have three weeks' leave left—you can take that as my notice." Lainey glared at her boss, flung her letter of resignation on his black ash desk and marched from the office. She was furious and she wanted out of Verdon Books Publishing Company, Ltd.

It didn't take long for her to clear out her bright roomy office. Lainey was a neat and organised person and her office reflected that. If only Patrick Nolan hadn't died last year after another stroke. Patrick loved books and the book trade, just like she did, and they had made a great team. But Peter, his son, had taken over the running of the company on his father's death and all he was interested in was cost cutting and making a profit.

That was all very well, but some costs paid dividends that were not easily reflected in the financial director's annual accounts statement. About six months after he took over, Peter called her in to his office and presented her with her last expenses sheet.

"Lainey," he said smoothly, looking out at her over his bifocals, "there are some fairly hefty expenses here. Perhaps you would run through the list with me to give me an idea of what company money is being spent on." She was flabbergasted! And then angry. Patrick had never questioned her expenses. He had trusted her implicitly and left her to do her job. She didn't let her anger show. Maybe Peter was just curious as to what the money was spent on. Well, she'd give him the benefit of the doubt this time. Politely she explained her expenses to him. Overnight stays. Dinners with wholesalers, retailers, authors, journalists. Petrol. Christmas gifts . . .

"What kind of Christmas gifts?" he interrupted her.

Lainey arched a perfectly shaped eyebrow at his tone. "Champagne. Whiskey. Brandy," she said coolly. His attitude left a lot to be desired. He was beginning to make her feel as though she was personally benefiting in some way herself from her expense account.

"Who gets champagne, for heaven's sake?" he queried testily.

"We always send our top-selling author a crate of Bollinger and some of our biggest wholesalers get one too. After all, Peter, if it wasn't for them, you or I wouldn't be sitting here," she retorted tartly.

"What's this bill from a travel agent?" He pointed a stubby finger at the offending amount.

"As you know, Michelle Powell completed *Career Girls* for us in six months, no mean feat for a six-hundred-page blockbuster, and it's walking off the shelves, just like her other one. And she had been approached by two other publishers but decided to remain with us. Patrick said before he died that he'd like to send her off on holidays as a little treat and I arranged it!" Lainey said icily. "And believe me, it paid off. She's halfway through her next novel as you heard at Friday's meeting."

"Typical of Dad!" muttered Peter. "What's this?"

Lainey stood up and looked at her watch pointedly. "I'm sorry, Peter. I've a meeting in town with the PR firm to discuss the publicity for Miriam Daily's new book and I'm meeting her first to sort a few things out for the press release. I'll be back later this afternoon if you wish to continue"—his cross-examination, she was sorely tempted to say.

"Yes, well, I think in future you'd better stick to a monthly budget. Then we'll know where we stand. I'll talk to the accountant about it. And I don't think we'll be sending any more authors on holidays." Peter puffed on a cigar and glared at her.

"Fine!" she snapped, "but if you don't look after your authors, don't be surprised if they move elsewhere. And it's not I who will be affected if my expense account is cut, but don't expect wholesalers and retailers to be quite so supportive. It's all part of the game, Peter. And treating these people properly pays dividends. Patrick understood that."

"Thank you, Lainey, I don't need a lecture on how to run the business."

"Well, Peter, as long as I'm sales and marketing manager for Verdon and as long as it's my department that's been targeted for cutbacks, I intend to give you my views, however unpalatable they may be."

"By the way," Peter raised his voice just as she was about to leave. "I'll be sending Damien to the London Book Fair from now on. It will be good experience for him. I'm sure you won't mind."

"Not in the slightest," Lainey said dryly, although she was absolutely furious. So Boy Wonder was off to London! The sneaky little scut. Ever since Peter had recruited Damien Lawson as administrative assistant, he had been poking his ski slope of a nose into her department, trying to muscle in. Obviously he was succeeding, she sighed, as she collected her briefcase and strode out of the office. "I'll be back by three," she told Margaret, her secretary.

Whereas once she couldn't wait to get in to work, she was finding it harder and harder to motivate herself and muster up any enthusiasm these days, she reflected glumly, as she drove around Stephen's Green looking for a parking place. Peter couldn't see beyond his nose, and in the conservative financial director he had an ally. No doubt smarmy Lawson was agreeing with everything they said. Maybe it was time to think of going somewhere else! she thought, faintly depressed. She had put a hell of a lot of work into Verdon Books. She had built up a great relationship with wholesalers and retailers and authors and artists and she had got an immense amount of job satisfaction. But if things carried on like this she didn't think she could handle it. To watch all her good work going down the Swannee because of unnecessary penny-pinching would be too hard to swallow. She must start keeping an eye out in *The Bookseller* to see what jobs were going, she decided, as she parked opposite the Shelbourne, which was really handy because she was meeting Miriam Daily in the Horseshoe Bar. Defiantly she ordered champagne for the author and toasted her success.

Lainey lasted another six months with Verdon, watching her publicity budget being slashed, watching Damien edging his way into her area with Peter's tacit approval. Not only did he go to the London Book Fair, he went to Frankfurt as well, and the last straw came when he took over the launching of Michelle Powell's latest blockbuster, something that Lainey had always taken care of with great flair. "It's as much an administrative function as a marketing function and I think Damien is showing great aptitude and initiative as well as keeping costs down," Peter had remarked snidely. Michelle's launch had been a disaster. Cheap wine, a few savoury snacks, a couple of balloons on the ceiling of the hotel room, and the people had started drifting off once they saw things were not going to improve. It had been tacky and tawdry and Lainey had been mortified, especially as a few people who thought that she was responsible had remarked to her that it hadn't been as good as other Verdon launches. Michelle had been terribly put out and Lainey couldn't blame her.

"It was dreadful," she told Peter angrily first thing the following morning.

"I didn't think so and we saved a fortune. Lainey, your launches are much too lavish. In fact I'm turning responsibility for all further launches over to Damien from now on, if you don't mind."

They eyeballed each other and finally Peter looked away. Silently Lainey left his office and went down to her own where she typed out her resignation on her shocked secretary's typewriter.

"What are you going to do?" Margaret asked in concern.

"I don't know yet. But I can't stick this," Lainey fumed.

"Me neither," muttered Margaret miserably. Lainey felt a pang. She'd miss Margaret. They had been a team since she had started to work for Verdon. And she'd miss her authors. She'd have to ring around and tell people she was leaving. After she presented a silent Peter with her resignation she tidied out her office and spent the rest of the day on the phone telling people of her decision. Without exception they were shocked, especially some of the authors she had been working closely with. They were even more shocked when they heard that Damien would be taking over her position as sales and marketing manager. "Not that little puke!" Miriam Daily howled in dismay when Lainey told her the news. "Oh, Lainey, please don't go. I couldn't work with him."

"I'm really sorry, Miriam," Lainey said regretfully. She liked the writer, who was a terrible panicker when she dried up and who would spend hours moaning about the pressure she was under. But she was a very successful author for them and Lainey had cosseted her through her last three books. Miriam wouldn't get much cosseting from Damien, Lainey reflected, and it would be interesting in a year's time to see how many authors had left the Verdon stable.

She went home that night by taxi, as she had to leave the company car behind her. For the first time, Lainey realised what she had done. She had no job, no car, and rent to pay. Fortunately she had a fairly healthy bank account so the wolf wouldn't be at the door for a while; and she'd get her tax back. She didn't know how she felt, she decided, as she sat curled up in her huge cane chair flicking idly through a few recent copies of *The Bookseller*. She was sorry to have left Verdon the way she had. It had been great working for Patrick but Peter was another kettle of fish and she could see that the company was slipping even in the short time that he had been in charge. Restlessly she got up and paced around. It was a pity Dominic wasn't there. At least she could talk it all out with him. She longed to ring him and tell him the story but she would never ring him at home.

It took her a while to fall asleep but after a few hours of tossing and turning she finally dropped off. The ring of the phone woke her and sleepily she stretched out a hand and picked up the receiver. Who the hell could be ringing at this hour of the night? She hoped there was nothing wrong at home. Unless it was Cecily making another one of her silent phone calls! Soon after Lainey had moved into the apartment in Monkstown she had started getting silent phone calls. She had an unlisted number so it had to be someone who knew her, she thought grimly after the third such call in a week. But why had they started now? And who would she have given her number to? Racking her brains it dawned on her that only the previous weekend when she had been home she had given her new number to Simon, in Cecily's presence. It couldn't be Simon and even Cecily couldn't be that pathetic. There was something disturbed about that kind of behaviour. But the calls had persisted and Lainey had had to get her number changed. She deliberately didn't give Simon and Cecily her new number for a couple of months and did not receive one call. Two weeks after giving Simon her new number, again in Cecily's presence, she started getting the calls again. Once she had dialled Cecily and Simon's number immediately after getting such a call. Cecily had picked the phone up on the first ring and when Lainey asked to speak to Simon, she had got so flustered she had started to stutter and stammer that he wasn't there and that she was just at that very moment going to ring "Mummy" in Dublin.

It was months before Lainey got another silent phone call but it didn't bother her anymore. If Cecily wanted to waste her money making silent phone calls for whatever weird reason she had, Lainey wasn't going to get upset by it. And she was damned if she was going to go to the expense of paying to get another new number.

It was a bit late even for Cecily, Lainey thought fuzzily as she picked up the receiver. "Hello," she murmured sleepily.

"I stood beside you today and smelt your fanny!" a man's voice said. For God's sake! thought Lainey furiously. She had been woken out of her hard-come-by sleep by a jerk making an obscene phone call. "Okay, so you're bloody Pinocchio! Bully for you!" Lainey snarled, slamming down the receiver and burrowing back under the bedclothes. A perfect end to a perfect day, she thought, thoroughly disgruntled.

## Saturday, September 10, 1988

Lainey sat in the minibus that was driving the flight crew to the compound in Jedda and yawned mightily. She was absolutely shattered as it had been a long and wearying flight from Manila. They had been flying a 747 and her zone in the first-class section had been full up and she had been kept going. She might be making a fortune in tax-free riyals as a stewardess with Eastern Gulf Airlines but she was working her butt off.

She clung on to her seat as the driver careered along, passing the Top Furniture store on Palestine Road. Then they were on the Corniche where the sunset was reflected in the marble-still waters of the Red Sea. It was the weekend and as usual hundreds had come to view the magnificent dusky pink and purple sunset. Sunsets were spectacular in the Middle East because of the light filtered through all the dusty particles and they always enthralled her. Lainey could see people resting against the metal and stone and marble sculptures as they viewed tonight's magnificent one. The wail of the muezzin rent the multicoloured sky as the call to prayer—a sound that she had grown so familiar with in her time in Jedda— told the faithful that it was time to pray to Allah. The driver honked at a driver edging in in front of the minibus. Travellers were exempt from stopping to pray but elsewhere the city came to a standstill. The minibus turned into Al-Suror Street and she could see white-robed figures hurrying towards the mosque.

Her uniform clung damply to her, her stomach and ankles were swollen from the long hours in flight. All she wanted to do was sleep. The heat was intense and smothering. At least the apartment she shared with three other stewardesses would be air-conditioned and cool. The traffic was bumper-to-bumper, horns beeping, angry drivers gesticulating. The rules of the road as she knew them did not apply here. Aggression was the thing! Beside her, Chloe, her French supervisor, nodded off to sleep. Lainey felt like doing the same. Ahead of her she could see cars stopped and she groaned. Not a bloody roadblock! That would delay them at least another half an hour. The minibus inched along. A sullen dark-eyed policeman boarded the bus, his gun swinging on his hip. Nudging Chloe in the ribs to wake her, Lainey got her papers ready for inspection. Roadblocks were a way of life here and she had got used to them.

The policeman gestured abruptly and she handed him her papers. He eyed her up and down and she stared determinedly ahead. Women really were treated like dirt in Arab countries. It was something Lainey would never get used to. Only the thought of the tax-free salary that was piling up nicely in her bank account kept her going. Another year or so of this and then she was getting out. The policeman handed her back her papers with a grunt and took those of the half-awake Chloe. Self-important little bastard! Lainey thought disdainfully. Just like that officious creep of a customs man it had been her misfortune to deal with when she had deplaned. After every flight that arrived in Saudi they had to go through crew customs. It was a real pain. It was bad enough having your luggage searched, bad enough that she couldn't wear the little gold crucifix that her mother had given her, bad enough that he had gone through her new *Woman's Own* magazine and ripped out pages which he had thought offensive, but when he held up a tampon and said, "What ees this?" Lainey wanted to strangle him with her bare hands. "Womanly things," she snapped.

"But what ees it for?" he persisted insolently. You know very well, you little prick, she almost hissed but had managed to restrain herself. No point in getting into a hassle. Management didn't like it and only last week one of the girls had been issued with a termination notice and been deported for being caught with a bottle of vodka. Stony-faced, she had stared at her interrogator until finally he had shoved everything back into her case and waved her on, muttering at her in Arabic.

Of the thirty that had started in her group only fifteen had stuck it out and Lainey was determined that only when she was good and ready to leave was she going to resign from Eastern Gulf Air—despite the insults and provocations and the stifling heat and dust and restrictions of life in Saudi. She had come here just three years ago to earn enough to buy a place of her own at home and she was well on target. She had planned to finish up and leave by Christmas but had been offered promotion to purser which was too good an opportunity to miss. Now, as second-in-command, working first class and making a mint in commission on the duty-free, she calculated that she could easily add another fifteen thousand to what she had already saved if she lived frugally. That would mean she'd have enough to buy a place and get a car as well. So one more year of hard work and hard saving and she'd be on the pig's back. It was a wonderful feeling having financial security. Never again would she be put through the anxiety she had experienced in the weeks that had followed her resignation from Verdon Books.

Lainey stared unseeingly out the dusty window of the minibus as the arching orange sodium lights of the freeway sped past and they headed for the compound. The first few days of her unemployment had been pleasant enough. It was delightful to linger in bed sleeping in as everybody else rushed out of the building and got into their cars or headed for bus stops and DART stations on their way to work. It was a joy to shower and slip into a tracksuit and watch morning TV while eating cornflakes and hot milk, a real treat. Usually Lainey grabbed a cup of coffee and breakfasted at her desk at work. The weather had been awful so she had been content to stay in, reading and watching TV and running up her phone bill. Dominic had come and played hookey from work and they had spent the entire day in bed. She had never made love in so many different ways. It had been glorious. But then he had had to go back to Cork and the weather improved and the walls started closing in on her and she had to get out.

It had been an awful shock to her system having to wait on buses again. She had been accustomed for so long to being her own boss and driving when and where she wanted to, and it was most unsettling to have a car no longer and to be at the tender mercy of the bus system. And the bus fares! Lainey had nearly fainted when she had handed the driver a pound and got a few pence change. Her electric and phone bill arrived, things she never normally gave a thought to, and she had paid them grudgingly, knowing that unless she got herself fixed up soon she'd have to eat into the money she had saved towards her mortgage. That was not the plan at all. It was such a pain. Here she was, having worked for ten years with nothing to show for it, no car, no house, damn all. True she had saved fifteen thousand which would get her a mortgage if she had a job but right now she hadn't got one and anyway she had wanted to try and save a bit more so she wouldn't have a big burden of a mortgage on her shoulders. Lots of her friends who had them were working just to pay the mortgage, and had precious little left after. It looked like London might have to be an option if she planned on staying in publishing. In her restless state the idea had seemed inviting. She had always wanted to travel and had enjoyed her foreign jaunts very much when she was with Verdon. Maybe a job abroad would be just the thing.

Dominic wasn't too thrilled when she broached the idea but as he said himself he had no say in the matter. Lainey was her own woman and she owed him nothing. If London was what she wanted then she should go for it. He was lovely like that. He never made any demands of her and he often told her to go out with other men, that it wasn't right that she should waste her life being with him if the chance for a good and happy marriage ever came along. Lainey told him she had no desire whatsoever to get married. She liked being independent. She had got used to living her life as she wanted and she had no broody maternal urges, so far anyway.

The day her last cheque from Verdon Books arrived in the post, she had ordered a taxi and hit Grafton Street and Dawson Street. A hair treatment in David Marshall's, a silk Armani blouse from Brown Thomas and lunch in Pasta Pasta soon put a sizeable dent in it. But what the hell! She deserved a little treat after what she'd had to put up with in the past few months. Cecily would go mad when she saw the Armani blouse. Her sister-in-law was so silly like that, always wanting what the other person had, always trying to keep up with the

Joneses. It was pathetic, really, and Simon was getting as bad as her. The last time she had been home, the carrying-on of them because they had got a woman "in" to help with Andrew, her little nephew, had been pitiful.

"It's so hard to get reliable staff these days!" Cecily declared.

"Indeed!" agreed Simon. "But we got a wonderful little woman in"—Lainey clenched her teeth—"a wonderful *little* woman." How condescending. Cecily was thrilled beyond belief. Apart from the fact that her wonderful little woman looked after Andrew, cleaned, washed and ironed and cooked an evening meal, Cecily was now on a par with Helena Mc-Grath who also had a "wonderful little woman." Lainey felt so sorry for her nephew. When he was a baby he had a Mother-care-decorated bedroom, with all up-to-date equipment, changing mats, playpen, mobiles, soft cuddly toys that matched the decor, and was dressed in his little Benetton romper suit. But Lainey had watched as Cecily tutted in disgust when he dribbled a biscuit on to his clothes. Now poor Andrew was growing up, fussed over by his parents, not allowed to get his good clothes dirty. He was being turned into a right little old man and it wasn't his fault at all, the poor child! When Lainey met them on their Sunday-afternoon "duty" visit to her parents, Andrew had told her solemnly that they had got a new maid. Cecily had cast a triumphant look in Lainey's direction as if to say, beat that! Then she described just how many people they had interviewed for the job and how hard it was to get someone just right.

"Just right for the measly pittance she's paying the poor woman," Joan whispered in the kitchen, where she and Lainey had escaped on the pretext of getting the tea. "She was only supposed to be minding Andrew originally but her ladyship has her doing the housework as well. A slave has nothing on poor Mrs. Maguire. And imagine having to put up with Cecily blowing all day! God help her, is all I say," Joan murmured as she buttered her mother's homemade brown bread.

Lainey sliced some cold chicken and ham. "I don't know

why I'm bothering. She'll sit there picking as if she's afraid she'll be poisoned."

"Would we be so lucky!" interrupted Joan with a grin as she snatched a slice of ham and munched on it.

"That's lovely!" Lainey said in mock disgust. "What a way to talk about your dear sister-in-law."

"Dear sister-in-law my hat!" expostulated Joan. "You're not constantly exposed to her like I am. Every blooming Sunday she's over acting the lady and wouldn't lift a finger to wash up. And that Simon fella is as bad, going around like Lord Muck. And you go over to their place and you wouldn't even be offered a cup of tea, let alone asked if you had a mouth on you. Then she might meet you in the shop, and if Helena's around Cecily wouldn't have a word to say to you, as if to let you know you're not lah-di-dah enough to move in their circles. You don't know the half of it, Lainey." Joan was angry now, banging the cups on the table as she set it. "And you know something else, Lainey? That Simon charged me for a filling. He let me off two measly quid! Big deal! It just sickened me. I can tell you one thing—I won't be going to him again. They're not going to swan around drinking champagne up in Fourwinds at my expense!" It was so unlike Joan to get angry. She was usually of such a cheery disposition and didn't let things get to her. Cecily and Simon were really getting her down and Lainey understood very well her sister's anger.

It was true. Lainey only saw them when she was on her occasional visits and Joan had to put up with a lot more than she did. And just who did Simon Conroy think he was, charging his sister for a filling? And just exactly *who* did Madam Cecily think she was, putting herself above Joan and treating her like dirt in public. What was she but a social-climbing little snob full of silly pretensions and the most self-centred person going? Who did she think she was kidding with her airs and graces? Lainey had been in the two-up two-down house in Dublin where Cecily was reared. And there was nothing in the world wrong with a two-up two-down, Lainey would be the first to admit. Their own house in Moncas Bay was nothing spectacular. But it was home and her family had nothing to be ashamed about. They were the equal of anybody in Moncas Bay, or anywhere else for that matter. And Cecily Clarke-Conroy needn't think she was impressing them with her carrying-on. The cheek of her! Lainey was just the woman to tell her so too! In fact she was going to have a word with Madam Cecily and Sir Simon right this minute, she decided furiously. Enough was enough. The pair of them needn't think they were going to get away with upsetting her sister.

Joan saw the look on Lainey's face and put out a restraining hand. "Where are you going?"

"I'm going to give that pair a piece of my mind. Just who do they think they are?" she said hotly. Lainey had a terrible temper when roused.

"Now calm down, Lainey!" Joan said hastily. "Don't cause a scene—that Cecily one is a troublemaker behind all her airs and graces. She'd fly off the handle if you started, you know what she's like!"

"I'd like to see her try!" Lainey was not to be mollified.

"Look, don't mind me moaning. I got my period today and I'm like an Antichrist," Joan explained. "Usually I couldn't care less about them. Please, Lainey, let it go, I have to live here—you don't. I was just getting it off my chest."

"Some day I'm going to tell that one *exactly* what I think of her," Lainey vowed.

"But not today?" Joan said anxiously.

"Not today," agreed Lainey, giving her beleaguered sister a hug.

"Phew!" exclaimed Joan in relief, wiping imaginary sweat from her brow. "The apocalypse has been averted for the time being. Lainey, you're something else when you're in a temper."

"I know," Lainey smiled sheepishly. It took a lot to get her going, but once it happened, the results could be awesome. "Mind," grinned Joan, "that lady won't know what's hit her if you ever let fly at her. Keep me a ringside seat."

"I've a good mind to put a laxative in her tea. That might clear some of the crap out of her," Lainey grumbled, as she arranged cucumber and tomatoes artistically around the plates of cold meat.

Sitting in Pasta Pasta, Lainey promised herself she'd give Joan a ring later to find out how she was. A few weeks after the episode, they had gone to Kinsale together for a long weekend and had a whale of a time, and Cecily and Simon hadn't been mentioned once. It had done Joan the world of good. When she got another job, they must do it again, she mused. She was just finishing a plate of delicious tagliatelle, wiping her plate with a piece of garlic bread when a familiar voice hailed her.

"Lord above, it's Lainey Conroy as I live and breathe."

Lainey looked up, startled, and her face broke into a broad grin. "Anne, how are you? You look sensational! What have you been doing with yourself?" It was her old friend from her library days and she was looking like a million dollars. Tanned, reed slim, dressed in a beautiful tailored suit, makeup impeccable, she looked as if she had just stepped out of a glossy magazine. "Are you coming or going?" Lainey demanded.

"I'm just going to have a quick bite. I've got to head off to the airport; I'm on standby for a flight to London. Can I sit here and you can tell me all the gossip." Lainey was delighted. She and Anne had always gotten on well because they shared the same sense of humour. Anne had left the libraries soon after Lainey and had gone to London. They had lost touch so it was really great to have the chance of catching up on the news.

"What are you doing? You look so well! Is that an engagement ring?" Lainey demanded as the waitress brought her a cup of coffee and took Anne's order. Anne laughed.

"To answer your last question first, No! this is not an engagement ring. There's enough people making idiots of themselves, thank you very much, without me adding to them. And I'm air hostessing for Saudia Airlines. I applied for the job in London three years ago and I'll do it for another few years. It's a fantastic way of seeing the world and I'm even saving money—and that's something for me to say." She laughed. Lainey smiled back, remembering how broke her friend always was when she worked for the corporation. "I'm based in London now so I actually live here in Dublin and commute. I'm flying over to London today and working on a flight to Jedda tomorrow. It's as cheap to commute as to rent accommodation in London. What are you doing?"

"Nothing at the moment!" Lainey said ruefully, and went on to tell her of her resignation from Verdon Books.

"Aw, that's a shame!" exclaimed Anne. "I know you loved it there."

"When Patrick was running the company it was great, but Peter hasn't a clue," Lainey said with a sigh.

"What are you going to do now?" Anne asked as she devoured a plateful of spaghetti bolognaise.

"I might go to London myself and see what's happening in the book trade over there."

"You could always go back to your permanent and pensionable job in the libraries." Anne's eyes were twinkling.

"No, thank you!" retorted Lainey in amusement. "Anyway things are so bad there. The cutbacks have really decimated them; there's an embargo on recruitment and the service is really being degraded. Marion Matthews, you remember her?" Lainey quirked an eyebrow at Anne who nodded, unable to talk as she forked spaghetti into her mouth. "Well, she was telling me they're even talking of shortening hours and making branches like Finglas and Drumcondra and Pembroke part-time! Isn't that woeful! She said they're run off their feet and no one's complaining. The public moan to them but won't bother to complain to their public representatives. I think we got out just in time."

"I think you're right. That sounds pretty grim. Although I must say I really enjoyed the fun when I worked there. I wonder did Mellory O'Neill ever manage to persuade 'gold medallions' to marry her?" Anne asked.

Lainey giggled. "Don't be so nasty. You haven't changed a bit."

Anne grinned. "Well, he was an awful dose so they were well matched. Do you remember how mad she was when Mariette Donohoe got engaged to Declan Brennan. 'I might have got my promotion but she's got her man,' she said one day at the desk. It's bad enough thinking like that, Lainey, but imagine saying it in public. I couldn't believe my ears!"

"You're joking! I never heard that," exclaimed Lainey, agog at this little tidbit of gossip.

"As sure as I'm sitting here," Anne assured her. "And she always pretends she's such a career girl. If he asked her to marry him she'd say yes so fast it would be indecent. And she wouldn't stay in the corpo either, for all her guff about getting to the top of her tree, as she used to put it. That one's as two-faced as they come."

"Yeah!" agreed Lainey of her one-time boss. "Remember how she used to do the real holier-than-thou bit at the staff meetings, telling us to keep up standards and how being late for work was as bad as stealing from the corporation. And that we were to remember that we were officers of the corporation and conduct ourselves as such. And then she'd be in making sneaky long distance calls to Manchester and down the country, and by God they never went down on the phone sheet. The old hypocrite!"

Anne guffawed. "Remember how we used to all stand at the desk, counting the clicks of the dial when she was ringing from the office and we always knew when she was making one of her 'illegals.' I wonder did she ever cop on that we all knew about her Wednesday-afternoon phone calls. We were bitches, weren't we?"

"Still are," Lainey said, grinning. "Did you know Lindsay Johnson got a big job in London? She was ever so impressed with herself. But then, of course, she always thought she was *it.*"

"Really!" Anne devoured this little snippet with relish. She and Lindsay had never got on. "Imagine her even going to the trouble of filling out an application form!" she remarked caustically. "I think she was the laziest one of them I ever worked with. She and her posters. She spent the day doodling and making out impressive reports that no one ever read. Remember all the time in lieu she used to take? She took more time in lieu than she ever worked. She really used to hog the office, didn't she?"

"She sure did," agreed Lainey who was thoroughly enjoying herself. There was something so immensely satisfying about a good juicy gossip with someone you hadn't seen for ages. Men couldn't possibly understand the pleasure women got from it. Catching up on the news was as good as going on a spending spree.

"Do you remember," Anne said with a laugh, "the time Anita Andrews was in charge and she was going on a date and wanted to go home and shower and change and she wanted to leave work an hour early. So she decided she'd pretend she was sick with diarrhea and she put on such an act that Lena Connolly felt sorry for her and made her some hot milk and pepper and she had to drink it."

Lainey shrieked with laughter at the memory. "And now look at her. I believe she nearly breaks her neck to get in to the office to draw the line at nine-forty. She's supposed to be a demon for giving lates." They chatted away until Anne had to leave, enjoying themselves hugely. Their gossip was interrupted by many a good laugh and when they parted they exchanged phone numbers, promising to meet up again.

In fact, a week later, Anne rang Lainey from London to tell her excitedly that Eastern Gulf Airlines were recruiting staff, and would she not give it a try. The conditions were excellent. The salary was tax free. The accommodation in Jedda was free if she was based there; otherwise she would get an accommodation allowance. All she'd have to pay for was her food, and anyway you ate free on the aircraft when you were working, so that wasn't a huge expense. The social life was terrific. Even though Anne was working for Saudia Airlines they'd still be able to meet up on stopovers and they'd have a ball. "Come on over," her friend urged. "You can stay in my friend's place and give it a try."

A month later Lainey was on a training course in Jedda in preparation for becoming a stewardess with Eastern Gulf Airlines. It was a six-week course. She shared an apartment with three other girls on a compound the size of a small town. It was a spacious apartment with two bedrooms, two bathrooms, kitchen, and living room. It was cleaned each day by a little Filipino maid called Scarlett. All the Filipino girls had names straight out of American TV. There were Crystals and Graces and Bettes; it was amazing. They were overworked, underpaid, and very badly exploited. Lainey always made her own bed and kept her belongings tidy, but it was sickening how some of the girls wouldn't even pick their dirty uniforms off the floor once they knew they had a maid to do it for them. It was far from maids they were raised. Cecily would love it out here, Lainey had written to Joan.

It was a completely different culture, one where women were very definitely second-class citizens. Once off the compound Lainey and all the other women had to dress with extreme modesty, wearing the abaya, the black cloak that covered them from head to toe. They could not be driven by a man other than their husbands and Lainey had been told of unmarried girls who were caught by the Muttawaah, the Saudi religious police, driving in the company of their male colleagues and they had been jailed, and then deported with the word "Prostitute" stamped across their passports. "Just be careful!" Anne had warned her. "And for God's sake whatever you do, don't stop to help at the scene of an accident. If the person dies you could be held responsible."

Of course they had been told all this at their orientation course in London, but to experience it all was something else.

The three b's ruled the expatriates' lives. No booze, bacon or broads. And no Marks and Spencer's products either. The Saudis were fanatically anti-Jewish like all the rest of the

Arabs out there and anyone with an Israeli stamp on their passport would not be allowed to enter the country. Lainey thought it was all pretty pathetic. She couldn't understand religious bigotry in any shape or form. What matter if you were Protestant or Catholic, Arab or Jew? Surely it was the kind of person you were that mattered, not what your beliefs were, or your sexual orientation for that matter. Tony had thrown up his hands in horror when he had heard what she was planning to do.

"No booze, Lainey! You'll never survive!" he exclaimed in horror.

"The cheek of you," she laughed. "You make me sound like a hardened alcoholic."

In fact the three b's might as well not have existed for all the notice that was taken of them on her compound. Practically everybody was an expert on home brew. Lainey had drunk some mighty potent concoctions at some of the parties she had been to. There were all manner of intrigues and affairs and she had even tasted bacon smuggled in by a stewardess under her abaya on a flight from London.

The training was demanding. They arose each morning at six, had breakfast, caught the seven-thirty bus to the training centre and finished around four. Then Lainey would lie at the pool for a couple of hours before doing a bit of study, or heading off to a party. The first three weeks had been in-flight service training, the last three weeks safety training. The customer was always right, they were told. Don't argue with the passengers! She spent her evenings practising with her colleagues in the confines of their living room. "*Shai/gahwa.*" The Arabic for tea or coffee became imprinted on her brain. Fortunately for Lainey she had always taken great care with her appearance. She was always well made-up and well groomed. The grooming checks were rigorous. She had seen girls given a grooming slip for a single chipped varnished nail. Too many grooming slips and you were called up and smartly told to get your act together or else. Lipstick had to match nail varnish. A ponytail could be six inches in length and no longer. Tights had to be a certain colour. Weight no more than 143 pounds. They were very strict. It wasn't a huge problem to Lainey, though many of the girls found it tough going.

Her first flight was to Kano in Nigeria. She was flying a jumbo. Her zone was full, she was kept going on the five-hour flight, and she didn't have time to be nervous. She soon got into the swing of things, bidding for her lines to take her all over the world. They would be given a sheet and could select the flight they'd like to be on. She stayed in five-star hotels in cities in every continent: the Singapore Meridian; the Gulf Meridian; the Holiday Inn in Madrid; the Soragaon in Bangladesh; the Sheratons; the Hiltons. Cecily was nearly apoplectic each time Lainey came home. She got home quite frequently and when, during her second year on the job, she was based in London she was home as often as when she had been in Dublin. Dominic was delighted when she was sent to London. He had really missed her, as she had missed him, and one of the delights of her homecoming, which she always tried to arrange for when he was in Dublin, was knowing that he would be there waiting for her. It was only in the last six months that she had been based again in Saudi and she'd had to get used to the heat and the lizards and the cockroaches and the invariable dust all over again.

Lainey had no intentions of staying a stewardess forever. She enjoyed the travel, enjoyed meeting people and was saving a lot of money, but in the end she wanted to go back to publishing. It had got into her blood, and she kept up with all the news and trends with subscriptions to *Books Ireland* and *The Bookseller*. Once she had the money to buy a place of her own she'd be back, she told Dominic with certainty when he was browned off at her having to leave London for Jedda.

He had bought himself a little apartment in a luxurious complex called Mountain View in Glasnevin and Lainey thought it was gorgeous. There was even a swimming pool in the complex and anytime she stayed over she always swam in it. Something like his place would suit her down to the ground, she had told him enviously. The one-bedroomed apartment had everything. A fabulous fitted kitchen. *En suite* bathroom. Small second bathroom. Huge living-cum-dining-room and, because he was on the ground floor, a lovely enclosed patio which looked out on the magnificent grounds. Dominic was very proud of it. It was his treat to himself, he told her, for all the years of slogging he had put in. His business was extremely successful and he felt he deserved more than just the room off his office that he had had for as long as she had known him. He had not told his wife about the apartment. That was his business, Lainey decided. Let him work it out his own way.

There was a letter from him when she finally got to the apartment in the compound, weary and suffering from aching feet. And one from home too. Oh, goody! she thought. Slipping out of her uniform, she sat down on the sofa and stretched. The apartment was cool and shaded, the air-conditioning on to the highest degree, the wooden slatted blinds drawn against the heat. None of the others that she shared with were home. They were all flying so she had the place to herself. She was beginning to get a headache and she'd no analgesic to nip it in the bud. Damn! she'd have to go down to the pharmacy. She wasn't getting into that uniform, she decided wearily. She'd just slip her abaya over her pale ivory silk camisole and briefs. It was handy in some ways, the abaya. It hid a multitude. She could be starkers and no one would know. It didn't take long and when she got back she decided she was hungry. She'd order a Chinese meal from the coffee shop which was open twenty-four hours a day and it would be delivered by a little Filipino boy on his three-wheeler bike. Lainey rang, placed her order, then went and got a basin of tepid water and plonked her aching feet in it. She wrinkled her nose at the smell and grinned. Once she had read a Mills & Boon novel in which the heroine had traipsed Rome, shopping with the hero. When they arrived at his villa he had begun to kiss her starting at her head and ending at her toes. This after a day on her feet! Well, if anyone attempted to kiss Lainey's feet right now, they'd expire. It never failed to amuse

Lainey watching the glossy soaps on TV just how immaculate
the heroines always were, always ready to be seduced, dressed
in freshly laundered underwear. Her La Perla lingerie was
sticking to her after her long flight and—wriggling her toes in
the water—she decided to have her shower before her Chinese arrived, so all she'd have to do then was eat her meal and
tumble into bed.

Ten minutes later, refreshed and dressed in a cool silk
nightdress, she was showered and relaxed and ready to eat.
Picking up her letters she read Dominic's first, lounging on
her bed. She smiled at his endearments as he wrote of how he
missed her and telling her the news about work and the
apartment and the like. Her mother's letter was full of news
too. Martin, Lainey's younger brother, had got engaged to
Maura and they wanted to know if she'd be free some time
next summer and to give them a date so they could arrange
the wedding. Lainey was delighted for her brother, and Maura
was sweet, a lovely girl altogether, the complete opposite to
Cecily in nature and temperament. Lainey looked forward to
having her as a sister-in-law. She smiled to herself. She'd keep
an eye out for something spectacular to wear. That was the
joy of travelling to the fashion capitals of Europe. She'd get
something nice for Joan and her mother as well. Give Cecily
something to annoy her. Yes, she was going to get Joan something exclusive and expensive. Something that Cecily couldn't
compete with, as no doubt she'd be determined to appear in a
designer label. Well, this time she wouldn't look down her
nose at Joan or her mother-in-law. The next time Lainey was
in Paris she was going to splurge. A Chanel suit for her
mother maybe. A Karl Lagerfeld creation for Joan and, her
own favourite, an Yves Saint Laurent for herself. It would cost
a mint but she didn't care. She'd saved really hard since she
got the job with the airline. If she couldn't treat her mother
and sister once in a blue moon, it was a poor lookout. And
Cecily, the silly snob, would be so put out. An added bonus.
Humming to herself, Lainey went to answer her doorbell and
pay for her dinner.

# Dominic

"Good night, Kimberly!"

" Good night, Kieran!"

"Good night, Mam!"

"Good night, Dad!"

"Good night, John Boy!"

"Go to sleep you pair!" Dominic admonished his two giggling youngest children as he switched off the light and put his arm around his wife. He hadn't slept in a single bed with Rita since he'd been a student, twenty-two years before. Imagine to think he was forty-one with four children. Where had the years gone?

"I hope to God Michael will be all right at home," Rita murmured drowsily from the crook of his shoulder.

"Why wouldn't he be all right? He's sixteen, big enough and bold enough to look after himself," Dominic assured her.

"He's probably having a party," Rita retorted.

Dominic laughed. "Michael's too lazy to go to the bother of having a party. He's probably sitting in front of the video with a few mates, eating chips."

"As long as he's not drinking," Rita said worriedly.

"Rita, will you stop worrying. I don't think Michael would drink behind our backs," Dominic reassured her.

Rita stretched, feeling cramped in the small confines of the bed. "No, I don't think he would," his wife agreed. "I hope Denise is okay."

Dominic sighed. "Denise is fine. She didn't want to come, she wanted to stay at Mona's and the way she's carrying on lately, it's just as well she didn't or there'd only be rows." His eldest daughter was going through a rebellious "I hate the family" phase and at fourteen, thought she knew it all.

"Ah, Dominic!" remonstrated Rita. "She's going through a difficult stage. Her hormones are awry."

"So are mine," he murmured, pressing close against her and nuzzling her earlobe.

"Dominic!!" Rita hissed in a shocked whisper, giving him a dig in the solar plexus. "The children!"

"Ouch! That hurt!" he whispered back indignantly. "They won't hear us. They're asleep. I'll close the door."

"Kieran might be afraid if he wakes up in a strange place. Leave it open and go to sleep, Dominic." Rita was not in the mood for fun and games.

So this was nothing new, Dominic thought discontentedly. There were times he felt as though he came a very poor second to his children. Were all marriages like this, he wondered in the dark as his wife began to snore softly. How did you keep the magic going in a marriage? Rita would never come away with him, being reluctant to leave the children for even the shortest period. Dominic loved his children and spent many happy hours with them. But he wasn't as completely engrossed in them as Rita was. He could contemplate a week's holiday away from them with equanimity. He didn't think he was in the slightest bit an unnatural father. He loved his children, he provided ably for them and would always be there for them. He didn't view their desire to become more independent of their parents as the disaster Rita did. It was the way of things. A week's holiday away from the kids would not cause major psychological trauma, he had assured his wife. But to no avail. "When they're older," she had been promising for the previous five years. At this rate, he'd be a geriatric before they ever got away.

Dominic shifted gingerly. He didn't want to wake Rita but his arm had got pins and needles from where she was lying on it. He should have insisted on going to a hotel but the kids had been all excited about sleeping in their sleeping bags on the floor of his new office.

He hoped he was doing the right thing opening the office in Dublin. Maybe he was overextending. But the business was definitely there—he knew that from the enquiries to his Cork office. He'd give it a bash for a year and see how it went. He'd leased this place for a year and if he didn't think things were going too well he wouldn't bother to renew it. Mind it was ideal and the rent wasn't bad. Fairview was an excellent location. Not far from the docks, less than ten minutes to the city centre. Plenty of shops and amenities. The sea and Bull Island within walking distance, and Fairview Park just across the road. It wasn't bad at all and he felt he was going to enjoy the few days a week he spent in Dublin. It was very handy too that there was living accommodation adjoining the office. Not much, but the room in which they were currently sleeping would do as a bedsit, with a small bathroom on the landing. It would suit him fine that he wouldn't have to go looking for accommodation.

That was why Rita and the two children had come up to Dublin with him, to do the place up and get him settled in. They had spent the day washing and scrubbing and unpacking bits and pieces and the place was quite homely now. Rita didn't really like Dublin. "It hasn't the class of Cork at all," she declared as they drove through the city streets to get to Fairview. Dominic liked it. He felt comfortable in its anonymity. And if he could build up a business here he could do it anywhere. He must arrange to interview a secretary, he decided sleepily, trying to find a comfortable position. Eventually he fell asleep.

## Friday, July 10, 1981

Humming to himself, Dominic patted some Old Spice after-shave lotion on his smooth jaw. It had been a recent birthday present from his younger daughter, Kimberly. Tonight, though, he didn't feel forty-two, he felt twenty-two. Mind he didn't look twenty-two, he thought ruefully, observing how grey he was at the temples. Still at least he hadn't gone jowly yet and he carried no extra weight.

What had got into him? Standing there admiring himself

like a fool. He was only going out for a friendly drink with a young woman whom he had got to know quite well since he had come to Dublin. "Lainey's almost young enough to be your daughter," he told himself sternly. Nevertheless he was looking forward, as always, to meeting her.

There was something about her that intrigued him. Despite her air of self-confidence, her classy elegance, her ambition to forge ahead in her career, there was a vulnerability behind it all that made him feel ridiculously protective. Even that very first time in Cork when he had helped her out by giving her the lift to the airport, he had sensed it about her. She had been so grateful for his help. They had chatted for ages afterwards and he had enjoyed very much talking to her. Lainey was an interesting young woman, clearly very involved in her career and, from what she had told him, Dominic could see that she was excellent at her job. He had found her easy to talk to and enjoyed telling her about his own career plans. He had been sorry to say good night to her, thinking that he would probably never see her again. Rita was tidying up after her Tupperware party and had only listened to him with half an ear as he told her of the events of the evening. Dominic felt his good humour fizzle away. He had spent the last three hours talking to a stranger who was more interested in what was happening to him than his own wife! It was enough to put a man in a bad humour.

When Rita informed him that she was planning a barbecue for Sunday lunch to which she had invited Mona and her gang, he went to bed in a foul humour. Christ! Could a man not get any peace in his own home! Mona had no control over her kids. They ran around like wild things, upstairs, downstairs, in, out, while she sat there moaning to Rita. Then his own crowd, seeing how their friends were getting away with it, would start, until Dominic would be unable to restrain himself any longer and let a roar out of him. Rita would glare at him, Mona would look hurt and reproachful, the kids would be quiet for five minutes or so and then they'd be off again. When he was growing up, his parents would have had a fit if he and his siblings had carried on like that. Going upstairs in someone else's house was a leg-battering offence and, by God, they had been reared to have manners. Nowadays people couldn't care less. Kids were let do what they liked with no respect for people or their property. Well, he didn't want his children growing up like that and he and Rita used to have some mighty big rows about what she perceived as his sternness. He just wanted his kids to have manners and respect. What the hell was wrong with that? Having to put up with Mona and her gang at a barbecue was not the way he wanted to spend his Sunday. He'd be better off in Dublin, he fumed, as he lay beside his sleeping, untroubled wife. And then the thought had struck him. He could drive up to the capital on the Sunday, instead of on the Monday, have a nice meal and a read of his Sunday papers and give that girl Lainey a lift as well. It would save her from going on the train.

Dominic had ended up enjoying his day immensely. Lainey had been delighted. The journey had seemed so short because of the company. She had invited him into her lovely little apartment in Monkstown for coffee, which he had enjoyed immensely. Then he had gone and had lunch in the Gresham, bought all the Sunday papers and gone out to Fairview and spent a lovely peaceful evening reading them. It had been one of the nicest Sundays he had spent in ages.

He had bumped into Lainey in the Country Club several times afterwards. He always entertained his clients there and when she was doing calls in Cork she always stayed there. When they both discovered that they were going to be in London at the same time on business they had been delighted and arranged to meet. They had spent a lovely few hours together and after that had got into the habit of meeting for a drink and going for a meal occasionally when he was working in Dublin. It was something to look forward to and he liked the company. Except for his business clients and Lainey, he never went anywhere. No night clubber he. The dubious delights of Leeson Street and the likes were not his scene.

Dominic was surprised that as glamorous and cosmopolitan a woman as Lainey would be interested in his company. He was sure she had men falling all over her. Then one night he rang her and realised that she was near to tears and went over to Monkstown to make sure that she was all right. She told him about that man Steve in Moncas Bay, who had married someone else, and he realised that there was no one else in her life.

That Steve was an awful fool to lose a woman like Lainey, Dominic decided, as he knotted his tie and put on his jacket. Whistling cheerfully, he drove into town to meet her as arranged.

## Monday, June 3, 1985

"Take care!" Dominic hugged Lainey tightly as he said good-bye before she flew out to Jedda. Although she was not going for a few days yet, she had to go down to Moncas Bay to say her good-byes to her family, who would be taking her to the airport.

He couldn't believe how shocked he had been when she had told him that she was going to Saudi Arabia to work. He was going to miss her like hell!

He had told himself over and over, from the very first time that they had become lovers, that he had no claim on her. He was a married man, she was young, single, and free. Just loving her and being with her was a bonus. But apart from that, forget it, he told himself.

Since they had become lovers on that wonderful magical night three years before, Dominic always expected Lainey to come and tell him that she was ending their affair, that she had met someone else. Someone more suitable than him, some eligible man! And so far, she never had. She seemed so content to be with him the times they were together. It was amazing.

Lainey Conroy had brought such joy into his life. He was a different man from the irritated restless person he had been, leading a different existence. When Lainey put her arms around him Dominic always felt as though he had come home to a restful haven where no one could disturb them.

He had been so shocked at himself in the beginning, after that first time that they kissed, when they realised that they were very much attracted to each other. Never, ever had he thought that he would commit adultery and betray his wife with another woman. Both of them had fought the attraction for a long while. Dominic had tried to talk to Rita about their relationship. He had tried to get back a sense of what they had had in those first few happy years of marriage but somehow, it evaded them. His wife was so busy with her own interests, so wrapped up in the lives of their children, and since he had started spending part of every week in Dublin, he had felt even less involved at home than before. All his kids ever seemed to want from him was money.

"Dad, can I have a tenner? I'm going hostelling."

"Dad, can I borrow the car to bring Cathy on a date?" Imagine, he had a son who was old enough to drive and go on dates. The feeling of growing older and not going anywhere hadn't helped him to stay faithful. Was it just a change of life type of thing? Did men go through a male menopause or was it just a fable? All he knew was that he felt lonely and rejected, just like Lainey. The time came when he didn't care about his guilt, didn't care that he was cheating Rita. Their marriage held no great meaning for him anymore. Rita wasn't that interested, so why should he do himself out of his last chance at a bit of happiness.

Dominic never regretted his decision to begin an affair with Lainey. It had brought him more happiness in the few years that they had been together than all the years of marriage. But he had no claims on Lainey and now she was going abroad and would probably meet some handsome single businessman on one of her flights who would sweep her off her feet—and that would be the end of their relationship. The pain in his heart was almost physical as he heard her reassure him that she would be home often and she would always love him. Watching her drive off in the taxi he had called for her,

he knew he could not concentrate on work that day. He told
his secretary that he would be out for a while, got into his car
and started to drive aimlessly around. An hour or so later
driving down the Old Finglas Road into Glasnevin, he passed
a recently built apartment complex. One apartment remained
to be sold. He could do with getting a proper place to live in,
now that he was firmly established in Dublin. After all, he was
doing so well. Besides, it would be an investment. On the
spur of the moment he drove into the luxurious grounds. It
was a nice spot, ideal for the airport and the city centre and
about a twenty-minute drive from his office in Fairview.
Lainey would get a great surprise if he bought a place. Because he had nothing better to do, Dominic decided to go and
have a look at the apartment for sale in Mountain View.

### Saturday, February 18, 1989

Dominic walked up the aisle of his parish church with his
twenty-three-year-old daughter gripping his arm tightly. He
could feel her nervousness. He couldn't believe that Denise
was getting married. Twenty-three was so young. It made him
feel so old and he wasn't really that old. Fifty wasn't considered old these days. But it was what she wanted and when he
had tried to persuade her to hang on a few years and enjoy
being single she had said, laughing, "But didn't you and Mum
get married when she was younger than me and you weren't
much older and aren't *you* happy?" He had no answer to that.
If he gave the appearance of being happy it wasn't because of
the state of his marriage to Rita, it was because of the role
Lainey played in his life.

Behind them, Kimberly, his younger daughter, dressed in
shocking pink, was enjoying her role of bridesmaid to the
full. Her twenty-first birthday was just a few weeks away and
she wanted a big party. Just as well he had the money to pay
for all these extravaganzas. His children thought money grew
on trees. They reached the altar and, kissing Denise on the
cheek, Dominic handed her over to her future husband. His

duty done, he returned to his seat beside Rita who was sobbing into her handkerchief. He put his arm around her. Poor Rita, she always took these things so seriously. When Michael, their eldest, had got married eighteen months before, she had moped around the house for days feeling depressed. Still, he thought wryly, his son hadn't wasted his time. Like father, like son. Rita had laughed when Michael told them they were to be grandparents. It was all settled. Michael's wife would continue to work and Rita would look after the baby. After rearing one family she was more than ready to take on another. So much for a nice peaceful retirement. Mona's eldest daughter was in the same boat and Mona too was going to mind her grandchild. So if things ran true to course, not only would he have to put up with his own grandchildren in the house, he'd have to put up with Mona's as well. What a prospect.

Rita found it so hard to let go of the children, whereas he was all for them spreading their wings and becoming independent. You couldn't be tied to the apron strings forever and they had been lucky, he told his wife. So far none of them had moved away from home into a flat, although Kimberly was chafing at the bit, wanting to get a place of her own in town. He wasn't too happy about that. If she was going to live with girl friends he wouldn't mind, but he had a suspicion that Kimberly wanted to shack up with that Senan McCarthy, whom she had been dating for the last few months. Dominic couldn't stand him. He was a lazy good-for-nothing and that was not what he wanted for his daughter.

As the priest spoke earnestly about the joys and responsibilities of marriage, Dominic sighed. He hadn't been a very good husband, he'd be the first to admit. Maybe he shouldn't have got married so young. His and Rita's needs were so different, they were such different people: Rita needing bustle and hustle and lots of activities to keep her occupied; he needing to succeed in his business, and longing for a life of relative peace and quiet. With Lainey he had found that. One of their greatest pleasures was to go for a long walk on Bull

Island on a Friday afternoon, a day he'd leave work early if she were home. They would let the wind blow away the stresses and strains of the day, listen to the waves pounding the beach and the screeching of the seagulls overhead, go into a pub for a quiet drink before the weekend crowds started coming and then home to cook something new and exotic. Cooking was a shared pleasure for him and Lainey. After their meal they would cuddle up on the sofa with a bottle of wine in front of a roaring fire to watch the *Late Late Show*.

Rita would have been bored out of her wits by that kind of thing. She far preferred to spend Friday and Saturday walking the length of Patrick Street going in and out of the shops and department stores, meeting acquaintances. She would buy handy frozen food, prepared dinners like lasagna and chicken Kiev that bore no more resemblance to the real thing than chalk did to cheese. The dinner would be cooked in a few minutes in the microwave, eaten on a tray in front of the TV while *Coronation Street* was on, and then he would be left to tidy up while she went off to her women's guild meeting or her school committee meeting or whatever. That's the way it had always been. Rita was Rita and he was he and the older he got the less he was willing to resign himself to that for the rest of his life.

Lainey's letter reposed in the breast pocket of his formal suit and later, when he had a few minutes to himself and all the speeches were over, he was going to sit down and read it again over a quiet pint. She was coming home for good. What joy! He had to admire her going out there to Saudi and working her butt off to achieve her goal. But she had achieved it. She had enough saved now to buy a place of her own without getting a horrendous mortgage, and even better, she was getting back into the publishing that she loved. Dominic was delighted for her. And for himself. He had missed her like crazy when she was away, even though when she had been based in London she had been home quite often. But it hadn't been the same at all. Now she was coming back for good and he wanted to spend more time with her. A lot more time.

Lainey made Dominic feel he was important to her in a way that Rita never had. But to be fair, Lainey hadn't to worry over and rear children like his wife had. It was just somewhere along the line that the balance had shifted and he had ended up at the wrong end of the seesaw. Well, life was not a dress rehearsal. One chance was all you got and he wanted to spend his time with the woman who understood him and made him happy. Beside him, Rita had started crying again as the rings were exchanged. Handing her a fresh handkerchief, he caught the eye of his youngest son, Kieran, as the sixteen-year-old, mortified, threw his eyes up to heaven. Dominic smiled at his son over Rita's head. At six feet he was already taller than him. He must give Kieran a few quid to spend on himself. Of them all, Kieran was the most like him and he was extremely interested in the business, working in the Cork office during his summer holidays. A thought struck Dominic and he smiled. Eventually Kieran might take over the Cork office and that would leave him free to spend the entire week in Dublin. Not even the thought of making his father-of-the-bride speech could put a dent in his good humour that day, he decided, as he took Rita's arm and led her to the altar to where they were to witness the signing of the register.

# Cecily and Simon

### Wednesday, November 12, 1980

There were crisps all over her good carpet, Andrew was bawling, terrified by the clown it had cost her a fortune to hire for his second birthday. Some horrible child had rubbed his dirty little paws on her vinyl silk peach and magnolia wallpaper and Simon was going to have a blue fit when he saw it.

It had seemed like such a good idea to have a party. She had seen some wonderful party ideas in *Good Housekeeping* and thought it would be a good way of getting one up on Helena McGrath. If Cecily threw the first party Helena would no doubt follow suit for her little girl, but the important thing was that Cecily would have done it first!

Motherhood was so demanding! She couldn't keep Andrew clean. He was always dribbling down on to his expensive little outfits, no matter how many bibs she put on him. And since he had started feeding himself it was a nightmare. She had never worked so hard in her life, not even for old sourpuss Muir. All that washing! The constant feeding. And changing those nappies—yeuch! Her lovely idyll of peaceful leisure was only a dream. Just as well Mummy came down from Dublin to help out. Otherwise, she'd go crazy. It was all right for Helena McGrath. The chef in the hotel cooked her food for herself and Steve, and of course she had breast-fed, so that meant she didn't have to go making up bottles and sterilising them and all that palaver.

Cecily supposed she could have breast-fed Andrew, but the thoughts of it made her queasy. And anyway, she hadn't wanted to have boobs as big as Dolly Parton! It was bad enough having stretch marks despite the gallons of baby oil she had rubbed on her stomach during her pregnancy.

Mind, it was lovely having people stop to admire Andrew and his little outfits every time she wheeled him down to the village. And if she did say so herself, he was an extremely pretty baby, compared to the scrawny offspring that Helena had produced. You'd think with Steve being so good-looking that the baby would have inherited some of his features, but no, the unfortunate child had her mother's pasty complexion and wispy, mousy hair that was going to give her dreadful problems when she got older. No! Andrew was definitely a handsome child but then he took after the Clarke side of the family, no matter how much Simon tried to say he looked like him.

Mrs. Conroy was delighted with her grandson. Cecily

supposed her mother-in-law wasn't a bad old stick really. But all she ever did was bake cakes and bread and go out and play cards two nights a week, and go to bingo every Sunday and Friday. She was so ordinary, not a bit fashionable or anything, not like Helena McGrath's mother who actually had a mink coat.

Still Mrs. Conroy was always willing to babysit for an hour or two if Simon and Cecily wanted to go up to Fourwinds for a drink or a meal. Simon loved bringing the baby home to show him off. Not that that Lainey one took much notice when she was there. Her own nephew, the first grandchild and she couldn't even be bothered to come to the christening!

Cecily had been furious. It had been just before Christmas and Cecily had had the house decorated to a theme, an idea she had got out of *Cosmopolitan*. Her tree was decorated with red and silver bows and balls, so tasteful and elegant. Helena had been so taken by it that she had actually stolen her original idea and decorated the foyer of Fourwinds in the same fashion. The red and silver theme had been carried right through. Red tablecloths to emphasise the gleaming silverware. Red and silver candles that Simon had been sent especially to Dublin to buy, with instructions not to come home until he found them. The house had looked exquisite. Lainey and the rest of the set in Moncas Bay would have to be impressed by this! So that everything would go like clockwork, and because Cecily couldn't cook much more than an egg, they had decided to get caterers in to do the buffet, something unheard of for a christening in Moncas Bay where most people just had sandwiches and cakes. Well Cecily and Simon were doing it in style and to crown it all they hired a photographer to take the pictures. And then that horrible girl hadn't bothered to come after all Cecily's careful planning. She was raging.

It was planning all of this and the desire to impress her sophisticated sister-in-law that had helped to banish the horrific trauma of childbirth from Cecily's mind. "Never again," she wept to Simon. "You'll just have to go and have the snip." Simon hadn't been too happy at the idea, but to show him that she was serious, she had cancelled marital rights until the job was done. She had been advised against taking the pill by her doctor, she couldn't bear fiddling with herself with that awful diaphragm, those condom things were revolting, and Andrew was the result of the Billings method, another distasteful carrying-on, taking your temperature and studying your mucus. It was enough to turn anyone celibate! What all the fuss about sex was, Cecily could not comprehend. *She* preferred a box of melt-in-the-mouth handmade chocolates any day! But Simon seemed to enjoy it and to be fair he was a most considerate husband. Nevertheless, it was up to him. She had told him, "Get the job done or no nookey!" He had lasted a year before taking the big step!

If he dared look for some tonight he would get an earful from her, Cecily decided grumpily, as she accidentally stood on a chocolate rice crispie, feeling it crunch under her patent high heels, right into her good Navan carpet. Where was Simon anyway? He'd promised he'd be home to blow out the candles. She'd kill him when she got her hands on him.

"Aaahhh!" groaned Simon as he came to a very satisfying climax inside the luscious body of Nurse Noonan, his receptionist and assistant.

"Simon, you're wonderful," smiled Máire, massaging his shoulder muscles just the way he liked. The pink lamp cast a warm homely glow in Máire's comfortable little bedroom. She had done the place up very well, made it very cosy altogether. He liked this bedroom. It was so easy on the eye, uncluttered and lived in, not like his own boudoir with its frills and flounces and those hideous Austrian blinds that Cecily assured him were the height of chic. The lamplight reflected on the polished glow of the old chest of drawers. Simon liked old furniture. Of course *his* marital bedroom was fully fitted in some cream melamine. Cecily wanted everything modern and matching. But as he lay contentedly beside Máire, Simon de-

ided why he was so comfortable and relaxed in this room. It
was because it reminded him of his old bedroom at home in
his parents' house.

When he gave Nurse Noonan the job as his receptionist/
assistant after his former receptionist left to go and live on a
kibbutz, he had never thought that he would end up having
an affair with her. He had leased her the rooms over his
surgery as a flat and she had made such a nice job of it that he
had taken to dropping in now and again for a cup of tea after
a gruelling day's work. He needed to relax for a little while
before getting home to Cecily and the baby. Cecily was not
the world's most natural mother, and indeed it had been a
heart-stopping shock for her to discover she was pregnant so
soon into their marriage. She had been enjoying her freedom
so much after the hard work she had put into her career in
Dublin. Simon had expected Cecily to be bored after dropping her career aspirations to marry him. But she had settled
into life as a housewife surprisingly well and seemed to be
thoroughly enjoying herself. It had given him immense satisfaction. Then she got pregnant and the cat was among the
pigeons.

Andrew was the joy of his life. He was a beautiful baby
and it gave Simon a secret little sense of satisfaction that he
and Cecily had produced a son and heir while the McGraths,
although they had a lovely daughter, still had to try for a son.
Just as well they had had Andrew because Cecily was adamant
about never getting pregnant again. And to prove it, she
hadn't let him near her until he'd gone and had a vasectomy.
Mind, after the nine months he had endured when she was
pregnant with Andrew, he was almost relieved to go through
with it. And anyway he was as horny as bedamned after ab-
staining for a year. It had been bloody sore for a few days after
the operation and he felt, much to his dismay, that he was no
longer the man he had been.

When Nurse Noonan had indicated that she was more
than professionally interested it had come as a welcome surprise to him. Cecily was much too harassed these days to

enjoy sex and now that he was shooting blanks, he might a
well get some benefit out of the operation. In fact it was th
ideal solution. Cecily was happy that he wasn't annoying he
He was happy because he was genuinely fond of Máire an
besides she had a ripe bosomy body that was made for lovin,
unlike his wife's model-thin angles. And Nurse Noonan wa
happy because she had cast the albatross of her virginity fro
around her neck, thrilled that at last someone desired he
despite the fact that she was two stones overweight and ha
thighs like tree trunks.

"I'd better go home," Simon murmured regretfully, a
most smothered between two soft bosoms. "It's my son
birthday and I've got to help blow out the candles."

"Soon," whispered Nurse Noonan as she tightened he
arms around him.

## Wednesday, June 8, 1988

The nail-varnish bottle slipped off the edge of the lounge
and Cecily cursed as purple varnish splashed on her whit
towelling robe and on to the red tiles of the balcony. Hastil
she got up from the lounger and, avoiding the purple puddle
went in to the villa to get some tissues and nail-varnish re
mover.

Just as well Simon was playing golf; he'd probably hav
hysterics. Hysterical Hilda she often called him when he go
excited over nothing. It took her a while to erase all traces o
the purple varnish and, slipping out of the towelling robe
Cecily placed it in the linen basket that Pepita the maid woul
be collecting a little later. She stepped into a turquoise swim
suit, poured herself a generous Malibu, added some ice, an
returned to her lounger beside the aquamarine pool.

She lay, relaxed, as the sun poured heat all over he
tanned body, planning what she'd wear to the party in Puert
Banus later this evening. Her Pat Crowley cocktail dress, defi
nitely. That could compete with anything the chic monie
Marbella set wore. It had cost an arm and a leg of course, bu

he had told Simon she wasn't going to Marbella unless she was dressed for it. Besides he was getting the villa for nothing, so the holiday wasn't costing him a fortune.

It had been most generous of Manus Burke to lend them his villa for a week, but then Simon had done some very expensive crown work for the cattle exporter and hardly charged him at all. You rub my back and I'll rub yours was Simon's motto in some cases. It paid better. You'd never believe Manus Burke was a millionaire to look at him. He was so laid-back. But he had a brain as sharp as a razor and he used it. No matter how hard Simon worked, he'd never be able to afford a luxury villa in Marbella, Cecily thought regretfully, as she rubbed on some factor six protection. This was so much more impressive than her usual package holidays to the sun. Still Simon was doing well enough. He had patients coming from as far as Wexford and her life-style was far removed from the one she had had before her marriage. Now she was *someone*, a leading light in Moncas Bay society, something she had longed to be from the time she had come to live in the village.

Her son Andrew was a model child and she had no problems with him. It was hard to believe he was nearly ten. They hadn't brought him on holiday—not that he had been disappointed. He had gone to stay with his grandmother. Andrew loved to stay with Mrs. Conroy although Cecily could not fathom why. He had to make his own bed, wash up and help his grandfather in the garden. At home Mrs. Maguire, her housekeeper, did all these chores, and they had a gardener call once a week to take care of the gardens. Children were funny. Cecily would never understand them. She took a sip from her Malibu. She'd been drinking it all afternoon and was beginning to get pleasantly woozy. This would impress the hell out of Lainey, she was sure. Her sister-in-law was due home for a visit from the Gulf, and Cecily would have a tan and tales about her holiday that would rival anything she'd have to report about her travels. It was such a pain, listening to her go on about staying in the New York Hilton and the like. And she only a glorified flying waitress for all her stuck-

up airs and graces. And some day Cecily was going to say thi
to her, she vowed. Mind, Lainey wouldn't take that lyin
down. She might retaliate. Somehow, Cecily felt she woul
never get the better of her sister-in-law in an argument. Still
Cecily would keep the insult in reserve, for when Lainey go
too big for her boots. Taking another sip of Malibu she sighe
with pleasure. This really was the life. A pity it was only for
week. She hoped Andrew wasn't missing them too much
Cecily's eyes closed behind her Ray Bans, as, nicely pickled
she began to doze.

Andrew was, in fact, having the time of his life. His Gran
Conroy didn't mind a bit if his clothes got dirty. She cooked
the most scrumptious dinners. And she always had tarts and
cakes in the pantry. Andrew loved his Gran's pantry, with it
jars of pickles and chutneys and jams and the big bread bir
that always had homemade brown bread. And the tin full o
scones and the plate of tart and, his absolute favourite, a big
chocolate sponge cake. The pantry was Andrew's idea o
heaven on earth. All they had at home was a huge boring
deep freeze and shop-bought biscuits and cakes.

At his Gran's he slept in his Aunt Lainey's bedroom
which had a little round window through which he could see
the sea. His Grandad had given him a pair of binoculars and
he loved watching the ships sailing past on the horizon. His
Grandad's shed was almost as good as the pantry. It had tools
and workbenches and Grandad was helping him make a
treehouse for the big oak tree at the end of his grandparents
big garden. As he hammered a nail into a sheet of wood that
was going to be the floor, Andrew smiled at his grandfather
delighted with himself. It was an awful pity his parents were
only gone away for a week. He only had a few days left to
enjoy himself so he'd better make the most of it. His grandmother appeared at the door with a mug of tea for his
Grandad and a big glass of homemade lemonade for himself
and two big chunks of chocolate sponge cake. "I thought the
workmen might be hungry," she said with a smile.

"And you're dead right. We're starving, aren't we, Andrew?" her husband replied, winking.

"We're starving, Gran," Andrew agreed, winking back as he took a mouthful of the creamy chocolate sponge cake and heaved a sigh of pleasure.

Simon watched in satisfaction as his golf ball arched and flew exactly where he wanted it to, right on to the eighteenth green. Just as well he'd got in a lot of golfing practice back home. He didn't want to make a show of himself here on this magnificent golf course, with all the jet-setters. He had tried not to gawk when he actually saw Sean and Micheline Connery, strolling into the clubhouse after a round. Even though balding, Connery was a fine-looking man and could still impress women young enough to be his daughter. Simon had got a bit sunburnt on his bald spot yesterday, he could feel it under his golfing hat. He'd put some cream on it when he got back to the villa. Although he was thoroughly enjoying his holiday, he was looking forward to going home too. It would be most enjoyable standing at the bar in Fourwinds casually mentioning that he had had a round of golf with Sean and Micheline. And telling about the parties on the yachts in Puerto Banus. All very casually of course. Most of all, though, he was looking forward to his reunion with Máire Noonan. He must buy her something really nice. Maybe he'd buy it after the game, seeing as he had a few hours to himself. Cecily had told him she intended to get some serious sunbathing done. And that suited Simon just fine. "Good shot!" his partner said.

"Not bad," agreed Simon with satisfaction.

# THE NINETIES

# Liz

*A*s she snuggled down into the comfy sofa, papers and magazines, a cup of tea and a chunk of pecan pie beside her, Liz reflected that she hadn't enjoyed herself so much in years. In front of her, a blazing fire roared up the chimney, the flames flickering and dancing, casting shadows in the lamp-lit room. Outside the wind howled and rain lashed in fury against the windowpanes. Liz didn't care; the storm added to her enjoyment and sense of comfort. In the background Dean Martin crooned softly, a selection of fifties love songs that soothed her spirit. This was, she decided, the perfect way to spend a Sunday evening. And she was going to have more of such evenings!

She couldn't remember the last Sunday evening she had spent by herself, just flopping. Mostly she accompanied Hugh to some do, or to the cinema, or a party. She was getting extremely tired of constant socialising. To Hugh it was a way of life and he thrived on it, but café society was beginning to bore her. All the same old faces at first nights and premieres and launches and lunches. The see-and-be-seen set always trying to outdo one another. She knew of women who had cracked up because of the pressure of the life-style of a social-ite. Liz grinned to herself—she'd never be that silly. Only last week she had been the cause of a heated argument at a charity do to which she and Hugh had been invited.

Liz had been wearing an emerald satin strapless sheath

dress that showed off her svelte figure to perfection. She loved the dress. "My dear, what a lovely gown! Is it a Bruce Oldfield?" Brona O'Malley, the hostess, inquired coolly as she inspected Liz from head to toe. Brona didn't like Liz, and the feeling was mutual. Liz thought the older woman shallow and superficial and she was well aware that Brona fancied Hugh like crazy and flirted quite blatantly with him in front of Liz, despite Hugh's obvious lack of interest.

"No, it's not a Bruce Oldfield, it's an Eve Clancy creation."

"Eve Clancy? I don't recall ever hearing of her. Is she a new designer?" Brona queried, perplexed, as she knew of and bought from most designers of note. Tonight she was wearing a Kanga original. It did absolutely nothing for her, the heavily patterned material swamping Brona's scrawny figure.

Stop being bitchy, Liz told herself—just because you don't like the Kanga label. Liz preferred a simpler style. "Eve is my sister-in-law," she said lightly.

"Oh! Homemade!" her hostess exclaimed patronisingly. "How quaint! Margo," she addressed a well-known fashion columnist who had just joined them. "Liz actually wears homemade dresses. You'd never guess, would you?" she added cattily.

"Really!" drawled Margo in her affected South Dublin whine. "How . . . unusual." Both women smiled, dripping condescension. Liz had had enough. She remembered Brona recently boasting that she had spent three thousand pounds on a Karl Lagerfeld creation. "I don't go in for haute couture much. I paid one hundred and fifty pounds for the material for this. I wouldn't dream of paying thousands of pounds for a dress. No matter how much money I had. I think it's obscene actually."

There was uproar.

"But, Liz, think of the work that goes into a designer original. All those seamstresses. The hand stitching, the unique design." Margo was incensed.

"This gown has been hand stitched. And it's an original," Liz countered.

"Oh, don't be silly, dear, that's different," Brona snapped.

"I'm afraid I don't see why," Liz said calmly. "You thought it was a Bruce Oldfield yourself. It's the label you're paying for and if you ask me it's all a great big racket and if people are daft enough to want to play that game just to impress other people, that's their choice. It's just not mine. Frankly, I'm not into that kind of snobbery."

The women were furious, Hugh and Incarna were highly amused and Liz was thoroughly browned off. Charity function or not, she was bored and restless and realised that this socialising had bored her for quite some time.

There had to be more to life than all this carrying-on, she reflected, as she sat at her table and watched various well-known people act out a game of charades, each contestant representing a deserving charity. "Try and look as though you're enjoying yourself!" Hugh murmured beside her. "Here's a photographer!" Dutifully she smiled. What was wrong with her? Hadn't she a life-style that hundreds of women would envy. Fame, fortune. A highly successful and lucrative career that was going from strength to strength. And an attractive desirable man at her side. Why was she so unsettled and fed up with her life?

"Why don't you go away for a few days and really think about what you want to do and what you want from life? Then you can do something about it," Eve urged her one day after a moaning session. "I've a surprise for you," she added, her eyes twinkling. "I'm pregnant again."

"Eve! Oh, Eve, that's wonderful!" Liz hugged her sister-in-law and Eve hugged her back hard in her warm affectionate way. "Just when I'd got down to a size twelve and all," Eve said in mock disgust. "So much for getting into a bikini next summer!"

"Fiona will be thrilled!" Liz remarked as she put the kettle on for a cup of tea. "I wonder will Caitriona be jealous. Is she awake yet?" Her niece was having her afternoon nap.

Eve laughed. "Is it me or the children you come to see! Go up and look." Liz needed no second urging. She took the stairs two at a time. Two big blue eyes were peeping out of the cot, and when Liz went over Caitriona broke into a delighted smile.

Liz's heart melted into a puddle. "You're beautiful," she smiled as she leaned down and lifted the child in her arms, inhaling the lovely scent of her. Caitriona nestled close, chattering away, her little hands playing with Liz's face. Inspiration struck. "Liz, what a brain wave!" she murmured to herself, nuzzling the little girl's neck, enjoying the laughs she was getting out of her.

"I was just thinking," she remarked casually, bouncing Caitriona up and down on her knee as Eve poured their tea. "Why don't you and Don take off for a few days while you can still fit into a bikini? I'll mind the girls."

Eve's eyes widened. "Are you serious?"

"Sure."

Eve flew out the kitchen door. "Where are you going?" Liz asked in alarm. Maybe Eve was feeling sick although that wasn't like her. She usually thrived in pregnancy.

"I'm just ringing Don and the travel agent before you change your mind," Eve said with a laugh, her fingers busy dialling.

Two weeks later Liz was ensconced in their big homely house. She had done as much work as possible the fortnight before. The only thing she had to do was to record her weekly art programme for TV and her mother had said she'd mind her grandchildren for the few hours it took. Liz thoroughly enjoyed the weekly television programme for children that she had been asked to do several months before. It was extremely popular, so popular in fact and the response so positive that the producer and director were seriously considering doing one aimed at adults. There was a resurgence of media interest and she was giving interviews regularly. Well, for this two weeks, she decided, she was going nowhere, doing nothing, just looking after her two adorable nieces in cosy domestic bliss.

"What about the Wexford Opera Festival?" Hugh exclaimed in dismay when she told him of her plans. "We were supposed to be going down on the special train."

"Bring Brona," Liz teased. "I'm sorry, Hugh. I just want a break from it all."

"A break! But you're going to be looking after two kids. That's no break!" He shook his head in disbelief.

"It is for me. It's just what I need right now. I'm really looking forward to it. And it will give me some time to think. I need to get things into focus, see where I'm going, assess what I'm doing. These two weeks will be just the time to do it."

Hugh put his arms around her and drew her close. "My complex little soul! What am I going to do with you?" He smiled, bending his head and kissing her long and passionately. "Will you think about coming to America with me?"

Liz stood contentedly within the circle of his arms. "I'll think about it." Hugh at long last had achieved his goal of getting a toehold in American TV. His two months in the States the previous Christmas had paid off and he was now spending increasing amounts of time there. Soon he was going to have to think about making a decision to go there permanently. He wanted Liz to go with him. She did not want to go. She had spent a month with him in New York last Christmas and if it was an indication of what their life together would be like in America, she knew she'd hate it. Hugh had been working continuously but that did not worry Liz so much as she was well able to entertain and amuse herself. She had seen old friends, visited the galleries and done some painting. It was their lack of time together and his increased use of coke that worried her. Liz knew the drug was so easily available in New York and she knew that Hugh would continue to take it despite her protests. It was a source of friction between them that would not be resolved. She understood his great need to make it in America, but knowing Hugh, once he

had made it there, he'd want to make it somewhere else. Tha
was the kind of man he was. There was no settling him.

She had felt vaguely depressed as this realisation hit he
after she came back from New York alone. It gradually bega
to dawn on her that lately she wasn't getting as much satisfac
tion from her work as she had been. The excitement of suc
cess had worn off somewhat and the hectic pace of her lif
was leaving her drained. Hugh, deeply preoccupied with hi
career plans, couldn't see her restlessness. Even after thei
lovemaking, where once they would talk for hours, he nov
fell into exhausted sleep, leaving her wide-eyed in the dark a
she listened to his slow even breathing and felt his thigl
heavy across her own.

"Liz, I think you're burnt out," Bryan Ross said to her on
evening shortly before her two weeks' baby-sit. They wer
having dinner and he was inviting her to exhibit in a galler
in London of which he was part owner. "Why don't you tak
a year off like you did before and go off somewhere and rela:
for a couple of months. Wind down, catch a few rays, hav
some early nights and regular meals and walk and swim an(
then start painting again."

"Hmmm. It sounds lovely," she sighed wistfully.

"Then do it!" Bryan commanded, tucking into Kung P(
barbecued pork.

"I love it when you're masterful. You remind me of In
spector Morse." Liz leaned across the table and sampled ;
forkful from his plate.

Bryan laughed. "It's a pity my wife can't hear you. If she
saw me eating this I'd get such an ear bashing! She's a terribl(
old bully."

"Barbara's a love and you're crazy about her, you
spoofer," chuckled Liz, enjoying being with him as usual.

"Think about taking that break!" he repeated as h(
walked with her to her car.

"I will," Liz said, smiling, but his words stayed with he
and the idea began to seem even more appealing as the lon;
cold nights drew in. Liz hated the winter—she was a real su

lover—and as the autumn progressed her thoughts turned back to that lovely six months in La Jolla when she had lived on the beach.

"Come and spend a few days with me in Mallorca when Eve and Don return," Incarna invited her when Liz told her all about what Ross had advised. "It will be a little break for you and you can think about your plans."

"I'd love to. Thanks, Incarna," Liz responded, delighted with the offer. "I haven't been over for ages." It was a few years since she'd been to the villa and the thought of a short break there in Incarna's effervescent company lifted her spirits.

"Are you absolutely certain you don't mind?" Eve said as she carried her travel bag out to the car. Don followed with the cases.

Liz laughed. "It's too late now, so go while the going is good." She held Caitriona in her arms, glad that she was wearing a sweater and jeans. She had food all over her, and Caitriona, who was now feeding herself, was trying to feed her aunt as well. Unfortunately her aim was not good and a mushy handful was currently reposing in Liz's black curls. Caitriona, at her present stage of development, was not for the fainthearted, but Liz, who had been puked upon and wet upon and dribbled upon by both her nieces when they were babies, was a sucker for punishment.

Waving the other pair off enthusiastically, she decided a bath was in order for Caitriona. Then she'd have to have Fiona's dinner ready as her elder niece had started school just a few months previously. Then maybe they might go out for a walk before tea and then it would be time for games before bed and Liz would spend the night reading the new best seller that everyone was talking about. Eve had given it to her before she left, telling her that she wouldn't be able to put it down. Then tomorrow was Saturday and they could do as they pleased. Organisation was everything, she told herself happily, as she filled Caitriona's bath. Twenty minutes later, she was as wet as her niece. By the time she had fed her and put her down for her nap, changed out of her own clothes and washed her hair to get the baby's food out of it, Fiona was home and the dinner was just in the preparation stages. "I'm starving. Is my dinner weddy?" her niece greeted her. She had been collected from her school by her granddad who was on his lunch break. He also gave her a lift in the mornings.

"It won't be long," Liz assured her cheerfully as she began to fry the plaice. The phone rang, there was a ring at the door, and the baby began to wail. "Oh, dear!" muttered Liz, turning down the heat, as she rushed to answer the door and the phone. She was a little behind schedule so she decided to skip the walk after lunch.

Fiona's face fell and her lower lip began to tremble. "But you said I could go on the swings in the park, Auntie Liz."

"I'll give you a push on the swing out the back," she cajoled.

"But you pwomised," Fiona said tearfully.

"All right all right!" Liz said hastily. After all a promise was a promise. It was dark by the time they got home, but it was lovely walking over to Johnstown Park, site of her many marathon tennis matches with her sister. The grass was covered with a carpet of dry red gold leaves that crunched underfoot and they enjoyed kicking their way through them. The mountains looked so clear and near in the late afternoon sun and the sky, a deep cobalt blue, was beginning to turn pink and gold as the sun sank lower and lower. Inhaling the crisp air as she pushed her niece on the swing, Liz sighed contentedly, thinking, this is the life!

As she settled down to her novel, admittedly somewhat later than planned, she wondered if Hugh would ring. He had flown out to Saudi two days earlier to do a programme on Iraq's invasion of Kuwait and the plight of the western hostages. He had promised he would phone at some stage. The children were fast asleep, the fire was blazing and she was as happy as a lark. Eve was right—*Career Girls* was unputdownable. When she had finished that she had Maeve Binchy's *Circle of Friends* to read and then she had a load of *Hellos* to catch up on. And Hugh was worried that she would be bored and lonely! If this was being bored and lonely it was blissful and she'd settle for it any day, she decided, as she threw another log on the fire and sipped a mug of hot chocolate topped with cream and chocolate flake.

It was one of the nicest times in her life, a time she would always remember with happiness. Things like washing the girls' clothes and hanging them out and bringing them in and ironing them gave her a great sense of satisfaction. One day she even painted a still life of a neat pile of her ironing. She actually enjoyed making beds and getting the house ship-shape, and standing at the door waving Fiona off to school with her "grandant," as she called him. Was it because it was all new to her and so it was different and not yet routine, Liz wondered as she repotted a geranium while waiting for a washing cycle to finish. Maybe. And why did she feel this secret guilt about enjoying it all so much? Was it because women were so conditioned in this feminist era of the career woman to think that housework was mere drudgery. Liz discovered that she could spend hours pottering around the house doing this and that and not feel the slightest bit bored. Maybe she was odd, maybe it was a phase that she was going through. Well, if it was, she was enjoying herself immensely and she wanted more of it.

"For God's sake, will you get Christine to baby-sit so we can go out for a meal!" Hugh grumbled over the phone during the middle of the second week, a few days after his return from Saudi.

"I'll cook you a meal here," she offered.

"Liz, no disrespect to your cooking but frankly I'm not in the humour for children and domesticity. We've stayed in every night since I came home."

"Well, you weren't moaning last night!" retorted Liz.

They had made wild and passionate love on the sheep-skin rug in front of the fire and afterwards as she massaged him with body oil to erase the knots of tension in his body he had looked at her with his heavy-lidded brown-eyed gaze and said slowly, "You look really well, very relaxed. You do really like this kind of thing, don't you?" He indicated Fiona's neatly pressed uniform lying on the back of a chair with her shoes and socks beside it, all ready for school in the morning.

"Yes," she said. "I do." Their eyes met.

"It will never be me," he said honestly, taking her face between his hands.

"I know that," Liz answered. It was the first time they had verbally acknowledged the differences between them and Liz knew that it was a turning point in their relationship. "I love you, Liz," Hugh said softly.

"I love you too," she murmured against his chest.

She hadn't gone out to dinner with him and he had rung off in a huff but the following morning a dozen yellow roses arrived for her and she smiled. Hugh could never stay mad with her for long and maybe she had been a bit mean. She asked Christine to baby-sit that evening and he took her to the Trocadero. Over dinner, Hugh proposed to her. Liz had kind of guessed it was coming. He had been putting so much pressure on her lately about going to America. She had managed not to think about it during her baby-sitting session but now he gave her no option—she had to sit down and think about and confront it and decide what choice she was going to make. "I have to think about it, Hugh," she responded honestly, her blue eyes wide and troubled.

"Well, I'm off to New York the day after tomorrow for ten days. You have until I get back. Is that fair?"

Liz nodded. It was time to make up her mind. She couldn't sit on the fence for much longer.

She resolutely put the decision out of her head as she enjoyed the final few days of the fortnight that had passed so swiftly. Don and Eve had phoned often from the Canaries and were having a wonderful time. They were stopping off for two days in London before coming home on the Monday, the following day. Upstairs, her two charges were slumbering contentedly after a thrilling day at the zoo. Munching a slice of apple tart, Liz sighed deeply. It had all gone so fast and she had still put thoughts of a decision out of her mind. Well, she wasn't going to decide tonight either, she thought stubbornly. Tonight she was going to enjoy her last few hours of solitude.

Picking up the *Sunday Independent* she put a cushion under her feet and two under her head and settled back for a read. A while later she came to the Living supplement and saw her own face smiling out at her under the caption "Nineties Woman." Liz groaned. She didn't mind giving interviews at all, enjoyed meeting new people and chatting with them. It was just reading them back afterwards that she never got used to. She was always slightly mortified by the whole thing. And then after her experiences with two-faced Polly and her "chocolate-box art" barb she had always felt a bit wary. But over the years she had done many interviews and most of the journalists had been extremely nice and friendly. When Susanna Nolan had phoned, asking if she could include her in a piece she was doing on successful Irishwomen, Liz had agreed. She had quite enjoyed the interview with the elegant journalist who had asked her intelligent probing questions without overstepping the bounds of privacy. Such a relief after some of the questions she had had thrown at her by others less polite. If she was asked once more when she and Hugh were going to tie the knot, she'd scream!

Studying the attractive brunette as her pen raced swiftly over the pages of her notebook, Liz reflected that Susanna, like herself, was a new breed of Irishwoman. There were so many successful Irishwomen around who really were getting out and achieving things and making their own choices. If she had a daughter, she'd have no fears for her growing up in Irish society. Fiona and Caitriona had everything to aim for in their future.

Liz smiled as she read the opening sentence of the article. "Liz Lacey is the personification of the new Nineties Woman," Susanna had written. "Unbelievably successful, independent and talented, she has overcome adversity and emerged a stronger woman. Some would say Liz Lacey has it made!" The rest of the article continued in that positive tone but Liz shook her head as she finished it. So many people thought she had it all, that she had reached the pinnacle, yet only she knew the emptiness she felt with increasing regularity these days. She threw another log on the fire and ran upstairs to check on the girls. Not a budge. After cutting another piece of pie and pouring herself a glass of milk, Liz returned to the sofa.

Picking up a couple of *Hellos* she flicked through them. She loved reading about the rich and famous, seeing the fashions, looking at their houses. Liz spent a happy three quarters of an hour dipping in and out of the magazines. Stretching her hand down to the floor she picked up the last one, which was also the latest. She felt a stab of empathy when she saw the bewildered and utterly shocked face of Princess Caroline as she stood watching her husband's coffin being carried into Monaco's cathedral. God love her, she thought sadly, knowing exactly what the bereft young widow was experiencing. Thinking back, she knew that she had gone around completely dazed for six months after Matt's death. She could see the same stunned expression on the grieving princess's face and pitied her from the bottom of her heart. "At least she has the three children," she murmured aloud, dropping the magazine. At least she would not be left empty and alone as Liz had been. The memories brought the tears to her eyes and in the quiet of Eve's and Don's sitting room she had a little cry.

Wiping her eyes, she put up the fireguard, switched off the lamp, washed up her dishes, put out the milk bottles and went upstairs to bed. Doing her last check, she smiled as she saw Caitriona with her little hands at the back of her head. No matter how often Liz put them under the quilt to keep them warm they would always be back behind her head the next time she looked in. Fiona lay sideways across the bed with her foot sticking out from under the cover, her cheek resting on her hand. Moving her gently and tucking the quilt tightly around her, Liz leaned over and kissed her very softly on the cheek. "I love you," she whispered.

As she lay in Don and Eve's enormous bed, thoughts

flitted in and out of her mind and her eyes grew drowsy. Hugh's proposal. She'd have to make her decision soon. He'd be home before the weekend. The interview that said she was a "Nineties Woman"· who had it made. Princess Caroline and her grief. Fiona and Caitriona fast asleep. Her eyes opened wide. "I'm going to do it!" she said aloud with conviction. She had been thinking about it for so long, pushing it away, drawing it to her, afraid yet excited. Well maybe she was a new breed of woman. It was a huge step to take, but this past two weeks had cemented the idea in her head. She'd go to Majorca with Incarna and really think it out and then she'd act on it.

Feeling as though a heavy burden had finally been lifted from her shoulders, Liz dropped off asleep, only waking once when Fiona crept in to her aunt's bed for a "cuggle."

# *Hugh*

### Sunday, December 30, 1990

*A*s he lay beside Liz's sleeping form, Hugh reflected that as long as he lived no woman would ever amaze him as Liz continued to do. She was something else entirely, he reflected ruefully, listening to her soft even breathing as she slept in the curve of his arm, their bodies entwined after a night of passionate lovemaking.

Who else but Liz would refuse his offer of marriage in one breath and tell him that she wanted him to father a baby in the next? Who else would consider the hare-brained scheme of giving up a fantastically successful career to go and live halfway up a mountain in Majorca to paint, with a baby in tow? Who else but Liz Lacey? And why the hell was he aiding and abetting her? And why the hell did America not seem as exciting all of a sudden? Women! They were nothing but trouble. She couldn't be serious about selling the apartment! There was no way she'd sell Apartment 3B! Deep down he had known Liz would never come to America with him and he couldn't in all honesty blame her. If he was to make it there he'd need to be unencumbered. He'd never be able to give Liz the attention their relationship needed while he was carving out his niche. He knew it and she knew it. He was what he was, just as Liz was what she was but it didn't lessen the love between them. That bond would always be there. If she got pregnant as she so desperately wanted he would be a father. Imagine. Hugh Cassidy. Father. It was a hard concept to grasp. His own father had died when he was young so he had never really had a role model. Maybe that was why he wasn't into settling down and having babies and things. He could always go into analysis when he got to the States, just for the fun of it! Everyone did it there. And he and Liz used to be highly amused at some of the crap they'd had to listen to that people took so seriously over there. Would he be hard to analyse? Why was he so determined to succeed, even at the expense of the most loving relationship he had ever had? Was he getting hooked on coke? He needed it a lot more than he used to. And he needed much more of it to get a buzz. What kind of a daddy would he make if Liz got pregnant? All those questions and answers to none! Sighing, Hugh turned over, drew Liz closer to him and fell asleep.

## *Claire*

Friday, March 23, 1990

"*I* walked up the path and opened the front door . . . and it was terrible . . . terrible! He was hanging from the bannisters. David. My son, my beautiful son. Oh, God . . .

help me . . . help me understand. Why did he do it?" Claire sobbed her heart out to the quietly listening woman who was stroking her hand. She lay on a couch in the small dimly lit room. This was her fifth session of acupuncture and there was something so understanding and caring about the petite dark-haired woman who was treating her that Claire found herself blurting out all about David. All the anguish that had been bottled up inside her since that terrifying October day almost six months before came rushing out in a torrent.

"I managed to lift him down. He was still warm but he wasn't breathing, and there was no heartbeat or pulse. I was screaming for help and one of the neighbours heard and came in and called an ambulance for me. We tried to resuscitate him but it was no use, he was dead. David was dead. My poor tormented son! What must he have been feeling to do such a thing? Didn't he know how much I loved him? Didn't he know I would have done anything I could for him? Oh, if only I hadn't sat daydreaming in Arnott's over my coffee I might have been home in time to save him." The tears were streaming down her face and her body shook with sobs, great gasping sobs as her grief poured out of her.

"You must not reproach yourself like that, ever," Emma, her acupuncturist said, quietly but very firmly. "There is a divine pattern to all our lives, Claire, and nothing or no one can change that. If you were meant to get to David in time you would have—if it had been God's plan."

Claire wept. "Oh, Emma, I try to accept it was the will of God but I am so tormented."

"I know, I know. But the fact that you are talking about it to me and expressing your grief is very good for you. It means that you are not bottling it up inside you where it can go repressed for a long time and end up causing physical illness. Look at the progress we have made so far with your periods and the bloating. We will work through this together. Never fear, Claire. You are not alone." She stroked Claire's hand gently until Claire, utterly spent, began to relax.

With quiet unhurried movements Emma expertly positioned the acupuncture needles. Then pouring a little scented oil on the palm of her hand she gently massaged Claire's forehead. The scent of roses filled the room and Claire inhaled deeply. "Relax now, Claire," Emma murmured. "Picture yourself in a beautiful rose garden. You are peaceful and untroubled and I am standing at the gate so no one can come and disturb you. Now say this little prayer. It might give you comfort and help when things seem to be overwhelming you. 'I cast this burden on the Christ within me and I go free.' Lie there, now, and let all the grief and sorrow flow out of you. I'll be popping in and out if you need me."

Claire lay inhaling deeply as Emma had taught her in one of their previous sessions. The breathing exercises were a great help. At least now when she woke up having one of her terrible panic attacks she was able to do something to control it. If it wasn't for Emma she would have gone out of her mind. Claire lay in the comforting darkened room, not wanting to leave it ever. Here she felt safe and protected from the horrors of her life outside. For the hour and a half that she was under Emma's care she always felt so peaceful. Despite the fact that Emma had other patients to treat and a thousand and one things to attend to, Claire never felt rushed or under pressure not to be taking up the acupuncturist's time, as she had so often felt in her doctor's surgery. But then the theory behind holistic healing was that the physical, mental, spiritual, and emotional states of the patient were all intertwined and that treatment of the whole person was the key to well-being. There was no comparison between a quick ten-minute consultation with her harassed and overworked GP and the hour and a half she spent every second week with Emma Morris. Emma had studied acupuncture in Singapore and nursing in Ireland, and blended the two traditions so skilfully and successfully that there was a three-month waiting list of people who were trying to get an appointment with her. Lying in the scent-filled room, Claire reflected that she had been lucky to get her appointment.

It was Rosie, desperately worried about her traumatised

friend, who had persuaded Claire to go to Emma for treatment. Haggard, exhausted from lack of proper sleep, drained, and worn-out from constant heavy periods and kidney infections, Claire had been a physical and mental wreck. Rosie herself went to Emma for treatment for a recurring sinus problem that conventional medicine had been unsuccessful in treating, and was delighted after several months of acupuncture to have her sinus problem cleared up. She finished her course of treatment feeling much healthier than when she started. Rosie knew that Emma was just what Claire needed.

Claire had been too apathetic to argue and had let Rosie make the appointment for her and drive her out to the clinic in Sandycove. At her first visit, the acupuncturist had advised Claire that she should continue treatment with her gynecologist and GP, explaining that the treatment she would receive at her clinic would be complementary to the conventional medical treatment she was undergoing. That first visit, Emma had not given her any needles. She had just talked quietly to Claire as she gave her new patient a thorough examination. "The first thing we must do is build up your immune system by good nutrition, supplemented by some vitamin therapy," Emma said. Claire listened with a complete lack of interest. She had come only so that Rosie would stop annoying her. If the doctors she had spent years going to and spent so much money on couldn't help her, she didn't think this quietly spoken woman with the firm handshake and calm aura could do much. It was probably more money down the drain. Well, she didn't care anymore. If it would shut Rosie and Suzy up, she'd go for a while.

She had never felt as ill in her life as during the week after she made her first visit and started following Emma's instructions. As she cleansed and detoxified her body, flushing out all the impurities, drinking gallons of water, not eating chocolate and junk foods, she felt so bad that she thought she could never go back. But some instinct of self-preservation kept her going and she persevered. The next week she got acupuncture and she began to tell Emma a little about her life. The other woman never probed; she just let Claire tell her what she wanted to tell her and they talked about it. It was their fifth session before Claire could tell her about David.

In the peaceful room Claire lay wide-eyed. All her crying and the exorcising of the pent-up emotion had left her drained but somehow the black unrelenting burden that sat upon her shoulders and weighed her down, did not seem quite as heavy.

Claire left the clinic a little later, having made her next appointment with Ann, the motherly receptionist, and decided to walk along the seafront for a little while. She wasn't in the humour for going home. It was only eleven-fifteen. She had had the first appointment, and it was her day off work. No point in rushing back to mope around a house filled with hideous memories.

Claire shuddered as she walked, the brisk March breeze catching her hair and whipping it about her face. She drew her collar up against the wind and walked along the sea-sprayed path in the direction of Dalkey. She wouldn't mind living beside the sea, she mused. There was something very calming to the spirit about the rhythmic ebb and flow of the tides. She'd like to live anywhere other than in that big cold house she had called "home" for so many years. Now, just six months after David's death, living there was like living in hell.

She bit her lip to stop it from trembling, as she walked, head bowed, shoulders hunched, hands clenched in her coat pockets. No matter what Emma said about trying to let the past be, and not to be holding on to bitterness and hate, Claire knew that she would never ever forgive Sean for the things he had said to her after their son's funeral.

"Bastard! I hate you!" she muttered aloud, wiping the tears from her eyes.

"It's all your fault, Claire!" Sean had accused her as they stood in the kitchen on the evening of David's funeral. They were still in their mourning clothes and Claire was making tea. Suzy was upstairs sorting out her brother's things for her mother, who couldn't bear to enter his bedroom. "If you hadn't been so selfish about going out to work and neglecting the children this would never have happened!" Claire couldn't believe her ears. Sean was blaming *her*. After the way he had treated their son: forcing him to study the maths that he hated, pressurising him about his exams and going to university, refusing even to consider the possibility of allowing him to become a carpenter as David so badly wanted. And then not letting him go away for the weekend to bring his girlfriend to the dinner dance, the last straw for her poor unhappy son. And Sean was flinging accusations at her! A red mist danced in front of her eyes and before she knew what she was doing she was on him, clawing at his face with her nails, screaming horrible obscenities at him as hatred surged through her and she struggled to wound him physically as he had wounded her mentally not only on this occasion but all through the years of their marriage.

Pulling off his glasses, she flung them across the room as Sean tried to defend himself from her fury.

"It is your fault!" he shouted. "You killed our son with neglect and you'll have to live with that!"

"It was you!" Claire screamed back, pummelling him. "You never gave him a minute's peace. You were always picking on him. You loved putting him down. You're a bully and a bastard and I'll hate you for as long as I live."

"Mam! Dad! Stop it! Stop it!" Suzy was standing white-faced at the kitchen door, watching them struggle and listening to them abusing each other. Rushing over, she dragged Claire away from Sean and put her arms about her shaking shoulders. "Don't you ever say anything like that to my mother again!" she spat at her father, who was trying to locate his glasses.

"Oh, typical!" he ranted. "Take her side as usual. Well, the two of you can go to hell for all I care. And don't you back-cheek me, miss, or you'll be sorry."

"Come on, Mam. Come in and sit down," Suzy urged Claire, ignoring her father. Claire sat shaking with her daughter's arms around her for a long time. To think that she was capable of such violence shocked her but she wanted to hurt Sean and if she had had a knife in her hand at that moment she would have stabbed him, so complete was her loss of control. She slept on the sofa that night—not that she slept much. Memories of finding David, his funeral, and then her horrific fight with Sean flooded through her mind and when she finally did sleep, she had terrible nightmares.

The next day Claire decided that she was going to go home to Knockross to her mother's house. Molly was deeply shocked by her grandson's death but had been unable to travel to the funeral because of an attack of bronchitis that had kept her in bed. Claire wanted to get away from the house where she was so tormented and would spend two weeks with her mother. Everybody had been extremely kind and understanding at work and her employers told her to take as much time off as she needed. Suzy decided that she was going too. Although she was in her last year at school, she was bright and had no trouble studying and her teachers assured her that they would give her extra tuition so she would catch up on what she missed. Sean didn't say a word when Claire told him coldly that she was going to her mother's for two weeks and that Suzy was going with her. His pale eyes glowered coldly at her from behind his cracked glasses and she knew that he would never forgive or forget her attack on him. She knew, too, that in his view she was responsible for his son's death, that it was something he had had to make himself believe to exonerate himself from any feelings of guilt. He would justify his treatment of David as that of a concerned parent and being a past master at self-delusion he would be able to convince himself of *his* innocence and *her* guilt.

It was a bitter, heartsick woman who got on the Waterford train that wet miserable October day. If it were not for Suzy Claire knew that she would never have gone back to Sean, or back to Dublin for that matter. She never wanted to see her husband again. Any feelings she had ever had for him had slowly been ground away over the years and now she hated him and she blamed him entirely for the death of her son. If Sean hadn't been so unreasonable and so tough on David and if he had allowed him to go to Knockross for his planned weekend he would never have taken his own life. Claire, uncharacteristically bitter, hoped that Audrey, David's girlfriend, who had been so annoyed with him for not taking her to the dance and who had hung up on him during their last telephone conversation, was feeling the worst kind of remorse. She had been at the funeral, but Claire couldn't bring herself to talk to her and had asked Suzy to keep her away from her. Sitting on the train, watching the countryside flash by in a grey rainswept blur, she was consumed with hatred for Audrey and for her husband.

Rosie's mother collected them off the train and drove them to the cottage, where they found a welcome fire and a supper that she had kindly prepared for them. Molly, wheezing but on the mend, was sitting wrapped in a dressing gown by the fire. She held her daughter tightly and Claire clung to her like a little girl. The two weeks at home helped her a little. The bond between Molly and her grew even stronger, as her mother tried to ease the pain of her child's grief. Suzy, though herself grieving deeply, was extremely protective of Claire and they too drew even closer, bonded by their shared loss. Claire could not have cared less what Sean was doing or how he was coping, and not once during her two-week stay did she contact him or he her.

When they did return to Dublin, Claire thought she was going to be sick as she walked up that garden path and was overwhelmed by frightening memories. Sean ignored both of them and she and Suzy spent the evening in the kitchen while her husband sat correcting papers in the sitting room. Once again, she slept on the sofa. The next day she went into town and bought one of those bed-chairs. She asked Suzy if she could put it in her room and sleep there with her. Never again would she share a bed with her husband. As far as Claire was concerned the marriage was over.

At least it helped a little when she went back to work. When she was busy she didn't have to think. In the evening she would cook dinner and silently place it before her husband. In silence Sean would eat it and then remove himself to the sitting room to correct his papers. Suzy spent most of her time studying in her room and Claire found the evenings spent in the kitchen, long and lonely. She began to have panic attacks, gasping for breath as her heart palpitated furiously and her knees turned to jelly. The first time panic struck, she thought she was having a heart attack as her chest got tighter and tighter. Claire managed to call Suzy, who summoned an ambulance. Claire lay breathing erratically as the ambulance sped to the Mater Hospital hoping that she *was* having a heart attack and that it would kill her. She was kept in overnight for tests but they found no evidence of heart trouble and the young hospital doctor told her to go and see her GP about her panic attack.

He prescribed tranquillisers and she swallowed them down gratefully. Anything to dampen her misery. But they only helped for a while and many was the night she lay in her bed-chair in Suzy's room listening to the soft even breathing of her sleeping daughter while her own heart pounded and terror filled her and her palms grew moist and sweaty and she thought she was going out of her mind.

Christmas came and went and that was another nightmare. Again, Claire and Suzy went to Knockross while Sean told her curtly that he was going to spend a few days with his unmarried sister in Drogheda. He could have gone to the moon as far as she was concerned.

At the end of January, Claire passed out at work one day while she was having a particularly heavy period. She telephoned Rosie to ask her if her friend could collect her and take her home. "Right! That's it," scolded Rosie. "You've *got* to do something about yourself. Suzy is worried sick about you and it's not fair to her. She has enough on her plate with David and with the way things are between you and Sean as well as having to worry about doing her exams. I'm going to make an appointment for you to see Emma Morris, the acupuncturist I've been telling you about. I know she'll help you get through this, and she'll be able to do something about your periods as well." She squeezed her friend's hand. "Trust me! I'll go with you the first time."

Walking along the seafront Claire smiled a little as she thought of Rosie, who never took no for an answer. She had even persuaded Ann, Emma's receptionist, to give Claire an appointment immediately, no doubt by telling her just how desperate Claire was. With a sigh, Claire turned around and began to retrace her steps. She was dying for a cup of tea. She'd have a snack in Dun Laoghaire and get the DART back to town and meet her daughter after school. Then maybe Suzy would take a break from her studies and they could go to a picture or something. What would she do when Suzy was gone? It wouldn't be long now. Her exams would be finished in June and she had confided to Claire that she was going back to France to work full time and to perfect her language skills. "Nineteen ninety-two is coming, Mam, and anybody with languages will have no problem getting a good job here," she declared confidently. Claire had recognised the wisdom of her daughter's words and wouldn't dream of not letting her go, no matter what Sean would have to say. And besides, anything had to be better for her daughter's well-being than living in the hellish atmosphere of her home.

But then there'd only be her and Sean, and endless days and years of misery seemed to stretch out in front of her. As she walked along Martello Terrace, past where the Mirabeau Restaurant, the most talked-about restaurant in Ireland, had once been, past Teddy's, that sold the creamiest ice cream on the East coast and where there was always a queue, and on towards the People's Park and the ferry terminal, Claire's resolve grew. She wasn't going to spend her life living as she was now. Anything had to be better than this. When Suzy went, her responsibilities as a mother would no longer restrict her. It would be time to make a decision as to what she was going to do with the rest of her life. She had three months to think about it and make her plans. Feeling hungry for the first time in a long while, after her lengthy walk and the bracing effects of the salty breeze, she turned left in the direction of the Marine Hotel. Whatever plans she was going to make for her future, lunch was the first thing on her agenda.

## Sunday, December 30, 1990

It was just the day to stay in bed, Claire decided. It was cold and blustery and she had no desire to get out of her cosy bed and go down to mass and listen to Christmas carols being sung. They always brought a lump to her throat anyway, and she didn't want to get sad and lonely. Old habits die hard though and she felt a twinge of guilt at the thought of deliberately missing mass. It would be the first time in her life that she had not fulfilled her religious duties. Still, God would understand, she assured herself, as she snuggled down, listening to the rain against the windowpane. Across the room the fire still glowed from the night before. That was one thing about the new smokeless coal: it was great for keeping an overnight fire. But it was terrible for spitting hot lumps. Several times she had been toasting her toes in the evenings after work and they had nearly been burnt off her by a shower of hot bits of coal. In a minute, she'd get up and put on another shovelful of coal and a couple of logs and that would keep the fire going for ages.

To think she had been living in the Drumcondra bedsit for six months. It was hard to believe, and hard to believe how much her life had changed since she had left Sean. It was a truly liberating, if sometimes frightening, feeling, to be in control of your own life. Especially after years of domination, first by her father and then by her husband, she mused ruefully. The decision to leave Sean had been the most terrifying Claire had ever made because it meant leaving her home and husband and standing on her own two feet and becoming responsible for herself. But Suzy and Rosie and Emma had all been there rooting for her, encouraging her to take those shaky first steps. And gradually she had lost her fear and, to her surprise, started to enjoy her independence. When she was living at home there was no chance that she would ever have got the opportunity of having a lie-in on a Sunday morning, or even considered not going to mass.

Every Sunday, week after week, year after year, she and Sean had gone to eleven-thirty mass and then she would go home and continue with her preparations for Sunday lunch. After lunch Sean would listen to the football match on the radio, if there was a match, and then they might go for a spin out to the back of the airport to watch the planes landing and taking off, and then it was back home for tea and a read of the papers before going to bed. As long as they had been living in Dublin the pattern of their Sundays had never changed.

Thinking of Sean, Claire sighed deeply. Now, over a year after David's death, she could pity her husband a little. The awful bitterness and hatred she had harboured towards him had gone, partly because she was no longer living with him and partly as a result of her continuing sessions with Emma at the clinic in Sandycove. "Whatsoever a man soweth that shall he also reap." Emma had quoted scripture to her one day as they talked about the feelings of hate and resentment that she felt towards Sean and her father and that had filled her to overflowing after David's death. "If man gives hate, he will receive hate; if he gives love he will receive love; if he gives criticism, he will receive criticism; if he lies he will be lied to; if he cheats, he will be cheated. That's what that means, Claire, and if you can get rid of all those negative damaging feelings and think and act in a positive way towards people, even those you feel hatred for, you will feel so much better and your life will be enriched many times over." Thus Emma had counselled her. It was a thought-provoking session— such a simple philosophy but so difficult to live by. But she tried hard, knowing that hatred was poisoning her, and as the months went by, Claire managed to find a serenity of sorts as she strove to change her life by thinking and acting as positively as she could.

Sean was deeply shocked when she told him of her decision to leave him. She had been thinking about it all the time in the months coming up to Suzy's exams. When she asked Emma about it, the other woman had told her calmly that the decision must be hers, but if Claire felt that by leaving her husband her life, and possibly his also, would be the better for it, she should think seriously about it. Rosie, loyal as always and unable to bite her tongue, had said briskly that she would have been gone long ago and that if Claire didn't do it now, she'd never do it.

Suzy, who was leaving for France immediately after her exams were over, urged her mother to go and make a new life for herself.

"Do it, Mum! You're still young and anything has to be better than this," she said one night as they chatted quietly in the bedroom after turning out the lights. In the room next door, they could hear Sean's snores. "When I'm gone there'll be just the two of you, and what kind of an existence will you have? You've got a job, you can support yourself, you've got Rosie and Emma. You won't be any lonelier than you are now, and you'll be able to come over to me on holidays. And I'll be able to come and stay with you when I come home." Suzy sounded positively enthusiastic about the idea.

"Do it, Mam!" were the last words her daughter had whispered as they held each other at Dublin Airport, prior to Suzy's departure for her new life in France. Watching her walk through the boarding gates, Claire's heart ached with pride and love for her beautiful, independent daughter. Well, if Suzy could make a new life for herself before she was even out of her teens, so could she, Claire decided. The next evening, after work, she bought an evening paper and set out on the trail of a flat. As soon as she found one and everything was settled she would tell Sean of her decision. He was furious that Suzy had upped and left, not even waiting for her exam results, and he blamed Claire for influencing her and encouraging her. The atmosphere in the house was poisonous and as Claire waited patiently with an assortment of other hopefuls to view the first flat on her list, she reflected that Suzy was right. Anything had to be better than the life she was living. But after she had seen five or six ugly flats that the landlords were charging an arm and a leg for, she wondered . . . Some landlords had such a cheek! Some of the places she had looked at weren't even clean. Of course, with the accommodation shortage and the new university, landlords were rubbing their hands with delight. Nowadays people had to take what they could get, and since she couldn't pay a huge rent for an apartment, she'd just have to put up with one of these flats.

As she walked down the Old Finglas Road towards Glasnevin on her way to see a flat on Botanic Avenue, she decided that she didn't care what it was like—she was going to take it. It had been a week of flat hunting with no success. Rosie had even driven her around on two evenings and when she saw what was on offer she had been disgusted and told Claire to come and stay with her for a while. But Claire was determined. She wanted a place of her own and she wanted her daughter to be proud of her.

She glanced at her watch as she passed the Met station. It was early yet, but then it was Friday, the most popular day for flat hunting, and there'd be plenty of others waiting, no doubt. Passing the well-kept grounds of a small luxurious apartment complex, Claire sighed. What a beautiful place that would be to live if only she had the money. She decided to while away a few minutes having a look around. There were beautiful wrought-iron entrance gates, which were obviously electronically controlled, and she watched a metallic grey BMW glide through them and thought, how posh! Walking through the small pedestrian archway, Claire gazed around with delight. Bathed in the afternoon sunshine of a scorching July day, Mountain View Apartments seemed to belong to another world. Paved walkways wended their way through lush emerald lawns that were surrounded by a profusion of flowering shrubs and bedding plants. The trees that had been on the site had been left there by the builders, and although it was only a relatively new development, five or six years old at the most—she could remember the derelict site that had been there—it now gave the impression of having been there forever. The pale yellow-bricked apartments with their huge flower-filled balconies looked serene and mellow. Claire rested for a little while in the shade of a huge oak tree that grew in the middle of the lawns and thought it was the most beautiful place that she had ever seen. Sitting on a carved wooden bench, listening to the birds singing and the soothing sound of water cascading over rocks in an ornamental pool, she breathed deeply for a little while and made herself relax.

On a balcony on the top floor of the centre block she could see a dark-haired young woman painting at an easel. The life of the idle rich, Claire thought in envy. Well, maybe some day in her successful future, she might be able to afford to live in a place like this. Especially if the business venture took off, that she was thinking of starting up.

She and Rosie had been discussing a business idea that had come to mind one evening when she had been styling her friend's hair. Rosie had broken two bones in her foot when a heavy cast-iron urn had fallen on it while she was gardening. Housebound for a while, which was not her style at all, she invited Claire and Suzy over for dinner one evening shortly before Suzy was to go to France. Rosie's husband was flying to New York and her children were on holidays in Knockcross with their grandmother and Rosie was feeling quite sorry for herself.

"Come on!" Claire offered. "I'll do your hair for you. I brought my gear with me in case you wanted me to do a job on you."

Rosie's face lit up. "You're a pet! There's nothing like getting your hair done to make you feel human again."

"Yeah, it's amazing the difference it makes," Claire responded as she began to snip. "It's all psychological of course. I've had customers in who've cut their own hair in desperation when they couldn't get down to us for a while."

"It must be awful for people who can't get to a salon because they're disabled or housebound or something," Rosie reflected as she sipped her martini, her leg resting on a foot-stool, as Claire worked away. "Aren't I lucky I've got you."

"Oh, there's a need for a mobile hairdresser and that's a fact," Claire replied as she ran her fingers through Rosie's hair to test the balance. "I visit a few old ladies not far from work, in their own houses and flats. Believe me, I could spend all day going around with the number of enquiries I've had. But I only do my few regulars. I'd be wrecked otherwise, although I might start taking on a few more. If I leave home, it would help pay the rent."

"*When* you leave home!" interjected Suzy from the sofa, where she was flicking through a pile of *Cosmopolitans*.

"*When* I leave home," Claire amended.

"You could start up your own business, do a hairdresser on wheels thing or something. There's a very good article here about starting up your own business," Suzy exclaimed, sitting up straight and staring at her mother.

"Would you go away out of that!" laughed Claire. "What would I know about setting up my own business and what money would I have in any case?"

"Borrow from the bank," Suzy said firmly.

"Sure I can't even drive! How could I be mobile."

"Learn to drive," her daughter challenged her.

Rosie smiled at her friend. "Suzy's right and, if you don't mind my saying so, I think it's a brilliant idea. If you can't get enough from the bank, maybe you would take me on as a partner and we could work something out. I've been getting bored lately. The business is practically running itself and I need something new. I'm itching to get my teeth into something else! Suzy, you're a perfect genius!" she beamed at her godchild.

"I know that!" came the smug rejoinder.

Sitting in Mountain View, enjoying the shade, Claire smiled to herself. What a pair! Suzy and Rosie. And yet it *was* a good idea and Rosie was a very astute businesswoman. She was working on the plan right now, doing market research, contacting residential homes and old people's flat complexes to see what the demand would be like. As a birthday present Rosie had given Claire a present of a course of lessons with a driving school. "Don't think you'll be getting the car!" Sean had warned her coldly after her first lesson. Claire had ignored him. She knew better than to think she'd be allowed to drive around in his pride and joy.

With a sigh, she got up from the wooden bench and left the apartment complex to resume her journey to Botanic Avenue. Passing the red-bricked apartments of River Gardens she saw a bikini-clad woman soaking up the sun on her balcony. They were lovely apartments too. It was funny, all the times she had driven past these places with Sean without giving them a thought and now that she was looking for a place to live, she'd love to be able to live in one of them. The woman oiled herself, toasting already tanned limbs. It had been a scorcher of a summer, the best since 1976. How lovely it would be to come home from work and sit on your balcony, relaxing in the evening sun. If she got into a bikini and lay out on the lawn Sean would have a fit. And she could quite easily get into a bikini now, she thought proudly as she passed the Pyramid church and turned left towards Botanic Avenue. She had stuck pretty well to the eating pattern that Emma had set out for her, and after the first few weeks of adjustment, it was amazing how her figure had begun to change and how her energy levels had risen. All the bloating had gone and all the fluid retention, and she was able to fit into clothes that she hadn't been able to fit into for years. The acupuncture was making an enormous difference to her physical well-being. Sometimes, despite David's horrific death and her troubled marriage, she actually felt quite optimistic because of this new sense of physical well-being.

Walking briskly towards the address of the flat, her hand clutching the evening paper, Claire hoped against hope that the place would be in a reasonable condition and that no one would be there before her. She was in luck. There wasn't another soul waiting and the landlord was actually there on time. He showed her into the bedsit, and her heart sank.

Olive green! A drabber colour could not be imagined. But it was clean and the room was big, with an open fire, which was an added bonus. A fridge, cooker, table and stools, and a sofa and bed filled the room. The man showed her the built-in cupboards. There was plenty of storage space, much more than in some of the ugly lodgings she had seen, and it was near enough to work. She could get the 19 or the 34 bus over by the Botanics. The rent wasn't the worst she had heard either.

"Could I paint it myself? The colour is a bit off-putting," she queried hesitantly.

"Sure! If you supply the paint yourself, you can do what you like," the man said briskly. Claire thought he looked like a guard. He was just a little older than her and he had the navy trousers and the cropped hair. Besides, weren't half the landlords in the city guards? The doorbell buzzed shrilly. More viewers. "Do you want it then? Before I let anyone else in to see it?" he asked.

"Mmm . . . yes . . . yes, I'll take it then," Claire agreed hastily, feeling absolutely terrified. In a daze, she heard him answer the door, heard murmured voices and heard him say that the bedsit was taken. Well, this was it! It was now or never. The man didn't seem to notice her panic. He was explaining that he would require a fifty-pound deposit plus a week's rent in advance. Feeling like she was signing her own death warrant Claire wrote out the cheque for the required amount. The first thing she had done when she started to work was to open a bank account and apply for a chequebook. This was the biggest cheque she had ever written. But then, this was the biggest step she had ever taken, she thought, as she stood alone in her new bedsit holding the keys the landlord had given her. Feeling like an intruder, she gingerly sat on the sofa. It was comfortable enough but Claire felt as though she was sitting on hot coals. She stood up and walked over to the window. The pocket-sized front garden had a scorched weedy lawn with a faded, dried-up cherry blossom tree in the centre. Claire always thought that cherry blossoms turned so ugly after their magnificent flowering for those few weeks in the spring. Would she be here in the spring to see it blooming? Feeling extremely apprehensive, Claire let herself out of the bedsit and began her walk home. Sean would have to be told of her decision, and now that the moment was upon her she dreaded the confrontation.

Many times, as she had lain in bed planning her future, she had practised how she would tell Sean. Always in her fantasy, she was calm, cool, and collected but when it actually came to it she just blurted out, "I've got a flat! I'm leaving you."

Sean was incredulous. "You can't do that! What about our marriage vows? We were married in the sight of God, for better or worse. You can't break the marriage contract, Claire."

"I'm not looking for a divorce, Sean," Claire snapped back, irritated by his hypocrisy. "I just think that it would be best for the both of us. Let's both try and salvage as much as we can from our lives. Don't worry," she added, "I won't expect maintenance from you, if that's what's worrying you."

Sean glared at her coldly. "Go, then, if that's what you want, but may God forgive you, because I won't." Claire looked at the bitter, mean man that she had lived with all those years and found herself for the first time feeling faintly sorry for him. Sean had nothing, absolutely nothing, except his regimented routines. He had no friends, his son was dead, his daughter had emigrated and his wife was leaving him. All he had were his bitterness and anger to keep him company. Well, she was leaving all those feelings behind her in this house. She was starting out afresh in the bedsit on Botanic Avenue. Squaring her shoulders, Claire went upstairs and began to pack. She packed her clothes, books, and personal belongings, her photos of David and Suzy, and the white linen tablecloth her mother had given her for a wedding present. Then she phoned Rosie and asked her if she could drive her to her new home. Claire left her marital abode with fewer possessions than she had brought to it but she didn't care. She was damned if she was going to be beholden to Sean Moran for one penny.

Slightly stunned by the news, Rosie arrived to assist with the move. Claire wrote her new address and telephone number on a notepad by the phone and told Sean it was there if ever he needed to contact her. Carrying her case out the door to Rosie's car, and then her box of belongings, and with Rosie's help, the bed-chair, she left the big redbrick house without a backward glance although her heart was aching. That house was her last link with David, however unhappy, but it was a link that had to be broken. In time, Emma had told her, she would be able to think of her son without grief. But now she felt very, very lonely.

"Stay with me until we've decorated the place a bit," pleaded Rosie, trying to hide her dismay at the sight of the olive green colour scheme. Claire was sorely tempted. But she knew if she didn't start as she meant to go on and stay in the bedsit the first night, she'd never stay there. Besides hadn't she paid her rent? No point in wasting hard-earned money.

"Thanks, Rosie, but I'd better stay and get used to it." Claire forced herself to sound cheerful.

Rosie shook her head. "You can be so stubborn, sometimes. But if that's what you want, okay. Just promise me one thing!"

"What's that?"

"If you get lonely or you want to come and stay with me for a while, promise you'll ring me. I'll be right over."

Tears filled Claire's eyes. Rosie had stuck by her all these years, offering unconditional friendship and support. Rosie was her Rock of Gibraltar, able to take her as she was, warts and all. With Rosie, Claire never had to be anything other than herself.

Hugging her friend, she sniffed and said, "It's a pity you can't marry your best friend. Think of all the hassles it would save."

Rosie grinned. "Mmm. If you had the right equipment

now, it would be perfect. The difference one little willie makes!"

Claire laughed, feeling better. Rosie always cheered her up.

They began to unpack, putting away clothes in the wardrobe. Claire put her photos on the chipped mantelpiece. Each week since she had thought about moving she had been buying sheets and towels and cutlery and the like on payday and she had accumulated a little cache of necessities that would get her started. She and Rosie worked companionably, cleaning out the presses and putting away the linen. They made up the bed and covered the duvet with the colourful floral cover with matching pillowcases that she had bought that very day in a drapery shop under the footbridge in Finglas.

"There, that looks better," Claire murmured approvingly as she stood back to admire their handiwork.

"Ah, when we've painted the place up a bit it will be fine," Rosie said reassuringly, always ready to look on the bright side. "Now let's go out and have a bite to eat. You didn't have your dinner, sure you didn't?"

Claire shook her head. She had been too sick at the thought of breaking the news to Sean to eat anything. But now, after the couple of hours of hard work on the bedsit, she was feeling hungry. "Where will we go?"

Rosie considered for a moment. "Well the Skylon Hotel is handy; it's just down the road." Then a thought struck her. "Do you like Chinese?"

"I've never tasted it," Claire admitted. Sean would no more venture into a Chinese restaurant than go to the moon.

"Oooh, you'll love it. Come on, get a bit of lipstick on. We're outta here, big time." Rosie rubbed her hands at the thought of food.

"Out of here—what?"

"Big time," grinned Rosie. "Isn't it the pits? They use the expression all the time in the States. My devoted husband told me that if I don't stop using it he's going to divorce me, citing mental cruelty. Come on, let's go and treat ourselves to a big meal."

Singing "Food, Glorious Food," Rosie drove down Botanic Avenue and turned left at the lights. As with the apartments, Claire had never given Drumcondra more than a glance whenever she had travelled through it, but now she noted with a new interest that there was a Quinnsworth supermarket, a fried-chicken place, Thunder's famous bakery, and lots of other shops around. There was a launderette too, the landlord had told her. That would be handy in the winter. Pulling up at the Chinese restaurant just across the road from the Skylon Hotel, Rosie said cheerfully, "Come on and we'll go into the hotel and have a drink first and then we'll nip across to the restaurant. We might as well make a night of it. After all it is a special kind of night."

"Okay," agreed Claire, hoping she looked dressed-up enough. She wasn't used to going into hotels. "Do I look all right?" she asked, patting her hair nervously.

"You're fine. When you're settled in we're going to go out together at least once a fortnight. It's time to have a bit of fun again," Rosie stated firmly. They went into the hotel and Rosie ordered champagne. Claire's eyes widened at this unheard-of extravagance. "A toast! To you!" her friend declared as she held up her glass of bubbly. "To the start of a new chapter in your life, Claire. I think you really are brave. I'm thirty-eight and I'm not sure I'd have the guts to do what you've just done after what you've been through. But things can only get better." Claire sipped her first-ever glass of champagne and hoped with all her heart that Rosie was right.

That night, as she lay wide-eyed and tense in a strange bed, listening to the unfamiliar sounds of her new home, wondering anxiously if the lock on her door was good and secure, she reflected that she hadn't enjoyed an evening out as much for a long time. Rosie was right: she thought the Chinese meal was delicious, especially the crispy duck, and it would be nice to do something similar on a regular basis with Rosie. The front door slammed shut as someone left the house, and she jumped in the bed. It was the first time she had ever been totally on her own at night. At least when she had been in lodgings in Waterford years ago, she had known her landlady and been treated like one of the family. "Oh, stop it! And go to sleep!" she scolded herself aloud, twisting to find a comfortable position. It was a really hot night but because her flat was on the ground floor, she was afraid to open the window in case of burglars. Tomorrow, she'd go and buy one of those little electric fans. She wondered how was Suzy getting on in Paris. She seemed to have settled in well with the family she was working for and she had phoned several times. Wait until Claire told her that she had made the move. She wondered briefly what Sean was feeling, alone in the house, but banished the thought. Sean had brought it all on himself and she had enough to do to try and find a little bit of happiness for herself.

Gradually she settled in. She and Rosie painted the bedsit lemon and white and the difference a new coat of different-coloured paint made was amazing. It had been some job to scrape and bond the walls before undercoating and finally painting it the fresh lemon colour that immediately lifted your spirits when you walked into the room. A few lamps positioned here and there instead of the harsh main light made such a difference at night.

She met the other people who shared the house. Rick and Pete were two students who lived across the hall from her and who came to her aid one day when her window had got stuck and she couldn't close it. She had made a cup of coffee for them as they struggled to get the window back on the runner. "Tell Rachmann to get that window fixed," Pete, the blond one, said, referring disparagingly to their landlord as he tucked into a plate of cookies. He looked as if he was starving, which he probably was. All the pair of them seemed to eat was burger and chips. They were nice young men, always ready to give her a hand with her parcels or whatever and Claire got friendly with them over the months. They always had a cheery word for her and one day she asked them casually if they'd like to pop over to her room for dinner one night. Eating on her own was something she had not grown accustomed to. They arrived with a bottle of wine and some chrysanthemums that Pete confessed to nicking out of someone's garden. It was the first time Claire had ever been given flowers, and nicked or not, she was touched. They devoured the lasagna she had prepared for them, lavishing compliments on her, and she hid a smile. David had always had a huge appetite and these two were no different; they just didn't eat properly. So occasionally she would have them in to dinner and they would take her over to the Addison for a drink and a bit of fun.

Miss Byrne lived down at the back. She was a small self-effacing woman who worked in the corporation and went to daily mass. She kept very much to herself but was always extremely polite and pleasant to Claire when they met in the hall or outside the bathroom that they shared with Rick and Pete. Miss Byrne made sure that the bathroom and hall were kept spotless. The Hoover that was there for their common use was taken out every Saturday morning at ten on the dot, much to the lads' annoyance as they were usually suffering from a hangover and tried in vain to have a lie-in.

Upstairs, four nurses shared a big flat which was the scene of a few noisy parties, much to Miss Byrne's dismay. The hallway was partitioned and divided off so that they had their own entrance and Claire didn't really get to know the girls, except to say hello if they were entering or leaving the house at the same time. It was nice, she decided, having other people in the building. Her nervousness at night diminished and she began to sleep much better as she settled in.

Suzy was delighted that she had finally taken the plunge and her letters were full of encouragement. Claire wrote to her daughter faithfully every Sunday night, fifteen or twenty sheets sometimes, as she told her about all the new experiences she was having: paying her first electric bill, having Rosie and her husband over for her first dinner party, going out for a drink with Rick and Pete, going swimming in the airport pool with Rosie, going shopping in Quinnsworth or Superquinn on Thursday night after work. It was all new and enjoyable. It had taken her so long to get used to the idea that she could put whatever she liked in the supermarket cart without Sean standing disapprovingly at her shoulder. The first time it really hit her was when she picked up a container of chicken liver pâté with garlic. She had tasted pâté at Rosie's several times and loved the taste of it. Old habits dying hard, she had put it back on the shelf and started to move along when it suddenly dawned on her that if she wanted the pâté she could buy it. She could buy a dozen cartons if she wished. Sean wasn't paying for the shopping, she was. It was *her* shopping. That night, a carton of pâté, a melon, and a package of assorted shelled nuts had gone into the cart. She had put back the pineapple; that was being wildly extravagant. She came home with her booty, lathered half a package of crackers with the pâté, cubed the melon, decorated it with nuts, made a pot of tea and went out to sit under the huge hydrangea bush in the backyard, with her tea and her library book. It was great having the library so near to work that she could pop up during her lunch hour to select a book. It was always hectically busy, particularly after the cutbacks, when it had had to close two nights a week and two mornings, much to the dismay of the Finglas community. Despite this, the staff were always extremely helpful. The smiling man at the desk had told her that it was quite possible to reserve a book if it wasn't on the shelf so she currently had about ten of the latest best sellers on order. And all for free, she thought contentedly, as she settled down to munch and read in the balmy scented breeze of an early August evening. She was reading *To School Through the Fields*, by Alice Taylor, and thoroughly enjoying it. Parts of it reminded her so much of home when she was young. Smiling, she remembered the exploits of old Mickey Hayes and Paudi Leary, the bachelors gay of Knockross. You could write a book about that pair and it would be a best seller.

She had gone down to Knockross a month after leaving

Sean, to tell her mother about it. Molly had just sat quietly holding her daughter's hand. "You were right, child," she said finally. "Everybody is entitled to try and find a bit of peace and happiness in their lives, no matter what the priests and the church say. I should have left Billy long ago, but what would I have done, where would I have gone? At least you have your independence, Claire, your own job and money in your pocket. It's different now—and about time," her mother said almost vehemently. Molly had come to Dublin to stay with Claire for a few days and had had a marvellous time, walking through the nearby botanic gardens, strolling around town on Claire's day off, going to the pictures and then for a meal, a rare treat for Molly.

"I love the city; I always did," she confessed one evening as they walked arm in arm around the big park beside Claire's bedsit.

"Do you?" asked Claire in surprise.

"Oh yes, dear. There's so much to do, without ever spending a penny. And you'd never be lonely," the old lady said sadly.

"Are you lonely at home?" Claire was ashamed that the thought had never really struck her.

"I missed you terribly when you left," her mother said with a smile.

That night, as she lay in the bed-chair, while her mother slumbered contentedly on the divan, Claire thought about what her mother had said. Although she was still extremely active and sprightly, the time would come when she might need looking after. Because of Billy and his drunkenness, Molly had never had a chance to make many friends, Rosie's mother being about the best she had. She'd never leave Knockross and come and live in Dublin, would she? Claire decided to ask her in the morning. They could get a place together. They had always got on well and it would be no hardship for Claire to have her mother living with her.

"What would you think of leaving Knockross and coming

up to Dublin to live with me?" Claire asked the next morning. They were getting ready to go to mass.

Her mother paused in the act of putting on her hat. "For good?" she asked, startled.

Claire nodded, smiling.

"You're a good daughter to me, Claire, and always have been, but I wouldn't like to be a burden on you," Molly said firmly.

"You'd be no burden to me. I couldn't think of anything nicer." Claire leaned over and kissed her mother's cheek.

Two bright spots appeared on the old lady's cheeks and her eyes became suspiciously bright. "I couldn't think of anything nicer, either," she agreed. "I'll put the place up for sale and see how we get on." Arm in arm they set out for mass.

"That was a lovely mass and wasn't the choir beautiful?" Molly declared happily as they strolled back to the bedsit.

"I thought you'd like it. That's why I brought you back to Ballygall parish," Claire explained. She could have taken her mother to the nearer church in Glasnevin, but the choir at the eleven-thirty mass in Ballygall was beautiful and there was something special about the warmth and community spirit of that parish she had lived in for so long that made her feel as though she belonged. When David died, the priests had been so kind to her and people she didn't even know had consoled her after the funeral mass. When people gave the handshake of peace in Ballygall it was genuine. She knew Molly would enjoy the mass. Claire was only hoping she wouldn't bump into Sean. After all it was the mass they had always attended throughout their marriage.

She had phoned Sean twice after she left him. The first time he had told her to leave him alone and not to be annoying him. The second time he had just hung up, his anger almost palpable on the phone. After that, she didn't bother. She didn't want any more rows; she just wanted to live her life in peace and quiet. She would have stayed in contact if he had wanted to. He didn't so that was that. Slowly, bit by bit, Claire began to make a new life for herself.

Molly went home and made plans to put the house on the market. She begged Claire to use the money from the sale to buy them a little house somewhere in the area instead of getting a flat together as Claire had planned. "Child, you'll be getting it anyway when I die. Wouldn't it be better for us to have our own place than to be paying money in rent?" Molly pointed out reasonably.

"But it's your money," Claire protested.

"If you don't agree I'm not coming to Dublin," Molly answered, but her eyes were twinkling. Claire could see that she was really looking forward to coming to live with her. It was as if she had taken on a new lease on life and she had gone back to Knockross on the train full of plans. Claire had never realised just how lonely her mother was. Molly had always seemed so self-sufficient. Claire began to look forward to the change herself. Just think, to be able to decorate a place of their own the way they wanted with no Billy or Sean to dictate to them. She began to frequent the estate agents. They wouldn't be able to decide on anything until they saw how much the house in Knockross would go for. But there was no harm in looking.

Then Sean had a heart attack. His headmaster rang her at work to tell her that he had been rushed to hospital and that she should go there as soon as possible. She left work dry mouthed. What would happen now? Was he going to die? If he lived, he'd need nursing. Was she going to have to give up her precious hard-won peaceful new life-style to look after her husband? After all, she was married to him and that's where her duty lay. Standing in the lift as it slowly made its way up to the coronary care unit on the seventh floor of the Mater Hospital, Claire felt as though she was starting to fall apart. Her palms were sweating and those old panicky fluttery butterfly feelings were coming back. "I cast this burden on the Christ within and I go free," she murmured aloud to herself in the empty lift, remembering the prayer that Emma had taught her to resort to in times of trouble. The place was so quiet! As she had been instructed, she pressed the bell for admittance to the CCU. A nurse met her and told her gently that Sean had suffered a heart attack and was unconscious but that they did not yet know how bad it was. He lay in a small cubicle with wires coming from everywhere and attached to the monitors that the nurses could see on their consoles outside. Numbly she sat beside him. She'd have to go home and get some things for him. In the raised bed he somehow looked small and shrunken and he had aged terribly. Although he was only fifty-six, he looked nearer to seventy at that moment. If he died, they would not have made their peace and she would have to live with that for the rest of her life. It would be another burden to be added to the ones she already carried. Claire left the ward and went to phone Rosie. Her friend came over immediately and took control of the situation as she saw the state of her shaken friend. "Right, we'll stop by the house and get Sean's things and you can ring Suzy."

"Suzy! God, yes, she'll have to be told," Claire responded, hating to have to ring her daughter with such news. Suzy, shocked, said she'd be on the next available flight. Claire felt physically sick as she walked up the garden path of her old home, remembering that awful day when she had found David. As quickly as she could, with Rosie's help, she packed all the things that Sean would need, reading from the list the nurse had given her. Rosie insisted that Claire stay with her in Howth that night. They met Suzy at the airport the next day and went straight to the hospital. There were no set visiting times in the CCU and as Suzy went in to sit with her father, Claire and Rosie stood at the big window on the seventh floor that gave a view of the whole of the city from Howth to Bray. "I'll have to go back and look after him if he gets over this," Claire said quietly.

"Now don't make any hasty decisions, Claire!" Rosie warned. "You owe him nothing. You've got to think of yourself."

"I'd feel as guilty as hell if I didn't." Claire bit back the tears that threatened. She had clawed her way to a semblance of peace and serenity after all these years and now it looked like her life was in tatters again.

"Dad's awake." Suzy came out to her mother, looking strained and tired. "He can't really talk much." Squaring her shoulders Claire walked down along the hushed corridor of the CCU, her footsteps the only sound. Standing by her husband's bedside, Claire saw his eyelids flicker. "You don't have to stay here," he said, gracious as ever.

"I know that, Sean," she said quietly, sitting down beside him.

"Suit yourself," he murmured and drifted back asleep.

As the days passed and the danger of another attack lessened, Sean was moved down to a general ward. It was as though an unspoken truce had been declared between him and Claire for the time being. They spoke about general things, never referring to their situation. Suzy stayed for a week and she stayed in the bedsit with Claire. When she went to visit him for the last time before her return to France, Sean kissed his daughter awkwardly and told her to look after herself.

"I'm going to go into a convalescent home for a month or two. The doctors think it's the best thing for me to do," he told Claire on her visit the next day, and a wave of relief passed through her. She continued to visit him two or three times a week after he was transferred to the small well-run convalescent home. And she had to admit that it was doing him the world of good. He was eating properly, taking regular exercise as prescribed by his doctors and after his brush with death he was much less regimented and repressed.

"I've decided to take an early retirement," he told her one day, several weeks later. "I'll be getting a good lump sum and pension and I've made quite a bit of money out of investments over the years." This was news to Claire, but typical of her husband, she decided. Well, good luck to him. She didn't want his money. "I'm thinking of going back to Drogheda to live with Martha." Martha was his unmarried sister and they were close in their own way.

"That's a good idea, Sean. You love Drogheda and it would be a nice place to retire to," Claire said.

"Do you want to move back to the house?" he asked her.

Claire shook her head. She could never live in that house again. It held too many unhappy memories.

"We'll sell it then. Whatever I get for it, you and Suzy can have to get a place of your own."

Claire couldn't believe her ears. Was this Sean talking? He saw the shock on her face. "Ah . . . I've been talking to a priest here, a very nice fellow. He made me look at a few things differently. You've as much stake in that house as I have and it's my duty to provide for Suzy. So that's what we'll do."

"God, it must have affected his brain." Rosie was stunned when she heard Claire's astounding news. "I hope you're taking the money and running!" she added sternly as she saw the look of confused indecision on Claire's face.

"I don't want to be beholden to him!" Claire murmured doubtfully.

"Beholden my arse! You're entitled to that money, Claire, for all those years when you never got a penny out of him! It's about bloody time he had an attack of conscience. Nothing like a near miss to put the fear of God in to you and make you mend your ways," snorted Rosie. "You take that money, my lady, and don't feel one bit bad about it! It's your due!"

"Mother, don't you dare refuse that offer," Suzy ordered, over the telephone line from France. "Dad's obviously trying to make amends and whatever you get you deserve ten times as much. For him to go and retire to Drogheda with his family is perfect for him. Now you think of yourself and go and get a nice place to live with Nana, some place where I'll be able to come and visit in comfort."

Claire put down the phone, not knowing whether she was on her head or her heels. Lying on her divan, listening to the relentless rain beating against the window, Claire smiled as she thought of Suzy. Her daughter hadn't come home for Christmas. She had gone skiing in Gstaad with the family she was au pairing with. At the end of January she was taking up a position as stewardess on a Cunard cruise liner. The world was her oyster.

Claire went down to stay with Molly on Christmas Eve, relieved to know that Sean was much improved and was quite happy to be back in Drogheda with his sister. Their house in Ballygall was up for sale. Molly, too, had a For Sale sign outside the cottage and she told Claire happily that she had several interested parties who were making good offers. "I'm really looking forward to going to live in Dublin but are you sure you still want me to come?" she enquired anxiously, after Claire had told her all about Sean and the house. "Sure, you might want to get back with him and start off afresh in a new place."

"No, Mum, I'd never go back to Sean. I could never live with him again. We're better off the way we are. We keep in touch by phone. He's happy in Drogheda and he's delighted to be retired from teaching—it was getting to be an awful strain on him. He can potter about his garden all day to his heart's content and I can get on and do something with my life. And more than anything I'd love to have you up in Dublin with me." They spent Christmas making plans, and Claire went back to her bedsit determined that the bad times were behind her and convinced that the only way she could go was up.

Now, listening to the rain drumming down, watching the flames flickering brightly in the grate, she stretched contentedly, reached down beside the bed and picked up one of the Sunday papers she had bought late the night before. It was one of the English tabloids with the magazine and she thoroughly enjoyed it. Sean had always called them the lowest of the low and wouldn't permit them in the house, but now that she was her own woman and could buy what she liked she always bought one of them, enjoying reading the gossip about Fergie and Di and the rest. Not that she didn't buy the other papers. She had read the *Independent,* and she'd keep the *Sunday Press* for later. Feeling peckish, she made a pot of tea, put some pâté and crackers on a tray and got back into bed. Later in the afternoon, she'd ring out for a Chinese meal to be delivered and that would take care of dinner. She was really pampering herself today, living the life of a lady.

And why not? You deserve it, Claire told herself firmly as she munched on her pâté and crackers. Laying down the tray, she picked up Suzy's stocking-filler of a Christmas present. *Be Your Own Boss, A Guide to Starting Your Own Business* by Terry Prone and Frances Stephenson. Claire plumped up her pillows and settled back comfortably. She was as far as Chapter Five which covered "Getting started." She was spending the New Year with Rosie and their plans for their new enterprise were well under way. Claire had handed in her notice at work and as she became engrossed in the book, she decided happily that 1991 was going to be the year her life would change completely.

# *Lainey*

**Thursday, August 2, 1990**

*L*ainey watched in disbelief as the television pictures showed Iraqi tanks rolling into Kuwait. It wasn't too long since she had flown into Kuwait International Airport and now here she was, sitting in Dominic's apartment, watching Saddam Hussein invade that small country. There was going to be trouble there, no doubt about it. Just as well she was home to stay.

She had made a lot of money in Saudi, especially in the last eighteen months that she had been purser, but she was glad to be finished. It had been an enriching experience. She had seen many places and travelled the world during her time as a stewardess, eaten the finest foods, gone scuba diving in the Red Sea, snorkeling off the Great Barrier Reef, visited the pyramids of Egypt, Paris in the springtime and New York in the fall. But she'd worked hard. It was tough being a stewardess on any airline but Eastern Gulf had been a tough number, with its male Arab passengers, snapping their fingers, calling, "Sister, sister, get me this, get me that. What is the direction of Mecca?"

"I'm not your bloody sister, thank God," she would swear under her breath, sorely tempted to point them in the wrong direction as they knelt, clogging up the aisles, when it was time to pray. Being an air hostess was not all glamour, Lainey conceded. Nevertheless it was an interesting, responsible job and she was not the "glorified waitress" that Cecily had called her during Martin's wedding reception.

That had been a day and a half and darling Cecily had certainly shown her true colours! Of course her nose had been mightily put out of joint when she saw the glamorous creations her in-laws were wearing. Lainey had hit Paris with a vengeance and bought designer outfits for her mother, Joan, and herself. Cecily had not been privy to this little titbit. She had gone to Dublin, to Penthouse and Pavement and bought herself a John Hagerty creation with a dropped waist and big shoulder pads. She thought she was the bee's knees until she arrived at the house on the day of the wedding and saw the style of the others.

"Did you see what Lainey treated us to? Isn't she the best in the world and isn't her Yves Saint Laurent suit gorgeous? And what do you think of the outfit she bought me from Chanel?" Mrs. Conroy asked her daughter-in-law, delightedly.

"Very nice!" clipped Cecily.

"Your dress is lovely too, dear," Mrs. Conroy added hastily, noticing the frosty tone. Cecily ignored her, sat down in an armchair and stuck her head in the paper. Mrs. Conroy raised her eyes to heaven as she caught Lainey's glance. Lainey could feel herself getting annoyed. Typical of Cecily! She couldn't stand for someone else to be better dressed than herself. Tony caught her eye, knowing exactly what was going through her head.

"Count to ten," he advised as he saw the glower on Lainey's perfectly made-up face.

"If that one starts her carrying-on today, I'm telling you she's going to get it from me," Lainey muttered as Tony led her over to the window seat in the sitting room.

"Oh, goody! I love when you cause a scene, but there aren't enough people here to enjoy it. Wait until we're in the church or the hotel or something," Tony urged wickedly.

Lainey started to laugh. Tony was irrepressible and just the antidote to Madam Cecily's rudeness. "You're looking extremely elegant, I must say." Lainey smiled as she admired her friend in his grey suit and embroidered silk waistcoat.

Tony smirked. "I didn't want to let the side down with all these designer labels and things. I'll have you know this is a Louis Copeland suit, and Jonathan bought me the waistcoat in New York."

Lainey looked at him affectionately. They had been friends for so long. They worried about each other and cared about each other and told each other everything. Tony had settled down so much since Jonathan came into his life and he had done very well in his accounting career. He was still game for anything, still incorrigible, but much more content and happy in himself now that he was in a loving, stable relationship that had lasted over the years. He had never been able to tell his family about his homosexuality and his mother and everyone else in Moncas Bay could not understand why Lainey and himself who had been together for so long and who always attended social functions in the village as a couple, were still not married. No doubt the tongues would be wagging again today when they were seen together in church and at the reception. It didn't bother them. In fact, Lainey enjoyed giving the gossips something to chew on. And it gave her a little added pleasure to know that Steve was as confused as everyone else.

She had seen Steve on many occasions since that night he

had kissed her and told her he still wanted her. She knew his desire for her had not waned one bit. And that gave her no small sense of satisfaction. Let him go on wanting her, because he'd never have her again. And besides she didn't want him anymore and that was a great freedom. Dominic was all she needed. Dominic and her independence. Steve McGrath could go and whistle! She smiled to herself. He had been practically whistling last night at the pool party at the Mangans', scene of their first meeting so many years ago.

Tony's father had thrown a party to celebrate clinching a business deal. No expense had been spared; a big marquee had been erected near the pool and the caterers called in. All the glitterati for miles around had been invited, including Cecily and Simon, much to Cecily's delight, and of course Steve and Helena McGrath. The two social butterflies had tried to outdo each other in stories of how good their "little woman" was. Lainey and Tony had been vastly entertained. Steve had not taken his eyes off Lainey all night, but apart from exchanging a few social pleasantries with him, she ignored him, much to his annoyance. When she went and changed into an emerald-green bikini, that showed off her stunning, long-legged, tanned figure to perfection, he couldn't hide the desire in his eyes. Eat your heart out, Steve, she thought grimly as she executed a perfect dive into the pool, where Tony and Simon and Cecily were already swimming around with several others. Cecily made sure to stay out of Lainey's way, not wishing to have her freckly paleness contrasted with her sister-in-law's glowing tan. When Lainey got out of the pool and dried herself off and got dressed again, Steve was waiting for her.

"Lainey!"

"Hi, Steve," she said with a studied casualness, not letting him even get started. Then she walked past him to where Tony was waiting for her at the bar. What her former lover had to say she had no intention of discovering. Maybe he wanted to apologise for his behaviour that day on the beach. Maybe he wanted to proposition her again. Lainey didn't care to find out. She still found him attractive, she couldn't deny that. It had taken her a long time to get over him and the only way she was able to do that was by keeping him at arm's length. That's the way she intended to continue. If he was suffering because of it, tough! It was his choice. At least he wouldn't be at the wedding and thankfully they were having the reception in the Arklow Bay Hotel—much to Cecily and Simon's chagrin as they much preferred swanning around Fourwinds in their finery. Lainey was delighted. Fourwinds was the last place she wanted to go. The Arklow Bay was a lovely hotel and the rest of the family was looking forward to the meal and reception.

The wedding mass was a lovely special intimate ceremony and Lainey had hugged her new sister-in-law warmly outside the church. Cecily had had a face on her in the church and it was obvious she and Simon were having a tiff.

"What's new?" Joan said, grinning and unperturbed, when Lainey mentioned it as they waited to get the photographs taken. Cecily stood with an expression that would have curdled milk while Simon's was not much better. Joan was thrilled to bits with her turquoise watered silk two-piece and white silk top by Dior. She had got engaged at Christmas, much to Lainey's delight. Cecily and Simon were the least of her worries. "Those two are always at it. Tidings of comfort and joy, I call them," she murmured out of the side of her mouth, causing Lainey to get a fit of the giggles.

The meal was delicious and Lainey had enjoyed herself dancing with a succession of partners. Tony and she had just finished a waltz and the band was taking a rest so they sat down at their table with Joan and her fiancé and Cecily and Simon.

"When are you two going to get married, anyway? Or are you going to live in sin forever?" Cecily enquired petulantly.

"I beg your pardon!" Lainey, stunned, couldn't be sure whether she had heard right. Joan's jaw had dropped five inches and Tony was quite unable to hide his amusement.

"You heard. When are you going to get him to make an

honest woman out of you and stop being the talk of the village?" Cecily eyed her sister-in-law coldly, taking a swig of her white wine and adding bitchily, "Your 'sell-by date' is long gone. If you're not careful you'll be on the shelf."

"How dare you, Cecily Clarke!" Lainey gritted. "What I do is none of your business or anybody else's for that matter. Looking at you would put anyone off marriage for life, believe me. And I'll tell you something else for nothing, Cecily. You are by far the most ignorant person it has ever been my misfortune to encounter. You could do with a few lessons in good manners because yours leave a lot to be desired." There! She had said what she had wanted to say for a long long time and boy, did it feel good.

"Huh!" Cecily said with a sniff, focusing her eyes with a little difficulty. "You think you're so high and mighty, the great Lainey Conroy. All you are is a glorified waitress." She smiled triumphantly.

"I'd far prefer to be a glorified waitress and have my own money than to be a lazy parasite to some poor unfortunate who'd have to work himself into an early grave to keep me in clothes," Lainey retorted. She was a little shocked to realise that her sister-in-law was as drunk as a skunk.

"You . . . you . . . bitch!" Cecily jumped up, enraged, her accent slipping to reveal her Dublin origin.

"Oh, behave yourself, Cecily. If that's the way you carry on at weddings where *you* come from, remember that we are a little more civilised down here," Lainey snapped, rising from her chair and leaving the table. If she stayed a minute longer, she'd slap the other girl's face.

"Round one to Lainey," said the hugely amused Tony with a grin as he caught up with her.

"Did you hear her?" exploded Lainey. "Did you see her? She's completely pissed!"

"Our Cecily's a right little drinker despite her little lady-like airs and graces." Joan arrived and they watched Cecily berating Simon, who was trying to get her to leave.

"Since when?" said Lainey in amazement.

"You're never here, of course," reflected Joan. "Oh, Cecily can lower it as good as anyone. I've never seen her this drunk, mind you. I think it was being outshone in the fashion stakes put her in a bad humour because she started lowering the G&Ts as soon as we got to the hotel."

"Silly bitch," Lainey retorted, hoping her mother hadn't witnessed the incident. But Mrs. Conroy was happily chatting to Maura's mother and hadn't seen a thing.

"This is the best wedding I've been to for ages. It's a pity there weren't a few fisticuffs. I'd have really enjoyed that now. It would have crowned it all nicely," Tony said, straight-faced.

"I'll fisticuff *you* in a minute if you don't shut up!" Lainey watched Simon leave the function room with his arm around a very unsteady Cecily. The remainder of the evening passed off peacefully. The next time she saw her sister-in-law, Cecily ignored her completely and that suited Lainey just fine. Simon started to get on to Lainey but she coolly told him to shut up and said it was nothing to do with him. Cecily was big enough and cheeky enough to fight her own battles. She was no shrinking violet despite her demure manner; that had been quite obvious at the wedding. Simon had been extremely put out and very cool ever since but that was his problem and Lainey wasn't going to lose any sleep over it. If he thought for one moment she was going to put up with any more of Cecily's impudence, he could think again!

A few months after the wedding, not long after Christmas, Lainey had got a very interesting letter from Michelle Powell. Lainey had kept in contact with the author, who kept her up to date with book world gossip. As Lainey had predicted, and it was something she took no pleasure from, several of Verdon's top-selling authors, including Michelle, had gone to other publishers. Michelle had written to say that the sales and marketing manager of Eagle Publishing, her present publishers, was leaving in the late spring and to wonder if Lainey would be interested in the job. The publishers would love to interview her, knowing of her brilliant track record at Verdon, and Michelle promised she'd dedicate her new book to her and that she'd never moan about anything again if Lainey would come back to Ireland and arrange her next launch.

Lainey jumped at the idea. She had a fine fat bank balance, more than enough to buy an apartment somewhere, and more than anything she wanted to get back into publishing. Eagle Publishing was a thriving company, just what she needed. There'd be plenty of travelling as well so she wouldn't be completely grounded. On her next leave she flew home and did an interview and was told the following morning that the job was hers.

Dominic was ecstatic. She had finished up with Eastern Gulf and taken a month's holiday in Greece, meeting up with Tony and Jonathan for the last week. Eagle Publishing had their offices on the Northside, so she rented an apartment in Griffith Avenue for the time being until she bought a place of her own. It wasn't far from Dominic and was ideal for the airport.

Before long it was as though she had never been away. She was welcomed back with open arms and all the contacts made while with Verdon stood her in good stead. She was given all the leeway she needed. Eagle Publishing were more than delighted to have a sales and marketing manager of Lainey's calibre in their company. When Annette Jackson, the hugely successful biographer, heard that Lainey was back in publishing, she promptly decided that she wanted to be published by Eagle and left Verdon with indecent haste much to their dismay and Eagle's delight. Lainey was in her element. Back where she belonged.

Watching the news about Kuwait, she shivered despite the heat of the evening sun. It had been the hottest day of the year, and she had opened wide all the windows and patio doors in Dominic's apartment to try to create a draught. She didn't expect Dominic home for another hour but she had a salmon salad all prepared, and wine chilling in the fridge. She could have had Dominic come to her own place but she hadn't unpacked half of her belongings in the new apartment as she didn't intend staying there that long. But she was so busy at work with all the new books being launched she just hadn't the time to go house hunting.

Happily she set the table on the patio. It had been as hot today as any scorcher in Saudi but a bit of a cooling breeze was beginning to blow up. People were saying it was the hottest day of the century and they could well be right, she decided, as she flicked a fly off the table.

Dominic greeted her with roses and a kiss and they sat down to dinner after he had showered and changed. They enjoyed their meal, chatting about their day's work and enjoying each other's company as they always did. Later in the cool of the night they made love and as they lay close together, caressed by the scented breeze that blew through the open window, Dominic took her face in his hands and stared down at her in the moonlight.

"Lainey, I've been thinking," he said, staring down at her. "I want to leave Rita. I love you so much I want us to be together for always."

# *Dominic*

Monday, April 8, 1991

Yawning, Dominic drove into Mountain View and saw a man placing an estate agent's For Sale notice up at the front gates. Oh! Someone's selling up, he thought idly. He had bought the apartment here in the mid-eighties and never regretted the buy. It was his haven from the world and it suited him perfectly. He yawned again. He was tired. It had been a killer of a drive up from Cork that morning. The fog had been a nightmare. The Monday-morning drive up was a bit of a killer really. He didn't usually come up to Dublin until

Wednesday afternoon, spending the first part of his week in the Cork office, but there was a big consignment coming in that needed urgent attention and so his presence was required. To be fair to Janet, his office manager, she was extremely competent at her job. Still Hillyards were important clients and he would be well paid for his labours.

He would have come up last night but his second grandchild was being christened. Kimberly had had a baby by Senan McCarthy and the bastard had run out on her and was now in London. Once she had got over the shock of her unmarried daughter becoming pregnant, Rita had everything under control and as well as minding their first grandchild, Michael's son, was in her element, changing nappies and feeding her new granddaughter. Kimberly and the baby had moved back home and the house was as chaotic as usual.

He sighed deeply. He had so badly wanted Lainey to say that she would live with him. He would have told Rita that he was leaving and paid her maintenance and come to live in Dublin. But she was adamant. She wanted a place of her own, wanted to be her own boss and wanted to be tied to no one. Trust him to pick someone like Lainey. Most women would be clamouring to have their lovers leave their wives and live with them. She had reacted in shock when he had told her he wanted them to live together and make a commitment. The irony of it. The wheel had come full circle. Women no longer needed men. They could live perfectly happily supporting themselves and if he and others like him didn't like it, that was tough! That she loved him he no longer doubted. But he realised that Lainey, after her experiences with Steve McGrath, was never going to allow anyone to have control over her emotions again. No one was ever going to have the power to be able to hurt her as she had been hurt so long ago. By keeping her independence and her career, Lainey felt she was in control and there was nothing he could say that would persuade her otherwise. When he had reminded her that she was in her mid-thirties and asked if she had ever thought of having children, she had told him with perfect truthfulness that she didn't think she would be a good mother. She had grown too used to being able to do as she pleased and, selfish though it might seem, she didn't want to have a child and end up resenting it for curtailing her freedom. She didn't feel any overpowering urge to become a mother and she felt no woman should have a child because it was expected of her, just because she was a woman.

Lainey was the most totally honest woman he had ever met. She had never been anything less than honest with him in regards to their relationship and she could face herself and her faults without flinching, believing that she was what she was and that if people didn't like her they could lump her. He didn't think she was being selfish not wanting a child. It was an awesome commitment to produce a child, and if she felt it was not for her, she was far more honest than some couples he knew who had children and paid other people to rear them while they carried on gaily working, socialising, and the like as though nothing had changed in their lives. Designer children he called them. It had become a status thing to have kids now. The new "in" accessory. From what he heard, Lainey's nephew, Andrew, was such a child, the poor kid. Dominic respected Lainey more than any other woman he had ever met and although he had been deeply disappointed that she would not live with him he knew her well enough to know that it was not a rejection of him and that their love was as strong as ever. Because he loved and understood her he had accepted her decision.

After a shower and breakfast he felt more alert and refreshed and ready to face the day. Driving out through the wrought-iron gates he noticed the For Sale sign again. A thought struck him.

Lord, it would be perfect. He jammed on the brakes, took a note of the name and phone number of the agents and smiled to himself. An apartment in Mountain View would be perfect for Lainey. It would be practically as good as living together. The next best thing. An ideal solution. He wondered which block it would be in. It was hardly someone in theirs.

He hadn't heard anything about anyone moving. Maybe Liz might know; she was having a management committee meeting at the end of the week. Thank God it was in her apartment; if it was in Al and Detta's he'd refuse to go. Those kids were the worst he knew, even worse than Mona's and that was saying something. Candine and Tralee Shaw were the best example of designer kids he had ever seen. Mind, the parents were something else. The kids couldn't be blamed, he supposed. Only last week Candine had thrown a flower pot down on top of Derek as he was showing his patio off to another new girlfriend. And Al and Detta had murmured something about childish high spirits and not lifted a finger to correct the brat! Al was such a bore. He had buttonholed Dominic the other day pretending to want to confirm that he had the right date for the committee meeting just as an excuse to fiddle with his new Psion organiser in front of him. He had been waffling on about how hard he was worked and how he had spent all of St. Patrick's weekend "reading on" stock onto the new computer Hanley and Mason had installed and how being an information scientist was no joke.

Wouldn't it be wonderful if Al and Detta and brats were selling to become even *more* upwardly mobile! Dominic liked the rest of his neighbours. Liz Lacey was terrific, with a great sense of humour; Derek, across the hall from him, was fine. He took himself so seriously and was sowing plenty of wild oats, but kept himself to himself. Maud and Muriel were very reserved with him, obviously putting two and two together where Lainey was involved. But they passed the time of day with him and that was all he wished for.

He didn't know anyone else in any of the other blocks on the complex. Anyway, to find out all he had to do was ring the estate agents and make an appointment to view. Then he'd ring Lainey with the good news. It was like fate, Dominic decided as he sped down Griffith Avenue towards his Fairview office.

# Cecily and Simon

### Saturday, December 29, 1990

**D**ressed in a pale peach Lacoste tracksuit, Cecily observed with satisfaction the controlled chaos that was her kitchen. The caterers she had hired were already hard at work and everything was progressing well. Simon was taking care of the drinks. She was looking forward to the party. Cecily loved entertaining. It gave her something to do, something to plan for and she always felt a great sense of satisfaction when a party went well. She entered her dining room and viewed it with an experienced eye. Yes, the table was fine, the flowers just right. This year her theme colours were gold and white. The cutlery gleamed and the crystal sparkled. She had decided on a buffet because of the numbers coming, and once the dividing doors were opened, there'd be plenty of room.

"Everything looks good, Cecily, up to your usual excellent standards," her husband commented approvingly as he passed by with a couple of ice buckets.

"Thank you, darling." She smiled, pleased. She was going to take a split of champagne from the fridge and relax in a warm bath for a little while before she dressed. "It will be time to dress soon. I must see how Andrew is getting on."

Her son was sitting on his bed with a face like a thunder cloud. "I really wanted to go and stay at Gran's. I hate it when you have parties," he moaned.

"Now stop that nonsense, Andrew," Cecily snapped. "You don't know how lucky you are. Now hurry and get dressed so you'll be ready to greet the guests. And don't forget to wear your new waistcoat," his mother warned him as she closed the door behind her. What had got into him, she wondered as she walked into her own bedroom and poured herself a drink. Andrew was so handsome and she was dying to show him off. She had bought him a lovely new suit and a gorgeous embroidered waistcoat to go with it. He would look quite the little man.

Andrew made a face at his mother's retreating back and let out a string of very satisfying curses. If he was heard using such language he'd be murdered, but in the privacy of his own room, he always indulged himself. That hideous waistcoat that his mother had bought in Dublin; Andrew hated it. Why couldn't he wear his new denim jacket and jeans that his Aunt Lainey had sent him down for Christmas. She really knew what a fella liked. He was twelve years old, nearly a teenager, in boarding school in Dublin. He was too old for his mother to be telling him what to wear. The blokes at school would give him hell if they ever found out. With a look of determination Andrew marched over to his wardrobe, took out his new denim outfit, found a crumpled T-shirt in his laundry basket and began to dress. When he was ready he went to his drawer and took out a little box. In it was his pride and joy. His gold earring. One of the fellas at school had pierced his ear with a darning needle for him. It had hurt like hell but it had been worth it. And at least he hadn't been called chicken like Ken O'Neill! Inserting his precious earring he took out some mousse and gel from his toilet bag. Industriously he set to work on his hair, stiffening it into spikes. Then when he was finally satisfied he delved deep into his wardrobe and brought out his precious Doc Martins that he had bought with the money his Grandad had slipped him at Christmas. While he was waiting, he decided he might as well have a fag. Taking one from the cache in his underwear drawer Andrew opened the window, lit up and began to puff away contentedly.

Simon hummed to himself. Thank God Cecily was in good form. She had been like an Antichrist lately. Of course that row at Martin's wedding hadn't helped. That Lainey had a mouth as big as the state of New York! Cecily had been right to get on to her about the carrying-on with Tony Mangan. It was ridiculous. They should have been married years ago, God knows, they were going together long enough. It might be the nineties, but Moncas Bay was a small enough place and people talked. The least they could do was to legalise things. Cecily had every right to remonstrate with his sister about her unseemly behaviour. After all it was Cecily who had to listen to the gossip about Lainey, while she was swanning around the capital doing the career girl. There had been no need for Lainey to attack Cecily so viciously. Mind she'd always had a very sharp tongue and a mighty temper. Simon sighed. It had been hell living with Cecily for the few months after the incident. But she seemed to be getting back to her old self. At least he'd had Máire to comfort him. She had been thrilled with the gold earrings he had bought her for Christmas. She was so easily pleased. It was a joy to be with her. Pity she had gone home to Wexford for Christmas. Still, she'd be back soon. Whistling cheerfully, Simon spooned a generous amount of caviar on to a cracker and ate with relish.

Máire Noonan smiled as the lamplight reflected in the sparkling diamond ring on her left hand. She turned it this way and that, watching it glow. Thomas had finally proposed on Christmas Eve and she had graciously accepted. She had been starting to get worried; after all they had been dating ten years and these farmers were awfully cautious. Anyway, he'd had to wait until his mother died and he got his hands on the farm. His mother had hung on grimly to her only son, but she was gone now and Máire had him at last. Thank God she wouldn't end up a spinster. Regretfully, she fingered one of the gold earrings in her ear. She'd have to tell Simon she was leaving to go home to look after her parents or something. She wouldn't like to hurt his feelings by telling him she was engaged. Besides, he might want all his presents back. He had been a more than generous lover. No, nearer the time that she was getting married, she'd tell him that she had to leave work to go home. It had been good all the years it had lasted. Now she had her reward for her patient wait for Thomas. Máire was going to become a married woman at last.

# TUESDAY, APRIL 23, 1991

# THE VIEWING

# Liz

"I'll have the deep cleanse facial with steam, the eyebrow shape, manicure, and full leg wax, please, Susan," Liz said as she mounted the grey-carpeted stairs of the salon, accompanied by the extremely attractive beautician. Dark and tanned, she always looked so well, and Liz had used her as a model for several sketches. Liz had already spent the last half hour at the tender mercies of her hairdresser, Nikki, and now, with her still-to-be-dried hair wrapped in a white fluffy towel, she was ready to be beautified. They reached the pink and green haven where Susan worked miracles on her clients.

"I'll get you a cup of coffee," the beautician said, laughing: "You might need it before you're finished."

"A cup of coffee is just what I need. Today's the day of the viewing. I've left them to it."

"You were right. It's awful having strangers poking around your house. By the time you're finished here they'll surely all be gone," Susan said sympathetically.

"That's why I'm having the whole works. It's a great excuse!" Lying back in the cream leather recliner as Susan went downstairs to get the coffee, Liz gave a deep sigh. She was doing the right thing, she was sure of it. John O'Malley, the estate agent, had arrived and she had left him the keys, much to his disappointment. He had been looking forward to a cosy chat. As she walked out of the complex she had seen a tall, thin blond woman get out of a car and look interestedly around her. She had a very sharp face and Liz, unreasonably, hoped she wasn't one of the viewers. She saw the woman look at her watch. She must be one of them! Of Hugh and his mother there was no sign, but as she crossed the busy road to the hairdresser's she saw Dominic's car in the car-park, so he and Lainey must be there.

Listening to the soothing music and the muted sounds of the hair driers in the salon downstairs, she felt herself relax. Whoever bought it, she wished them well. She had made the decision to sell after much soul-searching and she knew that what she had decided was what she wanted.

It had all happened very quickly, smoothly even, once she had made her decision. Poor Hugh, he had been hurt but not greatly surprised, when she told him that although she loved him she could not marry him and live in America with him. It had not been an easy decision to make. They had been together for a long long time, but his needs and hers were too far removed. If they married, the conflict could become too difficult to handle.

When she had told him she wanted to have a child nevertheless, he had been horrified. Liz smiled as she remembered the expression on his face when she had told him.

"Are you crazy, Liz? What would people say? Imagine if the newspapers got hold of it?"

"Hugh, I couldn't give a fiddler's for the newspapers and I've never worried about what people say and I'm not going to worry now. I've wanted a child for such a long time. I'm thirty-four. I can't leave it much longer."

"Don't you think it's being a bit selfish and hard on the child? After all, you won't marry me. I'm going to be living in America. You're going to have to rear it by yourself."

"I've really thought about it and maybe you're right, but Hugh, don't you think it's much better to bring a child into the world who's going to be very much loved and wanted even if I am single, than to have an unwanted baby just because you're married? I think there's a lot of hypocrisy around, and who's got the right to tell me I'm wrong? Anything that's one with love can't be wrong." She was pleading with him to understand.

"Ah, Liz, Liz, trust you to be different." Hugh shook his head thinking that as long as he lived she'd always surprise him.

Liz took a deep breath. "Will you think about it when I'm in Majorca?"

"Are you sure you won't marry me?"

"Hugh, we'd end up at each other's throats."

He smiled wryly. "I know you're right; I wish you weren't."

"We can always visit and keep in touch. You might get fed up in America and suddenly decide that domestic bliss is really what you've been wanting all along." Liz drew him close for a hug.

Hugh hugged her back. "Miracles do happen."

She had gone off to Majorca in a happy frame of mind, knowing that at last she was doing something about setting change in motion. Incarna and she had had a lovely time just browsing through the shops and taking long energetic walks. As they were walking down into Santa Ponsa one afternoon, Liz idly noticed a *Se Vende* sign. Peering through the wrought-iron gates she saw the little whitewashed villa with its oval turquoise pool and its flower-filled courtyards and reflected that it would be a lovely place to live. And it was only five minutes from Incarna's. Her eyes widened in shock. What was she thinking of? She hurried on after Incarna.

All that night she lay thinking about the villa. It would be perfect, really perfect. The climate suited her so well, she would be free to paint as never before . . . and Majorca was only two and a half hours from home. Casually, she mentioned the idea to Incarna.

"What a wonderful, wonderful idea," the Spanish woman enthused. "Come, let us go and find out all about it."

They had arranged a viewing, and Liz had fallen in love with the villa there and then. The views were magnificent and it was so peaceful. She could turn one of the bedrooms into a

studio. There was a bedroom for the baby, and one for he
self, and there was plenty of room for visitors. Don and E
and Christine and Liam would be able to spend long sun
holidays here. Liz began to get excited. And the best thi
was that the price was well within her means.

"It's a terrific idea," Eve admitted when Liz told h
"What will you do with the apartment?"

Liz hadn't really given it much thought. "Well, I ca
really sell it. I'll need a base here. I'm not decamping totall

"Hmm," mused Eve. "I know!" She grinned triu
phantly. "Sell it and come back to the flat. We're not letting
anymore—it's too much hassle."

Liz beamed. "That's a great idea, Eve!" She thought for
moment and said slowly, "Well, I don't know. I didn't tell y
this but I'm not going to go with Hugh to America and I'
hoping to have a baby."

Eve didn't bat an eyelid. "I was thinking that you'd
that eventually," she said, smiling. "And I think you're righ

Tears welled up in Liz's eyes. "Oh Eve, you're the bes

"So are you," replied her sister-in-law enveloping her in
hug. They talked about the baby for hours. Liz knew fro
being so deeply involved with her nieces that it was a hu
and awesome responsibility to have a child and raise it, ar
even more so without having a partner to support you. Sl
had sat worrying with Eve in Temple Street Hospital whe
Fiona was suspected of having appendicitis, and when Ca
triona's temperature had shot up to 104 and they couldn't g
it down. She had shared a few sleepless nights during teethir
time, and knew the worries that all mothers have. Liz had r
rose-tinted view of having a child. She knew what was
store and she was prepared for it. It was not a decision sł
had taken lightly. Nevertheless she knew it was a decisic
that would fulfil her more than any other.

To have a base at home with Don and Eve and the girl
What could be more perfect. It was this final slotting in
place of the pieces of her life that convinced her she wa
doing the right thing. Christine was delighted for her whe

ie told her of her plans. "No better woman to do it, and how
ioughtful of you to provide me with a holiday home in the
in." Christine was in no hurry to have children, but she
nderstood her sister's deep desire for one. Her parents had
een somewhat taken aback when Liz had broached the idea
f single motherhood. But, supportive as always, and know-
ig their daughter as they did, they told her that if she felt it
as the right thing for her they would help in any way they
)uld. Liz knew that deep down they probably didn't ap-
rove, but their loyalty to her would never let it show and she
new that once she placed their grandchild in their arms it
vould be loved and cherished by them as she was.

When Hugh had heard of her decision to sell Apartment
B and move to Spain, he was convinced she had gone crazy.
Give up everything that's happening here for you? As well as
aving a baby! Girl you really have flipped!" He was letting
is mews for a year until he saw what way things were going
) go in America. She knew he didn't believe she would really
o it, but she went ahead and made the arrangements to
urchase the property in Spain and set about finishing up her
ommissions. She had come off the pill and was hoping
gainst hope that she would get pregnant. Hugh would be
:aving for America in June and she had until then.

As it happened she got pregnant very quickly. On Valen-
ine's Day, she was told that she was six weeks pregnant and
he was so thrilled. Even Hugh, despite himself, was excited.
I'll take him or her for the school holidays," he grinned boy-
shly, running his palm over her still flat stomach. "You will
ome out to visit, won't you?" he queried a little anxiously.

"Of course, I will, daddy Cassidy," she teased him.

"You're not really going to sell 3B though, are you?" he
.sked.

"Hugh, as soon as everything is signed, sealed and deliv-
red in Majorca I'm moving all my stuff back to the flat and
'm out of here," she reiterated. She'd give him a surprise one
•f these days. He'd come to visit and see the For Sale sign up
ind then he'd be convinced.

It was the beginning of April before everything was se<br>
tled in Majorca. A week later O'Malley, Costello and Ryan ha<br>
a sign up announcing that Apartment 3B was for sale an<br>
Hugh found out that she was dead serious. "I really did<br>
think you'd go through with it," he confessed. "So you'<br>
going to sell?"

"Yep!"

He rubbed his jaw thoughtfully. "I wonder would Ma li<br>
it here. She's going on about selling the house and gettir<br>
something smaller."

"Well, damn you, Hugh!" Liz exclaimed angrily. "If I ha<br>
known that I'd have just sold the place to you privately ar<br>
not had to pay out a fortune to bloody estate agents."

"I only just thought of it now!" he protested. "Anywa<br>
haven't you told Dominic that his girlfriend could look th<br>
place over. You're better off in one way—at least you'll get th<br>
best price."

"Ah, Hugh, you should have told me you were inte<br>
ested," she said in disgust.

"Don't worry about it, Liz. It was just a thought. Mayt<br>
it's not what Ma's looking for. I'll have to see."

"Here's your coffee!" Susan interrupted her reverie. W<br>
Mrs. Cassidy in the apartment now? What did Lainey think<br>
it? Was the hard-faced woman one of the viewers? Who els<br>
was there? No doubt all would soon be revealed, Liz muse<br>
as she lay back resting her palm lightly on her stomach, dyir<br>
for the moment when she would feel the first flutter of h<br>
baby's life. Then Susan began her soothing beauty treatmen<br>
as Liz lay relaxed looking forward to the future.

# Hugh

**S**o she had been serious about selling, Hugh thought, as he helped his mother into the front seat of his Saab and gently fastened the seat belt around her. His mother was getting frail, he noticed. Liz's apartment would be ideal for her. No stairs, a lift that went right to her front door. All modern equipment. It would be perfect and if she liked it and the price was right she should have no problem disposing of the family home. It would be nice for him to know that his Ma was in Liz's old place. It would be nice for his child as well. He couldn't believe that Liz had got pregnant so quickly and he couldn't account for the sense of exhilaration he had experienced when she had told him about it on Valentine's Day. It was kind of exciting really and he didn't care what he was doing in the States, he was going to be home for the birth and that was final. If he was going to be a father of a child he wanted to be there from the word go. Bonding was extremely important and it was as important for a father to bond as it was for the mother. He knew, he had been reading up all about it in some books he had borrowed from the central library. Well after all, he was a journalist at heart; facts were important to him.

There was nothing to say that he had to stay in America forever or that Liz had to stay in Majorca. Maybe they could arrange something to suit them both—and the baby of course. He just wanted one bash at America and then he'd be satisfied. Then maybe they could work out something together. Whatever happened, Liz knew that she could always count on him for support and love in the rearing of their child. He would be as good a father as he could. It was the least the child deserved and, to tell the truth, he was rather

excited by the whole thing. Driving into Mountain View, as he
had done so many times over the years, he wondered if Liz
would be there. He vaguely remembered her saying she was
going to get her hair done. Anyway, they would be meeting
later.

His mother seemed most impressed by the grounds. He
smiled, watching her taking stock. The more he thought
about it, the more he felt Apartment 3B was ideal for her.
She'd have the two older ladies downstairs as neighbours,
surely they'd have something in common. The church, shops
and post office were right beside her. And there were plenty
of buses seeing as she didn't drive. It would be much better
for her than rattling around in that old house by herself. He
took her up in the lift.

Liz wasn't there but there were a few people looking
around already. He should have thought about his mother
buying it before Liz had put it on the estate agent's books.
Well, it was too late now. "It's really lovely, son, isn't it? I'd
love it," his mother whispered to him. He smiled down at her.
Well, that was that then. His mother wanted Apartment 3B
and Hugh would just have to make sure that she got it!

# Claire

Claire had visited three clients and shampooed and set
their hair before she set off for her appointment to view
Apartment 3B. She drove carefully in her little Fiesta. Well, it
wasn't hers exactly; it was a company car, Rosie's and her
company car. It was just great being able to drive. It gave you
such freedom. The years of waiting for buses and getting
soaked in the rain seemed like a bad dream. All of the past

few years seemed like a bad dream now. It was amazing how things had started to go right for her once she left Sean and started to be responsible for herself. CALL 'n' CUT, Rosie's and her business, had taken off beyond their wildest expectations. Every day they were getting more enquiries from potential clients.

Buying their own salon had been ideal. They had a base for their operation that dealt with ordinary clients and Claire took care of the travelling part of the business. Business was so brisk that they were thinking they might even have to get in another stylist. They had been in operation since the end of January and Rosie was even saying that they might break even in their first year of business!

Of course, Claire would have had to borrow a hell of a lot more from the banks had it not been for the money their house in Ballygall had made when it was sold. The property market was booming when Sean put the house up for sale. Properties were fetching outrageous prices and their big red-brick house in its desirable location was no exception. Even Sean had been stunned and for a moment Claire felt that he regretted his offer to her.

They had met the day the deal was being closed and Sean was looking better than Claire had ever seen him. All the greyness and strain had left his face, he had put on weight and he admitted to her that he was enjoying his retirement very much. He liked living in Drogheda again and his sister was very good to him. They didn't refer to David or their broken marriage and she was just as glad. She was anxious to have the old sores heal and she wished him well.

"Would you not take half the money?" she asked him as he silently handed her the cheque when they were alone, after the deal had been closed.

Her husband shook his head. "I'd only leave it in the bank, I'm not a great spender and I have more than enough with my pension, the lump sum, and the investments. It's for you and Suzy so go and get somewhere decent to live."

Claire silently took the cheque and put it in her bag.

"I know I wasn't the easiest man to live with. I've had a lot of time to think during the last couple of months. I'm sorry about the way things turned out," he said gruffly.

"So am I," Claire said quietly. "But it's in the past so let's try and look forward to our future."

"Good luck, then, with your house hunting," Sean said awkwardly and for a moment Claire thought he was going to shake hands. This was the man she had lived with and slept with and borne two children for and they were so awkward with each other. She felt a tremendous sadness. Leaning over she had kissed him on the cheek. "Take care, Sean. You have my number at work and as soon as I get settled I'll send you my new address." She watched him drive away back to Drogheda and felt relieved that at least they had had some sort of reconciliation. The failure of a marriage was always traumatic but she would put it behind her as best she could and get on with her life.

Driving up to Mountain View she prayed that there wouldn't be many people viewing it. It was like an omen that Apartment 3B had come on the market just when she had the money to buy it. Claire could hardly believe her eyes when she saw the For Sale sign one day when she was passing. She rang Molly in a tizzy of excitement asking if she would like to live in one of the apartments. "I'd love that. It's a beautiful place, Claire. I'll have the house sold in another month, so with your money and mine we'll surely manage to get it," Molly had said excitedly.

"It all depends how many people are interested and what kind of bids they put in," Claire cautioned, not wanting to get her mother's hopes up too high in case they were dashed.

Now, driving into the luxurious grounds, Claire offered up a little prayer that she would be successful. Apartment 3B was in the middle block and, pressing the intercom, she saw the TV monitors come on and was deeply impressed. What great security to be able to see who was ringing your doorbell. A man's voice, the estate agent's, responded as she announced herself, and the door slid quietly open. Claire stepped into a pink and grey foyer with an ankle-deep carpet. Hanging baskets of ferns adorned the walls and the place reeked of luxury. She walked to the lift which was waiting and pressed the button for the fourth floor. Swiftly she ascended and in a matter of seconds was standing in the private landing of Apartment 3B. The estate agent stood smiling politely in the doorway. "Mrs. Moran, good to see you," he said smoothly, handing her some brochures. "Do come in and feel free to look around."

Claire knew the minute she walked in that she would love it. It was so bright and airy and tastefully decorated. And the lovely fitted kitchen! And the views from the balconies! Molly would love sitting on the balcony in the afternoon sun, doing her knitting and looking at the view. The main bedroom was beautiful, so restful and feminine, and the *en suite* bathroom was everything her sybaritic heart desired.

A man and an elderly woman were in the dining room and she heard him say, "It's nice, Ma, isn't it? I think Liz is crazy to be selling it." Claire's eyes widened. She looked again and looked away hastily so she wouldn't be caught staring. That was Hugh Cassidy, the TV personality. He was gorgeous looking, even better in the flesh. Was he going to buy the apartment? Claire's heart sank. A tall, extremely thin blond woman in dusky pink pleated culottes was enquiring in a haughty tone about maintenance fees and Claire could see the estate agent diplomatically steering her out of earshot on to the balcony. "It's actually perfect for our requirements," Claire could hear her saying in a high-pitched nasal voice that was rather grating on the ears. Another couple had just arrived. A beautiful tanned woman and a distinguished older man who, to judge from the expression in his eyes, was crazy about her. Make the most of him, Claire advised the other woman silently as she went back into the kitchen to have another look.

Ten minutes later the estate agent was gathering them all together to show them the rest of the complex and the facilities on offer: the pool, tennis courts, activities room, and laundry. It was superb and Claire knew in her heart that she wouldn't view a place as nice anywhere else. This was what she wanted and if she had to go and get a mortgage to top up what she and her mother had between them, then she'd do it! To hell with it. She only had one life and for once she was going to go after something she wanted and she was going to get it. If Hugh Cassidy or the blond woman or the glamorous couple wanted to buy an apartment, they'd have to look elsewhere. Apartment 3B was going to be hers! Chin lifted in determination, Claire went in search of the estate agent to make her bid.

# Lainey

"Are you sure you won't let me buy it with you? Wouldn't you like to live with me?" Dominic asked for the thousandth time since he dropped his bombshell about leaving his wife. Lainey sighed. "All right! All right! Just checking," he smiled, as they drove in from the airport. She had thought about it so much, tried to work out what was fair for her, for him, for Rita. She loved Dominic very much. He was her pillar, her strength and she couldn't imagine her life without him. She had never put pressure on him to leave his wife, in fact Dominic had often complained laughingly that she wasn't like a proper mistress at all. She made no demands, caused no scenes, rebuked him for spending money on her and generally behaved in a most unmistresslike manner.

Lainey was nothing if not a realist. She always had been. She knew that at the age of thirty-five she liked her career and her independence more than she liked the idea of settling down. Being totally honest about it all, although she loved being with Dominic when she was with him, she also loved being on her own. In her own place, doing exactly as she pleased. With Dominic, she had the best of both worlds and she had been absolutely shocked when he had told her what he wanted to do. She supposed that most women would have been thrilled at what he proposed, after nine years of a relationship. But she wasn't most women. She was Lainey Conroy and a future of being single held no fears for her. And damn it, she *wasn't* a selfish person, she told herself when this unwelcome thought had crossed her mind a few times. There was nothing selfish about wanting to remain single and free. Why she should feel in the slightest bit guilty was beyond her. She was a woman of the nineties. Marriage or togetherness was no longer the be-all and end-all of a woman's life, no matter how conditioned women might be to think so.

Dominic had been stunned and shocked when Lainey gently tried to explain her feelings to him. "I thought you loved me," he said dully, drawing away from her for the first time ever.

"Dominic. I do! I do, more than I've ever loved anyone. You must know that," she pleaded.

"Then why won't you come live with me?" he demanded.

"Ah, Dominic! What's wrong with the way we are? What do you want to go upsetting everything for?" she said miserably.

"Because I want more," he said fiercely. "And I thought you would want it too."

"I never did anything to make you think that," she said quietly, hating to hurt him.

"I know you didn't." Dominic sighed deeply. "I was fooling myself."

"I love you. I've loved you for nine years that will never change for me, Dominic," Lainey whispered, leaning over to kiss him.

"I've never met a woman like you, Lainey Conroy," he murmured against her lips, holding her tightly.

Many times he asked her to reconsider and always she said no. When Apartment 3B came up for sale he told her as soon as he could catch hold of her. Ironically she had been in Cork on business, he had been in Dublin. Lainey had been so excited. It was precisely what she was looking for. The Mountain View complex was so classy and Dominic would be in the same building as her. Surely that would satisfy him. After all he still had to spend half his week in Cork, so she might as well have a place of her own for when he was away.

"Let me give you half the money towards it," he urged.

"Dominic, please! I really want to buy this place myself. It's an affirmation of all I've been through, of all I've achieved by hard work and years of planning. It's a dream come true. Don't you realise what this means to me?" Lainey willed him to understand.

Dominic smiled slowly, then nodded his head. "I understand much more than you know. It was the same with me and the business. Buy your apartment, Lainey, and be happy in it. You deserve it, God knows. And if you'll let me, I'll call up and borrow a cup of sugar or maybe a jar of coffee and who knows what might happen." He grinned. She flung her arms around his neck and hugged him tightly. He hugged her back and she had never felt so happy as she did then. He had been waiting for her at the airport, the old familiar smile lighting up his face when he saw her coming through customs.

"You should see what I bought in the duty-free," Lainey murmured against his ear as he embraced her.

"Sounds interesting. What is it?"

"Wait and see," she teased him, her eyes twinkling as she raised her mouth to his and kissed him passionately.

"You wanton woman!" Dominic murmured as he came up for air.

"Mmmm . . ." she murmured huskily. "I want you . . . it's been ten days. How much time have we got?"

Dominic looked at his watch. "An hour or so!"

Lainey smiled. "That's long enough to show you what I bought in London so let's get out of here quick!"

Speeding in towards the city, Lainey reflected how nicely

the motorway from the airport had been landscaped. In the distance she could see the vivid blue outline of the Dublin Mountains. With any luck she'd be looking at that view from now on as the owner of Apartment 3B. How fortunate that Liz Lacey had decided to sell right now. Of course, she was so successful, she was probably going to buy a bigger place. Dominic turned right at Whitehall and drove down Collins Avenue and then past the new university. Turning left on the Ballymun Road he sped towards Mountain View. Then he pulled in at the shops on the rise, turned to look at her and smiled. "Anything you fancy? I've got to get stamps."

"Just you!" She smiled back at him. He laughed as he went in to the Winkel to emerge five minutes later with a huge box of chocolate-covered Brazil nuts and two instant lottery tickets which he presented to her. To her delight, she won a tenner.

"It's an omen, Dominic. I can feel it in my bones. I'm going to buy that apartment," she declared happily as he gave her her winnings.

Five minutes later they were making love in the hallway of his apartment, hungry for each other as they pulled their clothes off. "I love you, I love you, I love you," she breathed as he came inside her.

"You should go to Rome more often," he teased her as he soaped her back in the shower a little later. "It does things for you."

"Just think of all the new places we'll have to make love in when I buy the apartment," she murmured, turning to face him, drawing him close again.

"If you don't stop, you'll never get to view the place and it will be sold," Dominic remonstrated as he turned off the shower and wrapped her in a large towel.

"Spoilsport!" Lainey exclaimed as she dried herself.

"The day isn't over yet," he warned. "And I've still got to see what you bought in the duty-free."

"Yummy!" Lainey laughed as she went in to the bedroom to dry her hair.

Twenty minutes later they were in the lift heading for Liz's apartment. The sunlight streaming through the French window was the first thing Lainey saw as she entered the apartment. She looked again to make sure. That woman on the balcony talking to the man looked terribly like Cecily. Imagine there being another Cecily roaming the earth. What a horrible thought.

"It would suit our needs perfectly," she could hear the Cecily clone saying. Her heart stopped. That was no clone. That *was* Cecily.

"Holy Divinity!" she exclaimed, shocked.

"What's wrong?" Dominic looked at her in concern. Pulling him back out into the hallway, unseen by Cecily, Lainey whispered, "That's Cecily out there on the balcony. What the hell is she doing here?"

"*The* Cecily?" Dominic was astounded.

"None other!" Lainey said grimly. "The nosy bitch! Ma must have mentioned I was going to look at this place. And she's giving it the once over." She frowned, perplexed. "But she was saying to the fellow on the balcony that it suited their needs perfectly."

"Maybe they're thinking of buying," Dominic suggested, just as perplexed as Lainey was. "That could make things awkward for us."

Lainey straightened her shoulders, the light of battle in her green eyes. "Over my dead body! This is going to be *my* apartment and Cecily Clarke can go and get lost for herself." Composing herself, Lainey Conroy strode through the door of Apartment 3B as if she owned it already.

# Cecily

$C$ecily drove through Bray like a demon. She was on her way home after viewing the apartment in Mountain View. And things had not gone as planned at all. That bitch Lainey had stared right through her as though she didn't exist, giving no indication of any sense of shock at seeing her there. Her moment of supreme triumph had turned flat. Oh, how she detested that girl. Always had and always would!

It was a relief, somehow, to know that the knives were drawn between them. No more having to pretend to be nice and polite. They had not spoken to each other since Martin's wedding and that suited Cecily just fine. Although it was infuriating sometimes if they were in company, because Lainey just treated her as though she didn't exist. And she could do it so well. It incensed Cecily.

She had made sure to be at the apartment much earlier than the appointment to view. In fact she had been the first there, determined to outsmart Lainey. Cecily had been exceedingly impressed with Apartment 3B. It was superb! And the swimming pool! What luxury. God, she could imagine the parties she'd throw there. The McGraths would be deeply impressed. The whole set would. It was perfect. She had had time to have a good look around before the next viewer arrived. A woman on her own, very attractive, but not very fashionably dressed. The clothes looked as though they were out of Dunne's! Then Hugh Cassidy and an elderly woman had arrived. And Cecily had been thrilled. If a celebrity of Hugh Cassidy's calibre was interested in the apartment even though it was on the Northside, that was good enough for Cecily! If only that stupid estate agent hadn't taken her out to the balcony to discuss the service charge, she would have been standing by the door when Lainey arrived. But still, you'd have imagined she would have been utterly shocked to see Cecily there. But no! Lainey had been as cool as a cucumber and looked right through her. It was sickening!

And *who* was the extremely distinguished-looking man her sister-in-law was with? He was a very handsome man indeed. Trust her of course. She always knew how to pick 'em: Steve, Tony, and now this mysterious stranger. And did Tony know about this man? Exactly what was the story? Cecily would give her eyeteeth to know.

In the end, every one of the viewers had wanted to buy the apartment and the estate agent had been practically rubbing his hands with glee. The result was, that it was going to tender. Sealed bids to arrive at the estate agents by the end of the following week. Well, Cecily didn't care. She and Simon were going to acquire Apartment 3B if it killed her. Lainey Conroy was not going to get the better of her this time. No way! Jaw set Cecily drove towards Arklow, stopping at an off-licence to buy a bottle of champagne, as she prepared her plan of campaign to get Simon to put in the highest bid for Apartment 3B.

# The Residents

Al and Detta drove home, weary from their day's work. Nicole Cullen, whom neither of them could stand, was leaving and they had to donate a fiver each to the collection. That had put Al in a foul humour. Detta hoped with all her heart that Tina, the nanny, had the children ready for bed. Passing the For Sale sign, she wondered if Apartment 3B had been sold and who had bought it. No doubt all would soon be revealed. Meanwhile she had to try and scrape together their next instalment of maintenance fees, if they didn't want to find *their* apartment on the market as well.

Despite its poor start, it had turned out to be a most interesting day. And Maud and Muriel, declaring a truce of sorts, had found the comings and goings fascinating. After breakfast, they had spent the entire morning at the window, peering down at the people toing and froing from their block. When they saw Hugh Cassidy, accompanied by an elderly lady whom they took to be his mother, there had been great excitement.

Imagine having a celebrity like that for a neighbour. It was almost as good as having Gay Byrne living next door to you. They had liked the look of the dark-haired woman who had come alone. But the sharp-faced blond woman in those dreadful culottes things had not appealed to them at all. Neither had the sight of Dominic Kent with his arm around his much younger woman. Such a carrying-on in public! Maud and Muriel were in perfect agreement for once. They wanted Hugh Cassidy to buy Apartment 3B. It would raise the value enormously.

Derek Sinclair had not had the best of days. Old Horton had eaten the face off him for being late. His VDU had had a nervous breakdown and expired at a crucial moment, causing the rest of the computers to go down. And when he had finally got away from the place to come home, his blasted tyre had gone flat again. What a life! As he drove into Mountain View he saw Dominic and Lainey driving out. What a beauty she was. And he had heard a rumour that she was interested in buying 3B. He wondered if the place had been sold. The idea of Lainey buying it cheered Derek up immensely. If she bought it, old Kenty had better watch out. All was fair in love and war! Whatever beautiful woman bought Apartment 3B, Derek would be the first to welcome her. And all the better if it was Lainey Conroy!

# THE DECISION